FRASER VALLEY REGIONAL LIBRARY

D0384804

BETRAYED

No one can touch Del Williams – the hardest gangster in Soho. He's got the monopoly on the drugs, the clubs and the girls – it'd be a mistake to underestimate him. The one person he'd take a bullet for is tough, beautiful Bunny Barker, mother of their daughter Star. Bunny is determined to shield Star from 'life', but Del has a lot of enemies. When a familiar face reappears, the family is put in terrible danger. Can Bunny protect Star from the demons of her own past, and her very worst nightmare?

BETRAYED

BETRAYED

by

Jacqui Rose

Magna Large Print Books
Long Preston, North Yorkshire,
BD23 4ND, England.

British Library Cataloguing in Publication Data.

Rose, Jacqui
    Betrayed.

    A catalogue record of this book is
    available from the British Library

    ISBN   978-0-7505-4017-9

First published in Great Britain by Avon
An imprint of HarperCollins*Publishers* 2014

Copyright © Jacqui Rose 2014

Cover illustration © Roy Bishop by arrangement with
Arcangel Images

Jacqui Rose asserts the moral right to be identified as the author of
this work.

Published in Large Print 2015 by arrangement with
HarperCollins Publishers

All Rights reserved. No part of this publication may be reproduced,
stored in a retrieval system, or transmitted in any form or by any
means, electronic, mechanical, photocopying, recording or otherwise
without the prior permission of the Copyright owner.

Magna Large Print is an imprint of Library Magna Books Ltd.

Printed and bound in Great Britain by
T.J. (International) Ltd., Cornwall, PL28 8RW

This novel is entirely a work of fiction.
The names, characters and incidents portrayed
in it are the work of the author's imagination.
Any resemblance to actual persons,
living or dead, events or localities
is entirely coincidental.

Acknowledgements

The more books I write the more I realise what a team effort it all is and I really couldn't have done it without everyone. So I'd like to give a huge thank you to, Lydia Newhouse, my editor, who has wonderful ideas and understands exactly what I'm trying to say in my books, bringing out the best in me. Thanks to the team at Avon/ HarperCollins, who have once again been so supportive, and forever thanks to my agent, Judith Murdoch, for everything she does for me.

On a personal note I want to thank my children, my family and my friends who all give me unwavering support, without which none of this would be possible.

Dedication

To Tim, my soul mate;
for everything you've ever, done. x

A false witness shall not be unpunished, and he that speaketh lies shall perish.

Proverbs 19: 9 (King James Bible)

1990

LONDON

'Come on out. It's not funny now, Bronwin. Mum said we had to be back by seven. She'll skin us a-bleedin'-live if were late.' The tall skinny girl shouted loudly in no particular direction before looking down at her bitten nails, peeling off the last of the pink nail varnish as she waited for her sister to come out of her hiding place.

Exasperated, Kathleen looked up again. It was getting dark, and even though she'd known it was cold before she came out, she'd only put on a thin t-shirt. Better cold than looking frumpy in the brown coat her mum had bought her last week. The thought of bumping into any of the boys from the Stonebridge estate looking like something left over from a jumble sale made her shudder more than the evening chill of the October air.

Peering into the darkness, she could just make out the dark silhouette of her sister, Bronwin, scuttling about in the thicket of trees, thinking she couldn't be seen. The girl sighed as she watched. What her sister found so exciting about playing in a stupid park was beyond her. Parks and swings and trees were for babies. And Kathleen certainly wasn't that.

There were only four years between them, yet her only sibling seemed so immature next to her. Ever since she was little she'd felt older than her years. And even though she'd just started second-ary school, she knew she wasn't a silly little girl anymore. Not now, anyway. Not now she'd lost her virginity with the boy across the landing. Although it'd lasted less time than it took the kettle to boil, and he'd only just managed to get inside her before he'd exploded, groaning and coming everywhere, it still counted. Counted enough to make her special. For the first time in her life she had something to brag about.

Kathleen knew she wasn't pretty like her sister, nor was she clever, and she certainly wasn't popular. Everything was always a struggle. Everything she felt ashamed of even down to the way she dressed. Hand-me-downs from anywhere and anyone. Musty clothes ingrained with the stains and smells of poverty, which brought nothing but ridicule.

But that was all going to change now. The sense of being a born loser had gone. She was proud of being the first one in her year to *do it* and envious word had got around the class. Now, the girls wanted to speak to her and the boys didn't avoid her any longer.

Looking back towards the trees, Kathleen realised couldn't see her sister now. She wasn't worried. This was how it always went. Her younger sister's idea of a joke. Hiding and making her search her out. Letting her be on the verge of panic before she'd appear, grinning all over her face.

As she stood waiting, chewing on her nails, Kathleen thought about her mother who was only fourteen years older than her and had decided a long time ago that even though she'd given birth to two girls, she didn't want the responsibility of caring for them, nor did she want the trouble of loving them; preferring instead to spend her time with any man who'd buy her a drink down the local. Kathleen shook her head in disgust and walked slowly towards the trees, resigned to the fact she was going to spend the next ten minutes searching for her sister in the woods.

'Bron!' She was getting pissed off now. She'd been looking for over ten minutes. Her arms had already been scratched by the bushes and she was certain something nasty had crawled down her top. She was cross, but she wouldn't let her sister know she was. They both had enough of their mother being cross at them without her adding to it.

Kathleen heard a branch snap just ahead. Her eyes darted towards the sound. In the shadow of the night, she saw a dark silhouette a few feet in front of her.

'Bron! Please stop messing, babe. I want to go now.' There was no reply. She edged forward, feeling the ground as she stepped carefully through the bracken, when suddenly she heard the breaking of another branch. Only this time it was coming from the side of her rather than in front of her.

Kathleen listened, waiting to hear the stifled giggles of her sister. In the darkness she could hear breathing, but it didn't sound like Bronwin's soft breath. This breathing was heavier, and she turned in panic. The next thing she felt was the taste of blood as the stinging blow of something hard landed on her lips.

She screamed as she felt her top being torn and rough hands pushing her down into the damp cold earth, tugging painfully at her pants, under her skirt.

As she felt the hands tighten round her neck, her breath becoming short as the life seeped out of her, it was of some small comfort to the girl that the last words she managed to cry were, 'Run, Bronwin! Run!'

Six-year-old Bronwin sat in the corner of the tiny room, watching the uniformed police officers milling about. Sitting by her was a plain-looking social worker.

'Bronwin, you really need to tell us what you can remember.'

'I don't think she's ready to answer any questions.' The social worker intervened as the large detective leaned in to question Bronwin. Annoyed with the interruption, the detective snapped back, 'I think that's a matter for Bronwin, don't you?'

'Detective, she's far too young to know what's best. She's had a traumatic experience and I don't think these questions will help, do you?'

'Listen, no one's saying she hasn't had a traumatic experience, but if we want to make sure the perpetrators can't get out of this we need to make sure she tells us everything she can remember. She's an important witness. Where's the mother anyway?'

The social worker flicked through the notes. 'We don't know exactly where she is at the moment; we've tried leaving her a message but we've had no reply. She told us she'd meet us here, but maybe it's all too much for her.'

'She's got responsibilities. This kid for one, and

another one lying cold.'

The social worker bristled, furrowing her brow angrily as she took a sidewards glance at Bronwin.

'That's enough, Detective. Not everything is so clear cut. The family are well known to us and there are problems. The mother's very young and, as I'm sure you'll appreciate, things can get difficult for her.'

The detective sighed.

'Fine, no more questions, but we need to take her to see the line-up. It's important; we can only hold the men for so long.'

The line-up room was dark and Bronwin wasn't sure what she was supposed to do. The woman who kept insisting on holding her hand smelt funny. A bit like the dusty old cupboard in the kitchen at home. She didn't like the smell and she didn't like the woman. She wanted to go home. Where was her mum anyway? She hoped she'd come and get her soon.

'All we want you to do is tell us if you remember any of the men's faces. We want you to have a good look and if you remember any of them, tell us.'

'Can I have a word, Detective?' A man with a loud booming voice appeared out of the shadows, making Bronwin step back behind the social worker. She couldn't really make sense of the words he was using, but he seemed to be so cross; like everyone else around her.

'Detective, my clients feel it's unfair they're not only being forced to be in the line-up, but that the "guilty" party will be decided on the say-so of a child. We all know what children are like. They choose things on a whim. I want a stop to this.'

The officer in charge rubbed his top teeth with his tongue. 'If they've nothing to hide, they've got nothing to fear.'

The man grinned nastily at the detective, his eyes reflecting the coldness in his smile. Bronwin took a sharp intake of breath. She didn't like this at all. Why wasn't anybody taking her home to bed? She was tired and wanted to snuggle up with Mr Hinkles, the teddy bear her sister Kathleen had got her. Where was her sister anyway? She'd heard people talking about her and they'd asked her a lot of questions, but she hadn't seen her since the woods. She didn't want to think about the woods; thinking about them gave Bronwin a funny feeling in her tummy.

Big tears began to spill down Bronwin's cheeks. Her eyes had adjusted to the darkness and she watched them fall onto the floor, right next to the man with the booming voice's foot. Cautiously, Bronwin looked at him from underneath her shaggy fringe. He was smart and clean and smelled nice.

Bronwin quickly dropped her gaze as she saw the man looking at her. Her eyes wandered to his shoes. They were black shoes. Shiny black shoes, apart from the bottom parts of them, which were dirty with mud. She looked up again, edging back as the man bent down to meet her stare.

'Would you like a hanky?'

Bronwin shook her head but the man insisted.

'Here, take it.' As he pushed the crisp white handkerchief into Bronwin's hand she noticed some letters embroidered onto it, but she wasn't good with letters, especially fancy ones that swirled and curled like those did.

'Now, is everybody ready? We need to get on with this.' The detective's voice had a tone of weariness. He was tired and didn't expect much from this line-up, even though in his gut he felt he had the right men; he knew only too well that with slick high-powered lawyers; like the one standing opposite him, even if the suspects had been caught with bloodstained knives in their pockets and the words 'guilty' written on their foreheads, there was still a possibility of them walking free.

'Are you ready, Bronwin?' The social worker pulled Bronwin up from her seat as the lights on the other side of the mirrored line-up room went on.

Bronwin nodded.

'All you have to do is pick out the men who you think you saw in the woods. Do you think you can do that, Bronwin?'

Again, Bronwin nodded. She stood on a chair and in front of her a procession of men began to walk in through the door on the other side of the glass.

'Don't worry; Bronwin, they can't see you or hear you.'

The men stood with their backs against the wall, staring ahead, holding up the boards they had been given. The detective adjusted the microphone as he spoke into it.

'Can you step forward, number one, and then turn to the left and to the right, slowly.' The tall man with dark hair stepped forward, nervously turning as instructed in both directions before stepping back to the wall.

'Number two, can you step forward and then turn to the left and to the right, slowly.' Without taking his eyes off Bronwin's reaction to the men the detective stood up slightly as he realised he was too near the mike.

'Number three, can...'

Bronwin's mind wandered off. Her legs were getting tired having to stand up and she thought it was funny the way all the men were staring ahead. The lady had said they couldn't see her, but she didn't know how that was possible if she could see them.

'Bronwin? Bronwin?' The detective was talking to her. She didn't know how long he had been, but she could tell he was cross; his cheeks were red like her mum's cheeks went red when she was angry with her.

'Do you recognise any of them? Were any of them there in the woods?' The detective's voice was urgent as he stared at Bronwin.

'Detective, let me handle it.' The social worker cut her eye at the detective. 'Bronwin, do you recognise any of them? Were any of them there in the woods?'

Bronwin looked first at the detective and then at the lady. She didn't know why they were asking her the same question and arguing about it.

The social worker sighed and looked at her watch. 'Bronwin, this is very important. If you can remember *anything*, you need to tell us. Can you remember who it was?'

24

Bronwin nodded her head.

'Show us then. Can you point them out?'

Bronwin nodded again, she raised her hand and pointed, speaking in a small voice. 'It was him.'

The officer sprang into action. 'Number eight.'

'Yes. And him.' She pointed again at the line-up.

'Number two.'

'Yes.'

The detective's face didn't give anything away. In a matter-of-fact manner he said, 'Well done, Bronwin. You've done great.'

Bronwin looked at him, her elf-like face turned to the side. She swivelled around, turning her back to the line-up and staring towards the door where the man with the booming voice stood. 'And him. I saw him in the woods as well.'

'Bronwin do you understand what happens to children who keep telling lies?'

'I ain't lying, Dr Berry. It *was* him, it *was* that bloke. Why won't you believe me?'

The psychiatrist tapped his pen on his leg absent-mindedly. 'We've gone over this before and we both know why I won't believe you, don't we?' The psychiatrist paused dramatically then said, 'Because it's simply not true. How do you think a person feels to be accused of bad things, Bronwin? How would you feel if I accused you of doing something bad?'

'But you are. You're saying I'm lying.'

'That's *not* the same, Bronwin, because you *are*.'

Bronwin's eyes were wide with fear as she

25

cuddled Mr Hinkles, her teddy bear. 'Please let me go home. I think I should go home now; me mum will be missing me.'

Nastily, Dr Berry spoke in a whisper. 'Bronwin, children who tell lies, *especially* vicious ones, don't go home. How would you like to never go home? I can make that happen you know. I can make sure you never go home, Bronwin, so you need to start to tell everyone you're sorry for telling lies about those nice men.'

'They ain't nice. They *ain't*.'

Dr Berry grabbed hold of Bronwin's arm and shook her hard, his face red with anger. 'I'm warning you, Bronwin.'

Bronwin didn't say anything. She didn't even know why she was here and all she wanted to do was to go home. She curled up tighter in her sadness as she listened to Dr Berry continue to rant. 'And you know what's happened now, don't you?'

Bronwin shook her head.

'Now everybody thinks you're a liar. The police, the courts, even your mum does. That's why they were found not guilty.' Hearing the psychiatrist mention her mother, Bronwin sat up, her face scrunched up in a mixture of hurt and anger.

'No she don't! She never said that!'

'Bronwin, *I* don't tell lies because *I* know it's wrong.'

Rubbing away a tear with the back of her sleeve, Bronwin yelled, 'You're a big fat liar.'

Dr Berry slapped Bronwin hard across her face, causing an angry welt to appear on her cheek.

Taking his glasses off to wipe them with the corner of his starched white doctor's coat, Dr Berry didn't bother to look at Bronwin as he spoke.

'That's why she hasn't been to see you, Bronwin, because she doesn't like liars. She told me she didn't want you to come home. *No one* is ever going to believe a word you say. No one *trusts* you, Bronwin, which means no one's ever going to believe you when you tell them what happened in the woods.'

At the word *woods,* Bronwin covered her ears.

'It's no good doing that, Bronwin. The only way to change this is by telling the truth and stopping these silly lies.'

'But I keep telling you, it ain't a lie. I want to go home. I want to see me mum and me sister.'

'Bronwin, I've told you this before. Your sister is dead.' Bronwin immediately began to scream. Her wail was fearful and high pitched; an adult's cry within a child's body. The scream resonated through her and began to take possession of her body as it started to shake, convulsing her into a fit. Dr Berry pressed a button and a moment later a white-gowned nurse entered the room.

'Give her fifty millilitres, nurse.'

The nurse picked up a full syringe from the silver drugs trolley nestling in the corner of the room, then quickly and expertly administrated the powerful drug into Bronwin's leg. Almost immediately, Bronwin's eyes began to roll back. Her shoulders began to slump and her mouth gently opened to one side as she lay on the bed in the tiny whitewashed room.

After a couple of minutes, Bronwin's eyes slowly

27

regained focus and she sat staring ahead at nothing but the blank wall.

Today was her seventh birthday.

In the next room, Bronwin's mother sat nervously pulling down the grey nylon skirt she'd bought from Roman Road Market the day before. She'd wanted to look presentable and it was only now she was realising that the skirt might be too short. Perhaps she should've got the other one, the longer one, but it'd been a fiver more and she'd needed the fiver for the electricity key. Taking off her jacket, she placed it over her knees.

She was nervous. Her hands were sweating and she could feel a prickly heat rash beginning to develop on her chest. She knew what these people were like. Knew how they judged; Christ, she'd been dealing with them since she was a kid herself, and now they had their hands on her daughter.

Week after week she'd called up to see Bronwin, but they'd told her she couldn't. She'd even turned up a few times, hoping someone would show a bit of compassion, but she'd been turned away, not even being allowed to step foot into the children's facility. All she'd been told was that social services and the doctors thought it was best for Bronwin to be taken into temporary care. That wasn't going to stop her though; she was going to get her daughter back and bring her home where she belonged. Today was the first time she was able to see the doctor in charge and, as her nan used to say, she was shitting bricks.

Gazing around the room made her feel even more nervous. There were paintings of men in gilded frames on the wall, looking superior and mocking. It surprised her to see the doctor's office void of any medical books, but instead filled with trinkets and thank you cards. She jumped as the glass door opened.

'Hello I'm Dr Berry, we've spoken many times on the phone. Thank you for coming.'

Refusing to take the outstretched hand, Bronwin's mum thought the doctor looked like he should've retired years ago. His white hair and stooped shoulders made her feel as if she was paying a visit to her granddad rather than a child shrink.

'I've been trying to come for a while now, but then you'd already know that, wouldn't you? What I want to know is when can I take Bronwin home?'

'Well, that might be a problem. Bronwin doesn't want to come home. She's a very troubled little girl.'

Bronwin's mother flinched. 'I don't want to hear about bleedin' problems mate. I just want to take her home where she belongs. She's my daughter, not yours, and I don't believe she don't want to come home. I want to see her.'

Dr Berry went round to the other side of his desk. He pulled out his chair slowly, staring moodily over his rimless glasses. 'How do you feel about your other daughter's death? Kathleen, wasn't it?'

'I ain't here to talk about me other daughter. In fact, I ain't here to answer any questions at all.

Just give me Bronwin so we can get out of here.'

As was his habit and his arrogance, the doctor ignored the interjection and continued to talk. 'Do you feel responsible for your daughter's death?'

Bronwin's mother stared ahead, painful, angry tears about to fall. She didn't know if it was her imagination or not but she was sure she could see a tiny smirk on Dr Berry's face as he asked about Kathleen.

She was pleased to hear her voice was steady as she made a concerted effort to stay calm. Her words punctuated the air. 'I'm not responsible for her death. It wasn't me who killed her.'

'But you were the one who let your daughters out. Surely you must hold some sort of guilt?'

Bronwin's mother blinked away the tears as she felt them burning. She bent forward, holding her stomach, and whispered almost inaudibly as her gaze found the window. 'Of course I do. Of course I do.'

'Then let us help you. You do want some help, don't you?'

Bronwin's mum nodded, trance-like.

'I still don't really know why she's here.'

Dr Berry's expression was patronising. 'I think you do, but if you need reminding again, why, I'll tell you. Myself and social services thought it was for the best, especially in the light of your past history with children's services. It's our job to make sure children are safe from harm. You know Bronwin is still very confused with what happened and *who* was there that night in the woods. Like I said before, she's a very troubled little girl. She insists on telling these lies.'

'Bronwin ain't a liar. That's one thing she's never done is lie. If she's telling you something then it must be true.'

'That's as maybe, but she's a child and all children lie.'

'She don't.'

Dr Berry sighed. 'Do you want us to help her and at the same time help you?'

'Of course!'

'I had another meeting with her social workers and they're in agreement with me that it's probably best for all of us, you as well, if Bronwin stays here with us. Permanently.'

Bronwin's mother stood up. Her body shook with fear and fury. 'Oh no you don't. You ain't going to mess my little girl up.'

'We won't be doing that; what we'll be doing is untangling the mess that has already been put there in her short life.'

'That ain't going to happen. You ain't going to take my daughter.'

'Of course not. That's why I'm asking you to sign these papers.'

'I'm not signing nothing. I want my daughter and I want her *now*.'

'I'm sorry, but that won't be possible. We've had an extension of the interim care, which means you can't take her.'

The shock and hurt on Bronwin's mum's face was naked. Dr Berry turned away quickly as the shouting began.

'You bastards. You *fucking* bastards.'

'We're not doing this to upset you, we're doing this for Bronwin's benefit. You'll be able to get on with your life, knowing Bronwin is getting the help she needs. She'll thank you in the end, I know she will. You can give her what you didn't have yourself. You can give her a chance and a start in life.'

'But I'm her mother. She should be with me.'

'Yes, but only if it's right for her – and at the moment, it isn't right.'

Bronwin's mother headed for the door, catching Dr Berry raising his eyebrows at her skirt. She pulled it down quickly.

'Well I'm sorry, but no way. I would never hand my child over to the likes of you. I might not be what you think a good mother should be, and I'm not saying I haven't got my faults, but I love Bronwin. I loved both my kids.'

Dr Berry's face was twisted with cruelty. 'Fight us? Fight me and you'll lose – and then you'll never see Bronwin again. Do it this way and you'll be able to see her. It's your choice.'

'You ... you can't do that.'

'We can and we will. Do you really think the courts will agree to you keeping her after both myself and the social workers give evidence of you being unstable and incapable of giving Bronwin what's needed?'

'I love her. Ain't that enough?'

'In an ideal world it is, but then we're not in an ideal world, are we? Can you excuse me one moment?'

Not waiting for any sort of reply, Dr Berry picked up the phone on his desk. He spoke quietly into it. 'Would you mind coming in now?'

A moment later the glass door opened. The

man who walked in didn't bother to introduce himself. He stood with a frozen frown on his face as Bronwin's mum stared at him. 'Who's he?'

Once more, Dr Berry chose to ignore a question he saw as irrelevant. He walked over to Bronwin's mum, picking up the papers as he passed his desk, then reached out with the pen that was always kept in his breast coat pocket.

'Sign them. It's for the best. If you say you love her, which I believe you do, you'll listen to me. No one's the enemy here.'

Bronwin's mother took in the doctor's face. Deep entrenched lines circled his eyes and cold small green eyes stared back at her. 'You'll let me see Bronwin?'

Dr Berry pushed the pen and papers forward. 'She'll be in good hands. There's nothing to worry about. I promise.'

Taking the papers, Bronwin's mother grabbed at the pen and hurriedly scrawled her name on the papers. Next, Dr Berry passed he papers to the other man, talking as he did so. 'We need another signature, you see, so that's why this gentleman's here. You'll get a copy of this for yourself.'

The other man took out his own pen. Bronwin's mother watched, loathing etched on her face as her eyes traced the flamboyantly written signature.

Dr Berry smiled, his tone overly jovial for the sentiment of the occasion and his clichéd remark inappropriate.

'Right then, that's all done and dusted.'

'Now take me to see my daughter.'

'You've done the right thing.'

'So why doesn't it feel like it?'

Staring through the glass pane of the door, Bronwin's mother wiped away her tears before opening it. Quietly, she walked into the room, feeling the air of hush as she entered. She stared at her daughter. So tiny. So elf-like. So beautiful.

'Bron. Bron, it's me.'

Bronwin's eyes stayed closed.

Dr Berry crept up silently behind her. 'It's all right, she's had some medicine to calm her down. She's just in a heavy sleep.'

'Can I wake her up?'

'It's best to leave her. She needs all the rest she can get.'

Leaningforward, Bronwin's mother swept her daughter's mass of blonde hair away from her forehead. She kissed her head before speaking to her sleeping child. 'Bron, Mummy's got to go now. But always remember I love you and I'll see you soon, and Bron ... I'm sorry.'

Turning to the doctor, Bronwin's mum stood up and went into the pocket of her torn jacket. 'Can you give her this? It's her birthday card.'

'Yes, of course. The nurse will see you out. The social workers will be in touch in the morning to sort the other details out.'

Once Bronwin's mother had left, Dr Berry took a quick glance at the card before throwing it into the bin in the corner. Deep in thought, he stood observing Bronwin as she began to stir.

The door opened, jarring him from his thoughts. He smiled at the entering visitor and reaching out his hand with a welcoming greeting. 'Thanks for signing those papers, by the way. I thought for a moment the mother was going to be difficult and start making a noise about her parental rights. I'll just wake her up for you.'

Walking across to Bronwin, Dr Berry gently nudged her. He spoke quietly. 'Bronwin? Bronwin? Hey birthday girl, you've got a visitor. Someone's here to see you.'

Bronwin slowly opened her eyes before rubbing them gently. She sat up, then screamed. It was the man from the woods with the black shiny shoes.

'She's all yours, come and find me when you've finished. Oh, and have fun.' Dr Berry chuckled unpleasantly, tapping the man on his back as he left the room, leaving him sitting on Bronwin's bed as he began to unbutton his shirt.

Nine years later

The bed was hard and the chair was too. Sparse and unwelcoming. And Bronwin didn't know why she couldn't go home, instead of having to stay in a house where she didn't want to be and didn't know anyone. It was the same recurring thought she'd had each time they sent her somewhere new.

She'd been in more care and foster homes than she could possibly remember and over time she'd developed a sixth sense. Knowing when people really wanted *her* or when all they *really* wanted was the few hundred quid caring allowance they got for taking in the likes of her.

How long had it been now? Eight years, nine even. Nine years of going from one home to another.

She no longer wanted to be, or to feel like, the unwanted teenager. The problem child. Hard to place. Hard to love. She didn't want to become bitter; hardened to life before she'd reached eighteen.

She was determined to change it. To take control. And as Bronwin stared out of the window at the rainy night she made a decision. The time was right. She was old enough not to have to listen to a bunch of jumped-up social workers telling her what to do. All they really did anyway was to find her a roof over her head – the rest of it was left to her.

Bronwin stuffed her clothes and the bedraggled Mr Hinkles, her childhood teddy bear, back into her bag, then opened the window. She felt the chill of the evening air and the spray of the rain on her face, blown in by the wind. Making sure no one could hear her, Bronwin shuffled onto the ledge. It wasn't so far down. Seven feet perhaps, maybe eight. Eight feet to freedom.

After a count of three in her head and then another one of five, Bronwin jumped, hitting the ground hard. She rolled on the grass and felt a sharp pain in her ankle, shooting pains up the outside of her leg, but she didn't care. All that mattered to her was that she was out. Out of the care system that had never cared for her and out of the system that had taken away her mother, the one person she'd cared about.

Getting up from the wet ground, Bronwin ignored the pain. She quickly picked up her bag, making sure no one in the house had seen her. The rain hit down hard on her but instead of it feeling cold, it felt warm, invigorating. She was free. She was finally free. Today was her sixteenth birthday.

PRESENT DAY

SOHO – LONDON

1

Bunny Barker lay back on the silk pillows and smiled. She stretched her long tanned athletic body out, enjoying the feel of her nakedness in the heat of the day. Her natural blonde hair cascaded over the side of the bed, almost reaching the expensive cream carpet that had just been laid.

It was only early July, yet the stifling Soho air made it necessary to have all the windows open, along with the three chrome fans switched to high. It was almost two o'clock, which meant she had another client in less than an hour, although she'd make this her last one of the day. That was the beauty of being her own boss.

No one to tell her what to do or when to do it. Though it hadn't always been like that. When she was younger she'd worked the streets along with the other girls. Night after night, freezing her ass off whilst fighting off punters, fighting off pimps, even fighting off the other Toms in the street who hadn't taken kindly to her being around. Then, fortune had come her way and everything had changed.

In the past seven years her life had become unrecognisable, bringing her things she'd never imagined possible. She had almost everything she could've wished for. Almost. Because Bunny knew there was one thing missing in her life. One thing life hadn't ever brought her. And that one thing was trust. Trust was something Bunny had never had.

She wasn't ever going to take her eyes off the ball. It'd taken her almost the whole of her thirty-three years to make something of herself and she wasn't going to let anything, even love, destroy that.

She knew a lot of people would argue that being a hooker wasn't making anything of herself, but Bunny had long ago stopped caring what anybody thought.

Looking round her sumptuous room, decorated in cream and gold, Bunny heard a knock on the door.

'Come in.'

The door opened and Claudia, her all-round helper, stood smiling. What she would do without Claudia, Bunny didn't know.

'Your next client's here, Bun. He's early; shall I tell him to wait downstairs or do you want to see him now?'

Stretching over, Bunny dragged on the lit Marlboro cigarette by the bed. She sighed lightly. She was tired. The familiar nightmares had kept her awake again and as a result she wasn't really in the mood to entertain. Besides, it was too hot and sticky, so the thought of a punter writhing and groaning as he pumped away on top of her didn't exactly fill her with enthusiasm. Still, at least she'd finish earlier than she thought she would, which meant she could go and pick up the last few bits for her holiday.

She caught her breath. It was silly, but the

thought of the holiday gave her butterflies in her stomach.

She'd never been further north than Edgware nor further south than Lewisham, but here she was, about to pack her bags for a few days away in Marbella. And as much as she was excited about it, the idea of it terrified her as well, and although it'd only be for a few days, the idea of leaving behind loved ones scared her.

'Let him in, Claudia, and once you've shown him up, you can get off early if you like.'

'Are you sure?'

'Totally, babe. This one's no trouble. If the last times are anything to go by, he'll be in and out within two minutes.' The two women giggled before Claudia left the room.

Leaning up on her elbows, Bunny braced herself as she always did before seeing a client. Of course she knew she could give it all up if she wanted, but she just wasn't willing to. No matter *what* anybody promised her. This was just something she had to do. She supposed it was no different to the people she saw every morning trooping off to work, wishing they were somewhere else.

When the suggestion of being a kept woman had been presented to her in the past, the idea of it had seemed very appealing at first. Not having to do anything. Not having to worry about anything. But then, as they always did, the old nagging doubts had entered her head and once again it'd boiled down to one thing. Trust. Or rather the lack of it.

She'd seen enough men promise the world to their latest bit of stuff, only for them to get bored of their dolly birds a few months down the line when a tastier sort came along. And there was no way she was going to get turfed out and end up back on the streets on the whim of a man. So, whether she liked it or not, Bunny continued to turn tricks, ensuring she was in a position to put money away for her future, which helped to quell her almost pathological fear of not having a pot to piss in.

In the past she'd tried to do other things but her lack of education and qualifications hadn't allowed her to; more importantly, her lack of confidence in who and what she was always led her back to this.

'Hello Bunny.'

Her regular punter stood by the door, as sinewy and pallid as ever. Even though it was the height of summer he wore a tweed three-piece suit and Bunny could see the tight starched collar and expensive silk tie was making him sweat. Word had it he was a judge but she didn't know if that was true or if it was just the Soho grapevine working overtime.

Though in truth, it didn't really matter to Bunny what her punters did. She wasn't interested in the way Claudia was, who got very excited by any sort of gossip. All that mattered to Bunny was that they paid her. Five hundred big ones a time. She wasn't cheap. But she shouldn't be either. She was good at her work and she'd never known any of her clients go away disappointed.

'Hello darling. It's good to see you, Peter.' Bunny smiled as she drawled her greeting, watching the man strip off his clothes hurriedly. He knelt

44

proudly on the bed with his semi-erect penis standing limply. Bunny inwardly shuddered but didn't show her disdain.

'My, my. What have you got there for me? I can see I'm in for a treat today, babe.' Bunny licked her lips, feigning excitement as the man's eyes lit up in delight. He smiled back, rubbing his sagging balls as he spoke.

'Bunny darling, I've missed you and so has Mr Torpedo here.'

Bunny stifled a laugh. She didn't want to be cruel, but the idea of him referring to his almost flaccid penis as some kind of lethal weapon amused her.

Holding a fixed smile, Bunny watched her punter crawl up the bed towards her on all fours with a leering, salivating grin on his face. Feeling his bony fingers making their way up her smooth legs, she closed her eyes, expertly shutting out the man in her head; concentrating instead on working out which suitcase to take on holiday. It was a skill she'd learnt a long time ago.

A moment later, and before she knew what was happening, Bunny heard the man let out a piercing scream. Jumping in fright, she opened her eyes to see the terrified punter being dragged off the bed by his hair and hit the ground, as a fist began to pummel his face. The splattering of blood on Bunny's legs was her cue to scramble up off the bed. Frantically, she shouted, remembering she'd sent Claudia home. 'Stop! Stop! Leave him alone.'

Racing towards the punter and his assailant, Bunny tried to intervene, but she wasn't any match for the other man. Desperate to stop the onslaught, Bunny looked round the room. In the corner, she saw her new and very expensive gold lamp. With a sigh of resignation, she ran across to grab it.

Running back and with only a small hint of a pause at the thought of her beautiful lamp, Bunny swung it with all her might, bringing it crashing down on the man's head.

Immediately he dropped to his knees, falling forward with a cry of pain. 'What the fuck!' The man turned round, his handsome face contorted with rage and his brown eyes full of surprise as Bunny stood panting above him, holding the remaining piece of the lamp. 'Hello Bun, how's tricks?'

'Don't give me *hello Bun*, and don't try to be funny! Look what you've made me do to me bleedin' lamp.'

Del Williams sat on the floor and rubbed his head. He grinned sheepishly and shrugged his shoulders as he stared up intensely with his dark brown eyes. His voice was gravelled and deep. 'I'll get you another one.'

Pouting, Bunny crossed her arms. 'I don't want another one, I wanted this one.'

'Don't be angry, babe; have a heart. What's a man supposed to do?'

'Stay out of me business, that's what. Why do you always have to do this?'

'Do what?'

'*This*. How many times have you come in here steaming like a bleedin' bull at a rodeo? I won't have any punters left at this rate. You're lucky

Claudia isn't here, she would've had your guts.'

Del smiled as he pictured Claudia. Over the past few years he'd had more barneys with her than he'd care to remember after the countless, and sometimes elaborate, attempts to barge his way in to see Bunny unannounced.

'Well, I wouldn't have to do *this* if you'd give it up like I asked. Like I *keep* asking.'

Bunny rolled her blue eyes and spoke gently. 'I told you how it's got to be Del. I know you...' Before Bunny was able to finish her sentence, a loud pained groan was heard from across the room. Del and Bunny looked over, grinning and catching each other's eyes as they realised they'd forgotten about the bewildered punter who still lay curled up on the floor.

Hurrying over and grabbing her grey silk robe to cover herself, Bunny bent down, helping the man sit up. She spoke with genuine warmth and concern. 'Are you okay? I am *so* sorry Peter, and so is my friend. Actually darlin', he's that sorry, he wants to apologise.' Bunny turned to Del, her blue eyes twinkling with mischief. '*Don't you?*'

Del looked down, wanting to avoid Bunny's eyes and definitely wanting to avoid having to apologise to some toffee-nosed geezer, who no doubt had a blissfully unaware missus and children waiting at home for him. But then, who was he to talk?

Continuing to avoid Bunny's eyes, Del thought about his wife, Edith. Spoilt, overweight and luxuriating in Marbella with a sour look on her face. He'd met her through a friend when she was barely twenty and she'd clung onto him like a leech, refusing to disappear when he tried to give her the elbow, until eventually he'd given up and she'd just become part of the furniture, placing her feet firmly under the table.

When he looked back on it, he couldn't even say she'd really been any different. Maybe not overweight, but the spoilt, sour expressions and the demanding ungrateful personality had always been there. Even when he'd lifted up her veil on their wedding day, instead of a smiling bride it was a pursed-lipped, angry woman who was never satisfied with anything he did. His friends had often asked him why he'd married Edith and his reply was always the same. Fuck knows.

He'd lost count of how many years he'd been married, like he'd lost count of how many years it'd been since he'd been able to look into Edith's eyes and feel anything but disgust and loathing for her. He'd tried not to. He really had. But however hard he tried, it didn't make one bit of difference.

He'd built his drugs and money laundering empire, working his ass off to provide for Edith and make a name for himself but it'd kept him away from her, and when he had gone back home laden with presents and enthusiasm, all he'd got in return was a long face and complaints. So gradually his visits had become less and less, until they were virtually non-existent, though the presents had continued and the money. Edith had made sure of that – Fedexed to whichever luxury holiday destination she was at.

And then, one Christmas, lonely and tired, he'd decided to go home. Wanting to spend some quality time with her out in his luxury villa in Marbella. But the person who'd greeted him wasn't his wife. She was a stranger. A greedy, selfish and ungrateful one – and in that moment he'd known he hated her.

He'd often laid in bed wondering why he hadn't left Edith. He wanted to. God, did he just. But when it came down to it, he couldn't.

Not leaving her was for one reason and one reason only. She could and would make his life very difficult indeed. She knew *everything* about him and *everything* about his businesses and when it boiled down to it, no matter how much money or how many houses he gave her he just couldn't do the one thing that would've freed him from her. He just couldn't trust his wife.

'Well?' Bunny's voice broke into his thoughts. He stared at her incredulously. She was seriously expecting him, one of the biggest faces in the country and certainly one of the biggest faces in the Costa, to apologise to some skank? But then, he guessed, that was love for you. It melted the toughest of hard men, and from the first time he'd laid eyes on Bunny as she stood on the corner of Greek Street touting for business, he'd been hooked, lined and bleedin' sinkered.

Winking at Bunny, Del Williams opened his mouth, not quite believing what he was doing as he began to apologise to the guy who'd been about to shag the only woman he'd ever loved in his life. The woman who completed him.

2

Teddy Davies put his head back and felt the burn of the coke up his nose and the bitter taste at the back of his mouth. It was good shit. Quiver, as he called it. Though it was almost the last of it, which meant he'd have to go back to the crap that was floating around Soho. Watered-down charlie with enough amphetamines in it to keep an elephant up all night.

He sighed as he tapped out the final line of the white powder on the top of the toilet cistern. Not a day had gone by in the past couple of years when he hadn't taken any quiver, but then he didn't actually *need* it. He only *liked* it.

Rolling up a twenty-pound note, Teddy Davies leant forward and hoovered up the cocaine expertly off the porcelain toilet top. He snorted hard, taking down the remnants of the quiver into his throat. As he closed his eyes, embracing the high, the cubicle door banged, making him jump. Angry at the broken sensation, Teddy snarled. 'What the fuck's wrong?'

'Sorry boss, we've got to go.'

'All right. All-fucking-right. I'm coming.' Teddy shouted an irritated reply as he grabbed the empty wrap, disposing of it down the grimy stained toilet. He opened the cubicle door and studied the bald-headed man who was standing nervously waiting for him.

50

Teddy nodded his head in recognition, straightening his clothes and wiping his nose with the back of his hand Taking out a comb from the inside of his jacket he looked in the cracked men's room mirror, brushing his wavy brown hair back. Detective Constable Teddy Davies was ready for duty.

Crossing over Regent Street, Teddy ignored the scream of the taxi horn. He strolled across, smiling sardonically as he cut his eye at the cabbie who was angrily waving his arms and mouthing unheard swear words behind the muddied windscreen. If it'd been dark, he would've been happy to wave his badge to pull the taxi driver over before giving him a slap. Still, he could always take down his carriage number and cause some aggro for him.

Whistling and loosening his tie as he mentally remembered the cabbie's number, Teddy turned off the heaving West End street, cutting through the back, quieter streets of Soho. Even though the quiver was wearing off he could still feel a buzz. But perhaps one more line wouldn't harm.

Walking along the shady side of Beak Street and turning right into Great Windmill Street, Teddy noticed a few girls standing on the corner. They couldn't have been older than sixteen, seventeen. Short skirts, tits pushed up to their chins and enough make-up to cover a football pitch. He didn't recognise any of them but he didn't have to guess very hard to know who they belonged to. He frowned, instantly knowing it was another new influx of Russian girls, which was the last thing he needed. There was already too many rumblings for him to deal with as it was.

The Russian pimps were difficult to deal with; they overcharged and ripped off their punters. Not to mention turning them over and leaving them half battered in alleyways, which lead to complaints at the station, bringing unwanted attention to the goings-on in Soho. The girls themselves were nearly as bad as their pimps. Hardened bitches, refusing to give pussy away for free.

Turning away and heading towards Old Compton Street, Teddy sighed. He'd have to deal with it later; find out what was going on. One thing he didn't like was being ripped off and not getting what was due to him. It'd taken him a long time to get control of the one square mile of Soho, making sure the pimps, hookers and launderers were all in their place. It was his territory and no one, not even the ruthless Russian mafia, was going to come in and piss on it. After all, he was Teddy Davies and if anyone got in his way, he was going to make sure they never got in his way again.

Walking into the cool air of Whispers bar, Teddy waved to Alfie Jennings, the owner of the club and a well-respected face in Soho. Teddy had a lot of time for Alfie. He was old school and knew the score. Pay up and shut up, and in return he kept the law off his back, which for Teddy was easy. He *was* the law.

Sitting down at one of the tables, Teddy knocked back the complimentary drink Ahie had just sent over; double whisky on the rocks.

'How's tricks?'

Teddy glanced up to see the grinning face of Del Williams. Of all the people he had to deal with, Del was the one who made him feel the most uneasy. It wasn't just because of his imposing physical presence. There was something else. Something about Del that told him he was only biding his time until he took over completely, that he was waiting to stab him in the back at any given opportunity, and for that reason, Teddy Davies had to watch Del like the proverbial hawk.

The problem Teddy had with Del was that he was one of the big ones. The biggest face and the biggest dealer around. He had influence and the kind of power Teddy could only dream of. He couldn't just get rid of him and get him banged-up, or dispose of him like some of the others who'd crossed him. He certainly couldn't risk having Del as an enemy, but then, Teddy also knew he couldn't just let Del do what he wanted either.

He needed to keep him tabbed, but increasingly Teddy was finding this harder and harder to do, especially as Del was now branching out with the Russians along the Costa del Sol. He knew it wouldn't be long until he joined forces with the Russians over here; that's if he hadn't already done so.

What he didn't know was how long Del would want or need to continue paying him the money to keep any shit from falling at his door. The idea of this rankled Teddy, kept him awake at night. If it wasn't for him, Del and his cronies wouldn't be anywhere near as big as they were now. And they certainly wouldn't have stayed away from the inside of a prison cell. He'd made them who they were today, and all he asked in return was a cut of their money. And a cut of their drugs. But what thanks did he get? He got as much gratitude as crabs on a whore.

With a tight smile and a begrudging handshake, Teddy greeted Del. 'Good thanks. Just come to collect my usual. We don't want to get behind now, do we?'

Del's features scrunched into a scowl. His face darkened, causing the twinkle in his eyes to disappear. 'Ted. Mate. Don't come here and talk shit. I don't like people who disrespect me. I value my reputation. Tell me something, *mate*. When have I *ever* got behind in anything I've owed you?'

Teddy Davies stared back, but not as hard and not as confidently as the penetrating gaze coming from Del Williams. He swallowed, and was almost able to hear the whisky going down above the music playing in the bar.

From the corner of his eye, Teddy could see Alfie Jennings watching with interest. This wasn't how it was supposed to be going down. How was he meant to maintain control when the likes of Del Williams thought he had the monopoly on Soho?

Unable to maintain the stare, Teddy turned away, muttering something inaudible.

'I can't hear you, Ted, you need to speak louder mate.'

Teddy looked at Del. He could tell he was enjoying this. Squeezing the balls out of him and making him grovel. And by the looks of Alfie

Jennings' grin, he was enjoying seeing his obvious discomfort as well.

Clearing his throat and cursing the fact he could feel himself beginning to blush, Teddy spoke, his voice laden with humiliation. 'Never, Del. You've never got behind with anything.'

'*Never*. That's exactly right my son, so *never* let me hear you say otherwise.'

It was all too much for Teddy, who went to stand up, wanting to get away from the mocking eyes as quickly as he could. He'd get his money later. But as he did, he felt the firm grip of Del's hand on his shoulder, pushing him back down into the purple velvet chair.

'Not so fast. I reckon I deserve something else, don't you? One little word beginning with *S* and then, Ted my son, we can put all this behind us.'

Teddy's head shot up and he saw that the twinkle had returned to Del's brown eyes. This couldn't be happening to him – and to make it worse, his whole buzz had left him.

'Well?'

Teddy glanced round nervously. Over in the corner of the bar, he saw Alfie had been joined by two other well-known faces of London, Vaughn Sadler and Freddie Thompson, all of whom were staring at him as if they were watching the Christmas episode of *EastEnders*.

Teddy turned back, taking in Del's face, which was now only a few inches away from him. 'I ain't got all day, Ted.'

It was almost choking him. Literally sticking in his throat and making it difficult for him to breathe.

'S ...s ... so ... sorry.'

Del Williams threw his head back and let out a huge roar – showing off his expensive set of veneers – as he slapped a tense Teddy on the back.

Teddy Davies watched with narrowed eyes as Del laughed. He watched Alfie, Vaughn and he watched Freddie. All laughing. All having a giggle at his expense. The fury rose inside him. He had to do something. Del had begun to cause him nothing but aggro and he certainly knew he couldn't trust him.

Somehow, he needed to rein Del in, but quite how, Teddy Davies hadn't figured out yet. But he would, and when he did, it'd be *him* throwing his head back and laughing as he wiped the stupid arrogant smile off Del Williams' face.

Standing in the afternoon sun on Drury Lane an hour later, Del was feeling pleased with himself. Very pleased. He was looking forward to the trip to Marbella with Bunny. In fact, he felt a bit like a school kid. They'd never been away together before, not that he hadn't tried to drag her away from Soho on many other occasions. He'd actually begged her, but it'd always been a firm *no* and then a dozen excuses. But this time he'd finally got her to budge. She'd promised and this time he wouldn't take no or an excuse for an answer.

Standing waiting in the London heat, Del's mind crossed from Bunny to the Russians. A lot of people he knew didn't want to deal with the Russian mafia, but they were the only people he *wanted* to deal with. They got things done and what they said was going to happen *did* happen. Everything was beginning to fall into place nicely. The deal he'd made with them to supply the coke for both the Costa and Soho had been a good call, though he could've gone for a better price. He didn't like to think of that too much; what was done was done.

These days he found himself being distracted, his mind wandering off elsewhere. Still, all in all it'd turned out well. Soon Soho and the Costa would be flooded with tasty coke instead of the shit that was flying about now. There were too many wannabe suppliers, too many pony outfits, which made it impossible to get the quality.

For the past year or so he'd found plenty of yes men. All who talked the talk, promising to be able to supply him with the amount and grade of coke he needed, but all inevitably never coming through with the goods, or if they did, the supply of coke ran out after the second or third run, making him have to go back to square one and allowing other runners to step in. The result of this being rather than him getting the whole pie, he ended up only being able to get a slice of it, as well as having to slice out to the likes of Teddy Davies.

All his other businesses were good. Money laundering, stolen goods and the different outlets he owned had made him a very rich man and a very powerful one. The one thing that had eluded him for years was the stronghold on the drugs trade – but now, thanks to the deal with the Russians, there'd be no more fuck-ups. The supply and the shipments would be constant, which meant he'd never have to deal with the other small-time suppliers and cockroaches who thought they were the big time.

Pulling out his phone, Del remembered that he needed to make a call to his lawyer. He'd been trying to get through all day. Each time he called the office he left a message, but no one called back, which had begun to piss him off no end. He needed some papers drawn up before he went to Marbella, which was now cutting it finely.

Just as he was about to leave another warning message, Del looked up. He smiled, waving as he caught sight of the person he was waiting for. The one other person who could compete with his affections as much as Bunny could, and only the second person he'd ever given his heart to. His daughter. Star Barker-Williams.

'All right darlin'.' Del winked at his daughter as she ran towards him, grinning.

Seven-year-old Star Barker-Williams looked at her dad and winked back. He'd taught her to wink and now it was her favourite way of greeting everyone, though her headmaster hadn't taken kindly to it this morning. He'd told her off and made her stay in at play-time. He was such a spoilsport. Even when she'd taken her pirate's treasure to school he'd told her off. Instead of being interested in seeing it he'd put it in his drawer until home time. The thought of it made Star crinkle up her nose in disgust. Still, at least she'd managed to take her spyglass to school today without being caught. She'd been able to keep it a secret and one thing Star Barker-Williams delighted in more than anything was secrets.

3

'One more time, Daddy. Do it again. *Please.*' The laughing request and exaggerated please came from eight-year-old Julie Cole as she and her brother, Zak, bounced up and down on their beds in manic delight as they watched their father, Gary, play air guitar to Robert Palmer's 'Bad Case of Loving You'.

'No, babe. It's getting late, sweetheart. You need to get some sleep.'

Disappointed, Julie sat down hard on the bed, her arms firmly crossed in disgust at her father's suggestion.

'What about sweets? You promised we could have some before we went to bed.'

'I ain't going out again, babe, I'm tired. I'll get you some sweets tomorrow. I promise.'

'You promised today. You said we could have them today. *Please.*'

Gary Cole couldn't resist it. He was as powerless to the charms of his daughter as he had been with her mother.

'Okay, okay. Bleedin' hell, you've chewed me ear off enough. But I ain't going. If you want them, you go. Here's a fiver; make sure you bring back me change.'

Gary sat back on the sofa and opened his fourth can of lager. Apart from the kids, getting lagging was one of Gary's few pleasures in life. It made him forget, and most of the time that's all Gary wanted to do. Watching the freshly opened beer's froth appear and bubble on top of the dinted can, Gary yawned. He lay back on the sofa not wanting to think anymore, instead drifting off to sleep.

Julie Cole skipped along the alleyway which ran behind the sprawling grey estate off the Euston Road. Even for her young age she knew it was a dump. She'd often heard her Dad say so and she guessed, but didn't know, if it was part of the reason her mum had left.

Standing at the top of the litter-strewn concrete stairs leading down to the canal walk, Julie looked around. It was quicker to get to the sweet shop that way, but her dad had told her to stay on the main road. But then, her dad wasn't here and when her dad wasn't here it meant he couldn't start shouting at her and give her a clip round the ear. It also meant she could do what she liked. The other good reason to go the short cut was being able to get home before Zak went to sleep. He liked sweets just as much as she did and she didn't want him not having his treats tonight.

With one more quick glance around and her mind made up, Julie Cole bounded down the stairs two at a time, jumping over the empty cans of beer and used syringes at the bottom.

Standing at the edge of the canal bank, with the sun still beating down, Julie crinkled her nose at a soiled nappy floating on top of the water. She

60

watched, fascinated, as a large water rat swam by, navigating its way through the rubbish and canal weeds.

'Dirty, isn't it?'

Startled, Julie turned round and saw a man standing behind her. She held her breath, frightened at his appearance. He stood a few feet away, staring hard at her. In one hand he held a fishing rod, in the other a plastic bag, which looked to Julie as if it was moving of its own accord. His clothes were old and torn and even though it was a hot summer evening, he wore an oversized trench coat. His face looked funny too. Scary. And his teeth looked like they hadn't been cleaned for a long time.

Julie began to back away, nervously.

'Do you want to see what's in my bag?' The man grinned as Julie shook her head, her eyes wildly focused on the dirty bag he held. It was definitely moving. Her dad had been right. She should never have come this way.

'Is everything all right?'

Another voice came from behind her. She turned round to see a tall well-dressed man coming out from the darkness of the canal tunnel. Julie let out an audible sigh of relief as he approached her.

'Is this man bothering you, love?'

Julie shrugged her shoulders. The well-dressed man turned to the man holding the moving bag and spoke in a firm authoritative voice. 'Maybe you should be getting on your way.'

Julie watched as the scruffy man, not bothering to say another word, hobbled off along the canal towards Kings Cross.

'Are you all right? Did he give you a fright? Sometimes people aren't as scary as they look but you should never trust anyone you don't know.'

Again Julie shrugged. 'Yeah, me dad's always saying that. He told me not to come this way.'

'Where is your dad?'

'At home with me brother. I'm going for sweets but I wanted to get back before Zak went to sleep, that's why I came this way.'

'Would you like me to walk with you? Make sure you're all right?'

Julie looked at the man. He was smart looking. Wearing a black suit. 'Okay.'

'Which shop are you going to?'

'Patel's on Eversholt Street 'cos they do the sweets my brother likes. Do you know where it is?'

'Yes, I know it, but I know a better way to go. Come on, let me show you. Hold my hand because it's dark under the tunnel. We don't want you falling over and ruining that pretty dress you're wearing, do we?' The man smiled as Julie Cole took his hand.

4

It tasted like garbage. If Gary were to bet what garbage tasted like, he would've said it tasted like his mouth did at that very moment. Scraping his tongue with his teeth, Gary lit a cigarette, hoping it would somehow remove the foul taste.

He looked round. The front room was strewn with cans and overflowing ashtrays. Gary couldn't remember anything about the evening and he wasn't going to bother to try. He could see the sunlight pushing through the curtains, but with his head pounding, causing his eyes to hurt, Gary had no intention of welcoming in the early morning.

The sofa wasn't the most comfortable place to sleep, but the effort required to walk up the stairs was beyond Gary and his hangover definitely felt like it was getting progressively worse with each waking moment.

'Fuck.' Gary Cole sighed heavily as he heard the small cries of Zak coming from upstairs. Lighting another cigarette, Gary took two attempts to prise himself off the sofa, wishing his son would either be quiet or realise the beauty of sleeping-in late.

Walking into the kid's bedroom, the huge grin given to him by his son went some way to soothe Gary's fatigue and pounding head. 'How are you, boy?' Bending down to hug him Gary pulled back quickly.

'Christ almighty. Smelly arse.'

Picking up his son and trying not to let the smell of Zak's nappy make him nauseous, Gary saw that Julie had already got up.

'Now then mate, where's your sister? Knowing Julie, she's already in Daddy's bedroom looking for extra pocket money.' He smiled at Zak, kissing him on his nose before adding, 'On that score son, she's very much like your mum.'

Opening the unpainted plywood door of his bedroom and expecting to see Julie rummaging through his things, Gary sighed. The last thing he felt like doing was playing hide and seek with his daughter.

'Julie, come on out now, doll, Daddy has a headache and really doesn't feel so well. *Please* babe.'

Trying to keep his patience, Gary went back to his bedroom and checked in the wardrobes, each time opening the door and each time saying 'boo' to an empty closet, much to the amusement of a giggling Zak.

Stomping down the stairs and thoroughly pissed off, Gary continued to call, hoping the game would soon be over.

'Julie, please babe, stop now, Daddy gives up... Julie? For fuck's sake. I give up, darlin'.'

Where the hell was she? He'd had enough now. He knew she wasn't in the front room, and the adjoining kitchenette was tiny; too tiny for a game of hide and seek. An old gas cooker stood against the side wall and the cupboards were high up out of reach on the right hand wall; impossible for any child to get to. So where?

A slight feeling of panic started to rise in Gary. He tried to quickly push it away but his heart started to beat faster as he thought about the events of the previous night. It was still a blur. Yes, he remembered Julie had gone out to get sweets, but he couldn't actually *remember* her returning. But she must have. The sweet shop was only ten minutes away, at most. He could've sworn he'd heard the front door shut. But then how could he? He'd been asleep. Pissed out of his mind.

'Julie?... Julie?' Running up the stairs two at a time, Gary went into the children's bedroom again, depositing Zak back into his cot who immediately started to scream.

Gary started to run, ignoring the pain in his head. He flung open all the doors, hearing himself breathing hard as he entered each room, feeling the sweat of cold anxiety run down his back as he looked under the beds, realising there was nowhere else for him to look for his daughter. In the background he could hear the hysterical cries of Zak compounding the terror in his own mind.

'She's gone. Open the fucking door, for fuck's sake, just open the fucking door.' The wild hammering on number fourteen was heard throughout the estate as one of Gary Cole's next-door neighbours came to the door.

Opening the door, the woman was astonished as she watched Gary fall to his knees, sobbing. She looked at him and something about the way he cried made her crouch down and hold him in her arms.

'What is it, Gal?' The pain that gripped his body made it nearly impossible for Gary Cole to speak, and when he did it was only a few words. 'Julie's gone. She never came back. She never came back.'

5

Julian Millwood felt like his face was about to explode. The throbbing ache not only encompassed his jaw but the whole of his body. He'd gnawed on the inside of his mouth, tasting his own blood. His lip felt like it'd swollen to twice its normal size. Goddamn tooth. He knew he should really go to the dentist but he hated them. To him, they were on a par with coppers.

With the curtains closed, he lit up a cigarette, exposing the gloom of the room and trying to ignore the pain now making its way up into his ear.

The thick grime in the bedsit was evident. Piles of old magazines and newspaper clippings were strewn across the floor and the tatty blue Dralon chair was full of papers dating as far back as three years ago.

The kitchen surfaces were covered in stinking takeaway cartons and the sink was full of dishes with the food so solidified on them it probably wasn't worth attempting to clean them. Julian groaned heavily. It was cleaner in the frigging nick, and that was saying something.

His time in prison had been a nightmare. It'd been the first time he'd served a long stretch but he knew it could've been worse, far worse, and with time off for good behaviour he'd only had to serve half of what the bitter man-hating female judge had given him. A result.

He'd asked his uncle to look after the place whilst he'd been inside, expecting when he came back out to at least see the stained sheets changed and the milk he'd poured on the cereal on the morning of his arrest to be thrown out. It hadn't. Everything was just the same, only with a more putrid smell.

It was as if his uncle had been keeping the place as some sort of shrine for his return, although Julian knew it was only because his uncle was a fat lazy bastard and as long as there was a free roof over his head, the man didn't care what condition the place was in.

Not that he was much better; he'd lived here for the past ten years and in all that time he'd probably bothered to clean it once, when his girlfriend had visited him. He hadn't dated her long, probably no longer than a month or so. He hadn't actually liked her. It was what had come with her that he'd liked.

But it'd all gone tits up when she'd come round for a surprise visit. She'd found some pictures and had quickly gone and rounded up her father and brothers, who'd given him the battering of his life.

He supposed it'd been his own fault. He shouldn't have left out things he didn't want prying eyes to see. And he'd known she was a nosy cow after he'd found her going through his mobile phone for text messages from other women. When he'd caught her she'd looked mortified, blabbing an apology, but he'd immediately laughed, knowing she couldn't have been further from the truth if she'd tried.

Touching his swollen mouth, Julian looked around again. He detested the flat. The estate. The area. But like a moth round a flame he was drawn back time and time again. He'd once tried to move away, but he'd only lasted a month. He hadn't known anyone and all he'd really done was swap one shithole of a place for another. At least this was an area he knew; he'd grown up here and he supposed it was what he was used to – and Julian Millwood was certainly a creature of habit.

Trying to light up another cigarette, Julian cursed as his lighter, running out of gas, gave out only a small spark. Remembering he had another one in his pocket, Julian put his hand inside his jacket and smiled when, along with the lighter, he pulled out a pink pair of little girl's knickers.

Alan Day was proud of his work. In fact he was very proud. He was one of the best at what he did. He was the defence. The barrister people loved to hate. The man who let the guilty walk. And Alan Day had been in the job long enough to know that the majority of defendants who walked into his mahogany and leather trimmed office were just that. Guilty. Violent partners, rapists, child killers, paedophiles – at one time or

68

another he'd got them all off.

Domestic violence was the easiest. Money for old rope. Take last week – he'd managed to successfully get the perpetrator off even though the man's own children had given evidence against him. But juries were hesitant to convict. They couldn't understand why women stayed. Why women couldn't seek the help they needed. Didn't understand and wouldn't understand, which played beautifully into his hands. All he needed to do was get the woman on the stand and make out she was either neurotic or embittered, and the jury would be happy to go along with it – and Alan was happy to be paid handsomely.

Rapists were nearly as easy to get off. Make out the woman hadn't really said no, just regretted it the next day. Had drunk too much; no one liked a lush. There were all sorts of defence strategies and again, all he needed to do was put a doubt, however small, into the jury's mind.

Paedophiles and child killers were harder to get off. The jury, especially the women, went gooey-eyed at a picture of a child. But then Alan did always like a challenge, and never did a malt whisky taste as good as when he managed to get the indefensible to walk free.

Leaning back in his chair, dressed in his tailor-made navy pinstriped suit, Alan lit a cigar.

A knock at the door interrupted his thoughts. His secretary put her head round the door. She was new and keen. Two qualities Alan Day liked. He felt the first stirrings of an erection. Give it a couple of weeks, she'd be begging for it. They always were.

'Mr Day. There's a visitor for you. I told him he'd have to make an appointment but he wouldn't go. I'm not sure quite what to do.'

'What's his name?'

'Julian. Mr Julian Millwood.'

For the first time in years, Alan Day felt nervous.

6

'It was this big.' Star Barker-Williams stood opposite a laughing Del and Bunny with her arms outstretched and her blue eyes wide open with excitement. Bunny grinned, speaking with warmth to her daughter. 'Are you sure it was that big, Star?'

Del laughed and nudged Bunny in her side. 'Listen, when the child says it was that big, it was that big. Ain't that right, Star?'

Star nodded profusely, a mop of blonde hair falling across her face. 'Yep. It was huge. Almost as big as this building.'

'And then what happened?' Claudia spoke as she leaned forward in her chair, getting nearly as carried away in the story as Star was.

Star looked round the room, delighting in everyone listening. She squeezed her hands together, her face lighting up. The nuns at school always told her not to be so silly when she tried to tell them about what she saw. To stop making things up. But she *wasn't* making things up. She really did see pirates. Pirates and cowboys. In fact, though she hadn't told anybody yet, she was sure the deputy head at school was a pirate in disguise. He had a glass eye and no one but pirates had glass eyes. The other girls at school said he'd been in a car accident but Star knew better. *She* knew how he'd got it. *In a battle on the high seas.* And one day she'd prove it, but for the time being it was going to be her secret.

Smiling, she turned back to Claudia, continuing with her story. 'Then when I went up to the pirate boat, I saw someone.'

Bunny grinned, 'Who? Oh wait let me guess ... a cowboy.'

'Nope.'

Del shouted out, 'A lion tamer.'

Star laughed. 'Nope.'

Bunny tried again. 'A fairy.'

Star pulled a face. Her mum was always trying to make her like fairies and dolls. And even though her mum bought her a new doll nearly every week she *hated* them nearly as much as she hated fairies. They were for sillies. She looked at her mum. 'No way!'

Bunny raised her arms up in the air, grinning. 'Go on then, we give up. Who was on the pirate boat?'

Star lowered her voice into a whisper. 'A little girl, and she was tied up.'

Bunny's smile dropped. She looked tense. 'That's enough, Star.'

Del's head whipped round to Bunny, surprised at the sudden change in her tone. As he frowned at Bunny, Star continued to talk.

'She looked dead scared and just as I was going to try to rescue her I heard a scream and...'

Bunny stood up, her face red and her voice raised. 'I said enough, Star! Don't you know when enough's enough? You have to stop with these silly stories. No wonder you're always getting into trouble at school.'

Star's eyes filled with tears as she looked at her mum. Annoyed at the way Bunny had spoken to Star, Del snapped.

'What the hell's wrong with you, Bun? She's only telling a story.'

'Well, maybe I don't want to hear her story at the moment.'

Claudia walked over to Bunny, speaking gently to her.

'Bun, you're being harsh, babe. Star's only having fun.'

Bunny said nothing. She looked at Del, who was staring at her in amazement, then at Claudia, before finally crouching down to look at her daughter, whose expression was a picture of hurt. Shame swept across Bunny's face.

'Star, I'm sorry. I don't know what got into me. Mummy's just tired. Can you forgive me, babe?'

Star wiped away her tears. She *hated* tears. A moment later she threw her arms round Bunny's neck in a loving embrace, but not before noticing the tiny glance exchanged between her mum and Claudia. A smile appeared on Star's face. There were secrets everywhere.

Teddy Davies adjusted his seating yet again in an attempt to get comfortable on the tatty sofa. He sat back watching Gary Cole crouched down against the wall, hugging his knees in despair.

Teddy rubbed his chin feeling his twenty-four-hour stubble and sighed. He hated missing children cases. They took too long *and* he was expected to be sensitive.

He had things to do. He needed to deal with Del. What had happened in Whispers was chewing at him. It was clear the man thought it was all right to humiliate him. He had a bad feeling about it all. Del was up to something and he wanted to get to the bottom of it before it was too late. He'd worked too long and too hard to lose control of Soho. But instead of being able to deal with it straight away he was stuck with Gary Cole, who was struggling to even talk.

He'd already wasted over an hour. He needed to speed things up a bit. Besides which, he could do with a few lines of quiver to pick him up, take the edge off his anxiety. Turning to Gary, Teddy spoke.

'Mr Cole is there nothing you can think of that may help?'

No answer.

Teddy tried again.

'Are you sure your daughter couldn't have just got up and gone out on her own?'

'No. I know she wouldn't have.'

Teddy indicated the rizla papers and beer cans on the table. 'So what went on last night, Gary? Looks like you had some sort of party.'

'What? Sorry. No ... no, there was no party. I had a few drinks. Oh Jesus.'

Teddy rolled his eyes, listening to Gary's sobs.

'You need to try to concentrate, Mr Cole. These melodramatics won't help anyone, least of all your daughter.'

The gasp in the room came from the other detective who held Teddy's gaze with a look of disgust. Teddy stared back, cutting his eye at his colleague. He didn't give a shit what he thought. Gary was gasping, clearly having some kind of panic attack.

'I can't breathe... I can't breathe.'

That was it. Teddy Davies had had enough. He walked towards the door. His colleague could do the rest. He had somewhere else he wanted to be.

'I think I'll be off now, Gary, the family liaison unit should be round shortly and if you do remember anything more, you need to contact me straight away. Oh and by the way, in my experience, if you can't breathe, you can't talk.'

Outside Gary Cole's flat, the summer sun pierced down into Teddy's eyes, eclipsing the depth of the squalor of the run-down estate. Striding back to the car and hoping to find the kids from the area hadn't taken his wheels off his new Range Rover, Teddy looked at his watch. A Rolex. Courtesy of Alfie Jennings for favours done. If he was quick, he could get back to Soho in time to speak to Del.

Teddy opened the door, going into the glove compartment. From inside he pulled out a wrap of quiver. Taking a quick look round he opened it, shovelling up the powder with his long fingernail, especially grown for moments like this. Within seconds the quiver hit the back of his nose, then his throat, until he felt the high take over his body.

Jumping into the car, Teddy smiled to himself. If Del Williams thought he could get the better of him, then he was more of a fool than he looked.

7

Edith Williams lay on the sun lounger and broke wind as she stuffed the last of the Godiva chocolates into her mouth. No matter how much she tanned herself in the heat of the Marbella sun her skin didn't turn any shade of anything, apart from red.

Her over-processed undernourished platinum hair hung like straw from under her hat. Her swollen size twenty body was squeezed into her expensive Pucci swimsuit, with the layers of fat straining to escape. Puffy fingers held an array of Bvlgari and diamond-encrusted Chanel rings. Her fingernails were painted a deep purple, matching the swollen veins on her hands and legs.

Feeling something warm on her chest, Edith looked down, and noticed that one of the chocolates had fallen onto her creped skin, melting and oozing dark liquid down her swimsuit.

'Oi, bleedin' hell. Look at the state of this. It looks like I've been shat on by a flying pig.' Edith spoke loudly to herself.

'Alfonso!... Alfonso! Bring a bleedin' cloth to

mop me up before the flies come and eat me alive.'

From inside the villa, Alfonso Garcia sat at the large marble kitchen table, finishing off his freshly squeezed lemonade, and rolled his eyes. He had no intention of moving until he'd finished his drink. At the best of times he didn't like to do much, but today it was especially true. He was tired and the Costa del Sol heat was, as it always did, getting to him.

He'd only just got back this morning from a trip to London. Another errand for Edith; bringing back chocolates from Selfridges. Why she couldn't be like anyone else and buy her chocolate from the local shop he didn't know. And now, even though in the last twenty-four hours he'd had less than two hours sleep, he was still supposed to be at her beck and call. Well he wasn't going to be rushed by anyone, least of all Edith Williams.

Spitting a lemon pip back into the iced drink, Alfonso listened to Edith's screeching, which was becoming louder and more hysterical with every call.

'*Alfonso!... Where the bleedin' frig are you?... Alfonso!*

'*Alfonso!... Stop bleedin' mugging me off... Alfonso!*

'*Alfonso!... Get your skinny arse out here... Alfonso!*'

Having given it another five minutes before going to see what Edith wanted, Alfonso walked out onto the pool area and was promptly greeted by an empty box of chocolates being thrown in his direction.

'Where the friggin' hell have you been Alfonso? I was calling that much and that loud I've got gut rot now. You know stress does funny things to me stomach. I'll have to go to the khazi now and do a banana split.'

Ignoring Edith's crudeness, Alfonso smiled a sickly smile. 'I didn't hear you.'

'I was calling loud a-bleedin'-nuff.'

'I was at the back of the house sorting out some of the deliveries that came this morning. Perhaps next time you should shout louder.' Alfonso held his smile for a moment before adding, 'What was it you wanted anyway?'

'Look at the state of me.'

Alfonso stared at Edith, trying not to show his disgust in his face as he looked at her beached-whale body on the sun lounger, covered in gooey chocolate.

'Come and help me clean myself up.'

Alfonso picked up a towel discarded on the other lounger and went towards Edith to wipe away the chocolate. Straight away Edith screeched loudly, brushing him away with her hand before he could wipe up the mess.

'Not with bleedin' that you silly sod. Get me some tissues. Oh and Alfonso. Where's my kiss?'

Alfonso's sickly smile reappeared as he inwardly shuddered. 'How could I forget?' Bending down he kissed Edith who, with shark-like speed, opened her mouth, pushing her tongue past Alfonso's tightened lips.

Coming up for breath, Alfonso took the opportunity to pull away. 'Now my princess, let me go

77

and get you those tissues otherwise like you say, the flies will eat you alive.'

Edith scowled. 'I thought you said you didn't hear me.'

'I heard you as I was coming through to see what was wrong.'

'But I said that when I first called you.'

Alfonso shrugged his shoulders. 'Edith my darling. I'm here now. Stop getting your pretty little head in a flap.' Alfonso winked at Edith who giggled in a childlike way, causing Alfonso to shudder again. 'Right, you'll be okay here for a moment while I go and get those tissues.'

Walking back into the villa with his back turned away from Edith, Alfonso's face changed into a nasty sneer. He'd been employed by Edith for the past three years, going from the maintenance man to the cook, to the chauffeur to the house-keeper and finally to her bed; not that there was any attraction on his part, quite the opposite in fact.

He'd stupidly thought becoming her lover would've given him a certain sway; imagining being able to do as he pleased – more to the point, being able to spend her money as he pleased. But he couldn't have been more wrong if he'd tried. Edith had become more demanding, both in the bedroom and with the things she expected him to do for her. Treating him more like the hired help than ever before. It wasn't as if she didn't have other staff working for her, yet she insisted on him doing it.

Going into the large, ostentatious gold-leafed bathroom, Alfonso grabbed some tissues. He stopped to look at himself in the mirror. He was naturally olive skinned but the years of living abroad had given his skin a constant dark mahogany tinge, making him look more Mediterranean than the locals and helping him turn from the East End-born Alf Garfield he really was into the suave, well-spoken Alfonso Garcia.

When he'd first come to Spain it'd been his intention to lie low and blend into the background, needing to be unseen, but he couldn't have imagined for a moment how well it would turn out. It'd worked out perfectly in fact.

Over a short period of time his skin had darkened, his mousey brown hair had been dyed to a jet black and he'd changed his name, picking up the local lingo along the way. He'd reinvented his life and erased the past. Changing his history from the life of crime he'd led – spending the majority of it going in and out of the nick – to a third generation Spaniard who'd come to live back in Spain with his mother who'd passed away ten years ago.

He'd picked up odd jobs, looking over his shoulder at first until he realised no one was actually looking his way. And over time he'd been able to put Alf Garfield to rest, and in his place the smooth-talking Alfonso Garcia was born.

Then one day he'd been in Puerto Banüs, the luxury marina south-west of Marbella. He'd bumped into an old acquaintance – a retired face from London that he'd done some work for when he first came to Spain – who'd told him about a job where they needed someone to keep their mouth shut and their eyes open. Alfonso had known this wouldn't be a problem; it'd been how he'd lived his life. A few days later a meeting had been set up with some cronies before he was actually taken to meet the man himself. Del Williams. Husband of Edith, and number one face.

Even though it paid well and the work came with living quarters provided, Alfonso hadn't seen the job to have any redeeming features; un-blocking toilets around the villa, changing fuses and whitewashing already brilliantly white walls as well as always keeping schtum to the comings and goings of the Costa del Sol's biggest faces, wasn't his idea of living the high life.

But then a couple of months after he'd started work at the Williams' villa, Alfonso had woken up to find Edith sitting in the kitchen, having re-turned from one of her luxury holidays. Within hours, Del had left the villa, going back to London, not being able to stand more than the minimum of time with his wife. So that had left Edith and him.

At first, Edith had viewed him suspiciously, but one thing Alfonso had always been good at throughout his life was reading people. Giving them what they wanted before ripping the granny out of them and taking them for everything they had. Edith was no different. Alfonso knew exactly what she needed to get *him* what he needed.

'Alfonso!... Alfonso! Where are those bleedin' tissues? Where the fuck are you?'

Alfonso scowled. The time was coming when he wouldn't have to jump to Edith's every whim. She was a fat, loud-mouthed cow – but a very rich one, and even though it'd taken longer than he thought it would, if he continued to play his cards right, he'd be able to get his hands on that wealth.

His phone started to vibrate in his pocket, breaking his thoughts. He answered, slightly annoyed.

'Yes.'

Alfonso listened to the caller for a moment, before growling down the phone. His voice changed from the feigned affected voice in which he spoke to Edith, into the heavy threatening cockney accent of Alf Garfield.

'Listen geeze, I told you to never fucking phone me... I'm warning you mate, don't press my fucking buttons, pal, otherwise I ain't going to be held responsible for my actions.'

Cutting off the call, Alfonso straightened down his clothes and walked out into the brilliant Spanish sunlight, trying desperately to ignore the nagging unrest that had just come over him.

Back in his office in London, defence barrister Alan Day slowly put down the phone as the line went dead. He had a bad feeling. A very bad feeling indeed.

8

'I wasn't expecting you to finish so early ... you all right, babe? You look tired. Do you want me to run you a bath, darlin'?' Claudia looked on edge but smiled as Bunny walked into the white and gold front room of the luxury apartment Bunny owned, but shared with Del on the west side of Soho. Bunny smiled weakly back, ignoring the question put to her. 'What have you got there, Claudia?'

'Where?'

Bunny looked bemused as Claudia shuffled awkwardly in front of the table. Of all the things Claudia was, it usually wasn't secretive. 'Behind your back. What's on the table, Claud?'

'Nothing.'

Bunny chuckled a little too loudly for it to sound natural. 'Claudia, it ain't nothing if I can see there's something there. What's behind your back, babe?' Bunny began to walk towards Claudia who turned towards the table and began quickly scooping up the contents of the box she'd tipped out.

'Claudia! What's going on? This ain't like you.'

Claudia shot round to face Bunny. Her face was red as she clutched hold of the shoe box against her breasts. 'And it ain't like you neither, Bun. Can't I have a bit of privacy without every Tom and Dick wanting to know what I'm doing? Is that too much to ask for? Or do I need to take me arse out of here to get some cop eye for meself?'

Bunny looked shocked. She'd never seen Claudia react this way. Well, not to her at least. She'd seen her fist down men taller and stronger than her, she'd seen her argue until the cows came home with Del and she'd always seen Claudia jump to her defence as if her life depended on it, but never had Bunny seen Claudia's formidable presence turn on her. Apologetically, Bunny spoke.

'I ... I don't know what to say.'

'Well don't say flippin' nothing then. Okay? Keep yer nose out.'

The moment Claudia said it, she wished she hadn't. She saw the hurt in Bunny's face as she turned to walk out.

'Bunny, I'm sorry. I didn't mean it... *Bronwin*, please.'

Bunny turned to look at Claudia, her face tense.

'Don't call me that. I told you *never* to call me that.'

'Call you what?' Del entered the room, over-hearing the last part of the conversation between the two women. His voice was loud and cheerful, startling both women.

Bunny glanced at Claudia nervously, then gave a smile to Del. 'Nothing. It's fine.'

Del grinned, relieved. The last thing he really wanted was to have his ear chewed off hearing about women's squabbles. He rubbed his hands together eagerly. 'Well in that case, who's up for a spot of lunch at The Ivy?'

Claudia picked up her shoe box and marched towards the door, pushing past Del. 'Not me.'

'Nor me.' Bunny turned and exited, leaving Del on his own wondering if there was ever going to be a time when he'd understand what went on in women's heads.

'I had the dreams again.' Bunny sat in the large white chair opposite the door, wringing her hands.

The place Bunny sat in was a tiny nondescript room with paint peeling off the wall, above a shop on the north side of Victoria Station, but it was one Bunny cherished coming to. It was away from everywhere. A room where nobody knew her or could find her, and it was this room she visited each week.

The one other person sitting in the room was a small hunchback grey-haired woman, dressed in unsuitable clothes for the heat of the summertime. Her black cardigan was buttoned up to the top and she wore a high roll-neck top underneath. She smiled at Bunny sympathetically as she looked over her glasses with a penetrating stare. 'Do you want to tell me about them, Bunny?'

'It's the same dream.'

'The one where you see him, the man from the woods?'

Bunny nodded, unable to hold eye contact with the woman, fearing she might cry.

'Have you told Del about the dreams yet?'

Bunny shook her head. 'No, not really. Not properly anyway.'

'I think you should. I'm sure he'll understand.'

Bunny looked down, noticing a line of ants

crawling along the skirting boards. 'Maybe, but...'

The woman pushed Bunny a little harder. 'Don't you want to? Is it because you don't trust him?'

'I do, but...' Bunny paused, not wanting to talk any longer, even though that was the reason why she was here.

'Go on Bunny.'

'How would I explain to him? I'm a grown woman, I shouldn't be scared of dreams. It's stupid.'

'Then why do you come here?'

Bunny shrugged, but didn't answer. The woman continued to talk in a soft and comforting manner. 'What made the dreams come back do you think?'

'The kid. The missing kid from Camden.'

'Julie Cole?'

'Yes.'

'Tell me what you see, Bunny. It might help.'

Bunny's blue eyes glazed over as she looked down. Her body became tense and she could feel her breathing becoming shallow as she began to talk, falling into the darkness of her own mind.

'It's cold and I'm wearing my dress. Brown dress, horrible thing.' Bunny gave a wry smile then continued. 'I don't have a jacket. Lost it or thrown it. It's dark and I can't see nothin' but I can smell everything. It's been raining and the leaves are really wet. I can smell the damp and the moss of the trees. I can feel my tights are damp because I'm kneeling down. And then I hear her calling. It's from a distance at first, but because I don't say nothing, I make her come to me. She's looking for me. Calling my name over and over again. I should've gone. I should've gone when she called me...'

Bunny stopped, unable to carry on, her eyes full of tears.

'Carry on, Bunny. Try to stick to telling me about the dream.'

'I can hear her calling my name as if she's right next to me, but I don't move. I stay perfectly still. I want to laugh but I know she'll hear me. And then I hear another sound coming from behind me. Other footsteps. Snapping at the twigs and crunching the leaves on the ground. The moonlight suddenly comes between the trees and I can see me breath in the darkness and just as I'm going to get up I see them. I want to call out to her for her to stop, to go back 'cos I know there's something wrong. But I don't. I can't because then they'll know I'm there. I'm looking through the bracken of where I'm hiding and I can see her face, she's still looking and she thinks it's me. She turns round and I catch the fear in her eyes. And then I feel something warm on my face and I know it's blood. Tiny splatters of *her* blood. I hear a gurgling sound and it's her throat being cut. I look directly at them, wanting to see them, but it's like they've got no faces. I can't remember their faces no matter how hard I try. Then I see her. She's just in front of me, lying on the ground. I can almost touch her. She's only a few centimetres away. So still. I see some of her hair has caught on the bracken so I stretch me fingers out to stroke it. I want to stroke it, to make her know it's all right that I'm there. But it's too late, she's gone. And then even though it's cold and

I'm afraid, I stay with her 'cos she pretends not be afraid of the dark, but she is and I know she don't like to be alone. I can't sleep, but it looks like she's asleep, so I just stay huddled up till the sun rises and she don't move and neither do I. Just me and her.'

Looking up, wide eyed, Bunny stared at the woman. 'I'm sorry, I've got to go, I can't do this.' Without waiting for a reply, Bunny grabbed her bag, running out of the door as she listened to the cries of the woman calling her back.

Bunny walked home slowly. She felt drained. Exhausted. And even putting one foot in front of the other seemed a huge effort. The memories of her childhood had reopened painful wounds.

She had once had dreams like her daughter Star. She had once believed that she could do anything. But she knew the debilitating shadow of her childhood had a lot to do with why she couldn't leave what she did behind. She certainly knew her past was why she couldn't allow herself to trust anyone, not even Del.

Being a hooker enabled her to give Star the things she'd never had. But it also allowed her to step slightly aside from the rest of society. She could hide away but still keep on living.

Though she wanted a lot more for Star. And for Star, Bunny would do anything. She'd keep on fighting to be a stronger. To be a better person. For Star, she needed to conquer her demons, so her child wasn't burdened with her ghosts from the past.

9

'What the fuck is that supposed to mean?' Teddy
Davies' face twisted in rage as he stared at the
small-time Soho dealer on the dusty floor of the
walk-up.

'I'm here to collect my money.'

'I ... I haven't got it.'

Teddy squatted down to where the man was
sitting. 'My money. My drugs. I want them *now*.'

'I can't ... he said I wasn't to give you any more.'

Teddy craned his ear towards the man. 'What
did you say?'

'I said I can't give it to you.'

Teddy stood up, slapping the man hard round
his head. He had a feeling he wasn't going to like
what he was about to hear. 'Talk then, I'm listening.'

'It's Del. Del Williams.'

Teddy spoke slowly. 'What about Del?'

'He's put word round we're not to pay you
anymore. He's told all of us if we get any trouble
from you just to contact him and he'll sort it –
but on the condition we give you nothin' or say
nothin', otherwise he'll do worse than the people
you know will ever do.'

Teddy stood up and stared at the man on the
floor. There was no reason for the man to lie to
him. But what he was hearing was unbelievable.
He put his fist in his mouth, chewing down on

his skin. Who the fuck did Del Williams think he was? He was not only trying to mug him off out of the picture with the Russians, he was trying to cut him out completely with everything. This was *his* patch. Not Del's. He was the one who'd seen it grow into what it'd become and now the likes of the flash Del Williams wanted to take it away from him. Well that wasn't going to happen. Not now. Not ever.

He needed to do something, and fast.

Teddy turned to the constable standing next to him.

'Cuff him.'

'What?'

'I said cuff him.'

'On what charge sir?'

Teddy rubbed his head. 'Intent to supply.'

'What the hell are you doing?' The man shouted in protest as the handcuffs went on him. Teddy grinned.

'I'm doing what all good coppers do; I'm getting scum like you off the street.'

'I ain't done nothin'!'

Teddy whispered into the man's ear. 'This is my patch, not Del Williams' patch, and the way I see it, if you want to play on his side then you're balling me and I don't like people who ball me, especially skanky toerags like you.'

'I dunno what you're talking about. You ain't got anything on me mate.'

'No? Well perhaps you'd like to come down the station and explain what this is.'

Taking a large white bag of quiver out of his own pocket, Teddy winked at the constable before placing it into the man's jacket pocket. He patted it. 'I reckon you're looking at least at a five-year lump for that. Take him away.'

'Don't think you're going to get away with this. Once Del finds out what you've done, you're a dead man.'

Teddy Davies yawned. 'Yeah, yeah. Save the movie line. Do you really think Williams gives a shit about the likes of you? Face it mate, you're well and truly stitched the fuck up.'

The moment they were gone, Teddy's face dropped. He couldn't believe Del was so blatantly making a public fool out of him. Telling the dealers not to pay him, like he was worth nothing. He'd helped to make Del who he was today and, just as he'd done that, he would now help to destroy him. And Teddy Davies knew exactly who could help him to do it.

10

A naked body has been found in Regents Park Canal. It is believed to be that of missing eight-year-old-school-girl, Julie Cole. No official statement has been made, but a police source tells LBC radio that an initial post-mortem examination shows she died from strangulation. It is also believed Julie had been sexually abused.

Bunny sat on the edge of her deep sunk porcelain bath. Her whole body was tense as she listened to the radio. Her head began to swim and the old familiar fear gripped her stomach.

'You look like you've seen a ghost, babe.'

Bunny looked up. It was Del. She smiled, pleased to see him.

'They've just said on the radio that kid, Julie Cole that went missing: she's dead.'

'I dunno why you listen to that shit, ain't nothing but misery and you know what you're like, Bun, anything to do with animals or kids and you're all over the place. Anyhow, forget that, I've got something that will put a smile on your boat. Someone's got something they want to show you.'

Del stood in the bathroom doorway and looked behind him. A moment later a little girl appeared, carrying a beautiful smile and a painting in her hand.

'Look Mummy, I did it at school.'

Bunny's sad eyes lit up as Star stood proudly, holding up the painting she'd done.

'Well come here then, let's have a proper butcher's.'

Star skipped to Bunny, her long blonde hair – identical to her mother's – flowing down her back. Her freckled button nose crinkled slightly as she laughed, delighting in the pleasure Bunny showed at her picture.

'Do you like it then? The teacher said she wanted to put it on the wall, but I told her she ain't going to do that, 'cos I wanted to bring it home to you and if she's got a problem with that she needs to speak to me dad.'

Bunny laughed loudly at her daughter's boldness. 'I think it's wonderful, babe. Who's this though, darling?' Bunny pointed to the indistinguishable mass of colours.

Star frowned at her mother as if she was crazy. 'That's you and that's Daddy of course, on an adventure. You're trying to get away from pirates.'

'You and your adventures. Couldn't you have drawn me in the beauty salon? I'm not sure if I want to go to sea.'

Star laughed with her mother. 'Nah, that would be boring. Who wants to get their nails painted when you could go exploring? That's what I'm going to be when I grow up. An explorer.'

Bunny looked at Del and laughed again. Star was certainly her father's daughter. Strong, wilful – yet she could charm any adult or child alike.

Even after seven years she still had to pinch herself at how everything had turned out, because Bunny knew only too well how it could've been.

She'd been a hooker since she'd left care and had always known how to look after herself, especially when it came to her health. She wasn't like the other girls, who for an extra twenty quid would do it bareback. Condom or do one. That was her motto and she religiously lived by it. That was, until she met Del.

She'd known who he was. Everyone knew who he was, he'd made it his business for everyone to know. And it was for this reason Bunny had stayed well clear of him, refusing to flit around him like the other girls did when she saw him in the clubs, flashing his money about and ordering bottles of Cristal champagne for everybody, giving it the big 'un.

The night she'd met him, business had been slow. She'd been touting on the corner of Greek Street for over two hours without a sniff of a punter when he'd pulled up in his grey Lamborghini. She hadn't been impressed and had seen him as she always had done before: flash and tacky. Still, that said, a punter was a punter.

To her surprise he hadn't wanted her to give him a blow job round the back of Soho Square – he'd told her later he'd been watching her for some time and had tried to think of ways for her to see him as more than just a punter. He'd taken her to Lola's Cafe on Bateman Street, where he'd bought her a cup of tea and a fried egg sandwich to warm her up. They'd talked for hours. About his business. About Edith. About everything. At first she'd watched the clock, working out how much money he'd have to give her at the end of the night, but soon she'd found herself forgetting about the time and had just enjoyed his company.

When they'd finished talking, he'd offered her a grand, pulling a bundle of fifty-pound notes out of his trouser pocket, but for some reason she hadn't been able to take it and had walked away, annoyed at herself, but also intrigued that for the first time in her life she felt something other than indifference.

The next night he'd picked her up again, this time spending the evening sitting in his car talking and eating chips. When he'd dropped her off back at the bedsit she shared with one of the other street girls he'd again offered her money, but again she'd refused.

The following evening she'd half expected to see him again and had found herself surprisingly disappointed when she hadn't seen his car drive slowly down the road. Trying to put him out of her head she'd turned two tricks and had been on her knees in the car park of Brewer Street, about to give a blow job to a South American punter, when the punter had been thrown across the bonnet of the nearby car with his trousers round his ankles and his penis standing to attention.

At first Bunny had thought they were being mugged, but when she'd turned around she'd seen Del, his face chiselled in fury, his fists battering the teeth out of the terrified man.

She and Del had spent that night together and it had also been that night that Star had been conceived. They'd been together ever since. Finding out she was pregnant had frightened the life out of Bunny. She'd never planned on having children; she was too worried about bringing an innocent child into the world, but mainly unsure if she could give a child a better start in life than she'd had.

She hadn't told Del, he'd guessed – or rather he'd looked in her bag and found the leaflets on abortion. Even though she was a hooker, he'd ranted and raved, jealous and hurt she'd been with someone else, not understanding she was pregnant with his baby. When she'd told him it was his, instead of him insisting she get rid of it, to her amazement, he'd begged her to keep the baby. And she'd liked the feeling; the feeling of someone wanting her, someone seeing her as more than just a fuck in the alleyway. But mostly she'd liked the feeling of him believing in her. Believing she could love and care for a child.

During her pregnancy she'd allowed him to look after her, letting him rent the flat in Soho and treat her like she'd never been treated in her life, but the minute Star had been born, she'd gone back to work, albeit in the flat.

Del had been furious. Ignoring her one minute, coming round to smash up the place in a jealous rage the next, begging her to stop work. Her heart had gone out to him, but no matter how much she'd wanted to make him happy, she couldn't do the one thing he wanted her to – give up work – because Bunny knew giving up work would've meant letting her nemesis come into her life; her nemesis being trust.

One day she'd got fed up after he'd yet again barged into the flat, throwing out the punter she'd been with. They'd had a row. Him scream-ing at her and she at him. It was then she'd decided to turn the tables. *'Okay Del. I'll do it. I'll give up bleedin' work if that's what you want, but on one condition.'*

'Anything darling, name it.'

'Leave Edith and tell her about Star.'

His face had drained of colour and it was then Bunny had known she'd been right not to trust him. Del would never leave Edith, no matter how much he loved her and Star, and she would never trust him, no matter how much she loved him and wanted to have a life like she read about in books. So they'd come to an unspoken agree-ment that no matter how much they didn't like the situation, that was the way it had to be.

Of course, Del still got jealous and he still made noises asking her to give up work, but there'd been a shift in balance. Del now knew what the condition had to be and, as Bunny knew he'd never agree to it, she felt safe in the knowledge that her having to trust someone would never be put to the test.

'So are you all packed then, Bun?'

'No, I ain't even got me suntan cream sorted out. Maybe you should go on your own; I'll come with you another time.'

'You ain't going to get out of it that easily.'

Bunny's tension came back in her body and a frown creased her forehead. 'What about Star? I don't want to leave her.'

'She'll be fine with Claudia. That women will look after her like she's one of her own.'

Bunny looked down, changing the subject quickly. 'There's some new girls on the block, apparently there was a bit of trouble with them. Chased off the regular girls: they're not happy.'

Del scowled. 'Who did you hear this from?'

Bunny shrugged her shoulders. 'Just one of the girls who covers the Berwick Street area. I use to work with her. She's a good un; don't cause trouble or go looking for it, but she's worried. Business is down because of it, so she asked me to have a little word in your ear. She said she thought it was the Russian lot. You know anything about it?'

Without answering, Del walked over and kissed Bunny on her head, before turning to Star and doing the same. It was all well and good letting the Russians come onto his patch and doing deals with them, but when they took the piss that was something else entirely. He turned and walked out, waving goodbye, then grabbing his car keys off the side.

Deep in thought, Del marched out into Brewer Street, not noticing Teddy Davies watching him.

11

Del Williams sat in Whispers club waiting for Milo Burkov to arrive. He didn't mind waiting for people – shit went down sometimes – but he knew Milo was late just to prove a point, and the point was to make Del sit waiting like a fucking muppet.

There'd been lots of times Del had tried to turn up later for their meetings than Milo; hovering outside or driving round Soho a couple of times, even having an unwanted brew in Lola's Cafe, all in an attempt to make Milo wait for *him*. But somehow Milo Burkov always got the upper hand, walking in a few minutes after Del did, a cheesy grin on his pocked Russian face.

It was an ongoing stand-off between the two of them, even though they both knew it was childish.

Sitting drinking neat malt whisky and trying to ignore the fact that he'd been waiting now for the past twenty minutes, Del thought of Bunny. There wasn't really any time he didn't think of her. It was all consuming. Each waking moment he wasn't with her he wondered what she was doing, where she was going and who she was with. It was like an obsession. This thought had crossed his mind before and he'd quickly dismissed it, not wanting to think of himself as some pathetic cunt, but if he were truthful, that was exactly what it was. Obsession.

So many times he'd snuck past the formidable presence of Claudia to break in and see Bunny, wanting to catch a punter with her so he could take out his frustration and batter him senseless. There were times when the red mist descended and he could've quite easily squeezed the life out of them – and if it wasn't for Bunny stopping him, he would've done.

It tortured him. Bunny fucking other men had almost broken him. Him. Del Williams. A man most men would be terrified of was broken by his woman.

Knocking back the rest of the whisky, Del sighed. He knew what he had to do if he wanted it all to stop. He had to leave Edith. But how could he? Edith would talk like a jack fucking rabbit. The only thing that would stop that mouth of hers was a bullet in her head.

The thought jolted Del. He sat straight up in the chair, putting down his glass carefully on the sticky table. He stared ahead at the velvet walls, replaying his words. *A bullet in her head.*

He'd often joked about doing away with Edith to his mates, but could he *really* do it? Really get rid of her once and for all? Of course he'd killed loads of people and had had loads of people killed, it wasn't the actual practicality of killing that bothered him. Once you'd done it once then the other times were never a big deal, not even when they begged and cried, wetting themselves like a baby. Business was business.

No, with Edith it was different. It was more about sweeping away any last bits of loyalty he still had for her. But it would be the solution. He could be with Bunny properly. More to the point, Bunny would give up work and he could get back to form, properly concentrate on the big deals he had coming up with the Russians. Not worry about Edith opening her big trap. He could feel like he was number one again.

Just as quickly as the idea began to form, it petered away again. He shook his head to himself. What the flick was he thinking? Of course he couldn't do it. Though it *was* a nice thought.

Turning his head at a sound, Del saw Milo walk into the empty club. He was tall and skinny with blonde, almost white hair, which looked startling against his dark brown eyes and olive skin.

Del nodded, raising his hand, but his mind was far from the business he had to attend to, it was on Edith – or rather, the disposal of her.

'Del. My friend. I'm sorry I'm late. You know how things are. Have you been sitting here long?' Milo Burkov spread his arms, embracing Del. His thick Russian accent cut mockingly through the air.

'No, not really. I got here late. Only just arrived myself.'

Milo slapped Del on the back and laughed, fully aware, thanks to his informant sitting in the far corner of the club, that Del had been waiting for him for almost forty minutes.

'Well, I'm pleased to hear it. I couldn't have you waiting for a Russian peasant like me.'

Trying to keep the annoyance out of his voice, Del spoke. 'Can I get you a drink? Vodka perhaps?'

Milo grinned again. 'Ah, the English stereotyping of the Russians. I'm good. I like to keep a clear head when I do business.'

As Milo pulled up a chair, Del began to talk.

'Let's get straight to it then. There's been problems with your girls. They've been chasing some of the regular Toms away. People aren't happy with it. There's been a lot of unrest.'

Milo shrugged his shoulders. 'And what would you like me to do about it? You know what women are like. Very territorial. I can't control what the girls do.'

Del leaned in. 'Bullshit Milo, you run those girls with an iron bar. We both know that. Don't play games. I let you come onto this patch as a favour for supplying the powder, not to let your girls crawl all over the place like fucking cockroaches.'

'I don't think your memory's serving you so well these days, my friend. You need to get your nose out of the pussy, too much can be bad for the old grey cells.' Milo winked at Del who gritted his teeth, listening to what else Milo had to say. 'The way I remember it, you didn't have a choice.'

Del bit his lip. 'You know that ain't fucking true. I saw a good deal and decided to run with it. I cut Teddy Davies out of the picture so we could do business directly and now you're mugging me off with the girls. Taking the piss. You need to back off Milo, or the powder deal's off. I'll find another supplier for both here and the Costa.'

Milo Burkov's face scrunched up into a sneer. 'Both you and I know there's no backing out. The shipment's already underway. Don't bring trouble on yourself, Del, not for a few whores,'

'Then don't fucking play me for a mug mate. Get your girls to back off and there won't be any problem.'

Milo shrugged his shoulders. 'You need to relax. The girls are small fry; they're not worth worrying about. But if it makes you happy, I'll see what I can do.'

'Don't see. Just do it.'

Milo clicked his fingers, gesturing the barman to come over. 'Fine. It's not good for women to come between us, especially when they're only whores. How is Bunny by the way?'

It was all too much for Del; he sprang up from his chair, knocking the barman who was standing nervously beside Milo out of the way. He bellowed, feeling the vein in his neck pulsate.

'Don't push it, Milo. If you don't want to bang me up the wrong way, some things are well and truly off limits and Bunny is one of them.'

From the far corner Milo's sidekick came running up. It was Del's cue. From the inside of his jacket he quickly pulled out a knuckleduster, aiming it at the sidekick. It struck the man's face – drawing blood immediately – and, as it did so, Del twisted it around, grinding the man's eye almost out of its socket. Blood oozed from his face as he screamed, falling onto the floor in agony. Bringing back his boot, Del kicked the man hard in the ribs to finish him off.

Out of breath, Del turned to Milo, expecting more trouble. Without reacting, Milo spoke to the barman, his voice soft and even. 'A double scotch and the same again for my friend.' Turning back to Del, Milo gestured his hand to the man groaning on the floor, and smiled. 'Forgive my men. As you see they're very loyal and sometimes a little, how shall I say it?... A little too enthusiastic for their own good.' With that, Milo kicked at the bloodied man who staggered up, stumbling and holding onto his face in an attempt to stop the blood flow.

Del watched Milo carefully as he signalled for him to sit back down. He was a cool character, he'd give him that much. Always playing his cards close to his chest. Milo was a nasty piece of work He'd seen him in action. Cold, ruthless and calculating but he chose his fights carefully. And unlike Del, Milo was clearly able to think first and react afterwards.

He wasn't sure if he could trust Milo, but that was the nature of the business they were both in. Always looking behind your back. Always trying to be one step ahead. And he'd rather deal with Milo than with Teddy.

Teddy had got greedy – both for money and in his liking for powder. He seemed to be on the edge, which made Del very nervous. The man was a loose cannon and in the business they were in you couldn't afford to be one, or for that matter to be around one. Not if you valued your life.

Del knew he had to distance himself from Teddy if he wanted to stay on top. The man had been all right at first. Another bent copper looking for his cut of things, and Del, like some of his associates, had been happy to pay him his due to keep the law off his back and run out any toerags who thought they could come on the turf.

It'd made his life easier. One less thing to worry about, but that had been then. Del didn't need the likes of Teddy now. He was too big for that. He had his own men watching his back. And so great was his reputation around the country, even his enemies weren't fool enough to try and take him on.

The main problem was that, somewhere along the line, Teddy had decided he wanted to be bigger than him. It was clear the man had become dissatisfied with the wad of money, drugs and girls that had been placed freely in his hand each week by Del and the other faces and dealers of Soho. He'd wanted more and now he was going to get nothing. Greed would be Teddy's downfall and Del for one wasn't prepared to go down with him.

Putting his glass down, Del spoke to Milo.

'When's the shipment hitting the Costa?'

'Any day now. Are you still going over there this week?'

'Perhaps, or I might leave it to my men to deal with it,' Del answered in a non-committal manner. Even though he was in business with Milo, he didn't want the man to know all his comings and goings. It was safer that way. The less people knew what he was up to the better; that's the way it'd always been and that's the way it'd carry on.

Looking at the time, Del got up. 'Shit. I've got to go, but Milo, sort those girls out. I don't want to be having this conversation again,' He nodded his head towards Milo's sidekick who was slumped in the corner. 'Take him to Doc's in Wimpole Mews and have him send me the bill.' Without waiting for a reply, Del walked out of the club.

From the other side of the darkened room the emergency exit door opened and Teddy Davies walked in. His face was flushed and sweaty from the quiver he'd just taken, but he felt good. Very good. Del Williams had thought he was going to pull a fast one and keep him out of the loop; well that was his first big mistake. And his second? Trusting Milo Burkov.

Sitting down at the table, Teddy smiled at Milo. 'Thanks for meeting me Milo. I've wanted to talk to you for a while. I've got a proposition for you; I was hoping we could come to some sort of arrangement.'

12

Julian Millwood suppressed his laughter as he walked up to one of the other residents of his estate. Gary Cole. He brushed his brown curly hair out of his eyes as he spoke.

'Gal. Have you got a moment?'

With hollow eyes, Gary nodded, listening but

struggling to concentrate on what Julian was saying.

'I'm sorry Gary, about Julie. She was such a sweet kid. If there's anything I can do, just let me know.'

Gary nodded but said nothing, and with his head down he failed to notice the slight smirk on Julian's face.

'Well, I'll let you get on and like I say, Gal, just let me know if I can help in any way.'

With large purposeful strides, Julian turned away, a huge grin appearing on his face.

Walking towards Camden Road, Julian opened another shirt button, exposing the mass of brown chest hair. He wasn't sure if it was the heat of the summer that was making him sweat or just the thought of *it*. The thought of *her*.

It was almost too much to bear; his excitement in the last week or so had put him on such a high he knew he could easily get careless. And he certainly couldn't afford to be that. He wasn't prepared to go back inside.

Hailing a cab, Julian's mind flicked back to earlier that morning when the police had knocked on his door. Routine checks, they'd told him. But he knew, like they'd known, it was far from routine.

They knew who he was and they'd been determined to find something, but like he'd told them, '*There was nothing to find.*' Not there, anyway.

He'd watched them pulling his already filthy flat apart; tearing the back of the cupboards out, chucking cushions and throws onto the floor, frustrated they couldn't find anything. He'd wanted to laugh at them as he listened to their snide comments and saw their cutting stares. But he'd said nothing, allowing them to get on with their job as he'd stood there. *Stupid ignorant pigs sniffing about in the wrong place.*

He'd presumed they'd come, but now that they had it meant he needed to get away. There was no way Julian was waiting around for them to keep coming back.

The best thing he could do was to get out of the country. He'd planned on it anyway, but it looked like he was going to have to do it sooner rather than later – and he knew exactly the person he needed to see to help him do that. His lawyer, Alan Day.

Ten minutes later, Julian's cab pulled up outside the drab offices off Gray's Inn Road. Even on the sunniest of days, the building looked cold and bleak.

Marching into the office, Julian stared at the receptionist. Tits, hair and no brains.

'Can I help you, Sir?'

With as much hostility as he could muster, Julian eyeballed the woman, before walking towards the double oak door.

'No, it's fine; I know where I'm going.'

'I'm afraid you can't go in there, Sir.'

'Watch me or try to stop me.'

Julian stood in the doorway and laughed out loud at the sight of Alan Day getting his dick sucked by a hooker.

Red-faced, Alan jumped up, annoyed not only by the interruption, but by the fact he was just about to come.

'Close the fucking door,' Alan roared as he saw the faces of the amazed clients waiting for him in the expensive, newly decorated waiting area.

Doing up his trousers, he pushed some money into the girl's hand, shoving her out of the door, along with the startled receptionist who followed closely behind.

Furious, Alan poured himself a large drink, his hand shaking.

'Look, I don't know what you want me to do, but it isn't a great idea for you to turn up like this.'

Julian smirked.

'I don't want you to do anything at the moment. Not yet anyway.'

'Then there's no need to be here is there?'

Julian lowered himself onto Alan's large leather office chair, spinning himself round.

'This is some place you've got here. You must charge your clients a fortune.'

Alan bristled. He didn't like the way the conversation was heading. 'I do all right.'

Putting his feet up on the desk, Julian kicked the pile of files onto the floor, scattering the papers everywhere. 'I'd say you do more than all right, wouldn't you?'

'What's this about, Millwood? Just tell me what you want and then get the hell out of here.'

Julian's mouth curled up to one side. 'That ain't a very nice way to talk.'

Alan's shoulders tensed up, but he spoke in a quieter tone. 'I'm sorry, but I haven't had a good day.'

'That's better, now we're getting somewhere.'

'Just tell me how I can help you.'

'Okay, so I lied. I do want something. What I want for starters is some money.'

Alan laughed scornfully. 'I don't think so.'

Julian narrowed his eyes. 'Don't be a fool, Alan. I'd pay up if I were you.' Julian winked at him. A long pause followed, before Alan spoke in a fluster.

'Fine, how much do you want?' Alan went into his pocket and brought out a small bundle of fifty-pound notes. 'Two hundred? Three? Here, take the lot.'

Alan threw the money down on the office desk in front of Julian, who picked it up and promptly took his lighter out of his pocket to begin to burn it. He watched Alan's stricken face.

'You insult me, Alan. I thought you could do better than that.'

'Then how much? How much do you want?'

'That all depends.'

Julian reached inside his jacket, pulling out a brown envelope. He opened it up and brought out some photographs. One by one, he laid them on the table.

'How much do you think they're worth, Alan?'

Wide eyed, Alan Day sprang into action and leapt forward, gathering them up in his arms.

'What the fuck are you playing at?' He twisted his body towards the door. 'Anyone could come in and see.'

Julian sniffed, picking up one of the photos Alan hadn't managed to scoop up. 'Has anyone ever told you that you take a good photo? Couldn't say the same for the girl. Looks a bit miserable to me.

Doesn't seem to want to give the camera a smile, can't see why not. Perhaps it's the position you've got her in. How old was she, Alan?'

Alan Day clutched the photos against his body. He could feel a shooting pain running down his arm. His chest began to tighten. '*Get out.*'

'Oh Alan, you'll have to do a lot better than that. You can keep the photos by the way. I've got copies. Shall we say one hundred grand by tomorrow?'

'I haven't got that sort of money!'

'There you go again. The defence barrister in action. You really are good at your job. If I didn't know you better I'd actually believe you, but lucky for me I know what a lying cunt you are. I'll be back round for the money.' Julian tapped Alan Day on the shoulder.

Julian walked into the waiting area, whistling, banging into a man who seemed to be having a row with the receptionist as he did so.

'Watch where you're going, pal,' Del Williams scowled. He pushed past the receptionist and Julian, shutting the door behind him with a bang.

'Alan, I was trying to get hold of you. What the hell do I pay you for if I can't get in contact when I need to?'

The shooting pain hit Alan again but this time it started from his left arm, making its way up to his chest. His hand involuntarily spasmed, cramping his knuckles into a clawed ball. The bundle of photographs Alan was trying to gather up tumbled down onto the floor.

The stress of seeing the photographs made Alan's chest tighten even more. He bent over, twisted in pain, unable to get to the fallen photos before Del. Watching in horror, he saw Del pick them up, but he couldn't move; Alan was sure he was having a heart attack.

Del kept his eyes on Alan, not bothering to look at what he was picking up from the floor. The man looked so grey and waxy. He had come to help him out, but seeing Alan now with things strewn everywhere and looking like a man under pressure, he thought he might leave it. The man looked terrible.

Del looked around and picked up a stray photo from the floor. Glancing at it, he saw it was a picture of a little girl and froze. He felt sick.

'What the fuck is this?' Del snarled.

'I ... I can explain. It's not what you think.'

'It's *exactly* what I think.'

Alan gasped, 'But let me explain.'

'There's nothing *to* explain. I don't want to know? With that, Del slammed the pile of photographs in Alan's hand.

Alan chanced to look more closely at the photo. Facing up was a photo of a naked girl, but the other person in the photo with her wasn't him.

'What sort of twisted fucks do you represent?'

Now it was Alan's turn to feel sick. Sick with relief. He wanted to laugh and cry all at once. Visibly shaken, he let out a huge sigh of relief. 'I know ... I know, but what can you do? Someone has to represent them. Innocent till proven guilty and all that.'

'But stone me mate, do you really need to keep all the evidence in the office?' Del shook his head. 'Fuck me.'

Alan scrambled the photos together, gathering them back into his arms and ignoring the pain in his chest. He went across to the safe and quickly stuffed the photos into it, instantly feeling more relaxed.

He turned to Del, giving him his best smile.

'Now, what can I do for you?'

An hour later, Del Williams stalked out of Alan Day's office. Walking down Theobalds Road towards the West End, he answered his ringing phone. It was Edith. He gave it five seconds before holding the phone away from his ear, not wanting to hear the usual list of moans and complaints from his wife.

He wasn't in the best of moods; Christ knew he needed all his patience to have any sort of communication with Edith and today he didn't have any. Lawyers, especially crooked barristers, had that effect on him.

He'd never liked Alan but then he didn't have to. He was good at his job and when you were looking at a five-year lump, liking someone didn't ever come into the equation. Over the years Alan had managed to get him off several charges – although he'd paid him his weight in gold for it – and as much as he was grateful to Alan for the way he did his job, that didn't mean he'd allow him to take the piss.

Sighing and feeling hot, Del put the phone back to his ear, just in time to hear Edith asking for more money. 'I'm like a bleedin' beggar. I'd be better off selling the *Big Issue*. How am I meant to keep a roof over me head? Clothes on me back? I'll be six feet under with the stress of it all.'

'I'll get one of my men to drop some money off to you, but I'm coming across in the next couple of days and I've got some business I need to deal with, so I need you to be out of the way for a while.'

Del pulled the phone slightly away again as Edith shrieked down the other end. 'Oh yeah, that'd be bleedin' right. Treat me like a fucking dog with fleas why don't you? First off I'm having to phone you up 'cos you leave me without a pot to piss in, now you want to throw me out. What am I? A fucking scrag end of meat?'

Del's tone darkened. 'Listen Edith, you can go on one of them cruises you're forever going on or you can come over here or even stay at one of them fancy hotels. The choice is yours. Whatever you do or don't do I don't give a shit; I'll pay for it, like I always have. All I'm saying is I want you out of the villa. Non-negotiable, darling.'

'Don't you bleedin' tell me to get out of me own house Del Williams. This villa is as much mine as it is yours.'

'I think you'll find it's not.'

'Oh yeah? Let's see if they say that in a court of law when I tell them exactly how you bought this bleedin' place.'

'Are you threatening me, Edith? Because both you and I know that would be a very silly thing to do.'

Standing in the air-conditioned villa in Marbella, Edith Williams swallowed hard as she listened to Del's tone. She'd be a fool to forget her husband was a dangerous man, but the feeling of him getting one over on her was stronger at that moment than the fear of antagonising him.

She'd been a good wife to him at the beginning of her marriage, but he'd been too busy wanting to make a name for himself. Within months of being wed he'd begun to build his empire, leaving her alone a lot of the time.

She'd been lonely at first, but then the local fishmonger had paid her some attention and after a few months she'd taken him as her lover. The first of many. Even though she was a large woman, she'd never had any problem attracting men. Maybe it was her money they were attracted to or maybe it was her confidence; whatever it was it didn't really matter as long as her insatiable sexual desire was satisfied. Of course Del had never known or even suspected. She was too careful and he was away so much, it was easy to hide it from him. And he was mug enough to think she'd wait for him like a virgin bride. She'd had her fun and doubtless he'd had his.

'Think what you like, Del. Just don't forget I know everything about you.'

Del closed his eyes for a moment. He kept his voice steady and spoke slowly. 'Just be out of my way when I get there.'

He clicked off the phone and kicked the wall he was standing by.

A bullet in her head.

As he crossed Southampton Row, Del Williams tried to put the ever-growing thought out of his mind.

13

Bunny Barker sat on the end of her bed, the warm summer breeze blowing through the room. Her grey silk dressing gown hung off her shoulder, exposing her soft pale skin. Her blonde hair was fixed up into a loose bun on her head and her lips were painted red.

For some reason she wasn't feeling comfortable, though she knew she didn't have anything to worry about; Claudia was just outside the door if she needed her. It was silly, but the reason for her discomfort wasn't because of a strange request by the punter sitting opposite her – it was because there was no request at all, which made the whole situation stranger than ever.

'You sure you don't want anything, babe? You know I'll still be charging you a monkey.'

'I know, but all I want to do is sit here and look at you.'

'I don't really do that.'

The man smiled. 'What, you don't want people to admire your beauty? You do know how beautiful you are, don't you?'

Bunny tried to stop feeling more uncomfortable than she already was. She lit up a cigarette, trying to look in control. 'It's just strange that's all, I don't usually have people wanting to just come and stare, but if that rocks your boat, babe, be my guest. Stare away.' Bunny smiled warmly, not wanting to be hostile in any way.

'Would it help if I touched you?'

Bunny shuddered although the heat in the room was stifling, requiring the chrome fans to be turned on high. There was something about his voice that she didn't trust. Perhaps she was tired, but she'd been in this game long enough to trust her instinct and know there was something unsettling about this man.

Bunny spoke, keeping her voice lighter and steadier than she felt. 'Do what you like darlin'. You're paying for it.'

The man reached out to touch her, but his fingers hovered in the air millimetres away from her skin. He cocked his head to one side, his brown hair flopping over his forehead.

'No, on second thoughts, it's okay. Perhaps next time. I'm a bit old-fashioned like that. I like to get to know a girl first before I screw her ass off.'

With that, Teddy Davies threw five hundred pounds on the bed before getting up and walking out of the room.

'Are you okay Bun?' Claudia looked at Bunny with a worried frown as she watched her pack her suitcase, folding and unfolding the clothes lying scattered on the floor.

'That last guy, he got me a bit on edge.'

Claudia's frown became deeper. 'Why didn't you call me?'

'Thing is, there wasn't nothing to call about. He just... Oh, forget it, it's me being silly. I'm just a bit tired. Poor sod probably can't get a shaft on

115

and that's why he only wanted to talk.'

Claudia smiled affectionately. 'If there is anything you wanna get off your chest darlin', you know you can chew me ear off as much as you like, don't you?'

Bunny nodded gratefully. 'It's this holiday. I'm a bit nervous. I dunno why Del won't go on his own, but he's insisting I go with him. You know I like me home comforts. I've tried to get out of it but he's hearing none of it. Plus I'm not looking forward to flying; worried we might crash.' Bunny shrugged her shoulders then looked forlornly at Claudia.

'See, I told you it's me being silly. But you asked and that's what's on me mind.'

'Are you sure it's only that, Bun? It ain't nothing to do with Star?'

'Star?'

'Drop me out girl. Don't give me that wide-eyed look of yours, missy. It might work with Del boy but it ain't going to work with me. I know when you're telling me porkies. Listen love, nothing's going to happen to Star; not on my watch.'

'I know, but I think if it can...'

Claudia grabbed hold of Bunny's hand. 'Don't, Bun. I don't want you thinking about anything bad. Go out there and enjoy yourself. Bleedin' hell girl, if I had some fella taking me away for a few days I'd be biting his hand off. Trust me, she'll be fine. I'll look after her as if she was mine.'

Walking down the street, Bunny held onto Star's hand. There was nowhere she'd rather be. It wouldn't matter if they'd been walking through a monsoon or waist high in mud; as long as she was with her daughter, it didn't matter.

She turned her head to look at Star who was happily chattering away to herself. It was a funny habit her daughter had. When she was little Bunny was sure Star would grow out of talking to herself, but she hadn't. Her daughter's imagination and her sense of adventure seemed to grow with each passing year, happily submerging herself in a secret world full of pirates and cowboys. A world where no one ever really got hurt or ever died; a world that Bunny could only dream about.

'Fancy some sweets, baby?' Bunny interrupted her daughter as they walked past the newsagents on Old Compton Street.

'Yes please, and can we get some for Dad and Claudia?'

Bunny smiled warmly. She loved that part of Star. She was a generous little girl, in both her material possessions and her thoughts; always thinking and wanting other people to have what she did.

'I'll take a packet of buttons for me dad, oh and some jelly babies. He loves them.' Bunny grinned as her daughter carefully studied the row of sweets.

'What about Claudia?'

'She loves them sherbet dip dabs, so I'll take a couple of packets of them.'

Bunny handed Star a five-pound note and watched as she went to pay. She could feel herself bristling as the middle-aged man behind the counter winked at Star. Her body went to grab her daughter but her logic forced her stay still. Star wasn't in any danger, she was here with her.

She had to stop this. Nothing could happen to Star while she stood here. Although knowing it was purely innocent, Bunny turned her head away, unable to watch the man grin at her daughter. Her phone rang.

'Hello?'

'All right, doll?' It was Del.

'Hello sweetheart.'

'What you up to?'

'I'm with Star, bringing the usual supply of sweets home for you.'

Del laughed affectionately down the phone.

'Put her on for me, will you?'

Bunny turned towards the counter. She froze. Star wasn't there.

'Bun? Bun?' Del's voice continued to be heard as blind panic took over her.

Bunny looked to her left, seeing only an old lady standing choosing between Rich Tea biscuits and Fig Rolls. To her right a group of boys chatted, pushing each other in a boisterous manner.

'Where did she go? Where did my daughter go?'

The newsagent shrugged.

Running out of the shop into the busy street, Bunny was met by a throng of summer visitors, milling slowly in dense crowds along the Soho streets.

Her head whipped from side to side, darting searching, desperate glances along the sleepy street. Bunny's heart raced. Sweat began to prickle under her armpits. Her mouth went dry.

'*Star, Star. Where are you?*'

There. Two feet ahead of her, Bunny got a glimpse of a mop of blonde hair. '*Please be her. Please be her.*'

Bunny pushed past the couple in front of her who blocked her view. 'Star! Star!' She felt sick as she saw her daughter talking to a grey-haired man.

Star Barker-Williams turned round, happily chewing on a candy bar. 'Mum, this is…'

Before Star could say another word, Bunny launched into a relieved tirade. 'What have I told you about going off on your own? Don't you know how much you frightened me? Frigging hell, Star.'

'But Mum…'

'No, Star; no buts. I ain't having it. You're always doing this. You and your adventures. That imagination of yours will get you into trouble.'

Star's eyes filled with tears. Her mum was always *so* over the top. 'Mum!'

'I don't want to hear another word. What were you thinking of, talking to strangers.'

'He's not a stranger. It's Mr Moore, our headmaster from school. I was only showing him what sweets I bought Dad and Claudia.'

Bunny stopped and looked properly at the grey-haired spectacled man who stood a few feet away, watching with a frown as the drama unfolded in front of him. Bunny could feel herself turning red. She felt foolish and angry that once again her past was affecting the present.

Too embarrassed to say anything, Bunny grabbed hold of a scowling Star's hand, hoping for a time, both for her sake and her daughter's, that she wouldn't see a monster hiding around each and every corner.

14

Julian Millwood sat listening carefully to Dr Berry. He'd aged badly over the years and had retired a long time ago from being a child psychiatrist, but his desire for young girls hadn't waned.

Dr Berry's voice was clipped and pompous. 'I've been speaking to one of my contacts, Julian. They're on the lookout for something special.'

Julian licked his lips, warming his hand on the side of his legs at the same time. 'What?'

'A blonde. Young. Very young.'

Immediately Julian shrugged his shoulders, slightly disappointed. There wasn't anything special about a blonde, it was such a cliché; everyone wanted them, whether they were natural or not. And it was usually more trouble than it was worth.

With a hint of boredom in his voice, Julian answered as he slumped down in the chair.

'Can't you just dye the hair of one of the Thai girls? Save a lot of troubles.'

'No, my contact doesn't want that. He wants a real blonde. An innocent. Some of those Thai girls have been at it since before they could even talk. They're born up for it. It's in their DNA. Makes the whores down in Soho look like Cinderfucking-rella.' Dr Berry laughed nastily, stroking the head of the young Filipino girl who was curled asleep next to him.

'So, can you help?'

Julian scratched his head, feeling the damp of sweat at the back of his neck. *A real blonde.* It was tempting to get involved, not to mention exciting, but the likelihood of being able to help was slim and it was also risky. Nevertheless, he liked the idea of it.

'I'll ask around, but I don't think so.'

'It'll pay well, Julian. Very well. This one they want to have for keeps.'

Julian raised his eyebrows, sitting up straight in his chair again. 'For keeps?'

Dr Berry's eyes glinted, mirroring the look in Julian's eyes. 'That's right. That's why they want the real thing. Like I say they'll pay well, so if you hear of anything or you can do something, let me know.'

Dr Berry turned away, focusing his attention back on the young girl who began to stir. Julian saw it as his cue to leave. Getting up, he walked out, leaving the judge to sit in the bare-roomed floor above the block of empty offices.

The bright sunshine hit Julian's face as he walked out into the middle of Soho. He couldn't get the doctor's words out of his head. *For keeps.* In that line of business you didn't often hear of such things. People talked about it and, like him, imagined it, but few actually managed to do it. It took a lot of planning, a lot of money and, to a certain degree, a lot of luck.

Dr Berry was right; getting any child for keeps

was something special. And the more Julian thought about it, the more he wanted a part of it. Perhaps it wouldn't harm to put a few feelers out – and he knew exactly the person to go to. Picking up the phone, Julian dialled a number.

Five people's phones began to ring all at the same time. Teddy Davies', Milo Burkov's, Del Williams', Alan Day's and Alfonso Garcia's – but it was only Alfonso who answered his phone.

'Yes?' Alfonso listened patiently then added, 'I can't hear you. The line's bad. You'll have to call back later.' Clicking off the phone, Alfonso smiled through gritted teeth at Edith who was sitting with a box of empty Kleenex on the marble table in front of her. The tissues had finished a long while ago and now she was reduced to wiping her nose on the sleeve of her expensive blouse.

'I'll go and get a hanky or some more tissues, Edith; you're ruining your top.' As Alfonso went to leave, Edith grabbed his t-shirt.

'Don't leave me, Alfonso. Sit with me, I can't bear to be on my own.'

'Darling, I was only going to…'

'*Stay!*' Edith's voice changed into a harsh order as she scowled at an impatient and exasperated Alfonso. The waterworks had been turned on all day; ever since she'd got up. And the wailing and whining of Edith around the villa was getting on Alfonso's nerves.

'How he has the bleedin' gall to tell me to get out of me own house, I dunno. Do I look like a frigging waif? Do I look like I'd be happy to do a shit on the side of the road like a bleedin' stray dog?'

Alfonso curled his lip. His facial expression was caught by Edith, who threw her arms up in an exaggerated gesture.

'Oh, that's right; pull a bleedin' face at me won't you? Turn on me when I've hit rock bottom.'

Alfonso gripped his fist under the table, but his smile was saccharin sweet. 'Edith, you mistake my look. I wasn't pulling a face at you my darling, it was at how your husband can treat such a...' Alfonso stopped and stared at Edith's ballooned body. 'Such a beauty as yourself.'

Edith frowned suspiciously at him. 'You really mean that, Alfonso?'

'You know I do, darling.'

With the speed of a gazelle, Edith Williams grabbed hold of Alfonso, clinging onto him in a tight embrace, almost winding him.

'Make love to me, Alfonso.'

Alfonso froze. He swallowed with a loud glug; his face rapidly draining of colour. 'Now?'

Irritated by the lack of enthusiasm, Edith snapped. 'Yes Alfonso; here. Right now.'

Without waiting for an answer, Edith began to unbutton her white Chanel blouse, exposing her gigantic breasts. They hung almost to her waist and she held them proudly, twirling her large nipples before quickly taking off her knickers – which were several sizes too small – to expose her red scorched sunburnt rolls of fat and a mass of dark brown pubic hair.

Edith grinned and winked at Alfonso seductively. 'Take me. I'm wet for you, Alfy.'

Alfonso could hardly speak as he stared at Edith, feeling his stomach begin to churn. He blurted out his words rapidly.

'I can't.'

A frown came over Edith's face and her eyes narrowed. She stopped caressing her nipples and folded her arms across her body. Her voice was tipped with angry hysteria.

'What do you mean, *you can't?*'

Alfonso tried to think quickly but he kept hold of his cool demeanour and smile. 'I can't ... I can't because... Because I just want to look at you. You're so beautiful, I just want to look at your body Edith. Allow me to do that.'

Alfonso could feel his smile waning as he tried to hold it. He locked eyes with Edith, feeling the tension in the cool air-conditioned kitchen.

A huge grin spread across Edith's face. She squealed in delight, clapping her, hands like a child. 'Well, why didn't you say so? I thought for a moment you'd gone off me, Alfy.' Edith pouted her lips, putting on the childish tone which Alfonso hated. 'And I couldn't stand that, baby.'

'Of course not. Why would you ever think such a thing?'

Alfonso paused and slyly looked at Edith. 'Have you ever thought about leaving Del? Have you ever thought about just you and me? Setting up somewhere together, alone, without having to worry about anybody else? What do you say, Edith?'

Edith threw her hand to the side as if she were wafting away a nuisance fly. She laughed in disdain. 'Don't be silly, Alfonso, how could I ever leave Del to come and live with you? It's a nice thought, but it ain't a very clever one is it?'

Alfonso absent-mindedly traced his finger in circles on the marble table. He was furious and he could feel the familiar rage, which he hid so well, climbing up the whole of his body. *Bitch.* Who did she think she was? He was expecting her to jump at the chance, not cut him down and laugh in his face.

His plan had been a simple one, but one he thought would work. Once he'd got her away from Del, little by little he'd make Edith totally reliant on him. Isolating her from her friends, breaking down her confidence and making her feel she couldn't do without him, until he had total control of her life and ultimately, total control of her money. And once that happened it'd be *adios senorita.*

Alfonso tried again. 'Is it about money, my darling, because I'm sure Del wouldn't leave you short and I have a bit of money put away?'

Edith sniffed loudly, picking at the peeling skin on her chest. 'Alfonso, I couldn't possibly run off with you. What would people think? Me and the handyman. Bleeding hell, I'd be the laughing stock of the Costa, not to mention Soho.'

Alfonso stared at Edith, unable to hide the hatred in his eyes. This wasn't how the plan was supposed to go and as Alfonso continued to stare, watching Edith walk across the room naked to pour herself a glass of fresh lemonade, he suddenly understood. Understood why Edith had never left Del. Edith Williams didn't want half of any money. She wanted it all. And that all was nothing to do with the pound and euro signs piling up in the bank. That all was the status that came with being the wife of London's number one gangster.

As much as he didn't want to, Alfonso knew there was nothing else for it. He'd have to go to plan B. The good old-fashioned practice of blackmail.

It certainly didn't fill Alfonso with pleasure at the thought of it. The problem was he valued his life – and Edith was cunning enough to try to turn it round and set her animal husband onto him.

Even if she didn't manage to convince Del it was all a huge mistake, Alfonso knew as well as anybody else that the only reason Del stayed with Edith was because of the information she'd collected on him over the years, and Del would come down hard on anything that threatened to make Edith open her mouth. Which meant there was little Del could do to Edith, even if it meant him turning a blind eye to her porking every guy on the Costa.

The baggage Edith had on Del was enough to put him away for life – or if she chose to put the information in the wrong hands, it could see him *without* a life. Unfortunately for Alfonso, what Edith had on Del she wasn't telling anybody else about. He'd tried to get little snippets out of her but she was as tight lipped as a choirboy's arse.

She was as shrewd as anyone he knew. But Alfonso wasn't going to be beaten. He was going to get his.

Edith walked back towards the table where Alfonso was still sitting. 'Alfey baby. Don't look so sad. You know I love you babes, but there's just no way I could *ever* contemplate leaving Del, darlin'.'

She paused, adding. 'I know what will put a smile on your face.'

Shuffling herself up on the marble table, Edith lay down and sprawled naked, pushing the porcelain bowl of grapes out of the way. She grinned, 'Come on baby, give me some sugar.'

With a heavy heart, Alfonso Garcia stood up from his chair. He closed his eyes as he stood over her then felt himself being pulled down. As Edith began to writhe and moan underneath him, Alfonso swore to himself that no matter how long it took, he would get every last penny out of Edith Williams and make her pay, in more ways than one.

Julian Millwood put his phone back in his pocket. He never liked speaking on them; he always felt it was too dangerous even though there were code words he used and anyone listening in would hear it as just an innocent conversation.

Looking at his watch, Julian headed towards Alan Day's office. He hoped the man had his money. He *needed* it. Once he had it he'd get out of the country. Even though Dr Berry had told him the blonde girl job would pay well, it was still only a pipe dream. Alan wasn't. He had the means and the contacts to help him, and besides, Alan owed him.

Julian knew he had to play it carefully with Alan. As much as he had stuff on Alan, Alan had stuff on him and he didn't want to push him too far into a corner and make him strike out. Alan was cold and clever and there was only so far the man would be cornered before he came out

127

fighting. After all, he was an expert on getting people out of almost impossible situations.

Walking into the familiar offices, Julian was greeted by the same receptionist from the day before. 'I'm here to see Alan.'

'I'm afraid he's not here. He was taken into hospital last night with a suspected heart attack.'

Julian's face darkened. He stared at the receptionist in disbelief. 'Well I need to see him. It's urgent.'

'Any urgent matters are being dealt with by the junior partner if you'd like to make an appointment with him.'

Julian shook his head and spoke through gritted teeth. He could feel himself beginning to sweat. 'No, I don't fucking want to see his junior, I want to see *him*.'

The receptionist began to become flustered. 'I'm sorry, Sir, but there's nothing I can do.'

Julian leant over the high walnut desk, picking up then slamming the phone down, which had just begun to ring. 'No, but you can tell me where he's been taken into hospital.'

'I'm sorry, Sir, I can't possibly do that.'

'I don't think you understand me. I'm not asking you, I'm...'

'Is everything all right, darlin'?'

Julian Millwood swivelled round at the interruption and came face to face with the man who'd bumped into him the day before. His face sneered in contempt. 'I don't think this has anything to do with you, mate.'

Del Williams stared at the sweaty looking man. He'd seen his face before, but couldn't quite place it. 'One thing I hate is people talking to people disrespectfully, I reckon you owe the woman an apology.'

'And I reckon you need to stay out of me fucking business.'

With a quick sweep of his arm, Del grabbed the man by the throat and was about to push him into the wall when he felt his shirt being pulled. 'Dad, Dad, we're going to be late for the cinema and I'll be bubbling if I miss it.'

Del and Julian looked down at Star at the same time. In his rage, Del had forgotten his daughter was behind him. He smiled bashfully at Star, slightly ashamed she'd seen his temper exploding out of control yet again. He glanced at the man who was staring at Star before turning his attentions back to his daughter to try to make amends. 'I'm sorry, darlin', we'll go in a minute, I just need to speak to Alan. Give me five minutes and I promise we'll go.'

Star put her hands on her hips in a manner much more appropriate for someone older. Del couldn't help grinning as his daughter looked up at him crossly. She reminded him so much of Bunny and even though she was only seven, she made her frustration known. 'Bleedin' hell Dad, the film starts in fifteen minutes and there's no way I'm missing the first part of the film so I can stand in some stinky old office.'

'Mind your language, Star, and the less you chew me ear off the quicker I'll be.'

Julian Millwood watched this exchange as he stared at the girl. She was small and beautiful; exquisite. If he were to bet, he'd say she was aged about seven or eight, but more than anything she was blonde. Blonde and innocent.

Julian licked his lips, taking in Star's long white socks, denim skirt and diamante t-shirt. He looked at the way her blonde hair fell in waves almost down to the base of her spine. He wanted to reach out and touch her but he resisted the temptation and began to change tack instead.

As he spoke he was unable to keep his eyes off Star. His tone was quiet and oily. 'I'm sorry, sweetie, it was my fault. I shouldn't have been rude to your dad.'

Getting no response from Star, Julian looked at Del. 'No hard feelings, hey?'

Del stood observing the man, who was reaching his hand out for him to shake. He didn't want to take it, he didn't have time for muggy cunts like him but then he supposed the man had backed down; not only that, he'd apologised to Star and in his book that went some way.

Taking a deep breath, Del made an effort to be cordial. 'Don't worry about it, pal, we all have our bad days. Anyhow what's the score?'

'This lady was just telling me Alan has had a heart attack and I've been trying to find out where he's gone, but she won't tell me.'

The receptionist smiled apologetically. 'I'm sorry but it's confidential.'

Del rubbed his chin. This wasn't good. He needed Alan to draw some papers up to get him into Spain without the authorities knowing. Without them he'd be leaving a footprint of his whereabouts. Of course he knew some people who'd give him false passports but good ones took time and that wasn't the same as having the official documents Alan always provided.

Turning on his charm he winked at the receptionist, who blushed, much to Julian's disgust. 'Listen darlin' I need to see Alan as well. I'm sure he wouldn't mind if you just gave us a squeeze. Why don't you just write down on a piece of paper where he is, and then no one will be any the wiser. What do you say?'

'No. I'm sorry, I couldn't possibly.'

'Dad! Dad! You said five minutes.'

Del turned to Star, who was pouting.

'Okay, okay princess, I'm coming.'

Quickly, Del reached over for a piece of paper. He scribbled his name on it, before passing it over to the receptionist. 'Have him call me. I don't care if he's tubed up. Tell him I need to speak to him. I need the travel papers sorted.'

Del walked out of Alan's office with Star, leaving Julian standing in the middle of the reception room, watching them.

15

Teddy Davies lay on his bed with his shoes on. He couldn't be bothered to kick them off; it was too hot and the action would require more energy than he had. Wiping his nose, he sniffed. The quiver had blocked it up, not allowing him to snort properly, which was pissing him off. He'd resorted to smoking a spliff, which had then resulted him in having to lie down.

Looking at the ceiling he thought about Del, then slowly his thoughts drifted to Bunny. Ever since he'd been to see her he'd been thinking about her. Screwing – quite literally – something Del held so dear, amused Teddy no end. Plus it certainly was an added bonus that Bunny was one of the most beautiful women he'd seen, with a body that made him go hard just picturing her.

The idea of sticking his cock into her whilst he thought of Del's soon-to-be fall from grace would be certain to give him the biggest spurt off ever; Teddy was quite certain of that.

If it hadn't been because of the puff laying him out cold, he might've gone to pay her a visit now. He knew that by having sex with her he wouldn't be following the plan he and Milo had worked out, but since when did he take orders from some jumped-up Russian?

Bunny and Claudia sat on the sun-crisped grass, eating a 99 ice-cream and giggling like a couple of teenagers.

'Star! Star don't go far darlin'. Remember what I said the other day. Stay where I can see you.'

Star frowned, annoyed with her mother's continual fussing. She'd been so embarrassed the other day when they'd seen her headmaster and her mum had turned into a worry pot, as her dad called it. She'd refused to speak to her mum that evening, until of course she'd curled up on the bed with her to read Star her favourite stories.

Her dad didn't fuss so much, in fact some of the time she knew she could happily sneak off and he wouldn't even notice she'd gone. But her mum was different; always worrying and getting upset if she went out of sight for just a moment, and now she was doing it again. Even Claudia wasn't as bad.

Summoning up as much hostility as she could for a seven-year-old, Star snapped at Bunny. 'I'm only here, Mum. I ain't going nowhere.'

'Well mind you don't, babe. You don't want to give me bleedin' shockwaves.'

Star stood with her arms folded, but soon her face changed into a grin. Even though her mum treated her like a baby, she loved her, and try as she might she found it hard to stay mad at her for long.

Skipping towards the swings, Star took a quick look round to see if her mum was still looking. She wasn't. She was nattering away with Claudia again. Walking backwards, checking to see her mum didn't look up, Star edged towards the woods. There was only one time she'd ever been able to go into them and that was when her Dad had been with her. Each time she'd asked her mum to go in them, she'd had a hissy fit. She didn't know why; they were only woods.

As Star approached them she smiled to herself, and not for the first time thought how exciting they looked. She decided now was the time to take the opportunity to explore.

Even though the weather was hot and sticky the shade of the woods cooled the air, giving it a refreshing feel. The trees were bent and twisted, straining under their own weight, and as Star walked deeper into them she imagined herself to be in a magical garden, rather than in the woods on the north side of Mill Hill.

Her small hands touched the tree bark, feeling the rough surface, exciting her with its smells and sounds It was one thing living in a beautiful house in Soho, but the nearest she came to seeing a tree was on the odd occasion she and her dad had walked through Soho Square.

Studying the tree carefully, Star watched in fascination, mesmerised by the tiny insects burrowing under the peeling bark.

'Clever, aren't they? Sometimes I think they've got more sense than humans.'

Star jumped at the deep voice coming from behind her. She turned and looked at the man, creasing her forehead in thought. Slowly, feeling unsure, she took a small step backwards.

'If you tear off this bark, you'll see a lot more of them. You're not squeamish are you?'

Star shook her head, not saying anything, only hearing the voice of her mother inside her head, telling her never to talk to strangers. She watched as the man winked, then proceeded to tear off the bark, uncovering a black mass of moving insects.

Star squealed then covered her mouth as the man laughed. He leant down towards her, leaning his face closer than she felt comfortable with. 'I thought you said you weren't squeamish.'

Indignantly, Star answered, her hands now firmly on her hips. 'I ain't. Just gave me a fright, that's all. Anyway, I have to go. Me mum will wonder where I am and if she tells me dad, he'll have me guts.'

The man gave a crooked smile that didn't reach his eyes.

'I'm sure he won't do that.'

Star shrugged her shoulders. 'You don't know me dad.'

'Well that's where you're wrong. I do know your dad.'

Puzzled, Star tipped her head to one side. She knew she shouldn't be talking to this man, but she couldn't help herself. She always did love games. 'What's his name then?'

'That would be telling.'

Star curled her lip, imitating the way her mother sometimes did. ''Cos you don't know, that's why.'

The man spoke, crushing one of the insects between his finger and thumb as he did so. 'Believe what you like, but I even know your name.'

Star's eyes lit up. 'What is it then?'

'I don't tell secrets.'

'My name ain't a secret.'

'But being here is, isn't it?'

Star looked down, feeling embarrassed that the man had guessed she wasn't allowed into some poxy woods at the age of seven. All her friends were allowed to roam about but she was kept on a tighter lead than her next-door neighbour's dog.

'Maybe.'

The man crouched down. Star could smell the overpowering scent of aftershave on him. It didn't smell anything like the stuff her dad wore. This made her want to cough, but she didn't want to be rude. Her mum had always taught her never to be unkind to people.

'So how about it stays your and my secret? I won't tell anyone that you were here and you don't tell anyone you saw me. What do you say ... Star?'

Star Barker-Williams took a quick intake of breath. The man really *did* know her name. Though she didn't know if this was a good thing or a bad thing because it meant he really *did* know her dad – which meant that if he found out she'd been in the woods on her own he'd probably not let her friends come and stay at the weekend when he and her mum went away.

'Okay. Cross my heart.' Star did a tiny cross on her chest. She felt the man clutch onto her hands tightly. He held them in his for a second, holding her stare with his. 'I think you'll find your heart is on the other side.' He moved Star's hand across her chest, then let go as suddenly as he'd taken hold of it. Star giggled and crossed her heart again as the man watched her closely. Taking a strand of her hair, he rubbed it, aware the squashed insect was still on his fingers.

'You've got beautiful hair, Star. Has anyone ever told you that?'

Star stared into the man's small narrowed eyes, holding his gaze for a few seconds. Slowly she pulled her hair away, touching it absent-mindedly. She wrinkled her nose.

'Yeah, me mum says it all the time, but you should see hers, it's longer than mine; nearly past her waist. Like Rapunzel.'

In the next few moments of silence, Star heard the birds singing, but she couldn't see them. It was much darker in the woods than she'd ever imagined, though she wasn't afraid of the dark like other kids, like her mum even. To her, darkness only made things seem more exciting; more like an adventure.

'I understand your dad's going on holiday.'

Star shrugged her shoulders. She didn't know this man and she knew not to tell her business to anyone. She'd always known that, ever since she was little.

'Are you going to go with him?'

Star frowned. She didn't like all these questions but she also didn't like the fact that she wasn't going to go away with her parents, despite pleading with them again and again. She didn't know why they were going to have all the fun and in the meantime she was going to be stuck at home with Claudia.

'If you were my daughter, I'd take you with me. Maybe I could have a word with your dad. Would you like that?'

Star's eyes gleamed. 'Would you? Would you ask him? But you can't say that I saw you.'

'I won't tell him. Like I say, it'll be our little secret. Are you good at keeping secrets, Star?'

Star went to open her mouth but the sound coming from behind her left her words stuck in her throat.

'Star! Star!'

It was her mother. She felt the colour drain out of her face. She'd wanted to come into the woods without her mum noticing. Looking at the diamond-encrusted Rolex her Dad had got especially commissioned for her, Star saw what time it was. She didn't realise she'd been that long. Now there would be no chance of her friends staying and even less chance of being able to go away at the weekend with her mum and dad.

'Trouble?' The man spoke with enough concern in his voice for Star to open up.

'That's me mum. If she finds me in here…'

The man put out his hand. 'I tell you what. I know a different route out of the woods. Why don't you come this way with me? Then your mum won't know you've been here. It takes you out to the other side of the park so she'll think you only went to the swings by the west entrance. It'll stop you getting into trouble.' The man smiled again and winked as Star looked at his outstretched hand. The high-pitched scream of her mother calling her name made the decision for her. Taking the man's hand, Star grinned.

'Come on, quickly.' The man pulled Star as he spoke, then started to jog through the trees. This was more fun than she'd had in a long time. It was a real adventure. Like the movie she'd seen last night about the girl stuck on a desert island.

'Star!' Her mum's voice shouted from behind, making Star pull on the man's hand as she turned round.

'Come on, you don't want to get caught do you?'

Star listened again to her mother's call.

'Star … please. Where are you?'

Star looked at the man who was trying to speed her up again. She spoke, her voice sounding older than she was. 'Mum sounds upset. She's worried.'

The man's voice had a firmness in it that hadn't been there before. 'Well hurry up then and once she sees you at the swings she won't have to worry, will she?'

Star shook her head. She stopped walking. She didn't like the idea of her mum being worried and the fear she heard in her voice was beginning to upset her. Before the man could stop her, Star shouted as loud as she could, 'Mum! Mum! I'm here.'

The man's face contorted with anger before panic gripped him. He quickly let go of Star's hand before running down the bank towards the thicket, leaving Star standing in the shadowed trees.

A moment later, Bunny came running up, tears pouring down her face. She ran up to Star, hugged her then slapped her hard on her cheek. Immediately, Bunny regretted her action. She dropped to her knees and grabbed hold of Star who looked as shocked as Bunny did with what had just happened.

'Star. I'm sorry... Bleedin' hell I'm sorry, but you gave me a fright. What the hell did you think you were doing? I told you never to go into the woods on your own. Horrible things can happen, Star, don't you understand that?'

Bunny shook Star, whose body was now racked with deep sobs. 'Star, are you listening to me? Star?' Bunny felt a soft touch on her shoulder. It was Claudia, panting and out of breath.

'Leave her, Bun. She's only a kid. She didn't mean any harm by it.'

Bunny's eyes were wide and fearful. 'But what if something had happened to her, Claudia?'

Claudia's voice was soft and caring. 'But nothing did happen, did it, doll?'

Bunny looked from Claudia to her daughter who stood crying, though Bunny could sense an air of defiance exuding from her. She stood up and yanked on Star's hand.

'Come on young lady. Just wait till your dad hears about this. I don't know what he'll say, but I do know he'll be blowing.'

Star said nothing, but as she was led away, she turned round to see the man standing behind the tree with his finger on his lips, signalling her not to say a word. She wouldn't. It would be her secret.

As Star walked away, the man watched and smiled. It had been easier to gain the girl's trust than he'd thought and once he got it fully, he'd put his plan into action.

'You've got to do something about her,' Bunny paced about in her bedroom, chewing her bottom lip. There was no answer, just a heavy sigh from Del. Bunny shot him a stare.

'Is that all you've got for me? A blow of air? Ain't you got anything to say?'

Del looked exasperated. He'd been sitting on the bed for the last forty-five minutes listening to Bunny going on about Star.

'Problem is, I dunno what you want me to say, darlin'.'

'*Something* would be nice. *Anything*. I don't understand why you ain't worried about it!'

Bunny held her gaze, looking at Del, who was now desperately searching for something to say that might placate Bunny. He rubbed the back of

140

his neck, wishing his phone would ring so he could make an excuse to duck out.

'Well, I'll have a word with her.'

Bunny's face flushed. 'A word? We've been having a *word* with her since she began to walk and it ain't ever done any good. It's those books she reads, her head's in the clouds. She thinks life's one big adventure and the world's hers to explore and roam about in.'

'She's just like me. When I was a nipper...'

Bunny didn't let Del finish. 'She's not you though is she? She's a little girl who only sees the good in everyone.'

'That's good ain't it? There's enough time for her when she's older to realise what a shitty world we live in.'

'It'd be okay if she didn't think she was bleedin' Marco Polo.'

'Who?'

'Never mind. Point is, she's got to stop going off like that.'

'It's only natural, Bun. She's a kid. Kids are forever wandering off.'

Bunny's words were filled with fear and anger. 'Don't you listen to the news? Only last week they found that poor little girl murdered.'

'Calm down, Bun. It's tragic, I know, but these things don't happen that often.'

Bunny exploded. 'What is *wrong* with you? You can't think like that. Don't you see? Don't you understand, it could happen to Star like it happened to that girl; like it happened to...'

Bunny put her head in her hands. Del sat on the bed, not knowing quite what to do. He spoke gently. 'Bun, what's going on? It's getting worse, babe.'

Through her tears Bunny spoke. 'I know. I know, but I can't help it.'

'Maybe you should go and see the quack. It could be hormones and stuff...' Del trailed off, realising that was the extent of his knowledge when it came to women's problems.

'It ain't hormones.'

'Then I'm stuck to know what it is, 'cos you weren't ever as bad when Star was a baby. You worried, yeah. But this? This is crazy Bun. You've got to stop.'

Bunny wiped her tears away. 'But when she was a baby she couldn't wander off, could she?'

Del got up and placed his hand on Bunny's arm.

'Nothing's going to happen to her. Trust me on that.'

Bunny scanned Del's face with her big blue eyes. 'How can I trust you on that? Because you don't know. You don't know what might happen.'

Del's tone was quiet and warm. 'Bun, this is doing me head in. It's not good for you to worry so much, and it's not good for Star either.'

'Because you don't understand.'

Del tried to keep the impatience out of his voice. There was nothing new about the conversation they were having. It seemed like a fortnightly event. 'Then tell me. *Help* me to understand.'

'I can't... I'm sorry.'

Del raised his voice, wishing he hadn't when he saw the hurt in Bunny's eyes. 'Can't or *won't*? Big-ass difference, Bun. You want me to understand –

142

but you won't tell me what you're thinking. It's all in your head, babe. There ain't no bogeymen hiding under the bed.'

'What's going on?'

Del turned his head and saw Claudia standing at the door with her face pulled tight and her lips pursed. This was all he needed.

'Nothing. It's a private convo between me and Bun. So if you don't mind…'

Ignoring Del's gesturing hand, signalling her to turn and walk away, Claudia bustled into the exquisitely decorated room. Walking over to Bunny with a concerned look on her face, she turned on Del. 'It don't look like nothing to me.'

'This has got nothing to do with you.'

Claudia saw the tears on Bunny's face. Her voice was accusatory. 'What have you done to her?'

Del opened his arms wide, taken aback. 'I ain't done nothing to her. Tell her, Bun. Tell her it ain't me.'

Bunny attempted a smile. 'It's okay Claudia.'

Claudia narrowed her eyes. 'Really?'

Bunny nodded. 'Yeah, really.'

Del growled. 'Happy now? Satisfied I ain't the monster here? Why is it you lot always presume it's us men who cause the problems? All we want is a peaceful life, but I can see there won't be any chance of that here.'

With that, Del grabbed his phone and marched out. The room fell silent. A moment passed before Claudia looked at Bunny. 'Was this about Star?'

Bunny nodded.

'Maybe you should talk to him, Bun. *Properly*.'

'No, I can't.'

'But if you don't you might drive him away.'

Bunny shook her head and walked towards the door, where she paused. 'Claudia, thank you. I appreciate you looking out for me, but let me worry about Del.'

Claudia stood looking out of the window, knowing there must be something she could do to help – whether Bunny liked it or not.

16

'Do you want me to get me ear chewed off?'

Star lay on her bed and watched her dad wave his arms up in the air for what must have been the twentieth time whilst he paced up and down in her newly decorated bedroom.

'I can't stop blowing now. Every time I think of it I'm bleedin' fuming, Star. What were you thinking, going into the woods without your mum? And what makes it worse is now I've got a truckload of grief from her. She's even talking about not coming to Marbella with me.'

'Yeah well, at least if she don't go I won't be left on me tod.'

Del stared hard at his daughter. It was times like this he wished he could swap her for a boy. Boys were much easier in his eyes. All he'd have to do was give them a clump and the problem would be sorted, but there was no way he was ever going to raise his hand to a girl.

Cutting his eye at Star, who'd now turned her back on him, Del walked across to the window. She had some front, but that was also what he found most endearing about her. She was a chip off the old block.

Del sighed. If he was truthful, he didn't know what all the fuss was about. All the girl had done was go into the woods and have a bit of fun. But try telling Bunny that. It was the same every time. He'd suggest she was overreacting, then she'd become almost hysterical. And hysterical women and Del just didn't go. It was all he could do not to walk out on her and go and have a drinking session with a few of his mates. But instead, like a mug, he always tried to listen and understand. But that was the problem. He *didn't* understand. And the worst thing was she became so unreasonable, not listening to sense. Quite frankly, it did his nut in.

He didn't actually know what was going on with Bunny. She hadn't been her usual self for a while and her fear surrounding Star was becoming over the top. She'd actually spent the last few nights lying on the sofa. When he'd asked her what the matter was, he hadn't been much help; his jealousy had gotten the better of him when she'd told him she was tired from too many clients. He'd stormed out and joined Alfie Jennings in a late-night poker game, topped off with copious amounts of the finest whisky.

When he thought about it, Del had a strong feeling Bunny wasn't telling him the whole truth. Sure, she was tired but there was something else going on as well – yet he knew it was pointless questioning her. He'd only be wasting his breath, which would end up frustrating him. Bunny had always been one to keep things close to her chest – unlike most women he knew who liked to verbalise every thought that entered their minds, no matter how trivial and tedious it was.

What Bunny needed was to get away; perhaps then he could persuade her to bang it on the head, give it all up and be the housewife he longed her to be. *Housewife*. The thought made him snort. What the hell was he thinking? He'd met her on a street corner and watched her entertaining punters day after day. And he'd accepted what she did when it'd suited him but now that it didn't how was he supposed to put up a fight about it and take the moral high ground? Bunny had an independent streak running deeply through her – asking her to part with her independence would be like asking her to give up her hands and feet.

Feeling his phone vibrate in his pocket, Del turned from the window, catching a glimpse of Star watching him. He winked, getting a scowl in return. Del laughed at his daughter, his cheeky grin making his dimples appear. The amount of love he felt for her always surprised him.

Looking at the caller ID of his phone wiped the smile away as quickly as it had appeared. It was Edith. He pressed the lock off button and glanced again at Star. She had no idea about his other life and although she was only seven she was savvy, and he was sure she wouldn't take kindly to dis-covering he had a wife.

146

'Hey Star. Fancy coming to do a few errands with your old man?'

Star, her grin almost identical to her father's, beamed. 'You mean it? What about Mum? She said I had to stay at home with Claudia.' Star pulled a face at the thought.

'You leave your mum to me.'

Star laughed. 'She'll have your bleedin' guts; you know that as well as I do.'

Del roared with laughter.

'Well I won't tell her if you don't.'

Star nodded, feeling very special. It was the second time that week an adult had asked her to keep a secret.

'Anything you see or hear...'

Star interrupted Del, 'I know Dad. Keep me trap shut.' Star looked adoringly at her dad. She always had fun with him but this was the first time he'd ever taken her anywhere important. Creeping down the stairs, Star took hold of Del's hand. She stifled a giggle when she saw a sleeping Claudia in the front room, her mouth wide open. She didn't know what Claudia would say if she caught them, which made it even more exciting.

Outside, Star let out the laughter she'd been holding in. She clung onto her dad's hand as they hurried along the tourist-filled Soho street. Even though it was still light, she loved Soho at night. Not that she had much chance of seeing it at this time; usually her mum made sure she was tucked up in bed by eight o'clock.

A few minutes later, they got to the corner of Greek Street where they waited, Del looking at his watch, in-between telling jokes and Star laughing at them raucously.

Del's phone rang, breaking the moment. It was Claudia. Certainly not someone he wanted to talk to, but he knew it was best not to ignore the phone call. Since he'd known Bunny, he'd known Claudia. At first Del hadn't liked her always being around, but then he'd seen how much she'd cared, not only for Bunny, but also Star, when she was born. Because of that he'd been willing to put up with her, and slowly he had come to respect and like her. He didn't much appreciate the way Claudia talked to him, but Bunny had asked him not to react to it. And for Bunny, he'd do anything.

Del stuck his tongue out at Star, who giggled again.

'Yes Claudia. How can I help you?'

Star felt as if she was jumping on air as her dad held the phone away from his ear, knowing Claudia was giving her father a mouthful. It was so exciting. Now she wouldn't have to watch movies wishing she was part of them, it was like she was in one of her own.

'Listen Claudia, she's with me. No need to panic.' Del paused for a moment then added, 'I'll do what I frigging well like with my own daughter. Don't tell me what I can or can't do.' Del cut the phone off, feeling anger swell in him.

Seeing a black Mercedes driving up the road swerved Del's thoughts away from Claudia. He nodded, then cautiously looked around as it pulled up slowly by the side of him. Opening the back passenger door of the car, Del gestured for

148

Star to get in before sliding onto the seat next to her.

'All right mate, I think we need to talk, don't you?'

As the man in the passenger seat turned round to speak to Del, Star covered her mouth. It was the man from the woods.

'This is my daughter Star, by the way.'

'Nice to meet you, Star.' Teddy Davies smiled, giving Star a knowing wink.

17

Alfonso Garcia stared down at his penis in horror. There were tiny red spots around the rim of it and a splay of spots down the shaft, pulling Alfonso in mind of the dot-to-dot puzzles he use to do as a child. Fuck. He knew he should've been more careful with the whore he'd picked up last week, but the idea of having a latex wall between him and a juicy bit of pussy hadn't appealed to him; so he'd taken the chance, and now he was going to have to deal with the consequences.

'Alfonso!'

Shit, it was Edith. What the fuck was he going to tell her? There was no way she was going to let him get out of sleeping with her, but he couldn't risk passing it on, that was *if* he hadn't already done so. He'd been a fool. He could've messed up everything, all for the sake of a cheap hooker.

The worst part was that the only person Edith

ever slept with was him. Del wouldn't touch her with the proverbial – which meant that, if she *had* got it, she would know exactly where it had come from. Then Alfonso could whistle a sweet bye-bye to anything he thought was coming his way.

Edith walked into the bathroom. 'There you are! I've been looking all over for you, like David bleedin' Livingstone looking for the lost world.'

'Don't exaggerate, Edith, there's only the bedroom and the bathroom to look in, and here I am.'

'Well that's as may be, but you didn't come when I called you; for all I knew you could've left me.'

'Leave you? Don't be silly, Edith darling. The only way I'd ever leave you would be if death itself parted us.'

Edith giggled childishly, making Alfonso grip onto the side of the oversized rolled top bath. The temptation of putting his fist down her throat was very appealing. His penis was throbbing and an almighty itch was beginning to start, feeling like it was coming from the centre of his urethra, so the last thing he could deal with right now was any of Edith's girly shit.

Before Alfonso had finished his thought, Edith rushed towards him, spreading her flabby bat-winged arms wide. Not noticing the corner of the bathmat turned up, Edith stumbled forwards, losing her balance, then finally tripped over the mat. She fell, knocking Alfonso into the gold-tapped tub.

Alfonso flew backwards, hitting his head hard on the porcelain. As the blood ran from his head he yelled loudly, not being able to keep control of his rage, and Alf Garfield's voice slipped out.

'*You fucking fat stupid bitch! I'll kill you.*'

The moment the words had come out of his mouth, Alfonso immediately regretted them. Edith stood over the bathtub staring down at him, her eyes a mixture of hurt and puzzlement.

Her voice was quiet and the shrillness that usually resided in it was gone. 'Why did you just speak like that?'

'I... I'm sorry Edith. I just got a fright.'

Edith narrowed her eyes suspiciously. 'But you didn't even *sound* like you.'

Alfonso knew he had to play this very carefully.

'If you want the truth, Edith, I'm angry with you. Hurt, angry and disappointed.'

Edith's puzzlement deepened, along with the crease in her forehead. 'Disappointed?'

'Yes, Edith. Look at this.' Alfonso awkwardly struggled out of the tub, pulling himself up with the help of the hanging towel on the rail. Unceremoniously he pulled his linen trousers down to reveal his throbbing penis in all its red-rashed glory. 'Look ... there.'

Edith stared down, then lifted her eyes up to meet Alfonso's gaze, her face turning a deep shade of red. 'I hope that ain't what I think it is, Alfy.'

'So do I – because the only way I could have got this is from you.'

'Oh no you bleedin' don't. I ain't been born blonde. This ain't got nothing to do with me.'

'That's what you say, Edith, but how else did...'

Edith cut him off, mid sentence. 'Listen to me.

I've been married for longer than I bleedin' care to remember so I've heard all the bullshit there is. Don't try to pull no wool over my eyes, Alfonso. You've been shag-nasty; dipping your dick in some dirty cow when me back's turned. But I ain't going to stand for it. It was bad enough having to suck it up with Del. But let me tell you, darlin', I ain't no one's mug; especially some toerag like you. Now do one. Get out of me face before I get the hotel security to throw you out.'

Impulsively, Edith grabbed hold of the rinsing glass on the side, throwing it in Alfonso's direction. He ducked, turning to see it smash on the far wall as it shattered into tiny fragments.

'You stupid bitch.'

As Alfonso charged towards Edith she ran for the bathroom door, but only managed to open it slightly before Alfonso slammed it shut, pressing his body onto hers.

He could feel her breathing hard, wheezing away as he pressed her up against the door. He gritted his teeth, spitting his words out savagely.

Alfonso growled. 'Don't push me Edith, otherwise you'll be sorry.'

'It won't be me who'll be sorry after I speak to Del. You've as good as hanged yourself, mate.'

Alfonso grabbed Edith's hair, pulling her head back before banging her, face forward, into the wooden door. She screamed, her top lip opening up in a bubble of blood. Bringing her head back once more, Alfonso yanked again on her hair and laughed nastily.

'Do me a favour. What are you going to tell

152

him, eh? That you and me have been screwing behind his back? Oh I'm sure he's going to like to hear that. If *I'm* hanging, babes, you'll be swinging right next to me.'

Through a shroud of tears and blood, Edith blubbered a reply. 'He'll never believe you.'

'Oh no? Well let's just tell him then. Go on babe. I dare you. But don't forget, sweetheart, I've got less to lose than you. All that will happen to me is I'll take a few clumps and then I'll be on me way. But you?' Alfonso grabbed a roll of fat from underneath Edith's armpit, squeezing it hard, causing Edith to yelp loudly. 'You, you fat greedy bitch, will lose everything.'

'He wouldn't dare. I know too much about him.'

'Then tell him.'

Alfonso swivelled Edith around. He curled up his nose in disgust as he witnessed the blood-drenched snot running down her chin. He could see the fear in her eyes.

'Things are going to change round here. You ain't going to call the shots no longer, not if you don't want me to tell our little secret to Del.'

'You ... you wouldn't, not if you care for me.'

'Care for you? Are you having a bubble?' Alfonso leaned in nearer, spraying saliva onto Edith's face as he spoke.

'Let me tell you something, Edith, I cared for my own shit more than I ever cared for you. Look at you, you're a disgrace. You make me sick. Every time I was near you it was like there was a bad stench.'

'You'll be sorry, mark my words.'

Slamming her head back against the door, Alfonso shouted.

'Ain't you heard what I've been saying? Don't threaten me darlin' – you're not making the marches anymore. This is how it's going to go. Until I decide what to do, I'm staying here. From now on, you don't give me orders. You don't tell me what to do. Don't ask me what I'm doing or where I'm going. And as for sleeping with you again, babe? I would rather stick my cock in a cold studded metal vice before I put it near your rancid pussy again. Then when I'm ready to tell you what I want, we can work out a nice arrangement.'

Still defiant, although in pain, Edith scoffed. 'Oh don't tell me, Alfonso. You're talking about money – well sorry to disappoint you, but I ain't got any. Not a pot, babe. I don't hold the purse strings, it's all Del, and he won't let go of his money in a hurry.'

'Then you'll have to find a way of getting to him, won't you?'

Edith's face curled up, her voice full of scorn and bitterness. 'You really don't know him at all. The only way to separate him from his dough would be a bleedin' bullet in his head.'

Alfonso stepped away from Edith, pushing her to one side to open the bathroom door. He turned to her and stared hard.

'Then a bullet in his head it is.'

18

'Come on then, move it. If we're going to get this plane we need to get a bleedin' jog on.'

Del Williams stood at the bottom of the stairs of Bunny's flat, dressed casually in a floral Armani shirt and dark blue Gucci jeans. He wasn't entirely convinced that what he was wearing didn't make him look like a muppet, but Bunny had bought the clothes for him. Up until now he'd kept them tucked away at the back of his walk-in closet, but today he'd brought them out, feeling it was the right day to wear them. Anything to humour her.

She'd been in an odd mood since Star had done her disappearing act and it'd taken him all his persuasion skills, along with the help of Claudia, to convince her to come to Marbella with him.

Even though Star had been the cause of the upset, she hadn't been much help in smoothing anything over; in fact Del reckoned she'd done everything in her powers to make Bunny stay. If it hadn't been for Claudia laying down the law, he probably would've been going on the plane on his own. Tears had been spilt and even an uncharacteristic tantrum had been performed on the new kitchen floor by Star.

Though he couldn't blame her. The girl wanted to come. Del wanted her to as well. He hankered after the idea of showing her off to his friends and acquaintances. Star was something he'd done in his life that he could say he was truly proud of. But one thing she could never find out about was his other life. Not just yet, anyway. And if he did take her across to the villa in Marbella, she would know.

He watched Star walk down the stairs with a glum face, carrying one of Bunny's Louis Vuitton bags. He chuckled warmly as Star scowled at him.

'Star, baby. Come and say goodbye to Mummy.' Bunny's face was full of love as she looked at her daughter. Always enjoying hugs from her mum, no matter how cross she was, Star ran into Bunny's arms.

'Promise me, Star, that you'll listen to what Claudia tells you.'

Claudia butted in. 'She won't have any choice, will you missy?'

Star scowled up at Claudia, making everyone roar with laughter and lightening the tension in the air.

'I'll be back soon. But call me any time, day or night. I don't mind. Remember to brush your teeth and try not to read so many of them adventure books.'

'Blimey Mum, anyone would think you ain't going to see me again.'

The smile on Del's and Claudia's face fell as they watched the fear come back into Bunny's eyes.

'I need to make a stop. Pull over here John-Jo.' Del tapped his driver on the shoulder, signalling him to park up on the yellow double lines. Bunny turned, her eyebrows raised in surprise. 'What now? Won't we be late for the plane?'

'Seeing as I've charted it I think it'll wait, don't you?'

'But…'

'I've got to pick up some papers from him, otherwise no one will be going anywhere.' Del tapped her on the leg then added, 'It'll be fine. Stop worrying.'

Bunny looked unconvinced, but then what did she know about travelling? This was all new to her and if she had her way she'd be at home with Star. At the thought of her daughter, her stomach turned over. She had to try to stay calm. Like Claudia had said, '*Nothing's going to happen on my watch, darling.*' Bunny knew Claudia she was right – but then why did she have this overwhelming sense of anxiety?

She had to snap herself out of this. She hadn't been sleeping well, which she was sure had something to do with it. Maybe Del was right, this holiday was something she, *they*, needed.

'Won't be a minute, babe. Then it'll be sea, sun and…' He leaned over and kissed her. 'Maybe you'll have to help me out with what the last s will be.' Del smiled, getting out of the car with the sound of Bunny's giggle echoing in his ears.

Even though the air-con was on, Bunny opened the window. She sat watching Del talking to the man, although she couldn't see him as he was blocked out by Del's large frame.

As if he could read her thoughts, Del moved to the side as he threw down the cigar he was smoking, giving Bunny a clear view of the man he was talking to. Straight away her mind started to race. Blurred memories began to fade in and out. She bent her head down, feeling nauseous, hoping whatever was happening would pass, but it was as if there was a strong smell making her feel sick. Sweet water entered her mouth as Bunny felt the colour draining from her.

She needed to get some air. Stepping out of the car, she looked in the direction of where Del and the man were talking.

'You all right, Bunny?' Del's voice penetrated her dizziness as she stood leaning on the side of the car. She attempted to nod but was afraid she'd lose her balance. What was wrong with her? It was like she was having a panic attack.

Del ran over to Bunny. The sweat was running down her forehead like rain drops.

'What's going on, Bun? You ain't just trying to get out of going, are you babes?'

Bunny gave Del a weak smile. The intensity of the feeling was beginning to pass. She gazed up and found herself staring at the man standing next to Del. His face seemed familiar, but from the distant past, a face blurred and shaded into a forgotten memory.

'No, I'm okay now. It's probably because I took one of those travel sickness pills on top of an empty stomach.' Bunny grinned meekly.

'Oh Bun, sorry. I haven't introduced you. This is Alan.'

Alan put out his hand for Bunny to shake. She took it and held his gaze, staring into the dark voids of his eyes. Almost too quickly she pulled her hand away as she felt she was being jarred by unwanted thoughts. She began to sweat again and her breath began to get short.

'Here you are.' From out of his pocket, Alan handed Bunny a hankie.

Bunny turned to go and sit back in the car.

Closing her eyes, Bunny welcomed the cool of the air-conditioned Aston Martin as she patted the sweat away from her forehead, trying to remember exactly where she'd seen Alan before.

19

Teddy Davies sat opposite Milo Burkov with just a small table and four fat lines of coke between them. It was quality quiver, the best Teddy had had in a long time, and even though the summer heat was muggy and the Soho streets below them were noisy, Teddy felt refreshed and mellow. The downside of it was that he was struggling to concentrate on what Milo was saying.

'What was it my friend had to say?' Milo spoke to Teddy, referring to the meeting Teddy had had with Del the other night.

'I saw the girl.'

'Which girl?'

'Star, Del's daughter.'

Milo banged his hand on the table, sending the coke up in the air before it sprinkled down like a snow burst.

'We agreed the girl's off-limits.'

'No, *you* agreed the girl's off-limits. I haven't got time for emotional squeezes. Nothing is off-limits when it comes to him. When he falls, I want to make sure he falls hard.'

Milo stood up, sweeping the coke off the table, much to Teddy's anguish.

'Detective Davies. I think the powder is starting to affect your brain. You aren't calling any shots with me. You don't decide what is or isn't off-limits. You were the one who came to *me* asking for my help, not the other way round. You would be wise to remember that.'

The quiver gave Teddy a false sense of confidence. He leapt up in anger. There was no way any foreigner was going to tell him what to do. He prodded his finger into Milo's chest.

'This is *my* manor, not yours. I could even go so far as to say this is *my* country, not yours.'

Milo looked round at his henchmen and burst into laughter. He gestured his head at Teddy, speaking in his native Russian tongue to his men.

Teddy's gaze went from Milo to the gargantuan men who edged nearer to Milo's side. His rush of confidence began to subside as the tight, intense feeling of the quiver started to wear off slightly.

Seeing the look of hesitation in Teddy's eyes, Milo grinned, showing off his gold tooth. His thick accent was almost cartoon-like. 'I suppose you are wondering what I said to my men. In English it is translated as *"Look at this fool, he is playing with the devil"*.'

With a quick right hook from Milo, Teddy shot across the room, landing on a pile of stacked-up boxes in the corner. He could feel his chin throbbing as shockwaves of pain shot up through the nerves of his teeth and he tasted blood in his mouth.

'In Russia we like to give the foolish one chance. So now my friend, you've used up that one chance. Another time, I will not hesitate to kill you.'

Grabbing his coat, Milo walked out of the room, followed by his men. Teddy could feel fury mixed with the pain running through his body. He felt humiliated. He was Teddy Davies and Milo thought he could do this. This was all Del's fault and he was going to make him pay a heavy price. There was no way Teddy was going to keep his family out of it. That's where he knew it would hit Del hard and the girl was the perfect place to start.

Soon his name would be known. Everyone in Soho would be talking about Teddy Davies – knowing they couldn't take the piss any more. It'd be his rule and no one, but no one, was ever going to take that away from him. Oh yes, when he'd finished with everyone it'd be him they were all talking about, not Milo, and certainly not the irrepressible Del Williams.

Half an hour later, Teddy sat in his car in Greek Street, thinking about Del.

Thinking of Del had Teddy reaching for the half-smoked spliff sitting in his ashtray. Taking the smoke deep into his lungs took the frown off his forehead and the twisted knot out from his stomach. He supposed he shouldn't get worked up. Wasn't that why he was here now, to lay the foundation of the first part of his plan? And what's more, he didn't care a jot what Milo thought.

Stepping out of the car, Teddy walked across the road, in the direction of the flat belonging to Bunny Barker.

20

Alan Day had been released from hospital and Julian Millwood sat opposite him, in a state of excitement as he sat in Alan's office. He was counting money, something he didn't often have the chance to do. In actuality he was counting it for the second time as Alan stared grimly, rubbing his chest. The stress with Julian wasn't helping Alan. Damn him. He sprayed two squirts of the nitrolingual spray he'd been given for his angina into his mouth, before taking a large swig of his brandy.

Julian raised an eyebrow. 'There's only eight grand here.'

Alan looked incredulous. 'You didn't really expect me to give you a hundred grand, did you? You're lucky you're even getting that.'

Julian could feel a sense of disappointment coming over him. Alan was spoiling the moment and he didn't like people spoiling things – especially criminals in suits. He went into his jacket pocket and pulled out a photograph.

'Hey, you'll never guess what I found. They just keep coming, don't they? Funny how our past sometimes bites us on our arse. Again and again

162

and…' Julian smiled and handed the photograph to Alan, who crumpled it up in his hands, face turning red.

'How old was she, Alan, I don't quite recall? Under twelve? Under ten? Under eight? Stop me when I hit the right number won't you? We take a good photo, don't we? I think I've put on a little weight since then and you…'

Alan kicked out at the chair next to him. He shouted loudly, much to Julian's amusement.

'That's enough! This is all a joke to you, isn't it? It's all highly amusing to know you could ruin my life. You've got your money, now get out. I want you to leave.'

Julian cackled at Alan's discomfort, then looked down at the money again.

'Well, I suppose this will have to do. For now, anyway. Thank you, Alan. But I'm sure I'll see you soon.'

'Get out!'

'Alan don't get so stressed – it won't be good for the old ticker. You used to like the adventure.'

'I said, *out!*'

Julian walked across to the door, pushing the money back in his pocket.

'Now stay away. No more money. No more favours. Like we agreed.'

'No Alan. *You* agreed.'

Alan snarled. 'Enough. I'm telling you now, I'm having nothing more to do with you. I'm washing my hands of it all. You've got your money, so I'd suggest this is the last time we speak.'

Julian laughed. 'I'll tell you when you wash your hands. Don't forget they're very dirty ones.'

'I won't be blackmailed like this. You'd be stupid to take me on.'

'Alan, Alan, Alan. Tell me, what exactly are you going to do about it. What? I can't hear you. Come on, tell me mate, I'd be very interested to know.' There was a long pause, then Julian added, 'That's what I thought. Nothing. Absolutely fuck all.'

Walking out of the meeting place Julian patted his pocket. He'd actually been surprised Alan had so readily agreed to give him money, and eight grand at that. Okay, so he'd asked for one hundred but he never *really* expected to get anything. Eight grand? Shit, he would've been happy getting a grand.

He wasn't going to ask Alan for any more. Not that he'd ever let him know that.

No, what Julian was going to focus on was making real money – the kind of money that would stop him from ever having to worry about money again. And the way to do that was to get a blonde. An innocent blonde.

Alan Day decided the pain in his chest had stopped enough to let him move again. Sweat sat on his top lip from fear and stress. He wasn't good at handling pain; he wasn't equipped for it. But what Alan was even less equipped for was being blackmailed by some low-life scum.

There were many ways to deal with people like Julian Millwood. He was stupid, brash and indiscreet and one way or another Alan would make sure he got his comeuppance.

21

The doorbell rang. In fact, Star knew it had rung four times because she'd counted it on her fingers. But she also knew she wasn't allowed to open the door. That had been the rule. Or rather it'd been Claudia's rule when she'd made Star promise she wouldn't answer the door to anyone.

'I'll swing for you if you do, Star. And then I'll get your dad to swing for you. Do you hear me?'

Of course she'd heard her, she'd said it loud enough. But Star hadn't argued. She'd nodded her head and given Claudia a hug. Star knew Claudia worried almost as much as her mum did.

Star let out a loud sigh. She was missing her dad and begrudgingly she had to admit she was missing her mum as well. But her mum was a spoilsport and had still been cross with her for going into the woods, not allowing her to have friends over for a sleepover or even a play-date. How unfair was that? So now she was stuck with Claudia.

The bell rang again and Star shivered. She'd promised not to open the door, but she hadn't promised not to look out of the window or through the letter box.

Star went to pick up her beloved spyglass. She loved it. It was just like the one Captain Jack Sparrow had. Her dad had bought it for her the last time he'd gone to Marbella and most of the time she never went anywhere without it.

Star tiptoed to the window. She hoped it was pirates. That would be fun. Stolen treasure, just like what her dad had sometimes. Star put the spyglass to her right eye, using the other end of it to draw back the blinds.

Circled in the spyglass, Star could see the people across the other side of the street. She could see them so clearly through the glass she could make out the lines and spots on all their faces.

Cautiously, Star went closer to the window and peered down from the first floor onto the busy street, turning the spyglass towards her front door. And then she saw who it was – it was the man from the woods and he was calling up to her.

Star called back down to him through the half-open window. 'Me Dad's not here, mate.'

Teddy Davies smiled. He already knew that. 'Oh, that's a shame. I really needed to talk to him. Star, isn't it?'

Star smiled, pleased that the man had remembered her name.

'Yeah it is.'

'Do you remember me?'

Indignantly Star replied, 'Of course I do. I'm seven, I've just had me birthday.'

'Can you open the door? I'd like to talk to you.'

'I can't – Claudia would go mad. I'm not supposed to open doors to anyone I don't know.'

'Well she's right, but you do know me. I'm Teddy.'

Star thought about this. It was true she *did* know the man but she didn't know him very well.

Nobody had told her what to do in this situation when she knew the person, but only a little.

'Star?'

'Yes mate?'

'Are you going to let me in?'

'Dunno. I'm thinking about it.'

'What are you thinking about, Star?'

'I'm thinking I don't know you very well.'

'That's right, Star – but I kept your secret didn't I? So you know me well enough to know that you can trust me.'

Star crunched up her button nose. 'Suppose.'

'No suppose about it, Star. I didn't *tell* your dad you were talking to me, did I? And I could've done, but I kept my word. It was our secret.'

Star didn't know what to do now. In a way she wished Claudia would come back from Mc-Donalds with or without the double cheeseburger she'd promised to bring, and then she wouldn't have to decide.

Star peered at Teddy again. He was right, he *had* kept her secret, but when her dad had taken her to meet Teddy in the car, her dad had spent the whole time shouting at him. And Star knew her dad really only shouted at people he didn't like – which meant she shouldn't like him either, and she certainly shouldn't let him in. But the problem Star had was that she *did* like him.

'Star?'

'Yes?'

'How about if I promise to keep this secret, too? I promise I won't tell anyone you let me in. How about that? Cross my heart and hope to blow a bullet in my head.'

Star laughed loudly.

'So what do you say, Star?'

Star backed away from the window and walked down the corridor. She reached up to the shelf, almost bringing the books and magazines down as she searched for what she was looking for – the key her mum hid up there.

Slowly she went downstairs to the front door and took a deep breath. She loved adventures, especially ones her mum and dad didn't have to know about.

Star slowly unlocked the door and faced a red-faced Teddy Davies.

'So what do you say, Star?'

Star looked up into Teddy's face; shielding her eyes from the bright sunshine. 'I say it's our secret.'

'Star! Star! What the bleedin' hell do you think you're doing? What did I tell you? I'm going to skin you like a bleedin' cat in China.' It was Claudia.

Star watched, her heart sinking as Claudia stomped up the street, rolling up her sleeves as if she was about to start a fight. 'Get inside now!'

'Sorry it was my fault.' Teddy spoke as Claudia poked him in his chest. 'And who the hell are you? You can't just turn up here. It ain't that sort of place and if I ever see you talking to her again, I'll flatten you. Count your luckies I'm not doing it now.'

'I only…'

'What? Only wanted to talk to some kid? You flippin' perv. Get out of here before I call the coppers on you and that's saying some.'

Teddy narrowed his eyes, hating this loud fat

woman in front of him. 'I *am* the police.'

Claudia's demeanour slipped slightly, though she still held firm. 'What? I'm supposed to be impressed? Jog on. I don't care if you're the friggin' fire brigade or the ambulance service for that matter, mate, you've no right entering into conversation with her.' Claudia swivelled round to glower at Star. 'And you miss, have no bleedin' right to open the door.'

Before Claudia could say another word, Teddy butted in. 'Well, that's my point. She didn't open the door. When I walked past, the door was ajar. You left it open. You should be more careful. I used to be a neighbourhood police officer and I know how carelessness like this can lead to all sorts of crimes.'

Claudia looked at Star, who put her head down. She then looked at Teddy and bristled. Her coldness was still present in her voice as she said, 'Thanks for the heads up. I appreciate it, mate.'

With that, Claudia pushed Star inside and quickly closed the door. She stared at Star, then smiled. 'When you speak to your mum on the phone tonight, I don't want you to mention this to her. It'll be our secret.'

Star hugged herself. She was collecting secrets like candy.

22

'I'm away, Alan. I don't want to be disturbed. And I certainly don't want to talk crap over the airways. Understand?' Del Williams clicked the phone off, using his thumb as hard as he could. That was the problem with mobiles. There was no slamming it down, unless of course you were willing to break the bloody thing, though the way he was feeling at the moment he would have broken it quite happily.

Alan was good at what he did, but in many other ways he was a muppet. What sort of guy talked about wanting to get someone weighed in on the phone – and a mobile one at that? Jesus, the man was a first-class looney tune to think that Del was going to indulge in *any* sort of conversation like the one Alan was trying to have with him. If the police had been listening in they would've been jerking themselves off to hear the convo.

'Everything okay?' Del turned and felt the soft touch of Bunny's hand on his arm. He smiled, trying to shake off the annoyance he felt.

'Just the usual shit. Nothing for you to worry about, doll. You look beautiful by the way.'

Bunny laughed warmly. 'Oh shut up. The bleedin' sun's hit your brain.'

Taking hold of Bunny, Del swept back her long blonde hair, away from her eyes. 'I know I don't say it a lot, but ... it's... I...'

Bunny could see Del was straining under the embarrassment of trying to put his feelings into words. She decided to come to his rescue and tapped his face gently. 'Have a day off, Del. I know how you feel about me and Star. You don't need to lay an egg saying it.'

Del burst into raucous laughter, showing the dimples in his cheeks. 'That's what I love about you, Bun. You let me be myself.' He winked at her and squeezed her bum at the same time.

'Well, what do you think?' Del wrapped his arms around Bunny's waist as he swivelled her round and stood behind her. He rested his chin on her shoulder, looking out to the sea from the whitewashed villa's large terrace, which was surrounded by landscaped gardens and tropical plants.

The panoramic view from Del's luxury hilltop villa was the most beautiful sight Bunny had ever seen. The only sadness was that Claudia and Star weren't there to share it with them. But there'd be another time, Bunny was sure of it. Next time Del offered to take her she wouldn't be so hesitant or afraid. For now though she was just going to enjoy and bathe in the beauty and seduction of it.

'It's exquisite, Del.'

'Now who's getting all soppy? It's not a bad view is it? I've never really taken much notice before, not when it was just me and Edith. She chewed me ear off so much about one thing or another it shit on anything nice. Turned it all into crap. But now I'm here with you, I can honestly say it's the dog's fucking bollocks.'

171

Bunny looked at Del, a mischievous twinkle in her eye.

'One thing though. The name of the villa. *Casa Williams*? Are you having a laugh?' Bunny raised her eyebrows and both she and Del giggled childishly.

'Bun?'

'Mmm?'

'Will you do something for me?'

Dreamily, Bunny answered, 'Yeah, of course.'

'Will you give it up?'

Lazily, Bunny turned her head to face Del. 'What you talking about?'

'I want you to give your work up, babes.'

Bunny's face dropped, and so did her hand from Del's. Disappointment and hurt showed in her face. 'Don't start this again. Why are you starting when we're having such a nice time?'

'It's because we *are* having such a nice time that I'm saying it. This is how it could be all the time, Bun.'

Bunny scanned Del's face, looking in his eyes for any hint of understanding. 'You don't get it. I can't give it up.'

'You can't or you won't, Bun? Two different things.'

'Isn't what we have enough?'

'I could say the same thing to you. This isn't just mine, it's yours as well. You and Star's. Anything I have, you have.'

Bunny shook her head, sadly. 'It's mine till you get bored of me. It's mine until you decide I'm not what you want.'

'That's never going to happen. I love you.'

'I learnt a long time ago that love should be enough, but it simply isn't.'

'I don't understand you Bunny.'

'Then stop trying to, babe.'

Del held onto Bunny's arms gently as he spoke. 'Do you trust me?'

She turned her head away. 'Don't ask me that.'

The hurt began to show in Del's eyes. 'Yes or no, Bun? It's a simple question. Do you trust me?'

'*Please.*'

The hurt turned into shock 'You don't, do you? Fuck me, you don't trust me.'

Tears filled Bunny's eyes. 'I told you, you just don't understand.'

'Do you know I'd give my life for you? I'd take a fucking bullet for you, Bun.'

'I know.'

'You can't know.' Del raised his voice for a moment and then saw the people he'd invited round for a few drinks looking over at him. Lowering his voice, he spoke again. 'You can't know, otherwise you would trust me.'

'Look, it's not you...'

Del broke into scornful laughter. 'Don't, Bunny. Don't fucking insult me by finishing that clichéd sentence.'

'Okay, no clichés, doll. But you haven't had my life. You haven't been where I've been.'

'Then tell me. Maybe then I'd understand.'

Bunny's eyes stared at Del. 'Just know I'm doing all I can to give Star everything I didn't have as a child.'

'You know I'll buy her anything she wants.'

'That's not what I mean.'

'Then what? *Tell* me.'

Bunny stroked Del's face. 'No. Let's just leave the past in the past where it belongs. Let's not disturb it.' Changing pace, Bunny tried to sound more upbeat. 'I'm here with you now. I love you, Mr Williams, and I love our daughter more than words can say. That's the only thing that matters.'

She looked behind her, seeing the group of people milling round the bespoke swimming pool; eating canapés, snorting lines of cocaine, drinking Cristal champagne and enjoying each other's company.

Seeing that he wasn't going to get any further with Bunny, Del took a deep breath to calm himself down. He didn't want the time with her to be ruined. He'd let it go for now but he'd try again.

Smiling, he chatted casually to Bunny as if the conversation they'd just had hadn't happened. 'You didn't mind me inviting some people? I thought then I could mix business and pleasure. I could do what I need to do, rabbit with who I need to, but still keep my eye on you.'

Bunny dug Del in his stomach gently. He proceeded to make a big show of it; bending over double as if she'd hit him hard and Bunny laughed, appreciating what he was doing. She knew he'd been hurt by what she'd said. And it'd hurt her seeing the look in his eyes. If only he'd learn to leave it and then everything would be fine, or as fine as it'd ever be.

Picking up his glass of champagne from the marble-clad stone wall, Del looked at Bunny laughing. He loved it when she laughed, though he could see she was tired. Maybe, as Claudia had said, she just needed to relax and get away from it all. But he wasn't so sure, and he knew the time he spent thinking about Bunny was distracting him in his work and making him sloppy.

He'd been worried about her in London. Worried she was getting tired of being with him. Perhaps that's why she was so adamant she wouldn't give up the game. He cringed when the word came into his head. He tried not to say it how it was, but amongst the beauty of the Spanish coastline hills, the word seemed uglier than ever.

'Are you okay?' Bunny's voice interrupted his thoughts and he realised he had crushed the glass of champagne he'd been holding in his hand. Not wanting to tell Bunny what he'd been thinking, Del shook himself, put the glass on the wall and smiled.

'Come on, let's stop the heavy. I want to introduce you to a couple of people.'

Taking Bunny by the hand, Del walked her over to a tall rotund man dressed in a garish Hawaiian shirt, standing over near the fairy-lit palm trees. As they approached the man, Del whispered. 'He's known as Fat Man Burke but no one calls him that to his face. Everyone just calls him Burkey.'

Bunny squeezed Del's hand, smiling warmly. She'd heard of Fat Man Burke. Everyone had – and not just people in the criminal underworld. She'd seen him in the papers many a time and she knew for a fact he was wanted by Interpol and the police for his involvement in a multiple shooting last year, as well as drug trafficking and money laundering.

'Burkey, can I introduce you to me…'

'Oh this is bleedin' nice, ain't it? Kick me out of me own home only so you can wine and dine a bunch of East End muppets.'

It was Edith. Loud, brash and very angry. Del stared at her, taking in her bruised swollen face. Curiosity made him want to ask her what had happened, but, first off, he didn't *really* care. Secondly, she was embarrassing him in front of his friends and business acquaintances and then lastly – and most importantly – she hadn't done what he'd told her to do. Which was, *stay the fuck away*.

'Edith. What are you doing here? Didn't we already discuss this? Didn't I tell yer what you were supposed to do?'

'What am I doing here? What am I frigging doing here? What do you bleedin' think I'm doing here darlin'? Shitting in the pool? No. I live here, don't I? So I've got just as much right as you to be here. More so than your bunch of frigging cronies.'

Del grabbed hold of Edith's arm tightly, his face flushed with fury. 'Don't make a fool of yourself, Edith.'

'You mean don't make a fool out of *you*. Well you're doing a good enough job yourself.'

Ignoring Edith, Del continued to drag her, pulling her hard by her arm along the palm tree-lined terrace. Edith opened her mouth as wide as she could and began to shriek like a banshee.

'You get your fucking hands off me, you bleeding gorilla. Get the fuck off me, you cunt.'

'I see your mouth is still as coarse as it ever was.'

'Fuck you,' Edith shrieked in Del's face as she trod her heels into the ground, trying to stop herself being dragged along.

'Leave her, Del,' Bunny's voice was soft.

Del turned to look at Bunny. Sensing Del was distracted, Edith took her cue and wriggled her way out of the grip. Free now to stand with her hands on her hip, Edith fixed Bunny with a steely gaze.

'Who the fuck is this?' Edith looked towards Del. 'Oh don't tell me, it's your cheap little whore. Jessica fucking rabbit.'

'My name's Bunny, actually.'

Edith roared with nasty laughter. 'What sort of fucked-up name is that? Turn it in, you sound like a poor man's porn star. Listen lady. I want you to get the fuck out of my house.'

'It's my house,' Del shouted angrily, not caring that everyone was watching.

'When it comes to your whores, it's my house.' Edith turned to Del, her eyes flickering with anger. 'I want her out. Get your whore out of here.'

'I say who comes or goes, not you. So it's you who's getting out. *Now!*' Del turned to all his visitors. 'I want all you lot out too. Out! Now!'

None of Del's visitors put up a fuss. They nodded to him in an understanding and sympathetic manner as they placed down their glasses and plates of food. At one time or another they'd all had their missus squeezing their balls and steaming off at whoever they were shafting. And as they watched Del, his face turning different shades of red, they were all grateful the scenario playing out in front of them was happening to someone else this time.

Edith prodded Bunny hard in the chest. 'Let me tell you something, Bunnykins, you're ten a fucking penny. I could buy you tomorrow. So don't come here thinking you're special, darling. Remember you're nothing but a whore.'

Del caught hold of Edith's arm. He spoke through gritted teeth, a mist of rage coming over him. He couldn't remember the last time he'd felt this angry. 'Do not put your hands on her. If there's any whore round here it's you, Edith. You're nothing but a money-grabbing bitch. A fucking leech, sucking the life out of everything.'

'Del, *please*. Leave it. You can see she's upset. I'm sorry Edith. I know seeing me here must be hard for you, babe.'

'You fucking tramp. *Hard for me?* You come into my fucking house with your arms draped around *my* husband like you're a fucking coat, thinking your pussy's made of gold and your tits are made of sugar candy, and you have the bleedin' front to stand there and say *it's hard for me?* You want me to show you what's really hard? Here's hard.'

With a swipe of her right hand and using all her force, Edith brought up her fist, smashing it into Bunny's face. The blow knocked Bunny sidewards. She staggered, trying to hold onto Del who put his hand out to stop her falling. Just as she was reaching out to him, Edith, not having finished yet, took hold of Bunny's hair and grabbed it hard, pulling Bunny into her. As Edith continued to shriek, Bunny cried out with pain.

'How does it fucking feel now, Bunnykins? Hurts, does it?'

Del sprang into action, attempting to peel Edith's fingers from Bunny's hair. 'Get yer hands off her, Edith. You're making a massive mistake.'

Not put off, Edith continued to tear at Bunny's hair whilst screaming loudly. 'Oh is that the big-shot gangster talking? Well you can fuck off too.'

'I said get off her, Edith.'

'No!'

Seeing that Edith wasn't going to budge and Bunny was still in distress, Del braced himself, feeling he had no other choice. With a quick flick of his head, Del side nutted Edith, whose nose exploded with blood.

It had the desired effect. Edith dropped hold of Bunny's hair, but as she did so, she fell into both Del and Bunny, who in turn stumbled backwards. Their arms flayed frantically as they stepped into nothing but mid-air, all three of them splashing down into the warm waters of the pool.

Spattering up to the surface, with his mouth spitting out water, Del pulled Bunny up. 'Are you okay, babe? I'm so sorry. Babe, talk to me.'

Bunny pushed her soaking mop of blonde hair out of her face. 'I'm fine. Really.' With that, Bunny waded out of the pool, with all the major faces from both London and the Costa watching her as the pink jumpsuit she was wearing clung to the curves of her body.

Del turned to look at Edith, her nose trickling with blood. He hissed through his teeth as he spoke. 'I want you to pack your bags and get out.

Then I never want to see your miserable face again. If I do I won't be responsible for my actions. And don't think you'll ever get a penny out of me, Edith. You'll get fuck all from me.'

'I want what you owe me.'

'I don't owe *you* anything, darling, and while I'm at it, I want a divorce.'

'You'll never get a divorce from me unless I get what I want. Don't forget I know *everything* about you. You should remember that.'

Del walked up to Edith in the pool. He took hold of her chin firmly in one hand, then turned her face towards him and leaned in, his face just centimetres from hers. 'Don't, Edith. Don't take me fucking on. And never, never threaten me.'

'Then give me what's mine.'

Del let go of Edith's face. He stared at her for a moment. 'You'll have to kill me, Edith, before I give you anything.'

Edith glowered at Del, hostility and hatred in her eyes.

'Be careful what you wish for, Del. You never know, it might just happen.'

Watching the commotion from the darkness, Alfonso slunk back into his room. His brain began to race. Life, he thought, had a funny way of turning out.

'What the fuck was that all about? I thought I told you to play it cool with Del not put a firecracker on his bollocks.' Alfonso growled as he sat smoking a Camel Light back in the tiny hotel room on the harbour of Puerto Banús.

Edith pushed a Dorito into her mouth. 'How

could I play it cool when I have to deal with that cunt?'

Alfonso shouted, 'Because that's what I told you to do, you silly bitch. *I* give the orders now.'

Edith pointed her red manicured finger at Alfonso. '*That's* where you're wrong Alfonso – because everything's changed now. You heard him. He's not giving me fuck all, and he wouldn't give a shit on a cherry pie if I'd been humping the whole of the foreign fucking legion. So you telling me what to do was short-bleedin'-lived mate.'

Alfonso could feel the rage inside him. The bitch was right.

Springing up, he pushed her hard.

'You stupid fucking cow. If you hadn't opened that fat gob of yours I would've been quids in.'

Edith tumbled backwards, crashing down on the floor. Alfonso's eyes were flashing with fury and he screamed as he kicked her in her side, his sinewy body jumping up and down with the energy he was exerting. He dived on top of her, insane with anger.

'There's another way! There's another way!' Edith screamed. Taking hold of himself, Alfonso stopped. He was sweating and panting hard. He wiped his lips, feeling the saliva running out of the side of his mouth.

'Another way how?'

Edith panted for breath. 'I made him what he is today. He owes me. I want half of what he has, but he ain't going to give it me no matter what. Even if I talk, spill what I know, I still ain't going to get it. So I'm not going for half. I'm going for it all. You following me?'

181

Alfonso got off Edith. He thought he was, but he wanted her to say it, needing to hear exactly what her plans were.

Edith sat up, pushing her tongue out to soothe her cut lip. Her broken nose throbbing. 'You said it. You said it in the hotel room, Alfonso.'

'I dunno what you're talking about.'

'*A bullet in his head.* Okay, let's do it. I want to put that cunt Del in the ground.'

Edith was surprised to see the slight hesitation in Alfonso. 'I don't know. He ain't just the postman. Your husband isn't someone we can blow away just like that. He's got a lot of people around him.'

Edith looked at Alfonso scornfully. She hated weakness and that was what she was suddenly beginning to smell, almost as if it was oozing out of his pores. 'I thought you were in. Ain't that what you wanted?'

'What I wanted was to get my money.'

Edith raised an eyebrow.

'You mean *my* money, Alfonso.'

'I don't want to be having to look over me shoulder for the rest of me natural.'

Edith stood up and walked across to the bathroom.

'Listen. We do it this way or no way, but whether you're in or out, Alfonso, I'm getting what's owed – and I know just the person who'll help me.'

23

'Can you believe it? Can you believe that shit?' Del Williams paced up and down, stopping for a moment to snort a line of coke.

'Del, you need to calm down, honey. Getting worked up won't do you any favours.'

'Calm down? Calm down? How the fuck am I supposed to do that? You saw what I've got to put up with. If it ain't Edith doing my head in, it's you.'

'*What* did you say?'

'You've lost your hearing now have you? That would make sense, 'cos you never listen to anything I say.'

'What are you talking about?'

Del raised his voice between more lines of quiver. He knew he shouldn't be getting arsey with Bunny, but what with being up all night thinking about his bloody wife and the charge of the coke running through his bloodstream he couldn't help himself, no matter how much he tried.

'I'm talking about you. You and your flipping pig-headedness. It does my fucking nut in, Bun. All your secrets.'

'Secrets?'

'Yeah, never wanting to tell me anything about what's going on in that bonce of yours. Always shutting me out. Well I'm sick of it and I'm not having it, you hear me?'

Bunny got up and walked to the balcony, looking out at the magnificent view across the dazzling Mediterranean Sea. She didn't like to argue with Del. They got on so well most of the time, arguing was rare. Though when they did fight, they had an established pattern – Del would blow off steam, stomping and crashing about and she would just listen, knowing eventually he'd calm down. But as she listened to him now, still hurt from what had happened the night before, he began to irritate her. '*My* pig-headedness? You want to look in the bloody mirror, Del. Maybe you might see some home truths staring back at you.'

'The only home truth around here is the fact you don't do as you're told.'

Bunny threw her head back and laughed. It pissed him off no end, not just because he hated how the argument was going but also, Bunny looked stunning, dressed casually in a plain t-shirt and cut-off shorts without a scrap of make-up on. Whether it was the effects of the quiver or not he was beginning to get a hard-on, which made everything even more frustrating.

'"Do as I'm told"? What am I Del, a child?'

'You might as well be; you act like one.'

Bunny's blue eyes opened wide. '*I* do?'

'Yes, you fucking do, darlin' The only reason you won't give up your work is because I've asked you. You like seeing me get pissed off over it.'

'Oh drop me out, Del.'

'No, 'cos I know what you're doing. You've been rumbled, doll. Ain't it every woman's goal

184

to make their man jealous? Ain't it?' Del paused dramatically, then opened his arms wide as he continued to rant. 'Well, babe. Well done, 'cos you've achieved your goal. I'm jealous. Fucking riddled with it. So now you know you can stop the spoilt little girl act and *give up yer fucking job!'*

Del shouted the last part then stared at Bunny, knowing that what he was saying sounded ridiculous, but as he heard his own irritation grow, so did his anger. He leaned in towards her.

'Now the truth's out. You can drop it, Bun. Give it up, 'cos I ain't standing for it no more. I ain't standing for me missus getting shagged day after day by someone other than me.'

As he spoke, images of Bunny with other men flashed into Del's mind. He turned away from her and smashed his hand into the wall.

The pain shot through him. 'See! See what you're doing to me, Bun. Is this what you want? I don't think you'll be happy until I clump some punter and end up killing them, will you? That's it, ain't it? I get locked up, then you're free to do what you like. Fuck as many men as you want.'

It was Bunny's turn to shout. 'Stop it, Del! Stop it! We're both tired. Let's stop.'

'Why should I stop it, 'cos I'm on a roll now, baby? Oh there's no stopping me, just like when I ask you to stop anything, you won't. But now all of a sudden you want *me* to stop. Well no can do, babe.'

Bunny put her head down, tears brimming in her eyes. 'You don't get it. You'll never get it. It's not about *you*, I keep telling you that. There's nothing wrong with you or us. It's *me* Del, *me*. So leave it.'

'Oh you'd like that. For me to leave it and turn a blind eye. Well sorry, doll. It stops right now.'

'Aren't you forgetting about how I met you?'

Del laughed ruefully, hating himself as he spoke. 'How could I forget? It's almost like you're proud of what you are.'

'I am who I am.'

'How frigging noble of you, Bun. Is that what you'll be saying to Star? *I am who I am?* You seem that comfortable with it I'm surprised you haven't thought about pimping her out yet, but I guess it's only a matter of time before you try.'

Bunny's blood ran cold. She gripped onto the side of the white drinks cabinet and spoke through clenched teeth. 'Don't you dare. Don't you *ever* say that to me again or I swear to God, Del, it'll be the last time you ever see me.'

'Too close to the bone, doll? Did I rumble you? Put paid to those long-term plans of yours? Were you hoping to have a mother-daughter thing going on to attract the punters?'

The sting in Del's cheek from Bunny's slap lasted long after the argument had finished, but as Del stood looking at Bunny's tears, watching her throw her clothes into her bag and collect up her purse and passport, he was driven on not by the physical pain but the emotional one.

'Goodbye Del.' Bunny opened the bedroom door and walked out without glancing back.

Del rushed to call her back, wanting to hold her in his arms, wanting to tell her he loved her and that he was sorry, but his anger and hurt made him call out words he knew he was going to regret for the rest of his life. 'That's it. Go! Go on Bunny. Go back to London. Fuck off back to where you came from. What do they say? You can take the whore out of the gutter but you can't take the whore out of the girl.'

It was definitely her. The whore. The bunny rabbit. Edith scowled as she looked across at Bunny as they sat in the first-class section of the plane. She'd thought it was her at the check-in at Marbella airport, with her long blonde hair, showing off her body as if it was a display cabinet. The last thing she wanted was to sit within smelling distance of Del's bit on the side, but she hadn't had much choice. The next flight wasn't leaving till tomorrow *and* they'd informed her there wasn't even a first-class section on that flight, which had made up Edith's mind.

Finishing off her neat gin and deciding she needed another, Edith took a sneaky peek at Bunny. She sniffed haughtily as she inspected her. She could imagine a lot of people would try to tell her Bunny was beautiful with her soft features, big blue eyes and pouting lips. Well that was them. Edith wouldn't. She looked cheap. Obvious. Who wanted a toned size ten body any-way? Men liked to grab hold of something. They liked a little bit of sirloin on their women. Like the kind of body she had. *She'd* never had any complaints. Oh yes, Edith could give the likes of Bugs Bunny a run for her money any day.

Laying back and stuffing a large handful of salted peanuts into her mouth, Edith smiled, imagining what Del would say if he knew she was about to go and plan his ultimate demise with an old acquaintance and lover of hers. Detective Teddy Davies.

24

He was lagging. Slaughtered. Pissed. And it didn't take the empty bottle of Hennessy by the side of the sun lounger to tell him that. His head swam, his vision was blurred and he didn't know what the fuck time it was. Furthermore, he didn't give a fuck either.

Del rolled onto his side and snorted some cocaine off a tiny marble table beside him. The quiver hit a home run but it wasn't enough for him to forget. He needed to get Bunny's face out of his mind – but more than anything else, he needed to get the last words he'd said to her out of his mind.

'Boss. Boss?'

Del paused. He could hear someone talking but he couldn't quite work out where the voice was coming from. Fuck it. He took another line, clenching his teeth as the coke exploded into his bloodstream. He could feel his heart working overtime but he could also hear the voice again.

'Boss?'

Shit. The voice was coming from above him. Del turned his body round. His head swayed from side to side and no matter how hard he tried he couldn't manage to keep it still. It was almost as if the damn thing had been loosened from his neck and any moment now it was going to roll straight off his body.

Giving up on trying to stop his head from moving, Del attempted to prevent his eyes darting around.

'Boss?'

Christ. There it was again. Focus. He had to try to focus. There. Right in front of him. There was someone standing there. Del opened his eyes wider, but it only resulted in him raising his eyebrows.

'Boss?' Alfonso Garcia stared at Del lying on the sun lounger. He curled his lip. The great Del Williams, the man most men feared, lying incoherent, sprawled out in the midday sun. He was a joke.

A thought passed through Alfonso's mind. How easy it would be to take Del out here and now. The man was in no fit state to defend himself. He was an utter mess. But to do anything to him would be like signing his own death warrant. Del's men were crawling all over the place, so for now all he could do was wait for Edith to be in touch.

'Yeah? What do you want? Is Bunny back?'

Del slurred his words to nobody in particular as he picked up and looked at the empty bottle of cognac.

'Pardon, Boss?' Alfonso couldn't make out what Del was trying to say.

'What?'

'I said pardon, Boss.'

'Why?'

'Sorry Boss.' Alfonso hadn't a clue what Del

had just said.

'Why are you sorry? I should be the one who's sorry. She'll never forgive me.'

'I can't understand. I'm sorry... I...'

Del roared loudly. 'I told you, I'm the one who's supposed to be sorry, not you pal. So don't you dare say sorry. It ain't got nothing to do with you, unless you've been fucking her too.'

Alfonso scratched his head. He was always lumbered with the shitty jobs – and having to deal with an inebriated Del Williams was almost as bad as it got.

After a moment of trying to think of what was best, Alfonso decided just to say what he was supposed to, hoping it might get through.

'Boss, I'm here to tell you we've got to go and meet the consignment. We've just had a call from the boat; it'll be in the bay in under an hour, so if you want to meet them at the warehouse then we'll have to set off now.'

'Well, why didn't you just fucking say that in the first place?'

Alfonso shook his head as he listened, still not understanding what Del was trying to say. The other thing he didn't know was if Del had understood *him*. If he hadn't, Alfonso certainly didn't fancy getting blamed for Del falling back to sleep and missing meeting the drugs drop.

With a sigh of resignation, Alfonso bent down and wrapped Del's arms round his neck, pulling him up from the sun lounger. As he walked from the pool area into the villa with the weight of Del leaning on him, Alfonso decided that between both Edith and Del he would've earned every single penny that was coming to him.

Two hours later, Del stood swaying on the sun-baked hilltops of Marbella, another bottle of cognac in hand and a large unlit cigar in his mouth. His men looked at him with concern on their faces. They'd never seen him like this before. He was a man who usually liked to be in control.

They nodded sympathetically when they caught his eye, knowing exactly what had happened with Bunny and Edith. They liked him. Respected him. Del was a good boss, a good man and he treated them fairly.

Eventually it was Fat Man Burke who walked up to Del. Seeing Del in such a state, he sighed, grateful his own missus was in the ground. Women were too much gut ache. They could bring down the hardest of men; hell, they could bring down a fucking nation. He didn't know why Del didn't just do what he did – fuck them and keep them at arm's length. And the moment you started to feel something for them, that was the moment you had to jog them on. Though in fairness to Del he'd seen Bunny and he could understand why he'd want to keep that bit of pussy all to himself. But to flick other women off? And put all his bollocks in one basket and get his heart involved? That was Del's mistake.

Fat Man Burke stood next to Del. He opened his mouth to say something to Del, but instantaneously started coughing and spluttering as a midge flew into his mouth. 'Fucking hell. What sort of a frigging hell hole is this? What I wouldn't give to go back to England.'

Del was still swaying. He turned to face Fat Man, almost losing his balance. 'Even your freedom, Burkey?'

'What?' Fat Man frowned. He couldn't understand a word Del had just said. He was more mangled up than he thought. Shit. They were about to do business with the Russians and there was Del out of his fucking tree.

'Fuck's sake, Del. You need to get a grip mate. They'll be here soon and how the hell are you going to deal with them?'

Del scowled. Or he thought he did. He couldn't quite tell what his face was doing. It seemed he had no control over his movements. Plus it wasn't helping that he wanted to take a piss.

'Listen, Burkey. One thing you ain't telling me is how to run my business. I run it. Not you. I was the one who set up the deal with Milo, so leave me to finish it.'

'Christ, Del. If I can't understand what you're saying, no Russian monkey will.' Fat Man glared at Del, then snatched the bottle of cognac out of his hands. 'I'll take that. Go and lie down in one of the cars. Get some sleep.'

'Fine, Burkey, but make sure you wake me up when they come.'

Fat Man Burke watched Del staggering over to one of the bullet-proof Range Rovers, not having understood a word he'd just said.

The dust clouds on the horizon told Fat Man Burke that the Russians were coming. Through his Leica Duovid binoculars he watched the large convoy of Cadillac Escalades making their way up the twisting off-road tracks. If they wanted to be discreet, they were going about it the wrong way. The clouds of Spanish dust billowed high into the blue skies, visible for miles around.

'The reds are coming!' Fat man shouted at Del's men, preparing them for the Russian arrival.

'What about the boss?'

'What about him?'

'Should I wake him?'

Fat Man looked across at the Range Rovers parked by the side of the derelict whitewashed outbuildings. He could see Del's feet sticking out from the driver's side as he lay sprawled deep in sleep across the two front seats. He wasn't sure what he should do. If he woke Del, he'd probably be in no fit state to deal with anyone, but if he didn't, he'd miss the handover. Still, it was only a hand-over. And surely he would've said if he'd wanted to be woken up? What harm was there to leave him to sleep? All the negotiations had already been done. It was only a question of exchanging money for drugs now. Turning back to Del's henchmen, Fat Man belched then answered confidently, 'No. Leave him. It'll do him good to sleep it off.'

Fifteen minutes later, the convoy of Cadillacs carrying the Russians – along with the kilos of uncut cocaine – arrived at the top of the hill, to be greeted by a wall of Del's men, with Fat Man at the front.

Fat Man rubbed the front of his teeth with his tongue. He had no idea why Del had wanted to deal with the Russians. Okay, they were slightly cheaper and the supply chain of cocaine was reliable, but when it boiled down to it they were foreigners. *Stick to your own* was his philosophy.

The one guy Fat Man had a problem with in particular was the main face. Milo Burkov. He'd only met him twice when he'd come over to Marbella to have meetings about a consignment of heroin they were pulling out of Morocco, but both times he'd detested him.

Milo had a fondness for speaking in Russian to his men, which pissed Burkey off no end. They all knew how to speak English perfectly well and each time it happened it'd made him feel uncomfortable, as if he they were mugging him off. Ripping the piss out of them whilst they sat there like a bunch of muppets, not knowing what was going on. Nope, he didn't like that at all, and it only added to Fat Man's distrust of all things that weren't draped in a St George's cross.

Trouble was, he was only putting in ten per cent of the money – which ultimately meant he had no say in who they dealt with.

Watching the Russians step out of their cars, dressed identically in dark t-shirts and dark trousers along with the obligatory Ray-Bans, Fat Man blew out his cheeks in frustration before muttering, '*twats*' under his breath, making himself feel slightly better.

'Burkey my friend, it's good to see you again.'

Fat Man Burke stared at the Russian. As far as he was aware he'd never seen this bloke before, but then to him all foreigners looked the same.

'No Milo?'

'No. Milo's otherwise engaged. No Del?'

194

'No. Del's otherwise engaged.' Fat Man held his smile for a moment before deciding *fuck it* and scowling instead at the tall well-built Russian. 'Right then, let's get on with it. Are we going to do this thing or not?'

The Russian turned to his men. He shouted, waving his hand. 'Ну, давайте это отсортированы. Спешите и получить вещи из машины.'

There it was again. That fucking foreign shit. Well, he wasn't going to stand for it. 'Oi mate, keep that bollocks to yourself. What the hell did you say to him? Come on, I want to know what you said about me.'

The Russian looked at Fat Man in surprise as his men walked past carrying crate-loads of individually wrapped kilos of cocaine.

'Fat Man Burke. I can call you that can't I?'

The snarl from Burke said everything. He ran at the Russian, stopping short of putting his clenched fist in his face. He held it millimetres from the man's cheek 'Who the fuck do you think you're talking to?'

The Russian, six inches taller and several inches wider, casually moved the fist away, closing his own round Fat Man's.

'My friend, I would be careful whose face you waved that fist into.'

Burkey was shaking with anger. He spat his words. 'I want to know what you said about me.'

The Russian put his arm round Burkey. Slightly too tightly for comfort. 'Paranoia is a terrible thing. Let me put that English brain of yours at rest. *Ну, давайте это отсортированы. Спешите и получить вещи из машины.* It means, *let's*

get this sorted. Hurry and get the stuff out of the car...
So you see Burkey, there is nothing to feel ill at
ease about.'

He laughed loudly, which annoyed Fat Man
even more and he threw the Russian's arm off his
shoulders, stalking off towards the outbuildings.

Inside the outbuildings was an escape from the
baking heat. Fat Man watched Del's men counting the kilos of cocaine. Eight hundred kilos, all
present and correct. He supposed it was something.

'Well?' The Russian who Fat Man had been talking to came up behind him. He didn't know his
name and he had no wish or intention of finding it
out. No doubt it was some unpronounceable shit
that would tie up his fucking tongue.

'Well what, mate?'

'Well, you've counted the coke and now we
count the money.'

'I want it loaded into my cars first. Then you
can have the dough.'

The Russian narrowed his eyes. A dark seething
anger displayed in them, but he answered cor-
dially, nodding his head.

'So be it. I shall tell my men to load it up.'

'No need. I'll tell my men to.'

'Your men? I thought they were Del's.'

Without a word and for the second time that
day, Fat Man Burke stalked off.

Watching the last of the cocaine being loaded
into the secret panelling under the Range Rovers,
Fat Man Burke couldn't shake off the feeling he
was being made a mug of by the Russian. He

196

took a sly glance across to where he was standing and immediately got a cheery wave in return. Fat Man turned away quickly, glowering. The man was a fucking wind-up. He'd be pleased when he could get back to his villa, shoot a bit of pool and get the housekeeper to make him some egg and chips.

A few minutes later, with the tension still sitting on his shoulders, Fat Man Burke nodded to Del's men to bring the black binbags full of money into the outbuildings.

'It's all there, but it's best if you count it mate. I don't want you and Milo to come back saying it was under the radar.'

The Russian flung his arms wide open dramatically.

'Burkey, you insult me. Surely we're amongst friends here.'

Fat Man raised his eyes to the ceiling. 'Just count it mate, and then we can all go home.'

There was a smash on the wooden door, startling all those present. It flung open.

'What the fuck is going on here?'

Both the Russians and Fat Man Burke, along with the other men, turned to the open doorway. It was Del. Del with a gun.

'I said what the fuck is going on here?'

No one moved as they stared at Del standing in the doorway, muttering to himself. In that moment Fat Man Burke finally found a common ground with the Russians. Neither one of them could understand a word Del was saying. What they did understand was the loaded gun waving in his right hand.

'Burkey? Where are you? I told you to fucking wake me up.' Del staggered into the cobweb-strewn outhouse. Everybody stayed frozen.

The Russian spoke slowly. 'There's no need for this, Del. Everything you want is here. Burkey's counted it. Milo made sure the deal was going to run smoothly.'

Del spun round, almost knocking into Fat Man. He could've sworn he heard a voice. He shrugged, then swivelled back round to face the Russian ensemble, his arms flaying like a conductor, the forgotten Colt 1911 bucking dangerously in his hand. Fear washed over the Russian's face. He held his arms up in the air.

Looking down at the floor, Del tried to remember where he was. Fuck knows. Where was Burkey? Where was anyone?

'Burkey? Where are you for fuck's sake?'

In his drunken state Del stumbled forward, pointing the gun towards the other Russians who in turn ducked then slowly raised their hands too. Thinking it was their cue, Del's men pulled out their guns; the metallic flutter of a dozen simultaneously drawn weapons echoed round the room.

Shit. He couldn't see what he was doing. Everything was a fucking blur again and God only knew where Burkey had gone. He needed to sit down. Maybe he shouldn't have drunk so much.

Del was sweating. A bead of perspiration ran slowly into his right ear. Hazily he rubbed it away. A second later his ear began to ring. Funny; he was sure he heard a scream. Christ. He needed to go and sleep again. Staggering out of the door, Del

Williams left Milo's lieutenant crying in agony with a bullet in his leg, unaware he'd inadvertently pulled the trigger.

Electric excitement bolted through Fat Man Burke. Del wasn't planning to do a deal with the Russians at all; he was planning to rip the fuckers off. The respect and pride Fat Man felt in that moment for Del pushed out his chest, jumping him into action.

'Okay guys, tie the buggers up.'

As Fat Man Burke stood by the Cadillac Escalades watching Del's men pile in and tie up the Russians in their own cars, he couldn't have been happier. He should never have doubted Del. He should've known he would've had a plan. A plan that showed the faces of the Costa not to mess with them. Fat Man slowly walked over to the cars and smiled at the remonstrating Russians. He slammed the door shut and winked at his own reflection.

25

One thousand and sixty miles away, Edith stood outside the John Snow pub on the corner of Lexington Street. Although the sun dazzled in the cloudless sky and the tourists and locals of Soho cheerily walked by dressed in pastels and bright colours, Edith Williams thanked her luckies that she no longer lived here.

It wasn't because she didn't like London any-more. She loved the place no less than when she'd left it all those years ago, but it was simply that she loved Marbella more. Marbella *was* her. The glamour. The luxury. The wealth Those things were in her blood; she was born to live there – though being *born to live there* was helped in part that Edith Williams conveniently liked to forget where she came from Her humble beginnings started not in a mansion, nor a stately home, but in a run-down council flat in the poorest part of the East End.

She looked down at her Hublot diamond watch. It was almost time.

Having ordered a double gin, Edith sat in the corner of the Soho pub and waited. Usually, waiting for people was one of her bugbears and something she never did. But then there was always the exception to the rules. And this time was certainly the exception.

'Double whisky, straight, no ice – and make sure you don't frig me off with the measures.'

'I'll get that. It's the least I can do for an old lover of mine, ain't it, babe?'

Teddy Davies span round and came face to face with Edith Williams. He hadn't expected, nor wanted, to see her. He blinked several times, not bothering to hide his puzzlement or shock.

'Well ain't you going to give me a hug, Edward, or are you just going to stand there like a fucking wilting plant on a ledge?'

Teddy bristled as Edith stood with her arms wide open. He glanced around the pub, catch-ing the eyes of the regular punters who seemed fascinated with this loud-mouthed, red-faced creature. Not liking to be the centre of attention unless he chose to be, Teddy grabbed hold of Edith's arm, pulling her forcefully out of the pub.

Edith chuckled, knowing exactly how to wind Teddy up. 'I see you still like it rough, Edward.'

'What the fuck are you doing here?'

Edith blew Teddy a kiss. 'Eddie...'

'Shut the flick up and tell me what you're doing here. And how did you know I'd be here?'

'Ed, is that any way to talk to a lady?'

'I said, how did you know I'd be here?'

Edith looked contemptuously at Teddy. 'I have my sources, just like you have yours, Ed.'

Teddy ground on his teeth. How the hell he'd ever put his dick in her he didn't know. Well he *did*, but knowing why and knowing he'd been sober at the time only made it worse.

'You know it's not Edward. It's *Teddy*. Not Eddie, not Ed, just plain Teddy.'

'Plain. Maybe,' Edith looked Teddy up and down. The sneer was apparent on her face as she stared at his brown suede loafers. It continued as her eyes worked their way up his body, scrutinising his appearance until she finally met his gaze.

'It's a shame when people let themselves go don't you think, babe? Let me give you a tip, darling, stick to Edward. Teddy makes you sound like a cunt. No grown man should have to be named after a stuffed toy, darlin'.' Edith raised one eyebrow then tapped Teddy on his chest before turning to cross Lexington Street. She called behind her.

201

'You and me have a lot of catching up to do, Edward. I'm booked in at The Dorchester. I'm in the penthouse. I'll be expecting you.'

Teddy Davies leant over the chrome and gold embossed toilet cistern, snorting up the last of the quiver he'd found at the back of his glove compartment. Between being on duty and having to deal with the problems of some of the Toms in Soho he hadn't had the chance to meet up with his dealer.

The lines he'd just taken were thinner than Victoria Beckham, which meant the buzz would only last for fifteen minutes, tops. He was tempted to go and pick some up from the estate on Camden Road, but curiosity mixed with slight anxiety as to why Edith Williams had reappeared had prompted him to walk into the Dorchester ten minutes ago, and he'd been in their toilets ever since. Combing his hair back and checking his nostrils for any tell-tale signs of cocaine, Teddy took a deep breath. He was ready to see what Edith wanted.

The penthouse. Teddy Davies took a deep breath, his hand hovering in mid-air. Just as he decided to knock, the hotel door swung open and Edith stood with an expectant look on her face, dressed in an almost see-through black negligee. Teddy gulped.

'All right, Edward. It's good to see you.' Edith winked, looking at Teddy like a hungry wolf. Teddy stared at Edith. He'd forgotten about her voracious sexual appetite and he certainly didn't want to be reminded of it.

He'd been thrown by seeing her earlier, but he wasn't going to be now. Del was a bigger clown than he thought, to send his wife. It was pathetic. Maybe Del saw it as a tactical move, but once Soho found out that the mighty face had sent Edith to talk to him, Del Williams would be a fucking laughing stock. Nevertheless, he was certainly interested to find out exactly what this was about.

'Edith, what can I say? This is unexpected – though I'm not sure yet if it'll be pleasurable or not.'

Edith licked her lips. 'Oh I'm sure it'll be pleasurable; wasn't it always?'

Before Teddy could answer, his mobile rang. He saw the caller ID. It was Milo. He needed to talk to him, but not now. He wanted to see what Edith had come for.

'I haven't come to play games, Edith. Tell me what Del has sent you to say then I can get the hell out of here. I must say, I'm disappointed that the big man has sent you.'

Without a word, Edith shunted Teddy inside her hotel room. It was enormous.

'Take a seat, darlin'.' Edith sat down at the table, pointing to the other dining-room chair. 'I didn't bother getting you a plate; I remember your tastes were more developed.'

Edith threw a small packet in front of Teddy. 'I thought you'd prefer that to a piece of cheese-cake, darlin'.'

Teddy looked down at the packet as Edith continued to speak. 'No tricks, doll. It's quality stuff.

It better be, otherwise my husband might have something to say about it.' Speaking as if Teddy needed clarification, Edith added, 'It's from one of his suppliers.'

Hungrily, Teddy opened the packet. He was an expert at seeing a weight of powder and knowing what it was. Four grams, give or take. He glanced up for a second, contemplating telling Edith to stuff her quiver; that he wasn't here for that. But how foolish would that be? And no one could tell him Teddy Davies was foolish.

Edith sat and watched Teddy as he began to snort lines of quiver. He hadn't changed. He was still a cokehead. Still a little man thinking he was a giant. But he was still someone she needed. She leaned across the table, her large breasts pushing the plate slightly, and grabbed Teddy's wrist, disturbing him from taking the next line.

'No one sends me to tell anyone anything, babe. You should know that, Edward. I do what I want and no one, especially me husband, tells me what to do. You following me, doll?'

'What's this about, Edith? I'm a busy man.'

'Oh I can see that, Eddie. I'm not here because Del sent me, though I am here because of him. I want your help, Teddy, and from what I hear you're just the man I need.'

Now this was beginning to get interesting. Not what he'd been expecting.

'It's been a while, but my feelings haven't changed when it comes to my husband. What *has* changed is that I ain't putting up with it no more. There's one thing him shagging whores both behind me back and in front of me, but it's another thing him not giving me what's mine. And I want it. But not only that; I want all of it.'

'What are you saying to me, Edith?'

'I'm saying I want Del dead. And I want *you* to pull the trigger.' Edith picked up her Chloé bag and emptied the contents on the table. Packets of fifty-pound notes tumbled out. 'I pawned me diamonds. I think that might be an incentive enough for you. It'll also help you pay for anyone else you need to help. So what do you say, Edward?'

Teddy rolled his head back and roared with delighted laughter. He didn't need an incentive and he didn't need to answer Edith. Quite literally, it was the best news he'd ever heard.

Milo Burkov threw his phone against the wall. Where the fuck was Teddy? He'd been calling him for the past few hours and the man had decided to do a disappearing act – today, of all days.

Picking up his espresso from the table, Milo walked over to the window. He could hardly believe what he'd heard; so much so that he'd had to ask his associate on the other end of the line to repeat what he'd said.

Del Williams had double-crossed him. He had not only ripped him off, but the prick had also shot one of his best men. Milo couldn't work out how the fuck it had all gone so wrong. Del must've got word that he and Teddy had been planning a move on him. Because what other reason was there for Del to react in the way he had done? The man had trusted him, then, from what seemed like nowhere, this had happened.

Until this had happened, even though Teddy had wanted it, putting Del in the ground hadn't been in his game plan. After this deal had gone through, Milo had been planning to run him out, to sink his business into the floor, but now the stakes had become higher.

Using his other phone, Milo dialled Teddy. He needed to speak to him. It rang, then went straight to voicemail. The man was a coked-up, small-time, big-thinking arsehole. What was the point in having him on his team when he never answered?

Shaking his head, Milo could almost hear the rings of laughter making their way across from the Costa del Sol. And as he stood looking out over Wardour Street it wasn't a question of *almost* picturing Del, he *could* picture him; raising his glass, toasting his success surrounded by the cocaine *and* the money. His money.

No one, but no one, betrayed him. The phone call from Marbella telling him what had happened had signed Del's death warrant. Now all he needed to do was get to him.

Teddy Davies bounded out of the Dorchester, partly from the quality quiver, but mainly from the conversation he'd just had with Edith.

He looked at his phone and saw twelve missed calls from Milo. He'd have to wait.

If somebody had told him this morning he would've been sitting down with Edith discussing her husband's hit, he would've thought they'd been tripping. Teddy Davies started to sing. He felt good and he was soon going to feel even better. Oh yes, Del Williams was going to be in for a treat.

26

Half a mile away, Bunny Barker was curled up on her bed, crying. Her favourite blanket covered her and Claudia sat by her side, concern etched onto her face.

'I want to string the bastard up. I've tried calling him, Bun, and he ain't answering. Probably too afraid to pick up the phone to me. He knows what a bleedin' earful he'll get. I'm blowing, Bun. Who does the man think he is, hey?'

Bunny tried to smile at Claudia but couldn't manage it.

'Leave it, Claud. It's okay. It was going to happen sooner or later. People let you down. I should know that. Don't know why it came as such a surprise.'

Claudia shook her head. She'd thought Del was different. She'd always given him a hard time, not because she'd thought he was like all the other blokes, but because he *was* different. Better than the rest. Solid. Well she'd fucking show him solid.

'What I don't understand, Bun, is why *now?* Why have the hump about what you do now?'

'It ain't just now though is it? He's always been on about it. He's never liked it, you know that.'

'Yeah but he's never been cruel with it.'

Bunny shrugged her shoulders. 'I guess he's under pressure. It's hard for him.'

'Don't start to make excuses for him. Story of women's bleedin' lives, making excuses for their old man. And where does it get them? I'll tell you. Up friggin' nowhere street.'

'I'm not making excuses for him and what he said...'

'I know, sweetheart.'

Bunny smiled and touched Claudia's hand gently. 'There's something else as well.'

Claudia's eyes were wide with curiosity. 'What?'

Bunny, spoke in a whisper. 'I'm pregnant.'

'I don't like to leave you, Bun. Not like this.' Claudia folded her arms, protesting as she stood by the front door.

'I'm fine. Go on Claudia.'

'No, it's not right. I don't want to leave you, babe.'

Bunny smiled then bent down and leaned her head on Claudia's shoulders. She closed her eyes, feeling exhausted but also comforted by Claudia's love and care.

'I really just want to be on my own. I've got a lot of thinking to do.'

I tell you what, why don't I take Star out with me. It'll do her good to get out for a bit, babe. Then you can relax and take a nice bubble bath or something.'

'Would you mind? Maybe you could take her to the cinema, then perhaps you could go to China-town and get something to eat afterwards. Just have a good time. I don't want her or you moping around with me. One of us is bad enough.'

Claudia gently pushed Bunny away so she could look in her face. 'I'm here for you. You know that.'

Bunny smiled. A proper warm smile, which for a moment wiped the sadness away. 'I know, Claudia, and I'm grateful.'

'What about this little one?' Claudia placed her hand on Bunny's stomach.

'I dunno. I can't get me head round it at the moment.'

'I don't like to ask and it makes no difference to me, you know that, but…'

'Is the baby Del's? That's what you're asking, ain't it.'

'Yes, but I'm not judging. Christ…'

Bunny put her hand on Claudia's arm. 'It's fine. I don't mind you asking, but yes. Yes of course the baby's Dell's. You know I never bareback with any of me punters.'

Claudia's shoulders visibly dropped, her face looking relieved. 'Oh thank fuck. Oh thank God for that Bun. You don't know how good it is to hear that. It's one less thing to worry about. Bleedin' hell.'

Bunny looked at Claudia and burst out into laughter. 'Go on, get on with you.' She then turned to call her daughter.

'Star! Star! Come on darlin', Claudia's going to take you out.'

As Bunny and Claudia waited for Star to appear, Claudia spoke. 'Bun. You are going to tell him, ain't you? I know he's been a fucker but he deserves to know.'

The laughter disappeared from Bunny's eyes. 'I don't know Claudia. Like I say, I've got a lot to think about.'

'But...'

Bunny interrupted her. She spoke firmly. 'I know you mean well, Claudia, but don't get involved. This is *my* problem not yours. I don't want you saying a word. Do you promise me?'

'I...'

'*Promise* me Claudia.'

Claudia scanned Bunny's face. 'Okay babe. I promise you. He won't hear anything from me. I just worry about you. I don't like to think of you on your own.'

'But I ain't on me own, am I? I've got you.'

Tears came to Claudia's eyes and she smiled. 'You have babe, and you know I'll help with the baby.'

Bunny lowered her head. 'Oh don't, Claudia, you'll have me filling up and I think I've done enough crying, don't you?'

Claudia gently put her fingers under Bunny's chin, lifting her head back up. 'Just tell me you'll be all right... *Bronwin*, please.'

Bunny stared at Claudia, but didn't react. She took Claudia's fingers away from her chin, but not before giving them a gentle squeeze. She nodded her head, then turned to call at Star again. 'Star! Claudia ain't got all day, girl. Hurry up, babe.'

Star Barker-Williams sat at the top of the stairs, just out of sight from her mum and Claudia. She hugged herself with excitement, not knowing how she was going to contain herself. She'd been there the whole time and had heard it all. Now she had another secret to put in her jar and this secret was simply the best one she'd ever heard.

Only a moment after Bunny had said her good-byes to Claudia and Star – who'd been acting even more excitable than usual – the doorbell went. Bunny smiled and turned back down the stairs.

'What have you forgotten?' Bunny opened the door with a large grin, expecting to see the harassed looking face of Claudia with Star by her side. She stopped, frozen.

'Oh. It's you.'

'Is that any way to say hello?'

Bunny crossed her arms around her, suddenly self-conscious that she was wearing a silk robe with nothing underneath it. Her smile was tight. 'I thought it was someone else.'

Teddy Davies gave a sly smile. He looked at Bunny, seeing the outline of her curvaceous body under the thin robe she was wearing. 'I wanted to come and pay you a visit.'

'I don't have my customers just turning up. You need to make an appointment.'

'Yeah, but I'm here now. Don't tell me you're going to turn me away and I've had a wasted journey.'

Bunny tightened the robe round her. She remembered this man from the last time. He hadn't wanted to do anything but talk. At the time he'd made her feel uncomfortable but looking back it was probably the way she'd been feeling. She hadn't known she was pregnant and

211

no doubt that was probably why she'd been feeling so strange these last few weeks.

'I don't know. I don't usually…'

Teddy put his foot in the door and winked. 'Oh come on. I don't bite.'

Bunny looked at the man. She wasn't really in the mood, but then she never really was. She rarely admitted it to herself, but she hated every moment of what she did. But now, more than ever, she didn't have the luxury of deciding if she was in the mood or not. She was properly on her own now. Yes, she had Claudia to help out with looking after Star, but when it came to earning money, it was all down to her.

Essentially it was Bunny who looked after Claudia, paying her a wage, putting a roof over her head – and soon not only would there be Star and Claudia to look after, she'd also have a baby. And in reality how long would she be able to keep on working for? She wasn't going to continue once she started showing so, if the last time was anything to go by, she'd only have another month or so before it was impossible to hide.

After the baby was born she wouldn't go back to work for a little bit so there'd be no money coming in; they'd all be living on her savings. There was no way she was going to rely on Del. She hadn't in the past and she certainly wasn't going to now.

Looking at the man again, Bunny knew there was nothing else for it. She needed to make as much money as she could whilst she still could, and what better moment to start than right now? She took a deep breath, bracing herself. She smiled a lazy smile – the feigned smile she'd fostered over the years and the one she only used for her paying punters.

Opening the door wide, she spoke. 'Come on then, but I don't want you thinking you can make a habit of just turning up like this. Next time you make an appointment like everybody else.'

Teddy grinned. 'Maybe there won't be a next time. Maybe this will be enough for me.'

Bunny didn't say anything. As she led Teddy up the stairs he watched her walk, her shapely backside moving under the robes. He could feel his erection beginning to start. He had no doubt it was going to be one helluva lay.

27

Del Williams couldn't believe what he was hearing as he sat surrounded by not only the shipment of cocaine, but also the money. He couldn't believe what he was seeing – and he certainly couldn't believe what he'd done. Sitting in the large back room of Fat Man Burke's warehouse hidden in the Sierra Blanca hills, he put his head in his hands for the twentieth time as he listened to Burke delight in what had happened.

He couldn't remember a thing. Not one iota. The last clear memory he really had was of Bunny walking out on him. That was days ago and everything had been a blur ever since. He felt a sickness in his stomach. Bunny. The thought of her was in the forefront of his mind, but it was driven out by the other hollow feeling in his stomach. Milo. What the fuck had he done? What had he been *thinking?* But more importantly, how the hell was he going to get out of it?

There was no explaining it; shit, he couldn't even explain it to himself let alone to one of the main faces of the Russian mafia. What was he going to say? *Sorry?* Jesus, he'd shot Mio's right hand man in the leg; apologies weren't going to cut it.

In the world Del lived in, giving the money back or even the money *and* the coke back wouldn't make any difference.

Inadvertently what he'd actually done was embarrass Milo and humiliate the Russian mafia, and the only sorry would be someone's claret being spilled. Specifically *his* claret – unless he spilled Milo's first.

'We need to sort out what we're going to do next.' Del growled at Fat Man as he threw back a double whisky.

Fat Man looked bemused. 'Push the gear out, what else?'

'You ain't hearing me, Burkey. I'm not putting the quiver out. Milo will just think I'm rubbing his nose in it.'

'And your fucking point is?'

Del raised his voice. 'The point is, Burkey, by not putting out the shit perhaps we can save our behinds. Damage limitation. It'll be the only way to show Milo that it's all been one massive fuck-up. And maybe, just maybe, we'll get away with our frigging lives intact.'

Fat Man Burke's face darkened. 'Listen, I ain't a pussy. No commie cunt is going to have me running for the hills.'

Del shook his head. 'What the hell era are you living in, Burkey?'

'The era that has us Brits standing on the frontlines and not being told by any Stalingrads what we can or can't do.'

Del decided to ignore Fat Man. Sometimes there was no getting through to him. 'It's a mess, Burkey.'

'What are you talking about? It's perfect. Pukka.'

'Perfect? Have you lost the plot? What part of ripping the granny out of the Russians then shooting one of them in the leg, before tying the rest of them up in their cars is perfect?'

Fat Man pulled a face, tilting his head to the side.

'Well when you put it like that, Del, I'd say all of it.'

Before Del could answer, his phone rang. Dragging it out of his pocket, he saw the number was withheld. 'Yes?'

There was silence on the phone. He felt his stomach wrench. 'Bunny? Is that you, doll?'

'Afraid not.'

Del sat up straight. He knew that voice and he wasn't interested in engaging with it. 'What do you want? Make it quick.'

On the other end of the phone Teddy Davies grinned. 'Is that any way to talk to an old pal?'

Del pulled the phone away, looking at it as if it was a wind-up. Putting it back to his ear he spoke, his tone threatening. 'I don't know if you're on something, mate, but who the *fuck* do you think you are, calling me up like this? I ain't one of your Soho muppets. Do yourself a favour, Davies, and jog on before it gets nasty.'

'Oh that is a shame, because I was actually calling to talk about Bunny.'

Del's eyes opened wide. He turned to Fat Man and gestured for him to go. 'Bunny? Who the fuck are you to talk about Bunny?' Del stopped as a thought entered his head. His whole demeanour changed. He swallowed, then took a deep breath.

'She ... she is all right ain't she? What is this about, Davies? Don't wind me up because I swear I'll come looking for you. You keep Bunny out of any of your pathetic games.'

'Del?'

'What?'

'I suppose fucking her is included in that?'

There was nothing but silence from Del.

Savouring the silence, Teddy listened to Del breathing, visualising the images that now must be exploding into Del's head.

'I fucked her.'

Del still said nothing.

'The oldest profession in the world; they say that about prostitution don't they?'

'I'm going to *kill* you Davies. Do you hear me? I'm going to kill you.'

Undeterred, Teddy continued. 'I had a nice chat with Edith the other day.'

'Edith?'

'Old lover of mine you know ... or maybe you didn't know. Though I must admit Edith's not in

216

Bunny's league is she? I can see why you're with her. That ass ... that pussy.'

'I'm *coming* to kill you.'

Teddy laughed. 'I'll be waiting. You know where I am.'

Fat Man Burke stood at the door of the warehouse, open-mouthed in amazement. Standing behind him were Del's men who stood equally amazed and equally open-mouthed. The only person within the warehouse who wasn't, was Del. *He* was too busy trashing the place.

No one could quite understand what was happening. And they certainly didn't know what to do. Fat Man Burke stepped forward, but seeing Del's wild eyes and the way he was swinging his arms around, he quickly stepped back to his original position.

'What are we going to do, boss?' One of Del's men whispered into Fat Man's ear.

Speaking out of the side of his mouth, Burke answered, 'How the fuck do I know?' And he didn't. But as he watched Del yelling and screaming, tears and rage spilling out of him with the kilos of cocaine being thrown and stamped on, bursting open like snow clouds, Fat Man knew he had to do something quickly, before all the coke and the money were destroyed.

'Get out of here guys.' Fat Man didn't bother turning his head as he spoke to Del's men, but he heard the scurry of feet. He waited until it'd stopped and he knew he was alone before he opened his arms wide to speak to his long-standing friend.

'Del? Del? You've got to stop this.'

Like an animal in a cage sensing someone was there to torment it, Del leapt forward towards Burkey. He snarled as he stared at him, saying nothing, before drinking down the rest of the whisky straight from the bottle. Wiping his nose and mouth on his expensive shirt sleeve, Del pushed the words out. 'She slept with him.'

Now this was difficult for Fat Man. It wasn't hard to guess Del was talking about Bunny. But Bunny was a whore. That's what whores did: sleep with people. So he couldn't see the problem.

He scratched his head, not quite sure what to say, but knowing if he said the wrong thing it could send Del off into another tirade. 'Ain't that a good thing? At least she's earning her keep.'

Del threw the bottle of whisky to the side then grabbed hold of Fat Man's Hawaiian shirt lapels. It occurred to Fat Man that he might have said the wrong thing.

'Don't fucking wind me up, Burkey. It ain't a joke.'

'Do I look like I'm fucking laughing, pal?'

'But you think I'm a muppet don't you? Giving me heart to some bird.'

Fat Man shook his head. *Fucking* women. 'Bunny's all right, she's one of the good ones, Del, but let's have it straight. She's a woman – and eventually they fuck you up or kill you.'

Del gaped drunkenly at Fat Man. 'But you ain't telling me what I should do, Burkey. Tell me what to do. She slept with him. With Teddy Davies. How the fuck can I *ever* touch her again, knowing she's been with him?'

'I dunno what to say to you, mate. I ain't good at shit like this. I don't even know what's gone on, but I do know you're letting some bird pull your fucking tail. Look at you mate. You're falling apart in front of me eyes.'

Del let go of Burkey, straightening his Hawaiian shirt for him. He took some deep breaths, nodding his head as he talked himself down. Breaking open a box of stolen whisky, Del grabbed a bottle, untwisting the top and gulping it down. 'You're right, Burkey. You're right. What the fuck have I been thinking? I'm going to sort it. One by one.'

Fat Man grinned, though it was followed by a nervous glance as he watched Del continue to down the booze. Once the whisky was finished, Del banged on his chest, letting out what sounded to Fat Man like a war cry. 'One by fucking one, Burkey, those bastard Russians won't know what hit them.'

Fat Man almost jumped in the air with delight. 'Now you're talking. Now you're talking.'

'But first I'm going to sort out that that cunt Davies. And I want you to sort out that two-faced money-grabbing bitch. She thought I'd never find out. I don't *ever* want to see her again. You understand what I'm saying?'

'You want me to get rid of Bunny?'

Del looked bewildered. 'Bunny? Not Bunny, you plank. Edith. Sort out Edith.'

It was Fat Man's turn to look bewildered. 'Edith?' He hadn't even known she came into the equation.

Del roared. 'Don't question me, Burkey. Just

sort it out.'

Fat Man shrugged his shoulders as he thought about it. Actually it wasn't such a bad idea at all. Life was certainly sweeter without his missus around. 'No problem. I'll sort it as soon as.'

Del staggered to the door. He held onto the frame, not noticing the tiny splinter going into his finger, and pointed at Fat Man. 'Don't mess up this time. I don't want a repeat of the Russians. Just let me know when it's done.'

28

Leaning over half a dozen fat long lines of quiver in his flat on the wrong side of Poland Street, Teddy chuckled to himself. Del Williams was going down. He would walk right into his trap. But before that could happen, Teddy needed to go and see somebody. And he knew exactly who that was. That someone was going to help put Del in his grave and then he, Teddy Davies, would be king of the castle.

'So is this your bedroom?' Teddy Davies had never been interested in interior design – quite frankly he didn't give a shit – but however un-educated he wanted to be, Teddy couldn't help admiring the room. The room belonging to none other than Star Barker-Williams.

Expensive handmade pastel yellow wallpaper dotted with silver bows matched the swathed curtains and bed linen that lay on the solid white wood four-poster bed. Cushions and throws were scattered on the long white leather settee, which took up the whole length of the back wall. A sixty-inch television was on the wall, with a three-sided open line fire completing the luxurious room.

'Yeah and I hate it. I wanted to have some wall-paper with pirates and ships on. Even skull and crossbones, but me mum said no, 'cos she thinks I'm too much of a tomboy as it is.'

Teddy picked up a silver-framed photo of Star and Bunny. 'Well maybe she's right. You're far too pretty to be a boy.'

'Yuk. I don't want to *be* a boy, but I do want to go on adventures, but me mum says they're dangerous. She's worried something will happen to me – but I told her nothing happened to Harry Potter, did it?'

Star pulled a face when she thought about it. Whenever she asked her mum to take her any-where they always ended up being chauffeur-driven in one of her dad's cars to the shops or to get manicures together, which wasn't the same as hiking over the hills and getting covered in mud. But her mum would never think about doing anything like that. She hated even a spot of dirt.

Star sighed and looked at Teddy. He was a funny-looking man. He reminded her of the man in the movie that her dad had let her watch and shouldn't have done. When her mum had come in she'd gone mad, and both Star and her dad had been in the doghouse. Sometimes her mum wasn't any fun at all, especially now. Since she'd

221

come back from Marbella, all her mum had done was cry. And all Claudia had done was try to stop her mum crying, then, when she couldn't, she started to cry herself.

Star pondered on this for a moment. Maybe her mum was missing her dad. She knew she was. Last night when Claudia had put her to bed, she'd had to bite down hard on her pillow to stop herself from crying. Crying was for babies. Star never cried. Well, almost never.

'So, tell me about your dad, Star.'

Star looked at Teddy quizzically. 'Me dad?' She didn't want to talk about him. It made her feel sad.

'Yes, what does he like? What does he like to do?'

Star shrugged. It was a funny question. She didn't really like to be asked questions. Not like this anyway. Her teacher at school did the same. Always trying to find out what her mum and dad did. Not that Star really knew.

Walking out of her room, closely followed by Teddy, Star went to get a drink from the kitchen. She answered matter-of-factly, 'Dunno. He likes the horses and he likes cars. That's about it really.'

Teddy leaned against the sink and squinted at Star. 'Yes, but what does he *really* like?'

Star looked puzzled. She had no idea what he was talking about and she was getting bored. She always felt bored when she was hungry. Claudia was taking too long to get back from the shops. She was always so slow.

'What I mean is, where does he like to go?

There must be some special place he likes to visit?'

'Dunno.'

Teddy snapped, irritated by Star's disinterest. 'Oh come on now, Star. You're telling me your dad doesn't have some special place he likes to go to and get away from it all?'

Star didn't like the feeling this conversation was giving her. The man was cross with her and she didn't know why.

As if reading her thoughts, Teddy changed tack He smiled, then whispered softly. 'I'm not being cross, I just want to know his special place because I want to give him a surprise. It's his birthday soon, isn't it? And I want to do something really special for him. Will you help me?'

Star chewed on her lip. This was more like it. This was something exciting and something that would make her dad happy. Her dad liked birthdays as much as she did and if this man, Teddy, was going to do something special for him, then Star would do all she could to help.

'Spain. He's there now.'

Teddy gripped his fists. Stupid kid. He spoke, desperately trying to keep his cool. 'I know he's in Spain, darlin' But I'm talking about somewhere here in England.'

Star paused, her face beginning to light up. 'Well there is somewhere. I dunno where exactly but he has a big house he likes to go to so he can get away from it. You know, from me mum chewing his ear off. It's somewhere in the countryside. Me mum don't like the countryside.'

'Where though? I need to know where.'

223

Star shrugged again and took a sip of her lemonade.

'Dunno.'

This kid was driving him crazy. 'Well, do you think you can find out for me, Star?'

'You mean ask me dad?'

'Yes, but don't tell him that I want to know. That would spoil the surprise wouldn't it?'

'Yeah, but I can't ask me dad, 'cos he's not answering his phone at the moment. Don't think he wants to talk to us.' Star looked down. She felt tears come into her eyes and furiously wiped them away.

'What about your mum? Would she know?'

'Yep, I guess.'

'But do you think you can find out today?'

'Maybe.'

Star's laid-back manner irritated Teddy. His voice showed it. 'Look, Star, if you don't want him to have a nice birthday then fine, I won't bother.'

Star's eyes pleaded with Teddy. 'No. No, I want him to. Maybe then me mum and him will stop fighting.'

Teddy slyly looked at Star. 'Are they arguing?'

Star wasn't sure if she'd said too much, but it felt good to tell someone about her parents. She hated it when her mum was cross with her dad. 'Yeah, a bit.'

'What are they fighting about?'

Star's walls came down again. She decided she didn't want to say anything else, so quickly changed the subject. 'So I should keep it a secret about his birthday?'

'Yes. It's our secret, Star, and nobody else's. You understand that?'

'What about me mum? I think she'd like to do something for him.'

Teddy raised his voice. 'No. You don't tell anyone. Understand?'

Star nodded enthusiastically as Teddy continued to talk.

'Do you know how to use a phone, Star?'

Star looked in horror at Teddy as if he'd just dropped out of he sky. 'Yeah of course. I got me own iPhone.'

'This is my private number, Star. When you find out where the place in the countryside is, I want you to call me. But like I say, you can't tell anyone and you need to find out today. At the latest, tomorrow. Can I trust you?'

Star's eyes gleamed. 'Yes.'

'Are you sure, Star? Cross your heart?'

Star winked at Teddy, proudly showing him she remembered which side her heart was on this time. 'Cross my heart.'

29

Milo Burkov cracked his knuckles as he rested his feet on the table, carefully avoiding the loaded machine guns lying next to his feet. He was smarting from the audacity of the man across the table from him.

Teddy watched Milo watching him. It was good

to be in such control. Everything was going better than he ever thought it would; finally, people were starting to eat out of his hand.

Milo, however, had already had enough of Teddy. 'My friend. You like to walk the tightrope of life I see.'

Teddy pulled a face. Metaphors were as bad as childish gibberish. He had no patience whatso-ever for them. 'Let's cut to the chase, Milo.'

Mb raised his eyebrows. He laughed loudly, heartily, looking round at his men, who followed his lead. The last time he'd seen this worm of a man he'd been scrambling about on the floor looking for sanctuary from his fists and now, suddenly, he had the balls of twenty men. 'Teddy. You want me to cut to the chase. What chase? There is no chase. As far as I recall we left it with you doing some groundwork. Since then a lot of things have changed. You never answering your phone, for one. I've been calling you for three days now and this is the first time I see or hear of you. It makes me nervous when a man does a dis-appearing act on me. I like my men to be visible, Detective.'

Teddy gave a supercilious smile. 'Oh don't worry about that. I was sorting stuff out.'

Milo couldn't stand it any longer. He banged his fist on the table but stared in amazement as Teddy did nothing. Milo nodded to his men. They ran forward, dragging Teddy off his chair. Milo walked round casually – still surprised to see Teddy wasn't showing as much fear as he should be – then drew his fist back and hit him in the stomach. Teddy bent forward, saliva running out of his mouth as he tried to catch his breath.

Milo lifted Teddy's head, holding his hair to do so. He stared into his face and spoke, contempt in his voice. 'Don't play games with me, Mr Davies. I don't like it I don't like an arrogant man who brings nothing but an empty plate to the table.'

Teddy began to splutter, but still he was grinning. 'Empty plate? I don't think so. You want Del, right? Well, I can give you him.'

Milo quickly gestured to his men to sit Teddy back down on the chair. He poured a drink of water then passed it to Teddy. Propping himself on the table, Milo cracked his knuckles, waiting patiently for Teddy to finish.

'You were saying, Detective?'

'I can deliver Del to you.'

'And what's in it for you? Although it's not really hard to guess.

'I want him dead just as much as you do.'

'No, Detective. I think you might have the edge on me there.'

'I can give you Del, but I want to run the show.'

Milo laughed scornfully. 'You? You really expect me to let you be in charge?'

Teddy looked at Milo as if it was the most natural thing in the world. 'Yes.'

'And why would I let you do that?'

'Because when it comes to Del Williams, I won't make any mistakes.'

'So let's just say I go along with this crazy idea. What would you want from me?'

'I'd need you and your men to turn up when I say and where I say – as well as do as I say.'

Milo blinked a couple of times, bursting into laughter at the little man with brass balls dressed in a brown mac in front of him. He looked round the room at his men. Twenty strong, fully armed Russian ex-military soldiers. Trained killers. Yet the pale-faced, sinewy man in front of him, sitting nonchalantly without a trace of fear, wanted to run the show. Well, why not? He liked men with courage; though Milo knew well enough there was only a fine line between courage and foolishness. But if that's what Teddy wanted and he could deliver, then it'd be worth it.

'Detective, you have a deal.' Milo walked round to the far side of the room and opened the black briefcase lying on the side. He pulled out a packet and threw it to Teddy, whose eyes gleamed.

'Half a kilo of the finest uncut cocaine. Deliver Del to us and there'll be plenty more where that came from.'

Teddy got up from the chair, the pain in his stomach almost forgotten. He tucked the cocaine into his oversized pocket, almost skipping out of the room. As he got to the door, Milo's voice stopped him in his tracks.

'But Detective. Don't deliver, and you, along with the enigmatic Mr Williams, will be a dead man walking.'

'Hello doll. You got something to tell me?' Del Williams sat in the large comfortable chair in Bunny's flat, the warm summer breeze coming in from the open window.

He'd been back in London for a couple of days now, but it was the first time he'd put his head above water. He had to be careful. He hadn't heard anything from the Russians, which wasn't a good sign.

Apart from that though, he desperately wanted some answers from Bunny, so he'd headed over to her flat.

Del stared at Bunny, refusing to acknowledge how beautiful she looked. Taken aback, Bunny stared at Del, refusing to acknowledge how good it was to see him.

'What do you want, Del? Make this quick, babe. I've got clients to see.'

It was a lie. Since the man the other night – Teddy, she thought his name was – she hadn't worked. She couldn't. After he'd left Bunny had been physically sick, at first putting it down to the pregnancy, but then quickly realising it was more than that.

The thought of strange men touching her made Bunny feel ill and the sickness went to the depths of her stomach, faded distant memories coming in and out of her mind. She didn't know what she was going to do. She *had* to work but something seemed to have finally snapped inside her.

Bunny spoke again, pushing the lie some more. She needed him to go. It was too painful to see him. 'Del, please. They'll be here soon.'

Del bristled, then took his anger and jealousy out on the handmade coffee table, which he'd never liked, kicking it hard across the room. His tone was harsh. 'I *said*, do you have something to tell me?'

Bunny's face paled. She had no idea how he'd found out about the pregnancy. 'How ... how did you know?'

Del could hardly contain his anger. She wasn't even trying to hide the fact she'd slept with Teddy.

'I got a phone call.'

Claudia. Bunny couldn't believe it. She'd promised she was going to keep out of it but within days she'd gone behind her back and called Del.

Bunny looked up at Del. She could see he was beside himself with rage. She hadn't considered what he'd do when he finally found out about the pregnancy, but she certainly hadn't expected him to react like this. Though now she knew his true feelings it told her everything.

'I didn't want you to find out. Not like this anyway.'

'Like this? It wouldn't have mattered if you'd said it with fucking flowers, Bun.'

'If I'd thought you'd take it so badly...'

'What, Bun? What?'

Bunny shrugged her shoulders. She didn't know what to say. This was the first time she'd seen him since Marbella and the way he was behaving cut deeply. She spoke, attempting to keep a lid on her emotions. 'You couldn't have called me?'

'Called you? Do you know the *shit* I've been dealing with? Everything's fucked up, Bun. I've got the fucking Russians out for me, not to mention Edith giving me the usual. And on top of all that, I've got you and all this crap.'

It was Bunny who raised her voice next. 'This "crap"? Is that what you call it? You have some bleedin' front.'

'Me?'

'Yes you, Del.'

Del stood up, red-faced, and stormed towards Bunny in fury. 'You can't even say sorry. Not that sorry would frigging cop it but it would be something, Bun. You could at least try.'

'Sorry? You want *me* to apologise to you? I've done nothing wrong, Del, so don't make me feel like I have. If anyone should be sorry it should be you.'

Del grabbed hold of Bunny's shoulders as an image of Teddy writhing on top of her came into his mind. He shook her, desperately searching for answers. 'Why? Why Bunny? Just tell me why.'

Bunny felt the tears run down her face. Her heart was breaking. The disgust she saw on Del's face was like a shooting pain through her. She knew they'd parted on bad terms in Marbella but she'd secretly hoped they may have been able to rebuild things. Talk, like they usually did. And even if the future was as she suspected it would be, her on her own, she thought at least Del would accept this baby as he'd accepted Star.

'It was an accident but I don't regret it. I'm happy it happened, Del.'

Something in Del seemed to flip and to Bunny's dismay he started to smash up the place. She watched in horror as he threw the silver-framed photo of them at the mirror. Smashed shards of glass flew everywhere. Del continued his rampage, kicking furniture and anything in his way. The lamp. The table. The large floor vase. Picking up a chair, he threw it, not caring where it landed. The leg of the chair hit the window, shattering it into frosted glass. He paused for a moment to spit words at her. '*Happy?* Do you want to kill me, Bun? Do you want to rip out me frigging heart?'

'Why can't you be happy about it?'

'Now I know you're taking the piss. You don't give a crap. You're a fucking ice queen, Bun. You've won, doll. You can have it. No woman is ever going to make me cry. I'm gone. I'm out of here, babe. I won't bother you again. I'll leave you to your whoring.'

'Dad?' Star stood at the door. She couldn't stop the tears rolling down her face. But she had to. Tears were for babies, but her dad wasn't a baby; he was the toughest guy she knew. But her dad was crying. Big splashing tears rolling down his face.

'Dad?'

Del looked at Star. 'Hello baby.' He looked around the room, seeing the destruction he'd caused. Embarrassed, he glanced at his daughter again as he began to head for the door. 'I'll see you soon, tiger. Be good.'

'Dad, don't go.' Star ran after her dad, she tugged on his clothes but he didn't turn round.

'Dad!' Star stopped as the front door closed in her face. She took several rapid deep breaths as her tears fought to escape. She had to make it better. She had to get her dad to be happy again. Running frantically into her bedroom, Star knelt down by her chest of drawers. She put her hand underneath it and scrambled around for a moment before pulling out a homemade box covered in shells. It was her secret box. Opening it, Star gazed at all the trinkets she'd collected, touching them gently, each one a memory.

Underneath the multi-coloured broken neck-lace she'd found in the park, Star found what she was looking for. It was a card. The card the man had given her. And written on it was a phone number that she hoped would make everything better and bring her dad back home. Tapping the numbers into her iPhone, Star waited for Teddy Davies to answer.

30

Julian Millwood leant across the counter in the betting shop in Chapel Market. 'I want my fuck-ing money back, pal.'

The shop assistant answered confidently, knowing that the partition divide would protect him. 'You know I can't do that, pal. Maybe next time you shouldn't put your readies on a three-legged horse.'

Julian scowled, hatred filling his eyes. He clenched his fist, smashing it down on the counter, and marched out into the throng of Chapel Market.

Fuck. Out of the eight grand Alan had given him, he only had just over a grand left. Fleetingly, he thought about going to Alan to get some more. But as quickly as the thought seemed like a good idea it just as swiftly turned into a bad one. Firstly, he doubted he could get anything else out of the tight-fisted cocksucker. Secondly, even if he did, how much would it actually be?

Another couple of grand at the most. What he needed was real money and as Julian passed a group of children crossing Penton Street dressed in their red and grey school uniforms, it hit home. There was only one way to get it. He needed to start making some calls.

31

Teddy Davies was like a pig in a trough. He'd given up lining the quiver up half an hour ago, deciding instead just to stick his nose in the bag. Two days had passed since he'd received the phone call from Star. Now all he had to do was wait, and waiting with a bag of quiver and a couple of ounces of skunk was the only way to go. Life was certainly turning out to be sweet.

'We need to meet.' The voice on the other end of the phone gave Del Williams pause for thought. Lying in the darkened bedroom of his friend's country estate in Kent, he couldn't quite place the caller.

'It's Milo.'

'How can I help you, Milo?'

'I would've thought it was obvious. We have a lot of things to sort out, but not on the phone.'

Del raised his eyebrows. He'd known this would come eventually. The call had been inevitable.

'If not on the phone, where?'

'I have the perfect place. In fact I'm here now.

Sitting in a lovely front room overlooking acres of land. Cream leather sofas, though sadly they're not as comfortable as they look. Still, it helps having these big green velvet cushions.'

Del sat bolt upright. He hissed down the phone. 'Where the hell are you, Milo?'

'From your reaction, I'd say you've already guessed.'

'I want you out of my house.'

'Not the response I was looking for.'

'Get out!'

'*Again*, not the right response. It seems you've forgotten what you did. It seems you have a selective memory. So let me refresh it. You owe me. Your life is in the balance, Del, so I would've thought showing a little bit of hospitality was in your best interests and the least you could do.'

'Don't cross the line with me, Milo.'

'Or what, my friend? You'll come after me? That would be a very foolish thing to do.'

Del got up from the bed, pressing the remote control to open the curtains. As daylight burst into the large lavish bedroom, Del took a deep breath to try to calm himself. He was playing right into Milo's hands by letting him wind him up. He needed to play this cool.

'Okay Milo. What do you want me to do?'

'I want you to come and see me.'

Del frowned. 'How do I know it's not a set up?'

'You don't, and I'm sure you know it probably is, but what other choice do you have? You of all people know how it goes.'

Del said nothing for a moment. That was the problem. He *did* know how it went. And he also knew there was nothing he could do. If he didn't go and see him, Milo would find him, maybe not as easily as he'd found his house in the country-side, but eventually he would and then there'd be no talking. No sorting it out. It'd be simply do or die.

Knowing he was cornered, Del spoke matter-of-factly.

'Just you and me?'

'Now you know I can't promise that. But I do expect *you* to come alone.'

'Wouldn't that make me stupid?'

'No more stupid than you've already been.'

'It wasn't like you thought it was, Milo. All of this is a huge mistake.'

'Then that's the one thing we do agree on, Del. It was a huge mistake. A *very* huge one.'

Del rubbed his head. It was pounding from all the alcohol he'd been consuming since he'd had the ruck with Bunny. Fuck. He didn't want to think of her. He didn't want her name anywhere near his head, especially when he had to deal with Milo. She was too distracting.

'Okay. I'll come and meet you.'

'Good. Now you're beginning to talk sense. Perhaps there is hope after all. Ten o'clock to-night shall we say?'

Unenthusiastically, Del answered. 'Ten o'clock ... but Milo, before you decide what to do, hear me out, pal. Let me sit down and talk. You and I, we go back a long way. Once you hear everything I'm sure we'll find a solution that makes you happy. Whatever it takes to sort it out.'

'Whatever it takes.' The line went dead.

Edith Williams pressed her stomach hard and farted, smiling with satisfaction. She'd been trying to dispel the trapped wind since yesterday afternoon when she'd eaten two double cheeseburgers.

Feeling more comfortable, she leant over to answer her ringing phone, almost immediately breaking into a smile as she listened to the caller on the other end.

'Edward darlin'. I'd thought you'd forgotten all about me. I imagined you'd be buzzing about like a fly on shit but you've proved me wrong. What news, Ed?' Edith paused, pushing her stomach again. Her eyes began to glint as she took in the information being recounted. 'I knew I could rely on you, Edward, but really, babe, you have to stop being so bleedin' prickly about your name. I've told you before, no one respects a man named after a bear.' Edith cackled, not bothering to say goodbye.

Gloating to herself, Edith dialled another number.

'Yeah? What do you want? What's the deal?' Alfonso's voice was gruff.

Haughtily, Edith replied, 'I was calling to say I'll be back tomorrow morning. Everything's sorted. I want you to pick me up at the airport.'

'And why the fuck should I do that?'

'Because I *told* you to, Alfonso.'

'I ain't your poodle any longer, Edith. We're in this together. We're partners.'

'Partners? We talked about this before. Del has no interest in what I do or don't do anymore.'

'I just want what's mine.'

'Well that's just it, ain't it Alfonso? Nothing is yours.'

Alfonso shouted angrily down the phone. 'That wasn't the deal, Edith. You know it wasn't.'

'Oh you mean the deal I made with you when you had me on the floor? Well I've been thinking about it, and I suppose you refusing to pick me up at the airport does me a favour darlin'. Saves me waiting to tell you. You're surplus to demands now, Alfonso. I don't need you anymore.'

'What?'

'You heard. I don't know what I was thinking. There was me making plans with you when I didn't need you at all. You're useless, Alfie baby. You'll never see a penny of my money, babe.'

Alfonso could hardly believe what he was hearing. 'You'll regret this.'

Edith continued to admire herself in the mirror, adding a touch more red to her already heavily made-up cherry mouth. 'No. No Alfonso, I don't think I will.'

'You'll pay for this.'

Edith sniffed. 'Again, Alfonso, I don't think I will. Now, it did cross me mind to get Del's men to throw you out, but I ain't a monster. I have a heart. So I've decided to let you stay on at the villa, for the time being anyway. I can't say fairer than that, can I? I'll even give you your old job back. You were so good at cleaning the toilets, Alfie. Oh and get your stuff out of the main house. I want you back in the west wing ... you know, the servants quarters.'

Alfonso Garcia threw the phone across the room

and watched as it landed on his bed, bouncing several times before it lay still. If it was the last thing he did, Edith Williams would get hers.

32

Del Williams sped towards his house just outside Rettendon in Essex. The electronic gauge on his bulletproof Range Rover showed ninety-five miles an hour. At first, he'd been driving well under the speed limit, hoping to delay his arrival and the inevitable showdown with Milo. Besides, he needed to collect his thoughts. But now he needed to get there.

The best approach was to offer Milo both the coke and the money. It'd be a massive loss, but in the long term what he'd lose would be nothing to what he'd gain. Being on an even keel with Milo was worth the loss of a couple of million pounds or so.

By sacrificing everything, Del would show Milo it'd all been one massive fuck-up. He'd even offer to push a couple of hundred thousand to the man he'd shot. Whatever it took to show the Russian mafia boss there were no hard feelings.

It might take some doing, but Del Williams was convinced that by tomorrow morning, he and Milo would be back to top drawer. Pressing his foot harder on the accelerator, Del turned up the radio.

Bunny Barker walked into her daughter's bedroom. She sat down on the end of the bed, giving Star a sad smile. She'd really been looking for Claudia, wanting to confront her about calling Del about the pregnancy when she'd given Bunny her word she wasn't going to get involved. She would've spoken to Claudia sooner but for the past couple of days she'd been staying with an old friend, so today was the first time she was going to have the opportunity to tackle her. To be truthful, she was dreading it. Bunny sighed. She still couldn't credit it that Claudia had betrayed her.

Bringing her thoughts back to her daughter, Bunny looked at Star. The freckles that were usually so tiny in the winter were now reappearing on her face, owing to the summer sunshine. Her blonde hair was even blonder. But her blue eyes – usually dancing and mischievous – were sad and almost lifeless.

'Hey babe, can I come in?'

Star didn't bother looking up from the treasures she'd tipped out onto her oversized four-poster bed. 'You're already in ain't ya?'

'Star, you don't have to be like that, doll. I just wanted to make sure you're all right. Can I give you a hug?'

Star shrugged her shoulders as her mum gave her a cuddle. She hated feeling like this and being rotten to her mum, but she didn't know how to get rid of the horrible feeling she had in her tummy. It was also in her chest. In fact all of her felt horrible, and the only time she didn't feel horrible was when she was asleep. But she wasn't tired. So all she could do was try to pretend the feeling wasn't there, but no matter how much she pretended, it didn't go away.

'Daddy *will* be back, Star.'

At the mention of her dad, Star put her hands over her ears and threw herself back on the bed. She didn't want to think about him because when she did all she could see was the front door shutting in her face. Him leaving. And that had frightened her. How could she tell anyone she was scared? Explorers didn't get scared and that's what Star wanted to be when she grew up. An explorer.

Star felt her mum touching her leg. 'Star honey, how can I make this better for you?'

Star said nothing. The only thing that would make it better was her dad coming back, but her mum couldn't make that happen. The only person who could do that now was her friend, Teddy. But she hadn't heard from Teddy like he'd promised and when she'd kept calling him, like her dad he hadn't picked up the phone.

'Maybe we can go to the movies, Star. How about going to see that new Pixar movie?'

Star sat up, her face contorted with rage. 'I don't *want* to see a bleedin' movie with you. I want to go and see it with me dad, but you made him go. You made him unhappy. I *hate* you. I hate you.'

'What's all this shouting?' Claudia stood by the door. She looked at Bunny sympathetically, then turned her attentions to Star.

'Star. You know Mummy didn't make Daddy go.'

Tears poured down Star's face. 'She did. She did!'

Claudia shook her head and spoke quietly as she sat next to Bunny. 'No baby, she didn't.'

'Then why did he go?'

'Sometimes adults are silly.'

Star shouted furiously. 'He's not silly. He's not.'

Claudia put her hand on Star's. 'I'm not saying he is.' She raised a glance at Bunny who was staring at her coldly.

'Claudia. I'll handle this. She's my daughter and I've always been there for her.'

The puzzlement on Claudia's face was so apparent even Star stopped and looked at her mum curiously to see what would happen next.

Claudia stammered. 'I... I... I ain't saying you haven't. I was only trying to help.'

Bunny's eyes were steely. 'It's a bit late to help now. You had your chance.'

'What's this about, Bun?'

Forgetting Star was sitting next to her listening, Bunny launched into an attack. 'It's about *you* Claudia and you know what, that's always been the problem. You've always thought it was about you. You thinking *you* know best. Making decisions without thinking about the consequences. Letting other people pick up the pieces for your mistakes. Well I'm done with them, Claudia. I'm not going to let you hurt my daughter as well.'

Claudia's eyes were full of tears. 'I would never do that, Bunny.'

'No, because I won't let you... I want you to go.'

'Go?'

Bunny couldn't bear to look at Claudia, to see

242

the pain in her face. 'Yes, go. Until I decide what I'm going to do, I don't want to see you.'

'Please, don't do this ... Bronwin.'

Bunny's head shot up. Her face contorted just like Star's had only a few moments ago.

'Stop it ... stop it! You always do that. You always call me that when you want something, but it don't work, Claudia. There is no Bronwin don't you get it? Bronwin died in me a long, long time ago. Now go. Get out!'

'No, not until you tell me what this about.'

'You told him. You told Del about the baby.'

Claudia looked stunned. 'I didn't. I told you I wouldn't. Please, you've got to believe me.'

'But I don't, Claudia. I don't. He as good as told me when he was smashing up the place the other day. You should've seen his face. I told you. I begged you not to say anything but you just couldn't help yourself, could you?'

'Bunny, you've got to believe me. I wouldn't lie to you.'

Emotionally exhausted, Bunny's voice dropped to a whisper. '*Please*, get out.'

Claudia silently got up and walked towards the door. She hesitated as if to say something but changed her mind, exiting the room without looking back.

A few seconds of silence passed as Bunny sat, her head bowed down. She kept her eyes closed before springing them open to look at her daughter, feigning a smile as her heart broke.

'So, tell me about these treasures then. What's this one?'

Bunny picked up a marble as Star looked at her

mum. She didn't know what had just happened between Claudia and her mum, or rather she didn't know why it had happened, but she did know by looking at her mum's face not to ask any questions. For now, anyway.

'That's a pirate's eye.'

'What happened to his other eye?'

'He still has it.'

'What about this? What's this?' Bunny held up a piece of cotton wool.

Star stared at her mum. Her voice was impassive as she said, 'It's a piece of cotton wool.'

A wry smile came to Bunny's face. Her daughter was something else. 'And this... Star what's this?' Bunny picked up a card with a number on it. Seeing what her mum had in her hand, Star tried to grab it but Bunny was too quick, holding onto it as she looked at the writing she didn't recognise.

'Give it me. It's mine.'

'Star. Whose number is it?' Bunny lifted her daughter's face to her. 'Star. Is it one of your friends from school?'

Star shook her head.

'Well, whose number is it?'

'Someone's.'

Bunny's voice pushed Star. 'Baby, this is really important. Whose number is it? You can tell me.'

'It's the man from the woods.'

Bunny grabbed hold of the bedside table to steady herself. Her head spun. Bile rose in her throat. Cold sweat prickled out of her pores.

'Mum?'

With great effort Bunny spoke, her eyes full of fear.

'What man? What man in…' She couldn't say it.

'That day you were looking for me, he was there.'

'A man?'

Star nodded. 'Yeah.'

Bunny knew she had to try to stop the panic taking over her completely. 'Oh my God. Can you remember what he looks like so I can call the police?'

Star was puzzled. She didn't know what all the fuss was about. But her mum always fussed. *Always*. 'Yeah, but he's my friend.'

Bunny shook her daughter. 'No, Star. Whoever it is, he's not your friend.'

Star raised her voice again. 'He is. He is my friend. He's been here to see me.'

'What?… What? Here?…' Breathe. She couldn't have a panic attack. She had to breathe. Bunny stared at her daughter.

'What do you mean he's been here?'

Star shrugged. 'He just has. He's Daddy's friend too. Daddy knows him.'

Bunny shook her head. This wasn't making sense. 'I don't understand, Star. Who is he?'

'I've told you, he's my friend. He's going to give Daddy a surprise for his birthday and then…'

'And then what, Star? What then?'

'And then Daddy will come back home because he'll be happy.'

Bunny grabbed hold of Star, hugging her tight in a loving embrace. She spoke again, trying to sound calm for her daughter. 'Star, why was he talking about Daddy's birthday? Daddy's birthday isn't till November, babe.'

Star, having got distracted by her treasures again, spoke absent-mindedly. 'He said he was going to give him a party he'd never forget.'

'Where, Star? Where did he say he was going to do it?'

'At the house in Essex, that's why I wanted to know where it was. Have I done something wrong?'

Bunny kissed her daughter on her forehead. 'No Star. No, you've done nothing wrong.' Bunny got up from the bed with the card in her hand. 'I don't suppose you know his name?'

Star nodded. 'Teddy, like my bear.'

A moment later, Bunny Barker vomited everywhere.

33

It was the fourteenth time Bunny had heard the ringing switch onto voicemail. None of them were answering. But she needed to speak to them – any of them. Del. Teddy. Claudia. It didn't matter who, as long as one of them answered.

She tried again. 'Hello?'

'Hello?'

'Del?'

'Nope.'

Bunny pulled the phone away for a moment to check which number she had dialled.

'Teddy?'

'Yep.'

On the other end of the phone, Teddy Davies lay staring at the ceiling.

'Teddy?'

'Mmm?'

'Teddy!' Bunny shouted down the phone, snapping Teddy out of his torpor.

'What?!'

Bunny's voice was dark and threatening. 'You listen to me. I want to know what the hell you're playing at.'

'Who is this?'

'Bunny.'

Teddy smiled. Ah yes, the beautiful Bunny, he could almost still taste her. 'How can I help you?'

'What the hell are you playing at?'

'You've lost me.'

Bunny shouted down the phone. 'What are you doing giving my daughter your number?'

'Oh, that.'

'Don't play games with me, but it's not me you'll have to worry about. It's Del.'

Teddy roared with laughter. A high-pitched, hyena laugh.

'Del? I don't think anyone will have to worry about him again.'

'What ... what do you mean?'

In a faraway place in Teddy's mind, a part of him knew he was saying too much, but he was past caring. 'Let's just say there's an early birthday present waiting for him – but something more than candles will get blown out.' The line went dead.

Del Williams kept his eyes on the road, but gave a quick glance to his ringing phone. He saw the caller ID. Fuck that. He'd lost count how many times Bunny had called. If she thought for a moment he was going to talk to her she must have her head up her arse. He threw the phone on the dashboard, pressing his foot harder on the accelerator. His phone rang again. What the hell did she want from him? What was she going to say to make it better? Nothing. Sweet F.A.

She'd told him that she'd been happy about sleeping with Teddy Davies. And he never wanted to speak to her again.

Pick up. Pick up. He needed to pick up. Voicemail. Shit. She dialled Del again. Voicemail. She had to get through to him. Bunny looked at the clock, her mind racing. There was nothing else for it. Running into Star's bedroom, she spoke in a rush. 'Star, I've got to go out. You stay here. Don't answer the door or the phone. I'll be back when I can. Claudia's going to be here in the next five minutes or so. Tell me you'll be okay?'

'I'll be fine.' Star smiled at her mum, then turned back to the cartoon she was watching.

'I love you, Star, always remember that.'

Bunny ran out of the room, grabbing the keys to Del's other Range Rover.

Del sped through the country lanes towards his house, taking the tight turns without slowing down. He turned right at the junction without looking, almost crashing into a car coming the other way. The constant phone calls were doing his head in. He couldn't turn his phone off in case Milo called, but it was distracting him and causing him to get edgy, which he couldn't afford to be. He needed to be sharp and he certainly wouldn't be that if he went headlong into another vehicle.

The turning at Rettendon village took Del towards his sprawling estate. Driving towards the beginning of his farmland the phone went again. This had to stop. Del grabbed the phone, pressing answer. 'What, Bunny? What the fuck do you want? What part of me not answering the frigging phone makes you think I want to talk to you?'

'It's me.'

Del slowed down the Range Rover. 'Who's me?'

'Burkey.'

Del let out a sigh. Christ, he had to stop getting so worked up.

'Bird causing you grief?'

Del snapped. 'Listen, I don't want to talk about it, mate. What can I do for you?'

'It's sorted.'

'What's sorted?'

'What you asked me to sort.'

'Sort?'

Fat Man sounded pleased with himself. 'Yeah, it's sorted.'

'Fuck's sake, Burkey. What are you talking about?'

'The thing you asked me to sort.'

Del lost his patience. 'Don't start all that again. I dunno what you're talking about. Spit it out.'

'I can't on the phone.'

'Then why the fuck did you call?'

'Because I thought you'd want to know.'

'Want to know about what?'

'The thing I sorted.'

Del yelled down the phone. 'Just tell me.'

'Edith.'

'Edith?'

'Yeah, what you wanted me to sort out about Edith.'

Del frowned. 'I never asked you to do anything. If she's giving you trouble...'

Sitting in the sun on his yacht docked outside Marbella, drinking a very pink pina colada, Fat Man interrupted Del. 'You asked me to deal with Edith. No mess-ups, you said. You wanted it finished once and for all.'

Del pulled up on the side of the road, his tyres churning up the sun-dried mud. He slammed his foot on the brake, lurching forward. 'Burkey. *Please* say you didn't do what I think you did.'

Fat Man spoke slowly. 'It depends what you think I did.'

Del bellowed down the phone. 'Did you or didn't you put a hit on Edith?'

'Yes. But only after you told me to.'

Del rubbed his face, trying to erase the stress. 'If I did, I was pissed out of my skull. Why the fuck did you listen to me?'

'Del...'

'I don't want to hear it. I just want you to stop it right now!'

'How can I stop it?'

'Phone them. You must be able to phone them.'

'I can't stop it. You know that as well as I do. It's

not like I have the number.'

'Get it. Someone must have.'

'Del, you know how it works. There is *no* number.'

Del exhaled, trying to steady himself. 'Okay. Okay ... where though? Where's it happening?'

'At her flat in Chigwell ... at ten.'

Del's wheel skidded as he put his foot on the accelerator, then he took his handbrake off as the Range Rover went into overdrive. Milo would have to wait. Fuck. Fuck. Fuck. He turned the leather steering wheel, U-turning towards Rettendon and out the other side towards Chigwell.

He reached for the phone, dialling Edith's number. Answer machine. It was typical of Edith. Del slammed his fist on the steering wheel.

The impact of the hit swerved the car to the right, edging it over to the other lane and making Del lose control for a moment as he only narrowly missed crashing into another Range Rover driving at high speed the other way.

Bunny swerved. Christ. Some drivers. She hooted her horn at the other car speeding past her in the other direction. Slowing down and regaining control of the car, Bunny tried dialling Del again. Voicemail. She wiped her eyes, not wanting the tears to blur her vision. She tried again. Please answer. *Please.* Voicemail. Looking at the car clock, Bunny put her foot down on the accelerator.

At the sign for Rettendon, Bunny checked the GPS. It was only another couple of miles. Speeding up some more, she turned left as she switched on the headlights and headed down the road as dusk began to draw in.

A few minutes later, she saw a dirt track heading off to the right and the GPS told her she'd reached her destination. She turned right into the private bridleway, slowing down further as the wheels of the Range Rover plunged into the dips and crevices of the uneven track.

The trees and high bushes almost enclosed the private road. Darkness began to cloak the night and Bunny felt a shiver down her spine. There wasn't a sound nor a light, apart from the moon high in the cloudless summer sky.

Just a few metres in front of her, Bunny saw a closed gate. She halted and moved to get out of the car to open the gate.

Putting her hand on the door, Bunny saw a bright light and then nothing... Nothing at all as a dozen Kalashnikov machine guns fired a hail of bullets, ripping through the metal of the car.

A moment later, Bunny Barker lay motionless in a pool of her own blood.

34

Del Williams didn't bother to wait. He didn't bother to ring. He just lifted his leg and kicked down the door, a Colt .380 Mustang in his hand. He ran through the corridor, pushing his body against the wall, his body charged. He could hear the television on in the front room and cautiously he edged towards the sitting-room door, cocking his gun, ready for action

'What the bleedin' hell are you...' Edith stopped as she saw the gun in Del's hand. Her face paled and she raised her hands.

'Listen babe, you don't have to do this. I know you and me have had our fallouts, but there ain't no need for this. It wasn't my idea, I swear darlin'. You know I wouldn't do anything like that to you. If you want to know whose idea it was, it was that toerag...'

Before Edith could finish her sentence, Del yelled, 'Get down!' He threw himself at Edith, pushing her into the front room. She banged to the floor as a masked gunman raced into the flat. Del rolled over as a shot fired out. He crouched down, aiming his gun at the legs of the intruder. His first aim missed. His second hit. The startled gunman, taken aback that there was someone else in the flat besides Edith, dropped to his knees, screaming out in agony as he held his leg.

Rushing across to the man, Del tackled the gun from him, slamming his head onto the floor and pressing his knee into his back as he held the gun against his temple. Hissing into the man's ear, Del snarled, 'Do not try anything, otherwise I will kill you. Do you understand me?' The man nodded.

'This job is finished, do you understand?' The man nodded again. 'You'll still get your money. I'll even double it up for the inconvenience, but I'm calling it off. The hit is *off*. I'll get my doctor to come and pick you up to sort out that leg. I'm

253

sorry I had to shoot you. You know how it is.' The man nodded, before falling unconscious in his own blood.

An hour and a half later, the doctor had come and gone and Del Williams sat on the chair in Edith's kitchen, spinning his Colt .380 round and round on the smooth and shiny surface of the kitchen table. His forehead was lined with a deep frown. 'What did you mean?' He looked at Edith, still with the hand on his gun. 'What did you mean Edith when you said *you wouldn't do anything like that? It wasn't your idea...* What was it you wouldn't do?'

Edith looked first at Del then at the gun. 'I don't know what you're talking about.'

'I think you do. I think you know exactly what I'm talking about – but the fact is, you just ain't saying. You need to start talking.'

For the second time that night, Edith Williams paled.

On the north side of Soho, Milo Burkov received a call from his men. 'It's done.'

On the south side of London, Teddy Davies received a call from Milo. 'It's done.'

On the west side of Chigwell, Edith Williams received a call from Teddy. 'It's done.'

Edith glanced across her kitchen at Del and simply replied, 'I wouldn't be so sure.'

35

Del was getting bored. It was clear Edith wasn't going to tell him a thing. Perhaps there was nothing to tell – but what she'd said had struck him as odd. He also wanted to confront her about sleeping with Teddy, but the last thing he wanted was for Edith to think he was jealous. It just pissed him off. Big time. All along she'd played the wronged wife, when in reality he'd found out she was humping anything that moved. But more importantly, he didn't want to confront her because then he'd have to talk about Teddy, which would make him think about Bunny, and he couldn't bring himself to do that.

Putting his gun away in his jacket pocket, Del stood up. He guessed there'd be plenty of time to pull Edith up about it once he'd got his head straight. Anyway, he had more to worry about than her. Thanks to Burkey's fuck up, he'd had to mug Milo off, and that was just what he couldn't afford to do. And looking across at his wife who was stuffing her mouth with a half-eaten cold kebab, Del Williams couldn't even say coming to save Edith had been worth it.

He gazed at Edith coldly. 'I'm off.'

Edith looked at Del slyly. 'I'm going back to Marbella tomorrow ... back to the villa.'

Del didn't have time for this. 'Do what you want Edith. You usually fucking do.'

As he headed for the door, Edith stopped him. 'You know what I'm curious about. I'm curious why that gunman came here looking for you. Why did you say he was looking for you, 'cos it just don't ring right with me? Why would anyone think of looking here for you, especially now you're shacked up with that scrubby little whore of yours? Bunnykins.'

Del stared at Edith, disdain on his face. 'You're right, Edith. I was lying. They weren't looking for me. They were looking for you. You and your big mouth. They were going to put a bullet in your head. And maybe I should've let them – but like a mug, I didn't think even *you* deserved that. So do yourself a favour, sweetheart, and keep your nasty comments to yourself, because if you don't, next time I swear I'll pull the trigger my-bleedin'-self.'

Del stomped out to his car, leaving Edith open-mouthed. His phone rang. Seeing the caller ID, he sighed. He wasn't in the mood for it. He pressed the red button sending the caller straight to voicemail. Almost instantly, the phone rang again. This was going to do his nut in. Del answered immediately, growling down the phone. He couldn't deal with constant calls; he had to think of his next move with Milo. There was nothing else for it. He pressed the answer button, snarling down the phone.

'Listen Claudia, I don't know what Bunny has told you, but I don't need you chewing me frigging ear off as well. Stay out of it, doll, okay? Just leave me alone and don't call my fucking phone. And that goes for both you and her. Is that clear?'

'Bunny's been shot.'

Silence.

'Del? Did you hear me? Bunny's been shot.'

'Del? Del? Listen to me. Del?'

Del began to shake with shock. He put the phone down on Claudia and held it close to his chest, hearing it ring. Feeling it vibrate against his heart.

The phone continued to ring over and over as he got in his car and began to drive, heading almost blindly for London.

At the traffic lights, he swerved off the road to a sound of horns. He grabbed the phone, slamming it against the dashboard. Both hands clung onto the steering wheel as he bent forward, his head leaning on the wheel. Del's whole body trembled. He gripped the wheel tightly, desperate to stop himself going into spasms.

The phone rang again. Del slowly raised his head, staring at it as if it was his personal Kryptonite. Eventually he reached across, scraping it along the dash. He swallowed, bringing the phone up to his ear.

'Just tell me. Is she dead?'

Del slowly pushed open the heavy frosted-glass doors. The scene that greeted him was calm and serene, the polar opposite of how he was feeling. He looked around. A metal hospital bed sat centre stage. Racks of machines and screens sat on the shelving units that hung either side of the bed by steel chains attached to the ceiling.

A variety of clear tubes and multi-coloured electric wires were draped neatly between the bed's medical equipment and the wall. And in the middle of the bed lay Bunny. Still and pale, her blonde hair matted and wrapped up to the side, her eyes shut, without a flicker of movement. The only movement came from the trickles of blood running down the many tubes, collecting in one of the several plastic bottles hanging under the bed. The smell of iodine was thick in the air. A long anglepoise lamp cast a yellow glow over Bunny's pale face. But to Del, Bunny looked more beautiful than she'd ever done. His very own sleeping beauty. The love he felt for her in that moment, as he stood listening to the sounds of the beeping monitors, almost overwhelmed him.

'You can talk to her. She'll probably be able to hear you.' The small grey-haired intensive care nurse smiled at Del warmly.

'Will she be okay?'

Earnestly the nurse answered, talking in a whisper. 'Yes, I believe she will. It seems the car she was driving was bulletproof so thankfully it took the brunt of the bullets. The ones which actually hit her missed her vital organs. They went into her sides, arms and lower back. We don't think there'll be any lasting damage, but we won't know for certain for a couple of days. But the doctors seem optimistic.' The nurse paused as Del went to sit down by the bed. 'If it wasn't for the car she'd be dead.'

Del waited for the nurse to walk away, then took Bunny's hand in his. 'Bun. I don't know if you can hear me, babe. But I'm sorry, doll. Not just for this, for everything. I've been a proper mug. I never meant any of the stuff I said. You know what I'm like; a bleedin' hot-head. Always blowing off. When Claudia called...' Del stopped and exhaled, his emotions getting the better of him. It took a couple of minutes to find his composure and when he continued, Del was aware his voice was cracking. 'When Claudia called to say you'd been shot, me whole world stopped. I can't imagine life without you. You gave me a right scare. I don't know what I'd have done if ... if...'

Del couldn't continue. He rested his head on Bunny's hand.

'Daddy!' Star ran up to Del, flinging herself on him and holding on for dear life. Del looked at his daughter, an exhausted smile on his face. 'I missed you, sweetheart.'

'I missed you too. I tried calling but you never answered. Did you lose your phone?'

Del gazed at Star. His eyes filled with tears as he realised she was giving him a way out from admitting he'd been a shitty dad. An arsehole. He nodded, ashamed of himself. 'Yes Star. Yes baby, I lost my phone.'

'That's what I thought.'

Claudia stood behind Star and Del. She bristled slightly at how easily Del had been let off the hook with Star. He hadn't seen the hurt in Star's face or listened to her cry. He was a chump. But then most men were, though she supposed in fairness to Del he was better than most of the chumps Claudia had met in her time. She pursed her lips, wanting to make sure Del read her disapproval of the situation.

'Del.'

'Claudia.'

'What about the baby? Will the baby be all right?' Star stood with her back to her dad, kissing her mum's hand.

Del started. 'What you talking about, sweetheart?'

'The baby, Daddy. Mummy's baby.'

Del turned Star gently round. He scanned her face. 'Star. I really don't know what you're talking about.'

'Come on, Star. Let's go and get a drink.' Claudia gestured to Star, wanting to break up the conversation. As Claudia placed her hand on Star's arm, Del brushed it lightly away. 'No, Claudia. I want to hear this. Star, tell me what it's all about.'

Star leant forward to Del's ear, cupping her hand round her mouth as she whispered very loudly, 'Mummy's got a baby in her tummy. I heard her talking to Claudia about it.'

Del immediately looked at Claudia, who looked uncomfortable. 'Well? Claudia?'

Claudia shrugged. 'I dunno.'

Moving Star out of the way, Del stood up, scraping back the chair on the highly polished floor. He walked to Claudia and grabbed her arm, not too hard, but hard enough to let her know he meant business. Pulling her out of Star's earshot, Del stared at Claudia. 'Don't mess about. If she is pregnant, I need to know.'

'I ... I...'

Del shook Claudia's arm. 'Claudia, *tell* me.'

'Yes. But she said you already knew. She was

angry with me because she thought I'd told you.'

Del looked bemused. 'Why the hell did she think that?'

'Don't ask me. She said you'd had a phone call about it. So I guess she put two and two together and came up with five. Apparently that's what you were arguing about when you ... well let's say it how it is, shall we? When you smashed the place apart.'

Del let go of Claudia as he thought. Arguing about it? They hadn't been arguing about that, they'd been arguing about Teddy. Del glanced over at Star who was busy playing with Bunny's hair. Oh Christ. It hit him. They'd both been talking about separate things. He'd been talking about her shagging Teddy Davies and she'd been talking about the baby. That's why she'd said she was happy about it. What had he done? Fuck.

'Claudia, have you told the doctor she's pregnant?'

As she shook her head, Del Williams charged out of the door.

36

Milo Burkov paced up and down the tiny flat, looking around him. At one time he was sure it'd been a decent place but it was clear the present occupier had let it get messed up. A bit like the occupier himself. Milo sighed, bringing his foot back to a kicking position. He booted as hard as he could, ignoring the squeal of the recipient on the floor.

Teddy rolled about in agony. He held onto his stomach, but realised it was his side that was aching. In fact, his whole body was in excruciating pain. He looked up just as Milo crouched down, grabbing hold of his hair.

'I'll ask you again. How did Del's girlfriend end up at the house?'

'I don't know. I swear.'

Milo stared at Teddy. He'd always thought he was a disgusting slug of a man. He slapped Teddy on the face.

'I want the truth, Detective.'

'I did what I said I'd do. I gave you Del on a plate. It's not my fault Bunny showed up instead.'

'So if I speak to Bunny, she'll tell me you had nothing to do with her being there?'

Now this was a tricky one. Teddy gazed at Milo through his one good eye. If he said yes and Milo *did* go and speak to Bunny, he'd be in more shit than he was already. He chewed on the inside of his mouth. If he admitted he'd said something to Bunny now, he was terrified what Milo might do to him. There was nothing else for it. Teddy closed his eyes and pretended to faint.

Milo had no time for cowards. He didn't know any Russian men who behaved like women.

Finishing off his cigarette, Milo pulled out his phone from his jacket. It rang and was answered almost immediately.

'Hello?'

'Del. It's Milo. I wanted to give you my condolences. *All of this is a huge mistake.'*

Del couldn't believe what he was hearing. '"*A huge mistake*"? You shot my woman. That ain't a mistake to me. That's a fucking tragedy.'

'And you shot one of my men. I think that makes us even, don't you?'

Del shouted down the phone. 'No, not by a long way, pal. It's only just getting started. You brought my family into it. You crossed the fucking line, Milo.'

Milo's voice was acidic. 'Don't let your ego get in the way, Del. I'm letting you off the hook. I'm giving you one last chance. We can draw a line under this. Shake hands and move on... You'd be very unwise to make us your enemy, Del.'

'No, Milo. *You'd* be very unwise to make *me* your enemy. This isn't over.'

'If that's what you want.'

'It is.'

The line went dead and both men looked at their phones, wondering which one of them had hung up first.

Del's face lit up as he saw Bunny's eyelids flicker. He watched her as she opened her eyes slowly, adjusting to the light and her surroundings as if she hadn't opened them in a hundred years.

'Bun. Bun. It's me. You've been shot. You're in hospital.'

A flat reply came. 'I know, Del.'

Del stood up, concerned, leaning over Bunny who kept her gaze fixed on the ceiling. 'The doctors say the baby's going to be all right. Why didn't you tell me? I mean I know you *thought* I knew, but

I thought you were talking about something else. I couldn't be happier, Bun. You and me. Well, you, me, Star and this little one.'

Del placed his hand on Bunny's stomach. She turned her head towards Del, wincing slightly at the pain as the drugs began to wear off, her eyes full of tears. 'No Del. There is no you and me.'

'What? You don't know what you're saying. It's all that medicine they've put in you.'

'No Del, I know exactly what I'm saying. You put our daughter at risk by your business deals and the men you associate with. I don't want to be with a man like you.'

'But they were never after her. It was me they were after.'

'But it's still me lying here, not you.'

'I ... I just mean, she's okay ain't she?'

Bunny's voice was full of scorn. 'And that makes it all right does it?'

'Of course it's not all right but she was never in any danger.'

'There you go again. Thinking you know everything. Telling me it'll be all right.'

Del sighed. He hadn't imagined that the moment Bunny woke up she was going to chew his ear off.

'But it will, Bun. Trust me.'

'Stop it. Stop telling me to trust you. I can't. I won't.'

'Well I'm *saying* it'll be fine. Star will be fine. I'll sort it.'

'How can you possibly say that? You don't know what's going to happen. Do I need to remind you that I've been shot? What if I'd had Star in the car? Would you still be saying the same thing then?'

Del exhaled heavily, trying to keep his patience. He knew Bunny was right, but he hated her being so angry with him. He'd been so worried about her; terrified she was going to die. Was it so bad to want her to be happy and try to reassure her everything would be all right? Instead of Bunny being as pleased to see him as he was to see her, she'd woken up and launched into one. *Women.* Even in intensive care she still managed to moan and do his head in.

'Bun, listen.'

'No, *you* listen, Del. I want you to take Star to Marbella. Get her out of the way for a while.'

Del looked stunned. 'I can't do that.'

'Don't give me that.' Bunny stopped. She was exhausted, drained and hurt and unable to think about what a narrow escape she'd had. She was furious with Del, but all she cared about at the moment was Star. It was always about Star. Her reason to keep on fighting.

'Bunny…'

'No, I want you to go. Please *go.*'

'I think you better do as your wife says.'

Del gave the nurse a steely stare as he thought better of ironing him out against the wall, then stomped towards the exit, purposely talking in a raised voice.

'Don't worry, I'm going, pal. And for your information she ain't my wife – but she might as well be 'cos I can't really tell the difference between the frigging pair of them. Do yourself a favour mate and stay well clear of fucking women.'

265

37

Alan Day reached for his nitrolingual spray. His chest was tight and to make matters worse he'd been suffering from a bad case of constipation. Papers and court documents were piled up on his desk with empty gum and Starburst wrappers scattered around, accompanied by coffee-stained mugs.

His mobile rang. It was Del. He answered, his oily court manner breaking through. 'Del. How can I help you?'

'I need you to sort out some papers for a passport.'

'Another one?'

'Listen, Alan, I pay you to sort things out for me. I don't pay you to be asking me questions.'

'Whatever you say.'

'I want to sort out a passport for Star. I'm taking her to Marbella.'

'No problem. You can come to my office any time.'

'Alan. I pay you enough to come to me. I'll probably be at the hospital or at home. Give me a call when you're on your way ... oh and Alan, don't make me wait.'

Alan held the phone to his ear long after Del had hung up, wondering if any of it was worth it.

Star couldn't believe what she was hearing. It was

turning out better than she had hoped. Her Dad was back. Her mum was all right – but best of all, she was going on holiday. Just her and her Dad. Cushty.

'I'm going to pack all me treasures and me spy-glass in case I see some pirates. Do you reckon we will, Dad?'

Del tried to show the enthusiasm Star deserved, but his mind was on other things; certainly not on pirates.

'I don't know, doll. We'll see.'

Del watched Star's face drop. She was such a good kid. She'd coped so well with Bunny in hospital. At first she'd panicked, going into hysterical crying when they'd told her, but once he and Claudia had reassured her that Bunny was going to be fine she'd cheered up, seeing it, as she did everything, as an adventure.

He tried again, trying to conjure up some excitement.

'Okay, I can't promise you pirates but I can promise you a good time. So why don't you go and get everything you need while I make a few calls.'

Star clapped her hands together and Del's gaze followed her as she skipped out of the room. He didn't know what Bunny was thinking. How was he expected to take her to Marbella when there was so much happening here?

His phone rang. Shit. It was Edith. He hadn't even thought about her. What the hell was he going to say to her?

Alan Day hated hospitals. He hated waiting – and

if he had known the woman who kept staring at him for no good reason, he most likely would have hated her as well. He turned to her, irritated.

'So you've no idea how long he's going to be?'

Claudia stared. She hadn't been able to take her eyes off this man since he'd walked in. He'd introduced himself as Alan but there was something so familiar about him.

'Why don't you call him? I've got his number if you want to try him.'

Alan went into barrister mode. 'I think you can safely deduce that not only do I have his number, but I've also tried calling him to see when and *if* he was going to arrive.' Turning away, Alan rolled his eyes.

'You don't have to do that.'

Alan looked taken aback. He blushed slightly. 'Do what?'

'Roll your eyes at me. I ain't done nothing to you. You asked me a question. I answered it. Show a bit of respect, mate.'

'I didn't roll my eyes.'

Claudia shook her head. 'I ain't stupid.'

Alan gave a tight smile. His face said it all.

Half an hour passed, and there was still no sign of Del. Alan looked at his watch. He really needed to get going. He was meeting another client on the other side of town soon.

Alan stood up and walked over to Bunny, who was still sleepy from the painkillers. She looked up, startled to see him.

'Bunny, I'm afraid I have to go. I've got another

client I need to see, so can you give my apologies to Del? I'm going out of town tomorrow. I'll be back the next day but that means I won't be able to get these papers signed for your daughter.'

'For Star?'

'Yes, he wanted me to sort out a passport so he could take her to Marbella.'

'Can't I do anything?'

'Well, you could sign the papers, but I have a feeling Del wants to do it himself.' Alan stopped. 'Sorry. Do you mind if I sit down? I feel a bit light headed.'

Alan day began to unbutton his shirt. He smiled at Bunny as she watched him, wide-eyed. A strange feeling came over her. Cold panic. She turned her head away quickly. Sweat began to appear on her forehead. 'Nurse! Nurse! I think I'm going to be sick.'

Alan reached for a hankie from his pocket, hastily passing it to Bunny. He stepped back as the nurse rushed across and drew the curtains round Bunny, then pulled a face as he listened to her start to vomit.

'I'll sign it.' Claudia stared hard at Alan.

'Excuse me?'

'I'll sign the papers for Star.'

'You?'

'Is that a problem?'

Alan gazed at Claudia, looking at her lazily. This place was making him feel queasy and all he wanted to do was get out of there. Screw Del – if he wasn't going to bother turning up, he wasn't going to bother worrying about who signed the papers. 'I suppose not.'

Alan took the papers out of his briefcase.

'Just sign here.' He handed his pen to Claudia. Slowly, almost trance-like, she moved towards him, her brain beginning to work overtime. She grabbed the pen and scrawled her name, passing it straight back to Alan. He gave a quick glance at Claudia, who still hadn't taken her eyes off him, and leaned over the paperwork as Claudia watched him sign his name.

Her eyes traced the flamboyantly written signature.

Claudia began to back away, her breathing becoming shallow. Walking backwards she shook her head, muttering inaudibly under her breath. Alan waved the paper in front of her. She could see his mouth moving but couldn't hear the words he was saying.

'You need to take them to give to Del.' Alan's face was lined with annoyance. He waved the papers again, shoving them into Claudia's chest before marching out of the intensive care unit.

Claudia didn't move for a moment. She clutched the papers against her body, leaning her weight against the wall.

'Are you all right?' The nurse looked at Claudia with concern. 'Would you like to sit down?'

Claudia's voice was breathy. 'I have to go... I have to go.' Without saying goodbye to Bunny, Claudia hurried out.

38

Edith was beside herself with fury. Nothing was helping to calm her. Not her favourite tipple of gin, not the handmade chocolates from Selfridges, and certainly not seeing Alfonso Garcia's smug face. On top of which, Del – the cause of her fury – wasn't answering the phone.

She'd been to the bank in Marbella expecting to withdraw some money; not much. Twenty thousand pounds. Twenty measly thousand pounds from her account. It wasn't much to ask for, but the bank teller, with her perfect English, had tapped away on the computer and pulled a sympathetic face. *'I'm sorry, Mrs Williams, you haven't got the funds in there.'*

Edith had known it was a mistake. *'Look again.'*

'Mrs Williams, I can see the balance here.'

'I don't fucking care if you can see the man in the frigging moon darlin'. I know the funds are in there.'

The manager had eventually been called, a po-faced man who walked as if he had something sharp sticking up his arse. He'd taken Edith to one side and explained all too clearly that they'd had a phone call to limit her weekly funds and cancel all her cards. Edith had spat her disgust, shouting and screaming abuse at the manager, to no avail – and all in front of a smirking Alfonso, who'd been demoted to driver.

'Then give me my weekly fund.'

The manager, sick of Edith by now, had delighted in putting one hundred and eighty euros in her hand.

'*What am I supposed to do with that?*'

With a glint in his eye, the manager had smiled at Edith and told her, '*I couldn't possibly say.*'

Standing by the pool in the villa, Edith wondered how it'd all gone so wrong. By rights she should be sipping martinis while looking out over the Marbella hills and playing the grieving widow, but instead she had less than one hundred and fifty pounds in her pocket and one very alive husband.

'Do you want me to get you something?'

Edith swivelled round and glared at Alfonso. 'This is all one bleedin' joke to you, ain't it?'

'Just doing my job like you asked me to.' Alfonso's beady eyes danced. Edith's humiliation in the bank was something he'd played over and over again in his head. It didn't come close to what she'd done to him, but it had still felt good.

Edith screamed hysterically. 'No, I don't want bleedin' anything – unless of course you know of a way of putting my husband in his place.'

Alfonso amused himself with his own insincerity. 'Now, I could've sworn you said it was sorted, Edith. Maybe that's me getting my wires crossed.' He grinned nastily. Edith leapt towards him. 'Get that bleedin' smile off your face.'

'You're the boss.'

Edith lost control of herself completely and she clawed at Alfonso, drawing blood on both cheeks. He touched his face, staring at the drops of blood on his fingers.

'That was a very silly thing to do, Edith.' Alfonso turned and walked back towards the villa, a sly smirk breaking out on his face.

Edith knocked back the gin in front of her, which was now warm thanks to the Mediterranean sunshine. She knew there must be something she could do to turn around her fortunes, but the problem was, she just didn't know what.

39

'Bingo.' Claudia got up from her bedroom floor, leaving her red shoe box of papers open as she clasped a handful of documents. She hurried out of her room and along the corridor to Del's upstairs office. Without knocking, she barged in, using her foot to push open the door.

'What the...?' Del sat at his desk staring at Claudia, his phone call interrupted by the intrusion. 'Listen, something's just come up. Can I call you back?' Del slammed down his mobile, glaring at Claudia. 'What the hell do you think you're doing barging in here?'

'You mustn't have anything more to do with him.'

'What?... What the hell are you talking about?'

Claudia stammered, her thoughts running faster than her unplanned speech. 'That man ... Alan Day. You can't have anything to do with him.'

Del looked at Claudia as if she were mad. His

shock at her bursting into his office was replaced by anger. 'Who the fuck do you think you are, coming in here and talking shit? Get out! Get out of my fucking house.'

Claudia stood her ground, even though her voice was trembling and tears were streaming down her cheeks. 'This ain't your house. It's Bunny's – and besides, I ain't going anywhere until you listen to me.'

Already in a foul mood, Del spoke through gritted teeth.

'I don't care whose fucking house it is. Whilst she's in hospital, *I'm* in charge. Now get out of this house before I physically remove you.'

Del moved towards her, but was stopped by another outburst by Claudia. 'That man, Alan Day, got my daughter's killers off.'

Del was taken aback but his anger was still present.

'Well I'm sorry to hear that, I really am, but what the fuck has that to do with *me?*'

Claudia shouted back, 'It's got *everything* to do with you.'

'Listen darlin'. You're not making sense. I'm trying to keep my patience here but you're pushing it. Say what you have to say, then *get out.*'

'It is to do with you!'

Del looked bewildered. Voice raised, he said, 'What the frig are you talking about, woman? How is this to do with me?'

'Because Bronwin's my daughter.'

Del looked baffled as he yelled back at Claudia, 'Who? Who the fuck is Bronwin?'

'Bronwin is Bunny. Bunny's my daughter.'

Claudia walked over, throwing the old newspaper clippings down on Del's desk. As he looked at the headlines he reeled in horror. *Suspected Child Killers Walk Free*. She slammed down the copy of Star's passport papers, followed by the document she'd signed all those years ago when she'd been forced to give up Bunny in the hospital. The two signatures, one faded, one newly written, were identical. Alan Henry Day.

Del looked up at Claudia's face, then down to what lay on his desk, then up once more to Claudia. He crushed the papers in his hand. Shaking with rage, he bellowed, 'Get out! Get of my fucking house!'

It was dark and Claudia sat beside Bunny, who was sleeping. The nurses' work-station lamp glowed, giving a dim light to the private side room. Claudia shook her head as her eyes dropped closed. She was tired. It was hot, and the chair was comfortable; a sure way of putting her to sleep.

But just as she was about to drift off, Bunny opened her eyes. Claudia smiled. 'Hey baby. I hope I didn't wake you? I was just trying to shake me bones from falling to kip.'

'You look tired.'

Before Claudia could answer, Del charged into the intensive care unit and marched towards Bunny and Claudia. 'Well, this is cosy. Mother and daughter.'

Bunny looked shocked and glanced at Claudia.

'When were you going to tell me, hey? Oh, didn't she tell you she let it slip?'

Claudia looked down, twisting her hands nervously. 'I'm sorry, I…'

Bunny continued to stare at Claudia, astounded. Unable to take the scrutiny, Claudia spoke rapidly, desperate to explain herself. 'The man: Alan. It's him, Bunny. Alan Day. Del's lawyer. The lawyer who got them animals off.'

Bunny's face drained. She picked up the handkerchief given to her by Alan, her fingers touching the blue embroidered initials – AD – as Del continued, furious.

'I don't even know who she fucking is anymore.'

'Don't talk about her like that. Like she ain't here.'

Del sneered at Claudia. 'It's a bit late now to play the caring mother card.'

Claudia visibly recoiled. 'She's still the same person.'

'How is she? Her name's *Bronwin*. Not Bunny. *Bronwin*. How does that make her the same person?'

'Didn't it ever cross your mind she had a proper name? No one's *actually* called Bunny.'

Del raised his voice slightly. 'In her passport, her name says, *Bunny*. Bunny Barker.'

'In *your* passport – or should I say *passports* – it has a variety of different names, depending who you need to be that day.'

'That's different, and you know it is.'

'So is this. You should've asked her.'

'So now it's *my* fault for not asking. I'm the one who's been mugged off here.'

Claudia snapped. 'Don't be so stupid. This was never about you, Del.'

'Really? For the past eight years or so me missus

has lied to me and so have you, then you have the front to say it's not about me?'

Claudia tried to appeal to Del. 'It wasn't a lie.'

'What would you call it?'

Claudia shrugged her shoulders. 'I dunno ... anyway, you can talk. You've got a wife over in Spain who doesn't know the half of it.'

'Not the same.'

Claudia's voice was full of sarcasm. '*Sure* it isn't.'

'Alan Day was one of the men in the woods.'

Both Del and Claudia turned to look at Bunny, who'd they'd partly forgotten about amidst their squabbling. It was Del who spoke, his tone hard. 'What?'

Bunny mumbled, 'His shoes. His shiny shoes.'

Del shook his head. He didn't know what the fuck Bunny was on or what she was talking about, but he didn't want to.

'This is doing my nut in. I'm going home to sort out Star. I've got to pack for tomorrow.'

Claudia spoke up. 'Do you want me to help?'

Del swivelled round. 'You stay away. You stay away from me and stay away from my daughter.'

As quickly as Del had charged in, he left. Claudia blinked away the tears. The sense of being a source of constant disappointment to Bunny began to overwhelm her.

Picking up her carrier bag, her deep feeling of shame didn't allow her to look at Bunny as she spoke. 'I'm going to go home now, but I'll see you tomorrow.'

Claudia hurried towards the exit, wanting to get out of the room before her emotions got the better of her. As she went to push open the door, Claudia heard Bunny whisper the word she'd hadn't heard for so many years.

'*Mum*... Wait.'

The tears distorted Claudia's ability to see properly, but she nodded her head as Bunny stretched out her hand for Claudia to take.

Wiping her eyes, Claudia walked over to Bunny and reached into her carrier bag. 'I brought something for you, but I didn't know whether to give it to you or not. But here you go...'

Within a second of seeing what Claudia had for her, Bunny's face crumpled. She brought up her hand – the thin drip line attached to it – and covered her face. She sobbed, deep and hard.

Eventually her crying stopped, and Bunny gazed at Claudia. She smiled, her voice choking back more tears.

'Mr Hinkles.' It was her childhood teddy bear. 'Where did you get him from?'

'I've always had him. I kept everything I could of yours. Remember when you first found me after you ran away from those people? I think you'd just turned sixteen?'

'Sort of.'

'Well, don't you remember you wanted to throw him away? Said he was for babies.'

Bunny gave a tiny smile as she looked at a very tatty Mr Hinkles. 'No, I'd forgotten all about him. But you kept him.'

'You're not angry with me?'

Bunny grabbed Claudia's hand. 'No, Mum. I never was.'

'I don't deserve you, Bunny.'

'Bronwin. It's okay, you can call me Bronwin.'

Claudia collapsed on the chair. 'I know we never talk about what happened all those years ago, but they told me it was for the best. They said you'd be better off with them. That's why I signed the papers. They didn't really give me a choice.'

Bunny spoke gently to Claudia. 'I know they did, Mum. I know. They lied to you and they lied to me.'

Claudia's voice was edged with panic again. 'If I'd known they weren't going to let me see you I would never have agreed, I swear. But you were okay though, weren't you, Bron? Tell me you were okay.'

Bunny stared at her mother. The woman she always called Claudia. She saw her eyes, frantic, desperate for reassurance. Desperate to be able to sleep at night, to know that the choice she made all those years ago when she was really only a kid herself, had been the right one.

Bunny knew her mum would be unable to take the truth of what had really happened to her within the countless care and foster homes, so she smiled. The feigned smile she gave to her punters and some of her foster carers; the same feigned smile she'd given to Alan Day when he and his friends had *visited* her time after time at the children's home run by Dr Berry, forcing her to do things she wouldn't allow herself to re-member.

'Yes, Mum. I was fine. Everything was fine.'

'Really? You ain't just saying that, Bunny, 'cos I know what those places can be like? I told you what happened to me when I was a kid in them and the idea that stuff like that...'

'Mum. It was fine.' Bunny smiled sadly, knowing it had been far from fine.

40

'*Now remember, Star, no wandering off.*' It was Star that spoke these words as she stood at the hospital bedside, imitating her mum. Bunny laughed, feeling a slight pain in her side as she did so.

'I'm not that bad, am I Star?'

Star nodded her head vigorously. 'Yes!'

'Well at least you're taking notice of me.'

Star's face turned serious. 'You will be all right with me and Dad gone, won't you?'

Bunny took in her daughter's face. The idea of her daughter going away hurt more than any bullet wound, but it was for the best. All that mattered was that Star was safe. Happy and safe.

'I'll be fine. Don't worry about me. Not only have I got the doctors to look after me, I've got Claudia.'

'And the baby? Will Claudia look after the baby in your tummy as well?'

Bunny nodded, twinkles of love shining from her eyes.

'Oh yes, Claudia won't let anything happen to the baby.'

Star shrugged her shoulders, up to her ears in excitement. She was going to miss her mum, but she was so excited about her new adventure she could hardly contain herself.

From her hospital bed, Bunny could see Del lingering outside the door. He didn't come in or even acknowledge her, but she was grateful he'd brought Star to say goodbye.

'You better go now; Daddy's waiting. Come and give me a kiss.'

Star held onto Bunny, who held on just as tightly, making the moment last as long as they could.

'Now, young lady. You look after yourself won't you? And look after your dad as well. Call me and tell me all about Spain. I love you, Star.'

'I love you too, Mummy.'

'That looks like me, Daddy, don't it.' Star Barker-Williams sat next to her Dad in the front seat of his Range Rover. Absent-mindedly, Del glanced across to see what his daughter was talking about, whilst also deciding whether or not to cut up the prick in the Porsche.

'Mmm? What does, darlin'?'

'This. Is it me, Daddy?'

'What, baby?'

Star tutted. 'You ain't listening, Dad. Look.'

Slowing down on the Strand to see what Star was showing him, Del turned his head. In her hands she held a newspaper clipping. The one Claudia had slammed on his desk and he hadn't bothered looking at. Del took it, placing it on the steering wheel as he tried to look at it at the same time as keeping his eyes on the road.

'Where did you get it?'

Star shrugged her shoulders, knowing full well

281

where she'd got it from. She'd found it on the floor of her dad's office when she'd been poking around, trying to find more treasures for her box. She hadn't read what the cutting had said because she'd heard Claudia come in, so she'd tucked it away in her box.

'I put it in me treasure box. See, I brought my box with me in case I see pirates – I might need some of my things...'

Star proceeded to pull other bric-a-brac out of her box as Del stared at the newspaper article. The photograph *did* look like Star. A mass of blonde hair. Big blue eyes. A button nose. But underneath the photo wasn't Star's name, it was Bunny's. *Bronwin Barker – Child Gives Evidence in Sister's Murder Trial*.

'Dad, ain't you going to move?' Star's urchin face looked at her dad as the traffic lights turned green. Del looked down again at the photo, realising where he'd seen a picture of Bronwin as a child before. He needed answers and was going to stop at nothing to get them.

'Yes darlin', but first, Daddy's got something he needs to do.'

To a cacophony of horns, Del Williams skidded his Range Rover into yet another U-turn.

The sight of Alan Day sitting on the toilet with his trousers around his ankles as he spoke on his mobile was almost laughable, if the situation wasn't so serious.

Alan looked up, astounded at the sight of Del standing by the door.

'Listen, Julian, I've got to go. But I've told you

282

before, there's nothing more to say.' Alan put down the phone, reaching across for the toilet paper.

'Client?'

'Something like that… How did you get in? The office is supposed to be locked… Anyway, do you mind?'

Del's tone was sardonic. His eyes glinted coldly.

'Not at all, pal.'

Alan went to get up from the toilet.

'No, I want you to stay sitting on the khazi, Alan. That's where a shitcunt like you deserves to be.'

Alan rubbed his chest. He could feel it getting tight again. 'What's this about?'

'I thought you would've known, Alan.'

'I haven't a clue what you're talking about.'

'Bronwin. Bronwin Barker.'

Alan shook his head, anxiety beginning to wash over him.

'Sorry, you've lost me.'

Del raised his voice. 'Then let me jog your fucking memory.' Del pulled out the newspaper clipping from his coat pocket and shoved it into Alan's face, almost knocking him off the toilet. Del's face sneered in hatred. 'You stink, mate. Every single part of you stinks.'

Alan glanced at the newspaper then up at Del, a glint of defiance in his eyes. 'I don't know what you want me to say. I defended them. Everyone has a right to a defence whether they're guilty or not guilty. I do my job and I do it well. I'm one of the best. Let's face it Del, that's why you come to me; because I can get you off. I don't see you complaining when the jury says "not guilty" for you or any of your men. So I don't see the problem. What's this really about?'

Del stood and clapped slowly. 'Have you finished? Because that speech right there mate; you almost had me ... almost. The jury might buy it – but I don't. Now, where do you keep them, Alan? Don't move.'

Del walked out of Alan's en-suite toilet, but turned back around as he heard a noise behind him. He turned and gave Alan an icy stare. 'I said, *stay* where you are, Alan.'

Del spoke loudly as he reached the safe. 'Are they in here, Alan?'

Sitting on the toilet, gazing through the crack in the door, Alan could see Del standing by the safe. 'I ... I don't know what you're talking about.'

'Don't you? I think you do. What's the combination?'

'I can't remember.'

'Alan. You know me – and you know when I want something I'll get it. *By any means necessary.*'

Through the crack, Alan watched Del produce a cosh from his jacket pocket.

'Okay. Okay.' Alan blew out hard. He could hardly breathe. 'Pass me my spray. It's by those files.'

Del glanced over to the desk. He walked over and picked up a bottle. 'You mean this spray?'

Alan nodded, gesturing his hand widely. 'Yes ... yes.'

Del looked at it and raised his eyebrows. 'I want the code.'

With his face covered in sweat, Alan struggled

to talk. 'Fine ... 16, 32, 12, 6... Now give me the spray.'

Del punched in the numbers. The electronic safe beeped, clicking open.

Del pulled out everything from inside the safe, throwing the numerous papers and documents on the floor. Then he stopped and closed his eyes. Leaning his head forward onto the cool metal of the safe door for support, he breathed deeply, calming himself before he dared reopen them.

The photograph Del had seen a few weeks ago here in Alan's office wasn't a nameless child. It was Bronwin. *His* Bronwin.

Unimaginable terror was visible in her big blue eyes as a man he didn't recognise did unthinkable things to her. There were other photos. Other children. Other men. And then Del was almost sick. He shook his head. There was Alan. Alan and a small child.

He hadn't thought. Hadn't known Alan was involved like *that*. Defending them, yes. Getting them off, yes. But being a part of it. Actually being a fucking part of it. Jesus Christ. He'd laughed with the man. Gone out to dinner with him and...

It was too much for Del to comprehend. He let out a deep primal scream.

Panting, Del put the photo of Bronwin in his jacket, then he paused, seeing another photograph. But this time it wasn't of Bronwin nor the unknown children; it was of another little girl, a girl who looked familiar.

'Who's this?'

Alan's words were staggered. 'Please ... give me the spray.'

Del put the spray in his pocket, crouching down on his haunches in front of Alan on the toilet. 'I don't think so.' He shoved the photo of the little girl in Alan's face.

Del whispered menacingly. 'Who is she, Alan? I'm going to kill you anyway but you might as well tell me.'

Alan's eyes flickered with fear. 'Julie ... Julie Cole.'

Del stood up. Julie Cole. How did he know her name? Oh fuck. Fuck.

'The girl from Camden? The girl who was murdered recently?'

Alan nodded.

'You killed her?'

'Not me ... not me, I swear... It was ... it was...' As Alan tried to finish his sentence he fell forwards off the toilet; a pitiful sight, his trousers still round his ankles. Del watched as Alan scrunched up his shirt, clawing desperately at his chest with one hand, the other stretching and searching for his phone. Just as his fingers touched his mobile, Del stood on his hand, bending down to pick up the phone, slipping it in his pocket.

The voice was almost inaudible. 'Help me, I'm dying... I'm dying.'

'Then it saves me the trouble of killing you.'

Star looked up at Del as he opened the car door, the warmth and love in her eyes pouring out. 'Everything okay, Dad?'

As Del put the Range Rover in drive he leaned over to kiss Star, trying to erase the horrors from his mind. 'It will be, babe. It will be.'

41

Star danced around in delight, skipping and hopping from one foot to another. She was in heaven. Her heaven. She twirled around, spinning and pretending to catch the cotton-candy clouds.

'I can see one, Daddy. I can see one.' Star stood stiff long enough to stare through the lens of her sailor's spyglass out at the Mediterranean Sea, watching as pirates in sail ships with skull and crossbone flags went by. 'Look, Daddy, look.'

Del smiled, taking the spyglass. He looked through it, seeing only the blue crystal waters of the Med with its yachts and speedboats.

'Did you see them, Dad?'

Del passed it back to Star and ruffled her hair. 'I did, mate. I did.'

Star looked delighted. 'Just wait until I tell Mum.'

Del watched with a heavy heart as Star did cartwheels on the immaculate lawn by the side of his villa. His head was wrecked. He hadn't even had time to think about the Russians properly. The past few days had been a living nightmare. It still wasn't over *and* he didn't know what to do about most of it.

He called Star over. 'Listen, Star, there's something I need to tell you, babe. I should've told you earlier but I didn't know how to tell you. It's just, well ... you know Mummy and I aren't married, well that's because...'

The words stuck in Del's throat as the double doors of the villa swung open. Edith stood there in all her garish glory. She stared at Del, then down at Star, and back to Del again.

Her voice was loud and coarse as she pointed at Star. 'What's that? I hope it ain't what I think it is.'

Del sighed. Things had just got a whole lot worse. 'I want her out of here. Do you bleedin' hear me?' Edith squawked at the top of her voice as Del sat at the kitchen table, knocking back his fourth glass of whisky.

Star lay on her back on the inflatable lounger, her hands submerged in the warm water of the pool, delighting in Edith's loud voice. She could hear everything. This holiday was going to turn out better than she could've ever imagined. Pirates and secrets. She let out a little squeal of joy, then continued to listen.

'Don't frigging go there with me, Edith.'

'Oh that's rich, ain't it? You bring your bastard offspring here and then you tell me not to go there with *you*.'

Del threw his glass against the wall.

'Oh I see, now you're going to start smashing up the bleedin' joint.'

'It's better than putting me fist down your throat. Don't push it, Edith. Have a go at me –

even at Bunny, but you do *not* fucking go there with Star.'

Edith snorted. 'What kind of name is Star? Bunny and Star? What you doing, Del, training them up to be in the movies?' Edith winked at Del, knowing they both knew what kind of movies she was referring to.

'That's it!' Del stood up, flipping the table over in fury. Edith waddled to the other side of the room.

'Don't come near me, Del. Don't you fucking come near me.'

'Oh you'd like that, wouldn't you? But I wouldn't waste my time laying a finger on you; I haven't done before and I ain't going to do it now. I don't need to. I'll just pay someone to fucking do it for me.'

Edith screamed, her strong Cockney accent punctuating the air. 'How can you say that to me, eh? How can you threaten me like that? 'Aven't I always been there for you? 'Aven't I always supported you? Keeping me mouth shut whilst you put it about. And how do you thank me? With a fucking kid.'

Del curled his lip at Edith. 'Well maybe if we'd had kids of our own, I wouldn't have felt the need to have one with someone else, would I?'

'I never wanted kids.'

'Not once we were married you didn't. Once you had the old ring on your finger. But before we were hitched you couldn't stop talking about bleedin' kids.'

Edith sniffed. 'I can change me mind, can't I?'

'You never changed your mind though, did you

Edith? You never had any intentions of having kids. You lied to me. It was all a fat frigging lie from beginning to end. The whole thing. Every month like a muppet I wondered if you'd be up the duff, and every month you weren't. Spending money on tests and Harley Street doctors, trying to find out what was wrong. But fuck all was wrong was it? The only thing wrong was you being on the pill. You mugged me off. But then I suppose if you had got pregnant you probably wouldn't have known who the daddy was anyway.'

Edith had the decency to blush slightly.

'Yes, that's right, I know. Well I know about one of your lovers, anyway. Tell me, Edith – how many more were there? Two? Three?'

Edith's look was supercilious. 'Lots. Lots and lots and lots. And I enjoyed every one of them.'

Del looked at his wife in disgust, then turned and walked away without another word.

'Me Dad says I can have some lemonade if I want some.' Star stood with her hands on her hips as she stared at Edith, who was sitting at the table, sipping a large glass of lemonade.

'There's none left.'

Star crinkled her nose. She didn't like Edith. 'It ain't finished, I can see some in the jug.'

Star reached across to the jug. Edith grabbed her wrist tightly. 'It's not yours. It's mine. So keep your hands off it.'

'But me Dad said I could have some.'

'Well Del's gone out and he ain't here is he? So keep your hands off *my* lemonade.'

Star said nothing. She stared at Edith then turned away and walked out of the kitchen. Edith smiled to herself. Bleedin' kid. She'd show her who the boss was. She took another sip of her drink, certain it tasted sweeter. Happily, Edith settled back down to read her magazines.

'Oi missus.'

Edith turned round in her chair to the sound of Star's voice. She came face to face with Star and a loaded catapult.

'Now don't be silly, put that down. I'll tell your dad when he comes back.'

Star shrugged. 'Tell him, I don't care, 'cos I'll tell him about you.'

Edith's mouth was tight with fury, her cheeks red. 'I said put it down.'

Star gestured her head. 'Not till you pour me a drink.'

'I think you better do what she says, Edith.'

Star jumped in fright as she heard a man's voice behind her. Alfonso Garcia smiled at Star. He walked over to the side, took a spare glass out of the cupboard then walked across to the table, picking up the jug of lemonade. He filled the glass almost right to the top. 'Ice?'

Star grinned. 'Yes please.'

Edith scowled. 'What do you think you're doing, Alfonso?'

'My job.'

Popping a couple of cubes into the glass, Alfonso scowled at Edith. He passed the glass to Star. 'I think it's all right to put your catapult down now. I should've tried that myself. I'm

Alfonso by the way.'

'Star.'

Alfonso put out his hand. 'Nice to meet you, Star. Not all of us around here are quite so horrible. Some of us actually like children.'

He smiled at Star as he walked out of the room, leaving Edith seething with fury as Star winked at her while she sipped her lemonade.

'I don't like her.' Star sat on Del's super-king-size bed playing with the snails she'd found on the wall near the pine trees.

'Who don't you like?'

'Edith.'

'Not many people do like her, honey.'

'She's mean.'

'Yup.'

'Is she *really* your wife?'

Del looked up from his newspaper. 'Someone's got big ears... You ain't angry at me, are you?'

Star looked puzzled. 'What for?'

'For being married to Edith and not to Mummy.'

'Do you love Edith?'

'You're having a laugh ain't you, girl?'

Star smiled. 'Well that's okay then ain't it?'

Del looked at Star, contented. If only other things in life could be so simple. He loved spending time with his daughter. Maybe coming here for a while was for the best. As long as Edith stayed out of his way, not only would it give him head space, it'd allow him to spend time with Star without Claudia or Bunny fussing about. Shit. He didn't want to think about Bunny. The images of

292

her being abused when she was not much older than Star, and images of her and Teddy were burnt into his mind.

'Baby, do you have to put them on the bed; they're all slimy.'

'No they're not. Look, this one's called Alfie and this one's called Teddy, after my friend.'

Del sat up curiously, but it didn't go unnoticed by Star.

'Teddy?'

'Yeah.'

'Star baby. I didn't know you had a friend called Teddy. Who's Teddy, sweetheart?'

Star shrugged her shoulders. She always knew when adults wanted her to tell them something. They spoke all softly and always put down whatever they'd been looking at so they could focus on what they were saying. But she wasn't going to tell on Teddy because Teddy was her friend. Her secret. He'd got her dad to come back like he'd promised so she wasn't going to break her promise to him. She wasn't going to tell her dad.

She knew exactly how to stop him asking.

'Can we talk about Mummy? Mummy and the baby? Maybe we can call the baby Sid?'

Del bristled. 'Why don't we talk about this later, Star?'

'No, I want to talk about it now. Can we call Mummy and ask her?'

'Listen, Star, Daddy's got to go and make some phone calls. Will you be all right here for a while?'

Star nodded. She watched her dad hurry out. Adults could be so silly.

42

Warm tranquil days drifted by in a haze of blue skies and clear oceans. Sailing and making sand-castles. Eating and drinking with long leisurely siestas in-between. The biggest decisions being made were whether to go swimming in the misty mornings or in the midday sun. Both Star and Del hoped the halcyon summer days would never come to an end.

Del had spoken to Bunny only a few times, their strained conversations amidst the Marbella sun casting a shadow on the otherwise bright days.

There'd been no word from the Russians and, for the time being, Del was thankful. He didn't have the energy nor the inclination to deal with Milo. He'd spoken to some of his men back in London and Alan's death wasn't being treated as suspicious. But it didn't make it any easier or less complex. He still didn't know what to do or who to talk to about Alan and his involvement with Julie Cole and Bunny.

Del wanted to forget it but his conscience wouldn't let him. He'd told himself it wasn't really his concern, that it was other people's problem now Alan was dead; he'd done his bit. But as soon as he'd told himself that, the images of horror rose up in his head. The innocence of childhood lost. Unrecoverable stolen lives.

So then Del started to think all over again about what he was going to do, but he was no further forward than he'd been before.

'Hey Dad, look at this.' Star held up a sun-bleached shell with her sandy wet fingers.

'That's pretty ain't it? What you going to do with that, doll?'

'I'm going to paint it and send it to Mum and Claudia. You reckon they'll like it?'

Del dried Star off with the large Ralph Lauren beach towel as she stood, dripping wet and shivering, on the beach. 'I think she'll love it, mate.'

'What are you going to send her?'

Del looked at his daughter. If only it were so simple. There was so much to get his head round he didn't know where to start, and because of that he was no closer to sorting the mess with Bunny – Bronwin – out. Even that. Even the name, it all felt so different now. Everything had changed.

Only a few weeks ago he was in blissful ignorance and now, like flipping Jericho, the walls had come tumbling down.

Turning his attentions back to his daughter, Del stood up, taking Star's hand to walk back along the jetty to his private sailboat – one of two boats he owned and a personal delight of Star's that seemed to hold no bounds.

'I dunno, babe. Let me think about it.'

'You could always send her a poem.'

Del glanced at Star and burst into laughter. 'Can you honestly see me sending your mum a poem?'

Star's forehead creased as she thought about it. She looked at her dad and grinned. 'Yeah, you're right. She'd think you were off your bleedin' nut.'

The harmonious laughter of father and daughter floated into the cloudless sky as Del and Star happily set sail towards the harbour of Puerto Banús.

'Wrap it round a few more times, baby.' Del gestured his head, interrupting his phone conversation to give Star the instructions she needed to tie up the boat properly.

'Is that better, Dad?'

Del looked and put his thumb up to show his approval. Star skipped on the spot. She hadn't known what a good sailor her dad was. In fact, she didn't even know he had a boat. But it didn't matter because now he was teaching her how to sail, and soon she was sure she'd be as good as him.

Since they'd been in Marbella, she'd been sailing every day, and she'd learnt a lot. How to tie up a boat. How to move the sail to make the yacht go in another direction. She even knew some sailing terms. The best term she knew was *ship ahoy*, though her dad said it wasn't really a sailing term, but she didn't care because it sounded good.

'Put that down, Star!'

Star looked up, hearing her dad's urgent tone as she stood on the deck.

'Now!' Her dad didn't often shout but when he did, Star Barker-Williams knew to listen.

'What is it?'

'It's dangerous, that's what it is. It's a flare gun. If you press the trigger and you're pointing it at someone, it can do a lot of damage. Take your eye out.'

'Or your nuts off.'

Del shook his head, taking the flare gun out of Star's hands. Going back to his phone call, he walked away, out of Star's earshot.

'Listen, Burkey, do me a favour will you? Speak to our courier and find out what the lowdown is on the consignment of powder coming in. I don't want to piss anyone off, but I ain't being out of pocket. And Burkey, this is a simple one. No mistakes, eh?'

Del clicked off the phone as another phone call came in. It was Bunny.

'Yes?'

'Is that what we've come to now Del, a *yes*, instead of a hello?'

Del rolled his tongue in his mouth trying not to say what he was thinking. He didn't need his ears chewing off.

Bunny was getting better and he could tell. She still had a long way to go, but the nearer she got to recovery the more distant they were becoming. She was getting stronger, but with it she was becoming harder. Or perhaps that was just him. Perhaps he just needed to tell her what had happened with Alan. What he knew. What he'd seen. But there weren't the words. Well, not any he knew anyway. So instead of talking, he'd retreated and as he retreated, Bunny slipped further away from his reach.

'Listen, is there anything in particular you

want, Bun, because I've got another call coming in?'

Before Bunny's reply came, Del switched over to the other caller. It was Edith. Sometimes Del wondered what he'd done in another life to deserve the shit that was being fanned his way.

'Edith?'

'I need some money.'

'And how is that anything to do with me?'

''Cos you've got your hands on it.'

'We've been over this before, Edith. Many a time. You ain't got any money. It's *my* money darlin', and you ain't getting your nasty paws on it.'

'How am I supposed to live, eh?'

'You get your allowance.'

Edith scoffed down the phone. 'You were always a cunt.'

'And you think calling me a cunt will help your case.'

Edith ignored Del's question. 'I *said*, I want some money.'

'Listen, doll. The weekly grocery bill, I pay for, so you ain't ever going to be out of food. The bills, I pay for, so you ain't ever going to be without electricity. Anything else – *you* pay for. It's not my problem.'

Del cut off the call. It rang again immediately. Angrily, he answered. 'Look, Edith, I've got nothing to say to you.'

'It's Milo.' Del sat down on the deck. So much for no phone calls and getting away from it all.

'Milo.'

'As you decided not to lay it to rest, I'm just

letting you know, I want my cocaine back and I want my money. With interest. Fifty per cent interest.'

Del laughed scornfully, shielding his eyes with his hand from the sun. 'No can do, Milo.'

'Is that your final answer?'

'It is.'

'Then I shall recover it whichever way I see fit.'

The phone clicked off.

The warm evening breeze drifted into the sun room as Edith, Star and Del stared at each other over sticky barbeque ribs and crispy onion rings.

'Would you like me to pass you some more?' Alfonso smiled at Star as he served the dinner to Edith, who'd insisted on joining Del and Star.

'Cheers.' Star grinned. She liked Alfonso, but for some reason she could tell Alfonso didn't like Edith. Though perhaps it was what her Dad had said before – no one liked Edith.

Chewing on an onion ring, Star looked at her Dad. He was drinking. And when he drank, it usually meant he was worried or unhappy, sometimes even both.

The happiness she'd felt this morning in her tummy when they'd sailed around the bay, stopping on a deserted stretch of beach, had disappeared. Star felt anxious. Sad. And she wished her mum and Claudia were there.

Since her dad had talked to some people on the phone this afternoon, he hadn't spoken much. And he hadn't said anything at all to Edith. Not even when she'd plonked herself down at the table and grabbed a handful of ribs.

After Edith had left the table, slamming her plate down as well as the door, Star went to sit on her Dad's knee. His head lolled slightly and his eyes lacked focus as the empty 1972 vintage cognac bottle sat in front of him.

'Dad, do you want to come and see how many stars we can count tonight?'

Del's voice slurred. 'Not tonight, baby. I'm tired.'

'You can look through my spyglass at them if you want.'

Del stroked his daughter's head. His eyes shut, leaving Star feeling very much alone.

43

Del opened one eye, trying to work out where he was; then opened the other one, hoping it'd give him some clarity. It didn't. He lifted his head, regretting it immediately as it began to throb. He winced, seeing for the first time where he was. He was still sitting on the chair. Still in the sun room. Exactly where he'd been last night when he'd decided to drink himself into a stupor.

Putting his head back down on the table, his phone rang. Slowly he raised himself up, cautious not to make any sudden movements. By the time he'd found the opening of his jean pocket, the phone had cut off.

Dropping his head back down on the table with a harder bang than he'd wished for, Del closed his eyes again, only for the mobile to ring again. This time he got to it. He licked his lips, trying to take the dryness away.

'Yes?' The word broke in his throat. He coughed, trying again. 'Yes?'

'It's Bunny.'

Shit.

Del attempted to sound awake. Awake *and* sober. 'Bunny. Hey.' The fewer words, the better.

'I'd like to speak to Star.'

Del rubbed his forehead, wiping away the cold sweat of a hangover. 'Sure.'

'Did I wake you up?'

'No ... no.'

'You sound funny.'

'Do I?'

There was a pause on the other end as Del pulled himself up out of the chair. The whole room swam before him. He leant his weight on the table, trying to ignore the vomit that was beginning to rise in his throat.

Bunny's tone was cold. 'Del, are you there?'

'Yup ... yup. I'm here.'

Another pause, and then the question Del was hoping to avoid being asked. 'Are you drunk?'

He swallowed, closing his eyes as sweet saliva seeped into his mouth. 'No ... no.'

Another pause.

'Just put Star on.'

'Okay-dokey.'

The distance from the table to the sun room door wasn't far, yet Del was dreading having to make the journey. Even though Bunny had refrained from saying anything else, he could sense the growing hostility on the line. Licking his parched lips again, Del spoke with great effort, his head pounding with every word.

'Bun? Why don't I call you back when I get her?'

'Why, where is she?'

Giving up and having to sit down, Del closed his eyes to try to elevate the dizziness. 'She's in her room. I'm on the other side of the house. I won't be long.' Clicking off the phone, Del rested his head back down on the table.

A few hours later, the vibration of the phone on the table woke Del up. Shit, what time was it? Ignoring the phone, he looked at his Rolex. Three-thirty. God, he must have needed that sleep. At least he felt better than he had earlier. The caller rang off, allowing Del to look at his phone. Twelve missed calls. Ten from Bunny. She'd be chomping at the bit, but at least now if she wanted to speak to him, he'd be coherent.

Standing up, Del waited for a second. He smiled. His hangover was gone. He had a slight headache but that was all; surprising, after how much he'd drunk.

He walked out into the pool area, squinting, adjusting his eyes to the brightness. He clocked Edith sprawled out on the lounger under the shade of the pine trees, reading yet another glossy magazine. She looked back at him haughtily.

'Star! Star!'

Walking into the kitchen, Del grabbed an apple, the crisp, sharp taste quenching his thirst.

'Star, honey.'

Del sighed. He walked along the long cool corridors of the villa, then opened her bedroom door. 'Star baby, your–'

The room was empty. Del might've semi-recovered from his hangover but he was in no mood to chase her around.

Del's mood began to darken as he searched the rest of the house. He was tired and hungry. Two things that were certain to make him pissed off. 'Have you seen Star?'

Alfonso shook his head, turning to the other gardener working next to him, who also shook his head. Del marched round the side of the villa, through the gardens and up the outside stairs, finally returning to the pool area.

'Edith, have you seen Star?'

Edith stuffed a sweaty marshmallow into her mouth. She shook her head. 'No.'

Del's heart banged in his chest. Panic rose up in his body as his men ran around the extensive grounds of the villa, calling his daughter's name.

'Sorry Boss, there's no sign.'

'There must be, she can't have just disappeared. You know what she's like; she's probably hiding somewhere. Look again. Go!'

Del shouted, watching his men exchange glances before they separated, each one going in different directions. He felt his phone vibrate. Quickly he pulled it out of his pocket, hoping it'd be Star, calling to say she could see him. Playing hide and seek as she watched, giggling.

He looked at his phone. His hopes quickly dispelled. It was Bunny. He couldn't answer it. Not before he'd found Star. And he would find her. Of course he would…

It was now six-thirty p.m. and Del's hopes of finding Star within the grounds of the villa were diminishing as quickly as his glass of whisky. With each moment, his fear rose; terror paralysed his thoughts as he walked along the marble corridors of his villa. He called out again, partly to himself, partly desperate to continue to hold on to hope.

'Star! Please. Just come out. Daddy's tired … please, baby. I just need to know you're okay.'

At seven p.m. one of Del's men spoke to him. 'Del we need to face it. Star isn't here. We've looked everywhere. We've turned everything upside down. There's nowhere else to look. I'm sorry.'

An hour later, Del leant over the sink. He looked in the mirror, staring at his own reflection. He didn't recognise who he saw staring back. It was almost if he'd aged within the past few hours. His face was drawn, ashen. His eyes were wide, fearful. Bending down, Del splashed his face, his tears invisible to any onlookers as they mixed with the cool water.

A little later, Del stared at Edith who sat at the table as he walked into the kitchen. 'Don't say a word, Edith. Not one fucking word.'

At nine p.m., one of Del's men ran up to him. 'Boss! Boss! We've found something. Boss!'

Del sprang up, and he rushed round to the side of his villa, running towards one of his men.

'Where was she? Where did you find her?'

Del's number four in command looked alarmed.

He glanced around for back up. 'Er ... no Boss, we haven't found her, we've...'

Del grabbed hold of the man, gripping his shirt hard. His words tumbled out as he shouted at the top of his voice. 'Why not? Why haven't you found her? What do I pay you for if you can't find a fucking little girl? My girl...'

Del dropped to his knees in the middle of the lawn. He covered his face, weeping into his hands.

'Take it easy, Del. It's okay, mate.' Fat Man Burke knelt down beside Del. 'We haven't found her, but she's okay. Everything's going to be fine.'

'*How can you say that when you don't know?*'

'Here, look.' Fat Man gestured at the fourth in command to give him what he was holding.

'It's a note ... a ransom note.'

Del snatched it. It simply read; *Four million to have your daughter back. We'll be in touch.*

Del's eyes scanned Fat Man's face. 'The Russians?'

'I think so, but at least we know we'll get her back. She's alive.'

44

Alfonso Garcia knelt on the floor. He cursed under his breath as the stain he was trying to get out of the cream shag rug refused to budge; as did Edith, who stood above him, giving orders.

He glanced to his right, staring at her large,

puffy ankles. He saw the blue veins running up and down her leg, pushing against the red taut skin, and her swollen feet shoehorned into a delicate pair of Jimmy Choo sandals – and every part of him wondered how long it would be until he could change his fortunes around.

He'd come so close to it. So fucking close and then Edith had double-crossed him. The thought sent rage through his body and Alfonso found himself having to breathe deeply so as not to turn and take a chunk out of Edith's ankle.

Managing to hang onto his self-control, Alfonso dipped the hard-bristled scrubbing brush into the bucket of soapy water just as Del walked in, kicking the bucket out of his way and all over Alfonso.

Alfonso flinched, his instinct making him want to jump up and iron Del out. Instead, he gripped onto his wet clothes, wringing out the water in his cheap shirt, pretending it was the neck of either one of the Williams'.

Del swivelled round and grabbed Alfonso by his shirt. 'Are you trying to break my fucking neck, mate?' Fat Man stepped in.

'Take it easy, mate, eh?'

Slowly Del released Alfonso. 'Next time you get in my fucking way I'll lift you off the floor, pal. You hear me?'

Alfonso nodded, hurrying to try to clear up the mess.

'Leave him. He ain't done anything to you.' It was Fat Man Burke.

'No? How about trying to trip me up in my own frigging house?'

'You're tired. You need to get some kip.'

'Don't patronise me, Burkey; you know better than to do that.' Del stopped, catching Edith's eye. He turned to face her, speaking aggressively. 'And what's your boat race looking at, eh? You got something to say to me, girl?'

Without saying anything, Fat Man gestured to both Alfonso and Edith to leave. Once they'd left the kitchen, Burkey, moving the bottle of brandy away from Del, spoke. 'It won't do any good taking it out on the people around you. It won't change things.'

'Maybe not, but it makes me feel a whole lot better.'

'Del...'

'Don't Del me! *Don't* try to make me feel better. It's been two days since Star's been missing and we haven't heard anything yet.'

'We will. We just have to sit it out. It's part of their game.'

The fear was apparent in Del's eyes. 'I just need to speak to Milo. Tell him the money's no problem. He can take it all.' Del pressed redial. The phone rang twice, then clicked onto voicemail.

'Why's he not answering?'

'Patience.'

Del kicked the kitchen cupboard doors, leaving his footprint on the handmade cabinets. He bellowed, giving the gardener who was working by the side of the house a scare.

'How can I have *fucking* patience when those cunts have Star?'

Fat Man shook his head. His heart went out to Del. It was a fucked-up situation, bringing kids into it, but he didn't put anything past foreigners.

The phone rang, and both Del and Fat Man froze for a second, before Del grabbed it.

Bunny. Again. He hadn't spoken to her. He hadn't told her about Star and now she was ringing up to twenty times a day. He'd given all his men instructions not to answer any calls from her either. He couldn't imagine what she was thinking, though it couldn't be any worse than the truth. But he couldn't afford to imagine what she was thinking. He needed to concentrate on keeping sane.

Closing his eyes, Del wondered when the nightmare would end.

Edith stomped down the road. She was sweating and she could feel chafing at the top of her legs. She tried to walk with her legs wider apart but it produced a waddle rather than a walk. Going back to a normal stance, Edith tried to ignore the heat of the burn between her thighs.

The furthest she'd walked for a good few years was a hundred meters. But now Del had refused her access to any of the cars she was forced to walk along the winding roads of the hot Marbella hills. Well, he'd pay for it. All the years. All the humiliation. Oh yes, he was going to pay for it in every way.

Alfonso walked down the quiet road, clenching his fists as he followed Edith at a distance. There was no one about. An opportunity. The perfect opportunity. He could get his own back in the way he knew how. The way Alf Garfield, his alter ego, would do it. And he'd enjoy every moment.

He narrowed his eyes as he followed her, his hand pulling out the flick blade from his pocket. Quick. Sharp and final. He was an expert. No one would know, but he would, and that's what mattered. He would have Edith's blood on his hands – and he would relish every second.

He'd given her every chance to sort him out. But with every turn she'd mugged him off. Making him her sex pet. Making him humiliate himself. Making him believe he'd have a share in the Williams' empire. Then she'd made the worst mistake of her life. She had screwed him over and where he came from you paid a price for it. If it wasn't paid by the greens, it was paid for in claret. Blood.

Alfonso held back for a moment as he watched Edith detour off the main road, across the tiny path and into the woods. He didn't know this side of the hills well, but he supposed it was a short cut down to the village at the bottom. Licking his lips, Alf Garfield followed Edith deep into the pine woods.

Coming to a small clearing, Alfonso flicked open the knife as he stood behind the tree watching Edith. He took a step forward then suddenly stopped, open-mouthed. He smiled at what he was seeing. He could hardly believe his eyes. He put the knife back in his pocket. *This* was going to be better than he'd ever imagined.

45

Julian Millwood stood in the middle of his flat, looking around in disgust at his own mess. The stench from the rotting food left on the plates was worse than ever thanks to the summer heatwave they were having in London.

Large black flies buzzed around the rooms and a trail of mouse droppings littered the kitchen. The stench also wasn't helped by the fact that the toilet had been blocked for the past few days. But as Julian stood in the run-down council flat, he could honestly now say he didn't give a flying fuck. It was no longer his problem. He was out of here and he certainly wasn't going to miss it. Not for one second. Not the flat. Not the area. Not even London.

Picking up his suitcase, Julian walked out of the fiat with a smile on his face, not bothering to lock the door. The crack-heads were welcome to it. As he walked along the stone corridor pulling down his hoodie, not wanting to be seen, he tried Alan Day once more. It rang, then quickly switched over to the familiar oily tones of the defence barrister's voicemail. Damn it. He had to speak to him. Urgently. Hailing a cab on Camden Road, Julian looked at his watch. He didn't even have time to swing by his office. He'd have to try him later. There was one last *favour* he needed Alan to do – only this time it was going to be a big one.

46

At five past two in the early hours of Sunday
morning the phone rang. Del scrambled to answer
it, searching for the phone he'd left on his pillow.
Christ, he must've dropped off to sleep. Something he hadn't wanted to do. His voice was
urgent. 'Hello? Hello?'

'Tomorrow. Seven a.m. Drop the money at the
bottom of *Calle de los Pinos*. Come on your own.
Once the money's dropped off you'll see the girl.'
The line went dead.

'Was it Milo?'

Del snapped at Fat Man. 'I guess. What fucking
difference does it make? As long as Star's returned
safely...' Del trailed off. He paced up and down by
the side of the pool and waved his hands, then
continued with what he was saying. 'He was using
a voice-changer device, so I couldn't tell.'

'Bastard. Fucking cowards that lot,' Burke replied.

Del stood staring at the lights at the bottom of
the pool, mesmerised for a moment.

'You want the men to come with you? We'll be
armed, and if we see anyone we'll shoot on sight.'

Del looked at Burkey and shook his head. His
mouth was dry with nerves. Star was close. It was
almost time to rescue her, to bring her home.

Pushing his fingers on his closed eyes, hoping

311

to avoid the tears spilling out, Del cleared his throat. He took a deep breath, adrenaline rushing through his body.

'No Burkey. I'll go on me own. I don't care about the money. I just don't want any fuck-ups. When we get her home we can think about what we're going to do next.'

'Okay Boss. And Del... It'll be all right.'

'I hope so, Burkey. Christ do I hope so.'

No. It wasn't possible. She was only here yesterday. Panic surged through her body as she saw what was in front of her. She began to run, stumbling forward; holding onto the pine trees for support as her breathing became deep and raspy. It was open. The door was ajar. The lock broken. Edith Williams staggered into the derelict shed. The damp tiny shed she'd kept Star a prisoner in for the past couple of days. It was empty. Star had gone.

47

Star opened her eyes but it didn't seem to make any difference. It was dark and she couldn't see anything. She lay still, until her back began to hurt. As she moved, she heard a voice.

'Hello Star, I've been waiting for you to wake up.' The light was switched on. 'Remember me?'

Star took a short breath as she saw who it was. It was her friend; Alfonso. He'd come to save her.

She was about to run to him but then she stopped. There was something different in his eyes. The way he looked at her. Almost in slow motion, she turned her head to see another man sitting next to him

Alfonso gave a hazy smile. 'This is my half-brother, Star. His name's Julian. He's come all the way from London to meet you. He's been wanting to meet a little girl like you for a long time.'

Alfonso stood up and walked towards Star. He knelt down, taking her hand in his, then stroked it gently, staring into her eyes. 'Don't be afraid, Star. As long as you do exactly as we tell you then you'll be fine.'

'Please let me go home. Me dad will be worried.'

Alfonso shook his head, stroking Star's hair from her face and tucking it behind her ear. 'That won't be possible, Star.'

Star began to shake. Tears rolled down her cheeks. She wrapped her jacket tightly round her as she felt her skin began to crawl. Alfonso put his hand on her lips. 'Shush, Star. Don't cry.' He traced his fingers round her mouth. 'No more crying. Understand?'

Star nodded frantically, her body trying to recoil from Alfonso. 'Good. You better get some sleep, Star. You'll need your rest, because in a few days' time we'll be going on a little journey.'

With a wink, Alfonso got up at the same time as Julian did. They walked to the door, but it was Julian who paused, turning round. He walked back towards Star, licking his lips.

'I almost forgot about your good-morning kiss.'

Star waited until she couldn't hear anything. As quietly as she could, she got off the bed – which wasn't a bed at all. It was a long box with a thin mattress on the top of it.

On tip-toes, she went to the door and put her tiny hand on the door knob, turning it as slowly as possible; terrified to make a sound. She twisted it both ways. Both ways were locked. She had to find a way out. To get back home. Wherever that was. She couldn't even remember how she got here, so how was she supposed to get back?

She tried so hard to remember. Remember something. Anything. But she couldn't. A tear ran down her face, which she quickly brushed away. Alfonso had told her she shouldn't cry and she didn't want them to be cross with her if they came back in.

Sighing, Star tried again to think how she'd ended up locked in the room by Alfonso and the other man with the horrible yellow teeth and bad breath. She shuddered.

All she could remember was her dad not wanting to look at stars with her, Edith talking to her in the kitchen and then and then, yes, she remembered. Edith had come into the garden where she'd been. Wanting to be nice to her. Wanting to talk to her. Wanting her to drink the pink lemonade she'd made for her. She'd drunk it to be polite. But it had made her feel sleepy and that was the last thing she remembered. Bugger.

As Star sat on the edge of the homemade bed

she held her tummy. She needed to go to the toilet. She opened her mouth to call out but snapped it shut as the thought of Julian came into her mind again, almost biting her tongue. Star rubbed her wrists. They hurt. She could see the red and the bruises on them and she didn't want to think about the other bruises, the ones on the inside of her legs. Covering her knees with her dress, Star curled back up on the bed. As she lay down, she felt something hard. She went into her jacket pocket and pulled out her spyglass. She still had it. Hugging it close, Star closed her eyes, dropping into an unhappy restless sleep.

'Keep your hands off her, Julian. That's what we agreed. They won't want her if she's been spoiled and then where will we fucking be? Julian, I'm warning you.'

Julian stared at his half-brother. He hadn't changed. Always telling him what he could or couldn't do. Even years back when they'd discovered they both had the same interest, Alf had told him what to do.

It'd only been by chance he'd discovered his brother's interest when he'd gone in his bedroom looking for any money he might have stashed away. He'd found his stash all right but it hadn't been money. It'd been photos. The same kinds of photos Julian himself had stashed away.

At first it had only been the two of them but as the internet had opened up, so had their world. Like-minded people. Like-minded groups from all walks of life. And it'd been through one of these groups that they'd first met Alan.

Alan had unlocked a lot of doors for them, able to use his position in life to get access to the weak and the vulnerable, as well as the downright naive. And it'd been Alan who'd taken them from just photographs and videos to the real thing.

Julian turned his thoughts away from Alan, whom he still hadn't managed to get hold of, to his brother. 'I brought you in on this, Alf, don't try to play fucking hard ball.'

'No, let's get it straight. You needed a girl for keeps. *I* found you one. I called *you*. I could've kept her all for myself but you know why I didn't?' Julian shook his head as Alfonso stared at him. ''Cos we're family. And family stick together.'

Julian thought of Star again and salivated. 'What harm can it do, Alf? As long as I don't actually put my...'

'No! No! Nothing. You don't go within a few feet of her. You've already been too rough with her.' Alfonso flicked open his knife, growling at Julian in his cockney accent. 'Are you listening, mate, 'cos I ain't going to say it again. Otherwise...' Alfonso trailed off as he held the blade in his hand, not needing to say any more for Julian to understand his intentions.

Alfonso stubbed his cigarette in the ground. Star had fallen into his hands thanks to Edith's greed. If he hadn't followed her, wanting to sort her out, he would never have known she was hiding Star. It was amazing what you found in the woods.

He looked across at Julian. There was no way he was going to miss out on nearly three quarters of a million just because his brother was too eager. Once they'd taken Star to the clients and they'd got the money, they could do whatever they liked. Go to Thailand. The Philippines. There were plenty of places where the government turned a blind eye to men with their tastes. But for now he was going to keep a close eye on his brother and in the meantime he had to think of the best way of getting Star out of Spain.

48

'Star's gone! Star's gone! She's fucking gone.'

Del stared in horror as he saw Edith stumbling out of the pine thicket covered in sweat, her clothes sticking to her body.

'What? What the fuck are you doing here? Get out of here. Get out of here. You'll fucking ruin everything.'

Edith struggled to get out her words as she grabbed hold of Del's arm. 'She's gone, Del.'

He pushed her off. Desperate not to be late. Desperate not to miss dropping the money off and the chance to get his precious daughter back. 'Get off me, woman.' With a huge effort he slung her off, sending her careering into the rocky wall.

Edith grabbed him again. 'No! Stop. Stop.'

His face red with rage, Del exploded.

'I swear to God if you don't get out of here, Edith, I'll knock you out. Now get the fuck off me!'

'But you don't understand. You've got to listen

to me. Star's gone. She's *really* gone. Someone's taken her.'

Both Del and Edith turned at the sound of the scream. They watched as Bunny collapsed into Claudia's arms.

Del stared at Bunny, not knowing where she'd appeared from. He hadn't wanted her to know. He'd wanted to call her when everything was sorted but now she was here, wailing in Claudia's arms. His head was wrecked, although he didn't have time to think about it now. He needed to go to the drop off, but Edith was in his way. 'Move, Edith. I've got to go.'

'Listen to me, you've got to listen. She was there, I swear she was and now she's not.'

'What do you mean she was there? You found her? Where? Edith, you're not making sense.'

'I'm trying to tell you.'

Del's voice was urgent. He shouted at her, fear causing him to look around him, agitated. 'Edith, I have to go. If you've seen Star somewhere...'

'She was in the shed.'

Del shook his head. 'Which shed, where? Quick, show me.'

'She's gone. She's really gone.'

Del looked at Edith as if she were mad. He didn't have time for this. He began to march down the road.

'She's gone – because I took her!'

Del froze. He stared at the ground for a moment, not allowing himself to turn round.

'It was me who took her. I was the one who wrote the note. You were always going to get her back ... but she's not there now.'

For both Del and Bunny, time stood still as the realisation of what Edith was saying sank in. Bunny, still on the ground in Claudia's arms, stared in shocked disbelief as she watched Del, in what seemed like slow motion, grab hold of Edith, then scramble to get his gun out of his leg holster.

Del held the gun, sticking it hard into the side of Edith's cheek, concaving the flesh. He shook his head; words were not enough.

'No Del, she ain't worth it,' Claudia shouted, leaving Bunny on the ground. She ran forward, trying to take the gun off Del, who began to speak in dazed bewilderment.

'You took my baby. You took Star.'

As Claudia tried to stop him, Del's strength overpowered her and with one shove he knocked her away. Turning back round, he pushed Edith into the gravelly ground, his knee digging into her side. His gun still pressing into her face.

'I'm going to kill you for what you've done.'

The sound of Del pulling the trigger back cut through the air.

'No, Del. No!' Bunny's voice was urgent but she managed to keep calm. She shook her head, her eyes focused on Del. She ignored Edith's terrified sweat-drenched face, continuing instead to talk to Del. She reached out her hand to him. Slowly. 'No, doll. Give me the gun ... give it to me.'

Del's face was a mix of rage and tears as his finger rested precariously on the trigger. 'But she took my little girl.'

Bunny bit on her lip, holding Del's wide-eyed, frightened gaze.

'I know she did... I know. And now I need you to help me get Star back. I need you to stay with me. Wherever she is, we'll find her. You and me. But I can't do it without you. I need you to be strong. Star...' Bunny's voice cracked. 'Star needs you to be strong. Now, more than ever. Can you do that? Can you give me the gun?'

'I...' Del trailed off.

'Don't do it, baby; she's not worth it, Del. Just give me the gun.' Bunny's outstretched arm hovered in mid-air. She spoke again, this time the desperation creeping into her voice.

'*Please*, Del. *Please* give me the gun.'

Like a child, Del nodded his head, handing the gun to Bunny in a blur of tears. He sat on the floor, burying his head into his hands.

Letting out a huge sigh, Bunny turned to Edith. 'After we find her, and we *will* find her, after that, Edith, I ain't going to stop him pulling the trigger.'

Fat Man leaned forward, looking puzzled as he whispered into Claudia's ear. 'So let me get this straight. Edith's working for the Russians?'

Claudia, talking just as quietly as Fat Man, shook her head as they sat in the kitchen. 'No. She took Star.'

'From the Russians?'

'No. *She* wrote the letter.'

'For the Russians?'

Exasperated, Claudia raised her voice slightly but immediately lowered it again as Del cut her a stare. 'No! She wrote it to get some money for herself.'

'So how do the Russians come into it?'

Claudia stood up, deciding not to bother answering Fat Man's question. She didn't want to be rude but her nerves were on edge and trying to explain to this man the ins and outs of the horrific situation they found themselves in was too much to deal with.

She walked across the large marble-tiled kitchen to pour herself a soft drink. At any other time she'd admire the luxury of the place with its wide sweeping views overlooking the hills and sea, but as she watched Del and Bunny, sitting, saying nothing, all she could focus on was the pain they were in.

Sitting back down, Claudia handed Fat Man a drink of homemade lemonade. 'Here you are, darling. I put some extra sugar in it. You need to keep your strength up if you're going to help look for...' Claudia stopped, finding she couldn't say her name.

Fat Man smiled sympathetically. He liked this bird. There was something straight up about her. She was old school.

He whispered again to Claudia. 'So how do you come into things?'

'I'm Bron– I mean, I'm Bunny's mum.'

Fat Man nodded, processing the information. 'Well it's nice to meet you, Bunny's mum, though it's a shame it wasn't under better circumstances.'

Claudia, grateful for Fat Man's warmth, smiled back. 'My name's Claudia by the way.'

Fat Man winked. 'And my name's Arthur – but

people call me Burkey.'

Bunny closed her eyes. She couldn't sleep. She almost couldn't think. It was as if her whole life had been building up to this moment. The fear. The guilt. The sense of powerlessness. But more than anything, her inability to care for and keep anyone she loved safe.

She could feel a stabbing pain. Her wounds, although almost healed, were hurting. By rights she should've still been in hospital, but as the days of ignored phone calls had gone by she'd began to worry. Finally the worry had got the better of her and she'd discharged herself, to the sound of Claudia's loud protestations. She'd allowed her to come to Marbella only if she came along too.

The doctors hadn't been happy with Bunny discharging herself either. They'd told her the baby was all right and everything looked normal but she had to be especially careful and rest a lot during this trimester due to the trauma already suffered. But she couldn't rest. She knew she would never be able to until Star was safe, happy, and back in her arms.

Bunny glanced at Del who sat as he had done for the past forty minutes, staring out into the distance. She had a sudden thought.

'What about Alan? He knew you were coming here. What if he's got...'

'Alan's dead.'

Shocked, Bunny sat up in her chair, looking around at Claudia who shrugged, mirroring the amazement on Bunny's face. Even Fat Man's face was a picture of surprise. This was the first time he'd heard anything about it.

'Dead?'

Del's voice was flat. 'That's what I said, Bun.'

'How ... how did it happen?'

'What difference does it make? That's what you wanted wasn't it? It's over.'

Angrily, Del got up. He didn't want to think about Alan because it caused the images of Bunny and the other children to pop up into his head. And now, more than ever before, he couldn't allow them to creep into his mind.

Stomping out into the kitchen, Del went into Edith's bedroom, where one of his men was keeping guard. He certainly wasn't going to let her sneak off anywhere.

'Tell me again. What happened?' Del yelled at Edith, pacing up and down in the large luxurious bedroom.

'I've told ya.'

'Then tell me again!'

Edith sighed, exhausted. It was never supposed to be like this. *This* was never supposed to happen. All she'd ever wanted was to get her money. No one saw how she'd been treated badly in all of this. Between Del and Alfonso... Where was Alfonso, anyway? She hadn't seen him for a while. Between both of them she'd been treated like a second-class citizen. Edith, working herself up, shouted back.

'If you'd just given me what was mine...'

'Don't you dare! Don't you fucking dare turn what you did around on me, you sick bitch.'

'How did I know someone would take her?'

323

Exploding, Del grabbed Edith. 'You're just not getting it are you?'

Edith sniffed. 'Perhaps you'd do better looking for Star than shouting at me. But then, that's what you've always done ain't it?'

Del covered his face with his hands, trying to contain both his fury and his fists. After a moment, he took his hands away from his face. 'I don't know what I ever saw in you. The best thing I ever did was leave you.'

Haughtily, Edith answered. 'I think you'll find it was *me* who left *you*.'

'At this moment, Edith, I don't give a rat's ass who left who. It could've been the fucking Israelites leaving Egypt for all I care.'

'Well living with you was like enduring the bleedin' plagues of Egypt anyway, I'd have gladly parted the fucking waves myself just to get rid of you.'

'Get rid of me? You've got some fucking front. I've been trying to dislodge you since we met, but you've clung on that hard you'd put a boa constrictor to shame.'

'She's not worth it.' It was Bunny's voice. She stood at the door, tired and full of fear. Edith's eyes glinted, hatred showing in them as she looked at Bunny.

'Well that's where you're wrong. I'm worth it all right. I'm worth every bleedin' penny ... you should understand that.'

'Why, Edith? Why did you do it?' Bunny spoke, her eyes pleading with Edith for answers.

'I ain't telling you nothin' darlin' Make up your own stories on it.'

Edith sneered as she saw Bunny take a deep breath, trying to control herself, but it was Del who leapt forward. 'What is wrong with you, Edith? When did you become so evil?'

Bunny walked fully into the room, taking Del's hand off Edith's top. 'Leave it. The authorities can deal with her.'

Del and Edith's heads shot round at the same time to look at Bunny in astonishment.

'Authorities?'

'Yes, Del. I'm calling the police.' Bunny got out her phone. Del looked at her, dumbfounded. 'You can't do that.'

'Can't I?'

'No. We'll find her ourselves. We don't need the police crawling everywhere. Someone will know something.'

Bunny's stared hard at Del, her tone full of amazement.

'Will they? They'll know where to find Star?'

Del said nothing as Bunny continued to talk.

'You're incredible. Our daughter's missing and you don't want me to call the police. Where are your priorities?'

Edith piped up. 'Money and his drugs empire; I thought you would've known that by now. Family comes second. Look at the way he treated me.' Del and Bunny ignored Edith's little outburst.

'That's unfair, Bunny. Star's my priority.'

'Is she? Burkey told me you didn't contact the police when you thought the Russians had her. Fine, that was your decision, you did what you thought was best, but now this is my decision. We need all the help we can get.'

'You can't call them.'

'Just try stopping me.' Bunny walked out of the room, followed by Del.

'Bunny! Bunny!' Del jogged down the corridor after Bunny who went into the master bedroom. The room they'd shared when they'd stayed here together in what seemed to be only a short while ago. So much had happened since then.

'Please, Bunny, just wait. I'm not telling you that you can't.'

'Aren't you?'

Del sat down, rubbing his head. 'No. I'm just saying...' Del gestured his arms, not really being able to put how he felt into words.

'What else would you have me do? Do you expect me to sit here and do nothing?'

'No...'

'What are you worried about – because it's clearly not Star.'

Bunny saw Del's face drop.

'I'm sorry, I shouldn't have said that. I know you care, but I can't just do nothing. Get your men to move everything out if that's what you're worried about, but I'm calling the police.'

'It's not that. Christ, as if I leave mountains of coke about the place. Give me some credit, Bun.'

'What is it then?'

Del shrugged. 'I dunno...'

'Then there's no problem, is there?'

'But the Spanish police, Bun?'

Bunny held Del's stare as she dialled a number. She walked out of the room as it rang. 'Hello? Hello? It's Bunny Barker. I need your help and *you* owe me big time.'

49

Star sat cross-legged on the grass and looked up at the sky, watching the clouds rushing by. It was only a short while ago since she'd lain on the beach with her dad watching them. She wondered if they were the same clouds being blown round and round or if they were different ones from the other side of the world.

Hearing a bird in the trees, Star turned her head, but quickly looked back down at the grass as she saw Julian staring at her. Even though she now knew Alfonso was mean, he didn't make her feel like Julian did.

'I wouldn't bother thinking of running away.'

'I'm not,' Star answered Julian without looking at him.

'Then why were you looking over here?'

Star shrugged. Julian cackled, spitting out the dried grass he was chewing. 'Seen something you like?'

'Leave her alone, Julian.' Alfonso spoke to his brother as he sat on the log.

Julian got up from where he was sitting. 'No, I want to know if she saw something she liked.' Julian walked over to Star, making her scuttle over to Alfonso who kicked her away gently.

'Don't be a mug, Julian.'

Julian didn't like the way his brother was speaking to him. He hadn't come over to Spain to be talked to like shit. He grabbed Star by her arm, leaning into her face. 'Come on, darlin', tell me what you were looking at.'

Star shook her head. 'Nothin'. I wasn't looking at nothin'.'

'See that. She thinks you're a nothing.' Alfonso let out a roar of laughter. He turned to his brother, then thought twice about it before twisting back round to Star. 'Is that right?'

Star looked nervously at Alfonso, hoping he'd come to her rescue. Alfonso grinned, amused by what was unfolding in front of him.

'No. I don't think you're nothing. I never said that.'

Julian smirked. 'So what *do* you think of me?'

Star could feel her heart pounding. She knew what she thought but equally, she knew what to say. 'I like you mister. I think you're all right.'

Julian looked at Alfonso triumphantly.

'Then how about a kiss?'

Immediately, Alfonso jumped up. Star heard the flick of the knife. She backed away slightly as Julian let go of her arm. 'I told you to stay away from her, Julian.'

Julian looked at the knife and then at Alfonso. 'I was only having a laugh with her, Alf.'

'Well, make sure that's all it is.' Alfonso sat back down, stabbing the knife into the log.

'Have you tried Alan again?'

Julian scowled. 'Yeah but there's no answer.'

'What about his office.'

'I'm not stupid. Of course I have, but no one's answering the office phone either.'

Alfonso shouted. 'Fuck. What are we going to

do? We're supposed to move her in the next couple of days. Without a passport for her, we won't be able to get her through customs. Keep trying.'

Julian nodded as he pulled out his mobile to phone Alan. He winked at Star, wondering when he'd be able to get her on her own.

50

Teddy Davies was drenched. His brown mackintosh stuck to him, and the handle of his luggage had broken, leaving him to tuck the bag under his arm. But the sudden summer downpour and the inadequate luggage were the least of his troubles as he stood on the doorstep, staring into the cold brown eyes of Del Williams.

'Weather's not very clever...' Teddy trailed off, feeling the squelch of the water in his sandals.

Del stared, saying nothing very loudly. He swung the front door wide open and turned, walking down the corridor towards the kitchen. *This* he couldn't get his head round. *This* was like something you read in a book or watched in a film, thinking it could never happen. But as he walked down the cool marble corridor, hearing Teddy's footsteps behind him, Del knew there was no getting away from how real it was.

They walked into the kitchen. It was empty. Del put his hand out and stared at Teddy. It took Teddy a moment to realise Del was wanting to take his coat. Quickly he took it off, passing the wet mac to Del, who held his gaze as well as the coat before dropping it on the floor where they were standing, prior to stepping on it as he walked across to switch the kettle on.

The next couple of moments saw Teddy standing in the middle of the room wondering whether it was wise or not to pick his coat up. Catching Del's unwelcoming gaze, Teddy decided it was probably best to leave it where it was.

'How do you have your tea, Teddy? Is this too strong? Come and see.' Del's voice was light as he made the drinks.

Taken aback by the change of tone, Teddy walked across and looked at the steaming hot mug of tea. Just as he was about to demand more milk, he felt Del's tight grip on his arm.

Teddy's face drained as Del spoke through gritted teeth.

'You being here ain't got nothing to do with me. If I had my way...' Del paused, taking a deep breath before continuing. 'Bunny's got it into her head that you can help. That's how desperate she is. So just make sure you do something. Oh, and I don't want her knowing that I know about you and her. Do I make myself clear?'

'Everything all right?' Bunny opened the kitchen door.

'Everything's fine, doll. Me and Teddy were just discussing if you put the milk in first or the water.' Teddy nodded, unable to raise a smile as he unsteadily went to sit down.

Bunny took the plates of biscuits over to the table, watching Del, who was now sitting out near the pool. She sat down next to Teddy. 'Biscuit?'

'Oh, don't mind if I do.'

Seeing that Del wasn't looking at them, Bunny's voice turned into an angry whisper. 'Del's none too happy about you being here but like I said on the phone, I'm going to keep my mouth shut about your involvement in my shooting if you help us, and you're going to keep yours shut about you and me. Do I make myself clear?'

'Everything all right?' Del walked back in from the pool area, eyeing Bunny and Teddy suspiciously as they sat at the table over a plate of chocolate biscuits.

'Everything's fine. We were just discussing if it's better to dunk or dip. Ain't that right, Teddy?' As if to prove her point, Bunny dropped a whole chocolate biscuit into Teddy's mug before getting up from the table and walking away.

Teddy Davies nodded, wondering what else could make his already shitty week worse. And he didn't need to wait much longer to find out.

'Bleedin' hell, look what the tide's brought in.' It was Edith.

Del sneered at Teddy and Edith. 'No introductions are necessary. Clearly you two are well acquainted.'

The silence that followed was excruciating and it was only broken by more awkwardness as Fat Man and Claudia came in. Claudia stared, recognising but not quite understanding why the copper from Soho was standing in Del's kitchen. Fat Man also stared, recognising not a copper from Soho, but the copper who'd once put him away for a five-year stretch.

Del saw the look on their faces. 'Don't ask me. Ask her.'

All eyes turned to Bunny. Even Teddy's, who was just as eager for an explanation as to why he had really been summoned, albeit *blackmailed*, here by Bunny.

'I know it's not ideal but everyone here wants the same thing.' Bunny paused for a moment, looking at Edith. 'Well, nearly everybody here wants the same thing. We want Star back. I thought because, for better or for worse, we've all had dealings with Teddy…'

Everyone at that point put their heads down, finding a sudden interest in the floor. 'But he knows the system. He has access to information we don't have.'

Bunny stopped, fighting the tears away. She looked round the room at everyone. 'Okay, maybe it was a stupid idea, but I'm just trying to think of anything that will help. It's better than doing nothing.'

Claudia stepped forward, putting her arms round Bunny. 'I know it is, babe. I know. We'll find her, won't we?' Claudia looked round the room, seeking reassurance. No one answered. No one was willing to catch her gaze.

'Coke, Teddy?'

'I never touch the stuff.' Teddy eyeballed Edith, watching the smirk appear on her face as she offered him a drink at dinner with a glint in her eye.

He looked along the table. Bunny, Del, Edith, Burkey, Claudia and himself – as well as some of Del's men, who looked like they'd stepped out of a guide book on Neanderthals. He was desperate for some quiver. He'd contemplated bringing some through customs but the humiliation of being caught with a few grams stuffed up his arse had stopped him. But it'd been hours now, almost twenty-four hours in fact, and he was beginning to feel it.

'Cold turkey?' Del spoke to Teddy, his face emotionless as he passed him the plate of meat.

Teddy gazed back. 'No.'

Del narrowed his eyes. 'You sure?'

'Perfectly.'

Fat Man nudged Claudia, who smiled back coyly. Silence fell once more in the room. No one ate the dinner, pushing it round their plates, deep in their own thoughts.

'Did you change your ring tone?' Bunny spoke to Del as she listened to the phone ringing out from the bedroom.

'It's not my phone, my phone's here.'

'Well, whose is it?'

Del pulled a face. It was the first time he'd heard it. Bunny got up, walking into the master bedroom, which was next door to where they were sitting. She followed the ring tone. It was coming from Del's suitcase. Quickly she opened it, rummaging amongst the clothes. It was coming from his fawn jacket pocket. Pulling the phone out, she looked at it and not recognising the number, she passed it to Del who was standing next to her. The caller ID had been withheld.

'Answer it.' Bunny urged Del.

He looked at her. He'd forgotten about this phone. 'It's Alan's.'

Bunny stared at Del as he pressed the green button.

'Hello?'

'Alan?'

'No...' Del paused, realising what he'd just said. Quickly trying to make amends he lowered his voice, trying to sound more like Alan. 'Yes, yes it is.'

He chewed his lip as he waited, hoping he hadn't given the game away. He was curious to see who it was. Patiently, he listened to the breathing on the other end, not wanting to scare the person off. Eventually the caller spoke.

'It's Julian. I've been trying to call you. I'm going to draw in my favours... I've got a keeper. I need you to get a girl out...'

The voice cut off and Del looked at the mobile in despair. The battery had gone.

'No!' Del yelled as Bunny looked at him, not understanding what was going on.

'Quick, get a charger. Now!'

Bunny looked at the phone, seeing it was a Samsung. 'I haven't got a charger for that.'

'Someone must.'

Bunny raced down the corridor, holding her sides as a pain ran through her. She burst into the sun room where everyone was still congregating. Her voice verging on the hysterical, she asked, 'Has anyone got a phone charger for a Samsung? Quickly!'

'I have.' Teddy stood up. 'It's in my case though.'

'Then get it!'

Teddy rushed to his bag, wishing he hadn't volunteered the information of his charger as he saw Del staring down at him whilst he pulled out everything from striped pyjamas to off-white Y-fronts.

'Can't you be any fucking quicker?'

Teddy nodded, his hand shaking from a combination of terror and lack of quiver. Frigging bag. It had too many compartments in it and now he couldn't find a thing. Continuing to rummage, Teddy pulled out a mini clear grip-seal bag. He stared at it as if hypnotised; seeing the remnants of cocaine inside. The moment was broken by Del hitting the bag out of Teddy's hand.

'What the fuck are you doing.'

'Sorry ... sorry.' Teddy blinked, delving deep into a side compartment. His hand hit on something hard. The charger.

Del grabbed it from Teddy's hands, not giving him a word of thanks. He rushed to the side and plugged it in. Impatiently waiting for it to charge up, Del's mind began to race. *Julian. Julian.* Why did he know that name? He looked at the phone, seeing a voice-mail message.

Please enter the pin. The woman's automated voice told him what he didn't want to know. Alan had protected his mail. Shit.

'What did the person say?' Bunny spoke to Del, breaking his thoughts.

'I don't know, maybe it's nothing to do with Star, but...'

'What?'

Del looked around at Teddy, Claudia and Fat

Man. 'He said he had a keeper.'

Claudia put her head in her hands, making Del feel the need to give her blind reassurance. 'Maybe it doesn't mean what we think it does. It could be about anything. So a guy calls and asks Alan for some papers for a kid. Big deal. He did it all the time. *We* did it for Star.'

He turned to look at Bunny, scanning her face. Seeing the pain, but also the strength in her big blue eyes. 'Don't worry, Bun. It's probably innocent.'

As he said the words, Del tried to ignore the sinking feeling in his heart.

51

The morning didn't bring any brightness. The sun hid behind the low clouds. The sea, usually sparkling and jewel-like, faded and merged into the grey sea mist. Del sat with Fat Man outside by the pool, the air thick with despondency.

'Do you think it was about Star?' It was the same question Fat Man had been asking since the phone call yesterday. Del stared at Alan's mobile, lying silently on the table. He didn't know. But what other leads did they have? Though the idea they *were* talking about Star was too horrific to contemplate.

'I dunno, Burkey. Like I said, it could be a pile up of coincidences.'

'Can I have a word?'

Del and Fat Man looked round. It was Teddy. They watched as he stood in a vest and striped pyjama bottoms, wrapping a blanket tightly round him, tears streaming down his face.

'Christ geeze, you need to pull yourself together.'

'I couldn't sleep. I feel terrible…'

He burst into tears again, dabbing his eyes with the hem of his string vest. Del and Fat Man looked at each other, embarrassed for Teddy.

Del, suspecting what was wrong, motioned the wiping of his nose to Fat Man, who nodded, grasping the situation. Del stared at Teddy with enough disdain for Fat Man to speak.

'Take it easy, mate. We're all under pressure.'

Del spoke slowly, not taking his eyes off Teddy for a second. 'My men will sort you out with what you need, but make sure you're not so coked-up you end up with shit for brains.'

An hour later, Teddy was singing. Life was good and the Marbella sun, although not shining, was beginning to break out. Yes, this is exactly what he needed. A rest from Soho. A rest from work and a few fat lines of quiver.

'Oi mate, I want a word with you.' Edith slid into Teddy's room, escaping from the hostage situation she regarded herself to be in. Teddy, glaze-eyed and annoyed at the interruption, snapped at Edith, 'What do you think you're doing?'

Edith, slanted her eyes. 'The question is, what do *you* think you're doing? I nearly had bleedin' calves when I saw your boat, walking in here.'

Teddy, rubbing some quiver on his gums, stepped forward to Edith. He whispered, 'How

337

do you think *I* felt? I'm the one who's been brought into the lion's cave, not you. I've got your gorilla of a husband breathing down my neck, expecting me to turn into Inspector Poirot.'

Edith pulled a face. 'Listen, Edward, I've got my own worries. Rambo out there thinks I've gone for a piss so I've got to make this quick. You need to keep your mouth shut about my involvement with setting Del up. You do that, I'll keep my mouth shut about yours. Do I make myself clear?'

Teddy nodded. In the last few hours, there had been a lot of people making themselves *very* clear.

The phone sat in the middle of the table with all eyes on it. No one moved. No one said a thing. The ticking clock was silent but the movement of the hands were clear and obvious to see. It'd been too long. Too long to hope the phone might ring again. They had no other leads. No other hope or life lines to Star.

'Don't you think you should lie down?' Del spoke to Bunny, who only just managed to shake her head. He implored to Claudia. 'Don't you think she should rest?' It was the first time he'd really exchanged words with Claudia since her revelation.

'I've tried telling her.'

Bunny snapped at Claudia, not appreciating her input. 'I'm not a child.'

'Your *mum's* only concerned about you.'

Fat Man spoke the word which hung in the air. A word layered with so much meaning, which for

338

so long had been left unsaid by anyone other than Bunny. Claudia, noticing Fat Man coming to her defence, smiled. 'Thank you Arthur, but it's fine.'

Before Del had chance to raise his eyebrows at the name *Arthur*, Bunny burst into angry tears, startling everyone in the room. 'Don't talk to me like you know me. You don't know *anything* about me, Burkey. You don't know anything about my mum and you certainly don't know anything about Star.'

'Burkey don't mean anything by it, Bun. Calm down. Think of the baby.' Del spoke, but seeing Bunny's head spin round towards him, wished he hadn't.

Rarely one to raise her voice, Bunny shouted loudly. The hurt and fear pitched high into her words. 'Don't make out I don't care. That's all I've ever tried to do.'

'I know, Bun, I'm not saying you don't care, I just...'

'You are. You are saying that. But you've never understood. You've never seen my whole life has been about making it right again. About caring for Star – but it didn't work because look what happened.'

'It isn't your fault. You couldn't have known.'

'It *is* my fault. It always was. I've fought my whole life and I wanted to give her better, but it hasn't worked because it's about me not being able to keep what I love safe. If it hadn't been for me she'd be here... They'd *both* be here.'

Del frowned, realising Bunny was talking about other things apart from Star, though he didn't understand quite what. 'Bunny, you're a good mother. The best.'

Bunny's eyes were filled with pain. 'Don't patronise me. Please, don't patronise me. I can't do this. I can't deal with any more guilt. Please Del, *please*. You have to find her. You have to bring her back to me. You promised me it'll be fine. You always said everything would be fine.'

Del stared at Bunny, his heart breaking for her. He felt helpless – he didn't know what to say, though he could feel everyone in the room willing him to find the right words to comfort Bunny.

As he stumbled about in his mind for words the phone rang. All eyes froze on it, then there was a mad scramble to pass it to Del.

Holding the phone in his hand, he put his finger on his lips, gesturing to the others to be quiet.

'Hello?'

'Alan?'

Del's eyes glanced round the room as he answered, trying to put on a refined accent.

'Yes.'

'It's Julian.'

'Julian?' Del said his name, an inflection in his voice.

'Millwood.'

'Of course.'

There was silence and once again, Del could hear the breathing on the other end of the phone of the caller on the line. The temptation to ask a question was overwhelming but Del waited, not succumbing to his feelings. Not wanting to mess up what could be their only chance of finding out if this was anything to do with Star.

'I need you to get some papers.'

'No problem.'

Again there was a pause. Del was beginning to panic but then he thought of Alan. The arrogant, narcissistic, manipulating barrister who'd he'd employed as his fixer for years. He thought of the way he'd spoken. Rude. Impatient and surly. And he thought of the phone call he'd heard Alan have with a man named Julian, on the night he'd died.

'What do you want, Julian? I told you, don't call me.'

'No can do, Alan, you owe me.'

Del nodded to himself. It was working.

'Nothing to say.'

'I want the papers for the girl.'

He needed to be careful. Trying not to sound too eager, he spoke, attempting to sound as calm as possible. 'Which girl?'

'You'd like her, Alan. She's your taste. Blonde. Blue eyes. An innocent.' Del's eyes widened and he squeezed the phone tightly, gripping on to it in anger. He felt Bunny's arm on him. He had to stay cool. *Stay cool.*

'She sounds perfect.' Del struggled to say the next words. 'Maybe I could have some of her myself.'

Julian chortled down the phone. 'Sorry, she's already spoken for.'

'Shame. I would've liked to have met her.'

As Del listened he heard the suspicion in Julian's voice.

'You've changed your tune. I thought you didn't want anything more to do with these things.'

'I didn't, but when you're dangling the carrot, it's hard not to take a bite. I need to know exactly what you need. Perhaps we should meet.'

'I can't, I'm in Spain ... with the girl.'

'I could meet you, it's no problem. I've got business out there myself. Just tell me where you are.' The moment Del heard the words rush out of his mouth, he knew he'd been too keen. The line went silent for a few seconds. Julian's voice was deadpan when he finally spoke. 'I'll call you back.' The phone went down.

'Fuck. Fuck.' Del slammed down his fist on the table.

'What's happened? What did he say? Was it about Star?' Desperate, Bunny stared at Del.

'I blew it.'

'How? Jesus, Del. What's happened?'

Slowly, Del looked at Bunny. Next he looked at Claudia, Fat Man and finally to Edith, skipping over the gaze of Teddy completely.

'He's got her.'

'Who?... Who's got her?' Bunny's eyes were filled with tears.

'I don't know him but he knows Alan. He says his name's Julian. Julian Millwood.'

Del Williams watched as Bunny collapsed to the sound of Claudia's piercing scream.

Twilight in Marbella brought a hue of flickering colours. Pale orange and yellow lights cast out from the seemingly distorted sun just visible above the horizon. Long shadows danced on the

342

walls as Del sat watching Bunny asleep. Beautiful and peaceful.

She stirred.

'Hello, sleeping beauty.' Del's smile was drawn with sadness.

Bunny tried to sit up but Del placed his hands gently on her. 'You need to rest, Bun.'

'How long have I been asleep?'

'A few hours or so.'

Bunny's voice was urgent, her blue eyes, deep pools of fear, scanned Del's face. 'What are we going to do?'

'We're going to talk.'

'Talk?'

Del nodded. 'Yes. Talk. I need to know everything. We should've done this a long time ago.'

'I don't know what you're talking about.'

'Don't you?'

'Tell me about Julian. Tell me about the men in the woods.'

Bunny vigorously shook her head as she hugged her knees, looking so much younger than her years.

Del took a deep breath and squeezed her hand, feeling a tight pain in his chest. He reached into his inner pocket, taking out the photo he'd found in Alan's office.

'Talk to me, baby ... please.'

Bunny blinked, staring at the picture of her with Julian. Del spoke in a hoarse whisper as his emotions drowned out his words. 'However long it takes, Bun. I'll sit here with you as long as it takes and then ... and then I'll go and find our daughter. I promise I'll bring her back to you.'

52

The early morning dew saturated the lawn. Glistening drops of water coated the delicate blades of grass as Del threw his cigarette down. He was exhausted. Bunny had talked all night, telling him things he knew he wouldn't, couldn't, forget until his dying breath.

'You all right, D?' Del turned, startled at the intrusion. It was Fat Man.

'You all right, Burkey?'

'Yeah. Couldn't sleep. You?'

'Not doing so good.'

Fat Man nodded, understanding. Del began to walk, getting into his Range Rover. Fat Man smiled and came up to the driver's seat door. 'Off somewhere?'

'Yeah.'

'Need me to come with you?'

Del looked at Burkey. He was one of the good ones and his constant presence, although he didn't know it, had been a source of comfort for him. 'No, I have to do this on my own.'

'You want this?' Fat Man took out a loaded Colt Combat Elite from his jacket.

Del shook his head. 'No, but Burkey ... thank you. For everything.'

'Go on, get out of here.' Fat Man shut the car door, worried how emotional he suddenly felt.

The drive down to Puerto Banús was long and dusty as Del cut through the hills overlooking the whitewashed buildings of Marbella. His open window let the heat of the morning blow in with the warm southerly breeze.

Heading down the hill, Del pulled up his Range Rover outside Dolce & Gabbana. He sat back in the cream leather seat and closed his eyes, partly from exhaustion, and partly what was in front of him.

Pulling up his trouser leg, Del took out his gun from his ankle holster, slipping it quickly into the glove compartment. He did the same with his phone and the tiny pistol he kept hidden in his leather waistband.

Okay, he was ready – or as ready as he'd ever be. Opening the door, stoking himself up, Del stepped out of the car. He wasn't sure how this was going to pan out, but it was certainly worth a try.

The water rose and cut in white crests as Del skimmed his twin engine Aquariva speed boat, custom made by Gucci, out across the crystal bay of Puerto Bands. The highly polished mahogany foredeck, inlaid with maple strips, sparkled in the sun. The opulent white leather, chrome and wood interior oozed 1950s Hollywood glamour. And the box of crayons next to the yellow bucket and spade oozed memories of the glorious day he and Star had spent racing round the coast; when she'd squealed with fear and delight as the boat had hit swelling surfs and waves at high speeds.

A few miles outside the harbour, Del began to slow down his boat. He looked in front of him and, like a steel block of flats coming out of the water, Del was dwarfed by Milo's luxury cruise yacht.

Four storeys of blacked-out windows and sparkling white metal towered above him. A grey and gold helicopter sat on the back of the yacht and a multitude of satellite dishes moved, circling round slowly: all making up the sleek five-million-pound ship.

Del turned off his engine and let his speedboat buoy from side to side on the gentle Mediterranean waves. The expectant sound of clicking metal made Del look up. There in front of him were four of Milo's men, aiming their sniper guns directly at him. With a sigh of resignation, Del put his arms up in the air as he watched the thin telescopic gangway purring forward towards him as it was opened.

Looking hesitantly at the water far below him, Del struggled to keep his balance as he walked up the gangway, which had rails on one side only.

Stopping just before he got to the boat's deck, Del shouted authoritatively, 'I want to see Milo. I'm not armed.'

Milo's men glanced at each other, then gestured Del with the nozzle of their guns to step aboard. The tallest man limped towards Del, recognition in his eyes that wasn't reflected in Del's. The Russian stood almost nose to nose with Del, a veil of hatred on his face.

He produced his gun, trailing it down Del's body. First to his chest, then to his stomach then finally stopping at his leg. 'I see your memory isn't as long as mine.'

Del stared at the man, recollections flashing into his mind. The outhouse buildings. The coke. The money. Shit. He held the Russian's gaze, not flinching, not retaliating as he felt the gun's hard barrel jabbing into his leg. 'No hard feelings, mate. As I said, I'd like to see Milo.'

A contemptuous smile crossed the man's face. He shook his head. 'I'll say who sees Milo and I'm also saying you're not. I want you to turn around and go back the way you came; only this time, you'll be swimming back... *No hard feelings.*'

Going round behind Del, he pushed the gun into his back, between his shoulder blades. Making Del walk forward, he pressed the button, closing the gangway. Once fully shut he forced Del towards the edge of the yacht, to the twenty-foot drop.

'Walk.'

Del didn't move. He felt the warmth of the Russian's breath on his ear. 'Walk or shoot. It's your choice.'

Del looked out in front of him. Nothing but sea. Nothing but a slow, exhaustive death as he drowned. Slowly, Del spoke. Emotionless. Clearing his mind of all thoughts. 'I'll take the bullet.'

'Enough. We've had our fun!'

The gun was withdrawn from Del's back. Laughter surrounded him. He swerved round and saw Milo standing a level above him, leaning over the silver railings.

'We meet again, my friend.'

It took all of Del's emotional willpower not to weigh into the Russian standing next to him, but he was saved by his sense of relief, albeit drained relief.

Del was walked to the middle of the deck, still with guns pointed at him. He looked up at Milo, despising his arrogance as he stood like an ancient Roman emperor addressing the masses.

Not wanting to waste any more time, Del went into his inner jacket pocket and pulled something out. The second he'd done it he knew he'd made a mistake. His call of, '*It's not a gun*' went unheard as his face hit the floor, smashing down onto the hard teak deck Milo's men piled on top of him. A knee ground into his spine. Feet kicked the side of him and four guns pushed into his body. His breathing staggered by his chest being compressed against the wooden deck, along with his head turned to the side and a Kalashnikov rifle pressed against it.

He heard footsteps and felt the vibration underneath his body. A pair of feet came into view along with a familiar sounding voice. It was Milo. 'Tell me why I shouldn't kill you right now?'

Del's gaze followed the length of his arm to what he'd pulled out of his jacket. It was a photo. The photograph of Julian Millwood and Bunny. 'Because this man has taken my daughter and I need your help to find him.'

Teddy Davies sat at the kitchen table eating breakfast, feeling just as much a prisoner as Edith. He'd been a fool to come, but then, what choice did he have? Bunny had told him in no uncertain terms it was either he came to help or she'd make sure Del dealt with him – in the way only Del Williams

348

could – for his part in her shooting.

He needed to try and think of a way to get out of there, and fast. He hadn't told anyone where he'd gone and the last thing Teddy wanted was to be found a few months from now in a gangster's graveyard.

Putting another spoon of muesli in his mouth, Teddy continued to contemplate his predicament.

'Hello Teddy.'

Muesli, milk and sugar flew out of Teddy's mouth, splattering the marble table. His shocked face turned red as his intake of breath at spotting the new guest turned into an uncontrollable coughing fit.

'Let me help you with that.'

Milo Burkov walked round to where Teddy was sitting. Bringing back his fist he banged it into Teddy's back. Extra firm and very, very hard. 'Better?'

Teddy shook his head, twisting out of his chair in an attempt to escape the pain. Milo's hand held him down. 'Oh no, I don't think it is better, do you Del?'

Del walked up to Milo. 'Why don't I see if I can make it better?' With a larger fist and a harder bang, Del hit Teddy's back, putting his entire weight behind it. Teddy shot out of the chair, almost being winded as the force of the blow ejected him across the table.

'I think that will do it, don't you?'

Del winked at Milo. Grateful, relieved – and no doubt eternally indebted to the man, but whatever the price, it was worth it. He now had the combination of his men and Milo's almost army-sized task force – and then that only left Teddy, who'd done little more than nothing since he'd arrived, unless of course you counted the quality grams of powder he was nostrilling. Why the fuck Bunny had asked him to come, he didn't know, but what was stranger than that was why he'd actually come. Del couldn't fathom it. He'd known Teddy for years and in all that time he'd never done anything for other people – unless of course there was something in it for him. For Teddy to put himself amongst them all like this, knowing how he felt about him, was completely out of character.

He supposed he could put it down to the powder. The man was clearly losing it, but then ... and Del didn't like to think of it, but there was always the possibility Teddy actually *liked* Bunny and sleeping with her was never about a wind up, it was about genuine feelings. Oh Christ, there he went again. He felt ashamed of himself for allowing these thoughts to enter his head when the people he loved the most were facing the cruellest of nightmares.

Wanting to channel his energy somewhere, Del turned on Teddy, who was struggling to wipe all the muesli off the front of his brown V-neck polyester top.

'This ain't a holiday mate.'

Teddy froze, realising Del was speaking to him. 'Pardon?'

Del sneered as Milo sat down, watching, as was his habit.

'I said, this ain't a holiday. I want to know what

you've been doing? What have you found out on Julian Millwood?'

Teddy opened his mouth before he'd thought of exactly what to say, leaving it hanging open. His eyes flickered round the room, then they settled on Del's phone, inspiring his next unconvincing sounding words. 'Phone. I've been phoning people.'

'People?'

'Yep ... er ... my ... er contacts.'

'Which contacts?'

'Secret ones.'

Del gave a suspicious glance to Milo and raised his eyebrows. Pushing him more, Del growled at Teddy. 'So come on then, why don't you call them?'

Teddy's face pinched in anguish. 'You want me to call them?'

'Yeah. Is that a problem?'

'No, oh no. Just ... er, maybe I should do it in the other room. It being confidential.'

'Confidential you say?'

'Yes, that's right.'

Del fixed his gaze on Teddy. 'I don't do secrets. Phone them here.'

Teddy swallowed. 'Here? Right now?'

'Here. Right now.'

Teddy looked at Milo who had a smirk on his face, the same smirk he'd seen countless times before. In a grand gesture, Teddy got his phone out of his pocket, waving it around before dialling. Turning to Del as he held it by his ear, he spoke in a self-assured manner. 'It's ringing.'

Del said nothing, only nodded, not taking his

gaze away from Teddy for a moment.

'Hello?... It's me. I'm wondering if you've had any luck on tracing the last whereabouts of Julian Millwood. The guy I was talking to you about.' Teddy put his thumb up to Del as he spoke. He paused, pacing round the kitchen, his face screwed up with concentration as he turned his back on both Milo and Del. 'Yeah... Ah-ha... Yeah... *What you doing?*' The last part of his sentence was to Del as the phone was pulled out of his hand.

'There ain't no one there, is there?' Del spat the words at Teddy before putting the phone to his ear. He glared at Teddy. 'The line's dead! You ain't got no juice in your battery.'

Teddy scarpered to the other side of the table. 'I can explain.'

'Explain? Star's missing and you're playing pussy-ass games. I should break your neck for that, mate.'

'I'm happy to lend a hand.' Milo spoke to Del as he stood up and walked towards Teddy. After all, Teddy and I have unfinished business, don't we?'

Teddy was about to bolt from the room in fright when a phone rang. Alan's phone. It was sitting in the middle of the table. Del cautiously picked it up.

'Hello?'

'It's Julian.'

Del's stomach lurched. Assuming Alan's voice as best he could, he spoke. 'Yeah, what do you want?'

'That's not very nice, Alan.'

'I'm busy, so maybe we should make it quick.'

'Fine, have it your own way. Those papers, how long will it take you to get them?'

'A day. Two days at the most.'

'Good because apart from having to get her out of Spain, I'm finding it rather difficult to stop myself.'

Del paused, then slowly answered. 'Stop yourself?'

'Well yeah, any other time I'd enjoy myself, but as she's a keeper, she's off-limits or rather, she's supposed to be.' Julian laughed nastily. It was too much for Del, who exploded.

'Listen, you touch her and I...' Del stopped mid-sentence, catching himself. He looked round at Bunny who'd just walked into the room. He saw her horrified face at what he'd just done. 'Julian, are you still there?'

'Yeah.' It was a one-word answer but the tone of suspicion and doubt resounded from it.

'What I meant to say was, you touch her and you'll fuck it up. Just looking out for you, Julian.' It wasn't convincing, nor did it sound it.

'Alan?'

Del answered nervously, ignoring the stares of everyone in the room. 'Yeah?'

'How much money did you give me?'

'Pardon?'

'It's a simple question Alan. *How* much money did you give me when I came to see you?'

He didn't know, how could he know? He would have to guess. Slowly, Del answered.

'Twenty grand. It was twenty grand.'

'Wrong answer ... you should've phoned a friend.' The line went dead.

53

'They're on to us.' Julian threw the phone onto the mattress in the corner.

Alfonso Garcia stared at his brother, a steely look in his eyes. 'What the fuck are you talking about?'

'That wasn't Alan on the phone.'

Alfonso flew forward, grabbing hold of Julian by his oversized t-shirt. 'You fucking idiot. What did they say? Who was it?'

Pinned against the wall, Julian argued back, 'How the fuck was I supposed to know, eh?'

'You're supposed to check who you're talking to.'

'I didn't give them any information. I never told him where we were.'

Alfonso flicked open his knife.

'You better not have done.'

'Screw you.'

Alfonso banged Julian hard against the wall, then turned to look at Star who was sat trembling in the corner, watching the scene unfolding in front of her.

'What are we going to do with her?'

'You'll have to get rid, Alf.'

Alfonso looked in amazement at his brother. 'I'm not doing that.'

'Why not? You killed Julie Cole without a second thought.'

'Who the fuck's Julie Cole?'

'The girl in Camden.'

'That was different.'

'Why was it? You hadn't planned it, just like you hadn't planned Star. Julie only happened because you'd come to London to get chocolates for Edith. So what's the problem? It's not like you haven't done it a few times before.'

'I ain't worried about doing it. Julie was different. That was pleasure. This is business – and I ain't throwing my future away. You can do what you like but I'm going to think of a way to get her out of here.'

'There's no way I'm going back to prison. She's a liability now.'

'Like I say, you do what you like, I'm taking her to the clients.'

Julian leapt towards Star, grabbing her arm roughly, pulling her towards him. She screamed loudly. 'Not without me you ain't. Do you really think I'm going to let you have my part in the money?'

Star began to cry, quietly at first then gradually louder.

'Then you better think how we're going to get her out of Spain without papers. The police will be crawling everywhere by now ... and stop that fucking crying, now!' Alfonso walked over to Star, slapping her hard across her face. He jabbed his finger into her chest. 'Shut it, you hear me?'

Star nodded, using everything she had to stop herself from screaming in terror. Closing her eyes, she thought of her mum and then of her dad, but that only made it seem worse. She tried to think of pirates, but that didn't help. She could feel the tears wanting to escape but she mustn't cry. She mustn't cry. Her face was still hurting and she didn't want another smack ... she wanted her dad.

Thinking about her dad was making Star's tummy hurt. She doubled over from the pain, then looked up and saw the horrible man with the bad breath staring at her, a funny look on his face. She watched as he began to breathe, hard and hungry. Looking back down again, Star hugged her knees tightly, trying to stop them from trembling; trying to let her imagination take her out of there as the man made his way towards her.'

An hour later, Alfonso Garcia sat at the tiny table scraping his knife into the wood. He'd been mulling things over and over in his mind and there seemed to be only one solution.

'I'm going back to the villa.'

Julian looked up from the mattress he was lying on.

'What are you talking about?'

'Hear me out. Star needed a passport to come here, right?'

Julian nodded.

'So the passport's somewhere in the villa.'

Julian sat up, beginning to follow the lead where Alfonso was going. 'We can't travel with her using her real name. They'll be looking for her.'

'It's better than not having any documentation. When we hit where we're going it won't be a problem.'

'And before that?'

'Let me worry about it.'

'I dunno what to say.'

'Look, no one thinks this is anything to do with me, right?'

'Yeah, I guess.'

Alfonso scowled. 'The only person who might've noticed I'm not there is Edith. Besides, I'm not planning on seeing anybody. I know all the security codes, and the blind spots for the CCTV cameras. If anybody does ask where I've been I'll just say I've been ill.'

Absent-mindedly, Julian picked his nose. 'I think you're crazy.'

Alfonso spun around and kicked Julian hard. His eyes were wild with rage. 'Have you got any better fucking ideas?'

Julian stood up to confront his brother but knowing the capabilities of his temper when pushed, he backed down. 'I just think it's risky, that's all. How do you know they don't think it's you?'

'Don't be a mug mate. How would they? All I need to do is wait for a quiet time. They'll be out searching for her, they're not likely to be sitting round the pool drinking fucking sangria.'

Julian shrugged. It was obvious he couldn't say anything to his brother to change his mind so he decided to say nothing. All he knew was he had a bad feeling about this. A very bad one.

Alfonso Garcia slowly walked round by the side of the pool. There was no one about, just like he'd thought. He'd watched them all drive out like something from out of a scene in a movie; a cavalcade of Range Rovers and Escalades driving purposefully down the hill. He looked up at the camera, knowing that where he was standing was a blind spot.

'Once a skiver always a bleedin' skiver. Where have you been?'

Alfonso froze as the sound of Edith's voice came from behind him. Slowly he turned round, watching her as she lay in a barely there black bandeau Herve Leger bikini, a glass of sangria in her hand. Although Alfonso felt disgusted to see Edith, her usual contemptuous greeting for him put him at ease. He was in the clear. Resisting the temptation to gloat about Star, he sneered.

'I've been looking for somewhere to live. Did you really think I was going to move into the servants' quarters?'

'So what are you doing here now then? You've come crawling back because you've got nowhere else to go, have you?'

A sickly smile crept over her face. She downed the rest of her drink in one, spitting the pips of fruit at Alf's feet from the sangria. Handing him the large glass, she crowed.

'Now you're back, you might as well make yourself useful. Go on then, Alfie baby; make me another one of these, lots of ice. I'll be here waiting.'

Alfonso crept silently along the corridor. His heart was pounding but seeing Edith had given him extra confidence. No one suspected anything. Perhaps it was all going to be easier than he'd imagined.

The door of Del's room sounded to Alfonso as if it was screaming rather than creaking open. He was terrified to make a sound. He froze for a minute in the doorway, making sure no one had heard him. Once he was certain the coast was clear, Alfonso tiptoed into Del's room.

The bedroom was large but he was familiar with it. The walk-in his and hers closet to the left. The luxurious cream bathroom straight in front and the super-king-size bed, parallel to the glass sliding doors.

Opening the drawers by his bed, Alfonso raised his eyebrows at the dozen or so Rolex watches. He was tempted to take one, but he wasn't here for that; he could buy all the watches he wanted when Star was delivered.

Closing the drawer and going into the next one, Alfonso rifled through it. Papers, documents and an expensive cigarette lighter but no passport. He had to think. Where would Del have put it?

Frowning, Alfonso walked across to the white tallboy drawers at the far end of the room. He opened them one at a time, rummaging through them as quickly as he could.

He stopped suddenly, hearing a noise. There were voices and they were coming from down the corridor. His eyes darted to the door handle of the room, desperate to not see it being turned. His whole body on high alert.

The moment passed and Alfonso's shoulders relaxed, hearing whoever it was walk past. He swivelled back round to the drawers to continue looking. This would be his only chance.

'What the hell do you think you're doing?'

Alfonso pushed the drawer closed, his back still turned on the person.

'I said what do you think you're doing, *pal?*'

Alfonso swivelled round, coming face to face with Fat Man Burke.

He brushed back his black dyed Brylcreemed hair and smiled, his eyes narrowing into tiny slits. 'Del's asked me to do something for him.'

Burkey looked unconvinced as he put his hand on his waistband, exposing the top of a gun handle.

'Why would he ask you to look through his drawers?'

'He didn't.'

Self-congratulatory Fat Man nodded his head. 'I didn't think so? He pulled out his gun on Alfonso. 'Move it. You've got a lot of explaining to do.'

'No, you don't understand. He didn't tell me to look anywhere at all. That's my problem. He just told me to get it and do it. No disrespect to the boss but he's not really in the frame of mind to have any patience and explain stuff.'

'Get what and do what?'

Alfonso's eyes gleamed. 'The passport. He wants me to get flyers made of her, put them round the town. He asked me to get a copy of her passport photograph to use for them, 'cos it was only taken a few weeks ago, so its a true likeness. But like I say, he didn't tell me where the passport actually *was* and I hate to let him down, especially at a time like this when he needs us to rally round the most.' Alfonso beamed a smile and held it, not moving a muscle as he held the gaze of Fat Man.

'Of course. Of course. No one wants to let him down.' Fat Man nodded vigorously as he spoke, putting his gun back in the holster. 'I think I can help. I know where it is, mate.'

Fat Man smiled, walking across to the painting on the wall. He put his fingers underneath it and un-clicked a lock, enabling him to pull it open, revealing a safe behind it.

Knowledgably he keyed in the code. Turning to Alfonso with a wink.

From where he stood, Alfonso wanted to whistle. He could see bundles of fifty-pound notes and knew there must be at least half a million inside it.

'Here you go mate.'

Fat Man Burke held Star's passport in his hand, along with another one. 'You don't need his as well do you?' The other one was Del's. Alfonso stared at the passport, amazed at the stupidity of Fat Man. He wanted to get out of there as soon as possible. Lifting Star's passport out of Fat Man's hand, his heart pounding, he answered, trying to sound as casual as possible. 'No, just this one. I better be going. Bang these out ASAP.'

Fat Man stood by the safe he'd just relocked and frowned, the man's words running around in his mind. Something didn't feel quite right but he didn't know what. Looking across at Del's tallboy drawers, he suddenly realised what it was. Grabbing the car keys from off the top of them, Fat Man Burke ran out of the bedroom as fast as he could after Alfonso.

Swinging open the front door, he yelled. 'Oi, stop. Wait! I said wait!'

Alfonso turned round and saw Fat Man at the door, demanding he stop. He wanted to run but there was nowhere to go. Security men lined the gates and front walls. Fuck. Even he would struggle to get out of this. He closed his eyes and waited.

'What the fuck? Didn't you hear me calling?' Fat Man stood opposite Alfonso, resting his hands on his thighs, breathing hard.

'I ... I...'

'I thought you might want these. It'll be quicker.' Alfonso's eyes opened wide at what Fat Man held in his hands.

'Save you walking, pal.' Alfonso looked at the keys. The man was a mug. He began to back away, but Fat Man caught him by the arm.

'Oh and I wanted to thank you. I appreciate your loyalty to Del.' Fat Man tapped Alfonso on the back, pointing him in the direction of the Range Rover parked in the corner of the large courtyard.

He couldn't believe it. He couldn't believe his luck His laughter echoed round the luxurious inside of the Range Rover. *Edith's* Range Rover.

As he drove out of the courtyard he saw a procession of cars coming up the road. He heard a beep and without wanting to look properly he raised his hand up in a wave of acknowledgement. Putting his foot down on the accelerator, Alfonso looked in the rear mirror. All clear. He had done it. He had actually got away with it.

Standing in the courtyard, Fat Man looked up at the sky, feeling slightly more positive than he had done when he'd got up. He hadn't fancied the idea of the Russians being about, in fact he'd hated it. He could only liken it to what the British in World War II must have felt when they'd had to converse with the enemy. It almost sickened him. He'd held off saying anything to Del, not wanting to add anything more to his plate. Hopefully with the flyers more publicity could be generated and they'd get Star back, and then the Russians could crawl back to where they came from.

Deep in thought, Fat Man watched Del drive in, followed by a dozen other cars. He waved, walking slowly to where Del had pulled up.

Bunny got out of the car, looking drained. She forced a smile.

'All right, Burkey.'

'All right, Bun. How's it going?'

Bunny shook her head as she helped Claudia get out of the back of the Range Rover. 'Don't ask.'

Fat Man gave a coy smile to Claudia.

'Hello Arthur.'

'Hello.' Fat Man looked at his feet, taken aback at feeling himself blush.

'I better go in; Bunny's not feeling so good.'

Fat Man's words sprung out. 'Yes, of course. I'll catch you later.'

Walking up to the side of the open driver's window, Fat Man leant on the side of the car, speaking to Del who sat motionless, his head resting on the steering wheel.

'How's it going, mate?' Through the window, Fat Man patted Del on the back. Without raising his head, Del spoke, sounding exhausted.

'Not good, mate. Not good at all. We're chasing fresh air.'

'I know, pal. I know it's tough.'

There was a gentle silence before Del responded. 'It's killing me, Burkey.'

The kindness in Fat Man's voice made Del squeeze his eyes tightly. 'I know, Del. I know, but I'm here for you, mate.'

Another silence passed before Burkey, trying to conjure up some enthusiasm, spoke.

'Let's hope that these flyers will help.'

'What flyers, Burkey?'

'Don't worry. I lent him Edith's Range Rover, so he's on his way now. He only left five minutes ago but hopefully, he'll have them up in the next few hours.'

Del sat up, staring straight ahead. His hands holding onto the top of the steering wheel.

'*Burkey*, what flyers?'

Burkey swallowed. 'The flyers you asked the dago-looking guy, Alfonso, to do.'

'*Burkey.*'

Fat Man's voice began to become smaller. 'We found her passport.'

Del's breathing started to get heavier. '*Passport?*'

Burkey's forehead was beginning to break out with sweat. He wiped it away, almost speaking in a whisper now. 'Yeah, you asked him to take Star's passport.'

For the first time, Del turned to look at Fat Man. A statement rather than a question. 'What have you done?'

A second later, Del span into reverse, causing Fat Man to jump out of the way. He held his fist on the horn, bringing attention to himself.

Everyone milling around in the courtyard looked up, their faces a picture of concern.

Milo and the others ran up to the car. 'What's going on?'

Speaking hurriedly, Del looked at Milo. 'I think we've got a lead. I need everyone in their cars. We'll probably need your helicopter as well Milo. The guy we're looking for only left five minutes ago. Suntanned-looking, oily cunt. White Range Rover, gold roof.'

'*Gold roof?*'

Del rolled his eyes 'It's Edith's.'

The men all looked at each other, nodding in understanding.

'Everyone keep in contact. He can't have got that far. So let's move it.'

Putting down his foot, Del drove off and almost immediately skidded to a halt. He leant his head out of the window as Bunny stood a few inches from the front of the car.

'What's going on?'

'Christ, woman, I could've killed you. I think we've got a lead. He's in Edith's Range Rover.'

Bunny ran round. 'What? Who?'

Urgency was in Del's voice. 'I'll explain later. Bunny, I have to go.'

'I want to come with you.'

'No. No way. You need to rest.'

'But…'

Del didn't wait to hear the end of the sentence

365

as he put the car in drive, hurtling out of the gates, followed by the others.

Bunny stood for a moment, hearing the sound of engines disappear down the hill. The sense of powerlessness and desperation hit her. She had to do something. She couldn't just stand here doing nothing. She looked around the courtyard. It was empty apart from a van Del's men used for grocery shopping. She suddenly had a thought.

54

Hiding underneath a hot furry blanket, Teddy Davies wondered what was happening. He was being thrown side to side. There was nothing to hold onto. He felt the driver go over a bump before he was thrown in the air, banging down hard on something sharp. Trying desperately to cling on, he was involuntarily rolled to one side as whoever was driving sped round a tight corner.

He'd been planning to see if he could scale the side wall. Anything to get away from the villa and what he saw as his impending doom, but then he'd heard Fat Man come into the courtyard shouting after someone, followed shortly by Del's procession of cars. Panicking, he'd jumped into the back of one of the parked vehicles and before he knew it, Teddy Davies was being flung without dignity amongst boxes and bottles in a van stinking of what smelt like rotten meat.

As a box fell on top of him, spilling out cabbages and cauliflower all over his head, it suddenly struck Teddy that maybe he needed to re-evaluate his life.

Del Williams sped across the tiny roads of the Sierra Blanca hills, dust billowing out behind him as his tyres churned up the sandy tracks. He sped past lemon trees and olive groves, through small villages, beeping his horn in desperation as he became stuck behind herds of goats. He tore along tight bends, ignoring the hundred-foot drops on one side of him. Ignoring his electronic speedometer hitting one hundred and twenty miles an hour. And all the time, frantic in his search for a white Range Rover with a gold roof.

Looking in his driver's mirror, he saw one of his men still behind him. The others, along with Milo's men, had dispersed along the way, spreading out in different directions, desperate to spot Edith's car. He looked up, hearing the loud sound of a helicopter hovering above him.

Del's phone rang. He answered it straight away. 'Yep.'

'It's Milo. I haven't spotted anything yet but I've got my helicopter out as well.'

'Yeah, I can see it. It's just flown over me. Is everyone still in contact?'

'I've been speaking to my men all the time. Don't worry, between us all there's no way we won't spot him soon.'

'I hope so, Milo. I really do.' Cutting the call off, Del pressed his foot down as he cut off the road, towards the top of the hill.

At ninety miles an hour, the van bounced over the uneven sandy dust track, the engine struggling with the back wheels spinning in the dirt. Bunny Barker crunched it into fifth gear, certain she'd just seen Edith's white Range Rover. She'd been turning right at one of the many tiny white-washed villages dotted outside Marbella and from the corner of her eye she'd seen the dazzle of reflected speckled gold as the sun bounced off the roof of the car, emitting a beam of light. She'd lost sight of the car but she could still see the dust clouds.

There was no signal on her phone but hopefully once she was at the top of the hill that would change. Pushing the van to its limit, Bunny tried to ignore the pain that was beginning to start in her stomach.

Bunny turned off the engine. Down the cart track, just in front of her, Bunny saw the white Range Rover. It was definitely Edith's. And it was parked outside a small run-down villa.

She could feel the adrenaline rushing round in her body. Something told her she was so close to finding Star. She looked at her phone again; still no signal. Looking around her, she saw there was nothing but lemon and olive trees. No other house or car in sight. Rubbing her stomach, Bunny breathed out as a sharp pain shot through her body.

Stepping out of the van, Bunny rushed over to the trees, her eye focused on the villa. As she watched, she crept forward, scratching her legs on the brambles. She squatted down, trying to stay unseen, but also from the pain, which was getting stronger.

A sound behind her made her jump. She heard a noise and stared in horror as she realised it was the sound of her van being driven away. She struggled to get up, holding onto the tree for support, trying to see who was driving it, but it was going too fast.

As Bunny watched the tail lights head down the track, she froze as she saw two men come running out of the dilapidated villa.

She couldn't breathe; bile was rising up in her throat. She began to grapple for the tree she was leaning on, needing support. Her hand gave way, bringing her down to her knees as it scraped down the jagged tree trunk. She could see tiny cuts on her hand as she held her stomach, memories and visions coming into her mind. She tried to get up again but the searing pain in her abdomen was merciless.

'What have we got here then?'

Bunny looked up. And then she saw him. Finally she saw him. Older, but still his face. The face of one of the men who had killed her sister. As Bunny knelt on the rough ground, she didn't see Julian through her adult eyes, but through the child she once was.

Terror gripped her body. She was back in the woods. Back to that night. There was her sister. Still, cold ... dead. She saw the blood oozing amongst the autumn leaves. She felt the cold of the night. And felt the fear of being alone, wondering if the men would come back for her.

'What's going on?'

Alfonso's voice came from behind Julian, flicking open his knife. He bent down and Bunny felt the flat edge of a steel blade on her cheek, then on her neck. Slowly and bluntly, it glided over her skin. Her eyes flickered as she stared at the other man.

Alfonso answered the unspoken question for Julian. 'It's Del's missus. Where did she come from?'

'Beats me, but we better get the fuck out of here. What do you want me to do with her?'

Bunny continued to stare, unable to say anything as the agony in her stomach as she began to haemorrhage made her almost black out. He didn't know who she was. *He didn't know who she was.* She wanted to scream and tell him. Tell him it was *her*. Tell him it was *her* sister he had taken a knife to, cutting her throat with one vicious stroke. And with that cut, he had killed part of her as well. Yet he couldn't see it in her eyes who she was. He couldn't see her pain. For Star. Her agony for her sister. The child she'd been when she'd given evidence against him. He was blind to it. Blind to the suffering of it all.

Alfonso stared at Bunny but spoke to Julian as he put his knife away. 'Leave her, she's not worth it. We'll be long gone, and she doesn't look like she's going anywhere fast. Come on.'

Leaving Bunny on the ground, Alfonso and Julian hurried back to the villa. She watched in horror when a moment later, she saw Star being dragged out of the house. Her daughter was only a few feet away. There was Star – and she was unable to help her.

Bleeding heavily, Bunny began to lose consciousness as she tried calling out the words, '*Run, Star, run.*'

Teddy Davies drove the van at high speed down the road. He wanted to put distance behind him before he decided what to do. When the van had stopped, he'd let himself out of the back. He'd actually been going to head off on foot, but seeing the van abandoned with the keys in the ignition had been too tempting. He hadn't known who was driving it and he hadn't bothered to wait around to find out.

Slowing down a little bit, Teddy looked across to the horizon. Holy shit. Rising up in the distance, like a vision from hell, were a dozen large black Escalades. The Russians. Looking in his rear mirror, Teddy saw three black Range Rovers heading over the hill. With a quick turn of the wheel, he swerved to the side of the road. Getting out of the van, he began to run.

The cars were getting nearer but there was no hiding cover, so he headed towards the side of the hill, looking at the drop below. As he contemplated what to do, he heard the approaching sound of a helicopter and as he looked up into the sky, Teddy began to lose his balance. He stumbled backwards, slipping as he desperately tried to hold onto the grass, which came away in his hands. With a scream of terror, he tumbled down to the beach below.

'We've got a sighting!' The words which Del had needed to hear but didn't think he would were growled down the phone in a heavy Russian accent.

'Where?'

'The helicopter's just seen it. He's hovering above it now. Apparently the car's driving erratically, he's probably got a blowout from the off-road terrain. It's up on the hills, roughly three miles outside La Virginia. Head towards there and I'll keep you updated.'

He could see it, sparkling in the sunlight as they drove off-road across the hills. The white distinctive Range Rover which had cost him a fortune.

Behind him were the rest of his men in Range Rovers; to the side of him, the Russian Escalades, and above him, the hovering helicopter. He pulled out his gun, aiming to shoot at the car tyres. With one hand on the steering wheel Del leaned out of the window, still keeping up his speed. He fired, hearing the shot but missing the target. Again he fired, hitting up the dirt track. He tried again. This time, the bullet hit. There was a squeal of the tyres, followed by a bang as the rubber exploded.

The white car veered to the right, careering across the sandy ditch, finally stopping as it crashed into an olive tree.

Del got out of his car, his gun pointed at the Range Rover. He signalled his men to move forward and form a circle around it. He watched as Milo did the same – only the guns *his* men carried were military issue.

'Get out of the fucking car.' He edged forward, not wanting to shoot in case Star was behind the blacked-out windows. There was no sound. Del motioned to Fat Man to stay back as he crept forward. He pressed his body against the side of the car, moving along it. With a quick movement, he opened the driver's door. What he saw made him jump back in horror. Falling out of the driver's seat was Bunny, covered in blood.

'She's been shot! She's been shot!' Del yelled, holding Bunny in his lap as he knelt on the ground holding her head up. Milo rushed up to him, crouching down to look at her.

'No, she hasn't been shot. She's bleeding.'

Del looked at Milo in horror. 'Oh my God, the baby.'

55

Julian Millwood sat back on the deck of the boat, feeling the sun and warm wind on his face. They headed out into the Mediterranean Sea and he couldn't help being impressed. 'I hate to say it, Alf, but you pulled a blinder sorting this out.'

Alfonso grinned as he drove the boat on the crystal waters. 'It's not over yet but once we hit Morocco we can relax a bit. I can almost smell the money, little brother.'

Star sat at the back of the boat, watching the coastline of Spain fading into the distance through her telescopic spyglass, along with the fading of hope that she'd ever see her mum and dad again. At first they weren't going to allow her on deck but she'd been sick several times and eventually they'd let her get some fresh air as they sat and watched her every move.

She could feel herself trembling with fear even though the sun was beginning to beat down. She found every time her thoughts moved away from watching the sea she began to cry, so she stayed looking at nothing in particular, desperate to keep her thoughts away from home.

She glanced at Julian and Alfonso, feeling a shudder. They were mean and they scared her, but she didn't know what to do to get away. And now they were on a boat she didn't think she'd be able to get away at all, especially as she didn't swim very well. Since they'd been here her dad had begun to teach her, but she much preferred splashing about looking for shells. She didn't think pirates needed to swim. She'd *never* heard about one swimming so she supposed it was all right. The teacher at school had said she could try in the deep pool next term but she didn't really know if she wanted to.

Walking right to the back of the boat, Star looked down at the water. She could see the propeller frothing up the water into white bubbles, and the little dinghy that was tied to the yacht dancing along on top of the water behind.

Star let out a small cry as an idea came into her head. Her hands shot out over her mouth and she quickly looked round at Julian and Alfonso, making sure they hadn't heard her.

Slowly she crept nearer the edge. She looked behind her again and saw Julian lying in the sun with Alfonso concentrating on steering the boat. Turning back, she pulled the rope, bringing the dinghy close to the yacht. Star's head whipped round again. No one was paying her any attention.

She looked at the water below. It looked so deep. But she had to be brave. That's what adventurers were and that's what her dad was. He was brave and strong. And her mum always said Star was like him.

With one more look behind her, Star Barker-Williams closed her eyes and jumped off the yacht into the dinghy below.

It was like a trampoline. Her body bounced on the floor of the dinghy. Once. Twice. Three times, before she managed to scrabble up, quickly holding onto the side to regain her balance. Silently she stretched forward, her tiny hands easily untying the knot of the nylon rope. She watched as the rope dropped into the water, her dinghy slowing down as the other boat, driven by her capturers, continued to sail into the distance.

Teddy Davies couldn't believe his luck. Though it didn't surprise him. It was just the kind of luck he'd come to expect after the last few weeks. But even he couldn't quite have guessed how bad it could really get. He looked to the left of him and to the right of him, but didn't bother looking behind or in front of him because he knew what was there. Water. Oceans of the stuff. The only thing surrounding him was sea – and not a centimetre of dry land in sight.

When he'd tumbled down the hill to the beach below, his fall had been broken by several bushes and trees. He'd ended up with only a few scrapes and an angry bruise on his right knee. That hadn't been the problem. The problem had been that there was no way to get back up the slope. Although it hadn't been steep enough for him to be really hurt, it'd been steep enough for him to fail several times in his attempt to climb it.

Thankfully he'd seen a small motorboat pulled up on shore, probably left, though not abandoned, by one of the private yachts. At the time he'd been thankful, knowing Puerto Banús wasn't too far away. But as Teddy sat floating in the middle of the sea, miles from anywhere with the petrol run out in the small outboard motor, thankful certainly wasn't the first word that came to mind.

56

She didn't know how long she'd been on the dinghy but she was starting to get tired and the sky was turning dark. She was hungry and thirsty. And even though she'd got away from the mean men, looking into the sea, which now looked so deep and black, was beginning to scare her.

She thought about two-headed sharks, monsters with one eye, fish with teeth so long they were nearly as tall as her, all swimming about just below her, waiting till she fell asleep to sneak into the boat and eat her. She shivered, huddled up in the dinghy and for the first time since she'd been taken by the men, Star Barker-Williams allowed herself to cry loudly, knowing she was in the safety of the middle of nowhere. The noise of her cries soared high into the air as all her stored-up tension and fears were let out. All she wanted to do was go home but she didn't know how to get there.

Calming down slightly, Star wiped away her tears. She sniffed, wiping her nose on the dress that she'd been wearing for over a week. Staring into the distance, Star sat up. There, she could see a boat. She stood up too quickly, almost losing her balance as the dinghy tipped slightly to the side.

She began to wave, slowly at first, then more quickly as the boat approached her. Then she stopped. Her hands stayed in the air; frozen. She could feel her legs beginning to shake. There, standing on the deck of the boat approaching her, were the bad men.

'Please you're hurting me,' Star cried out as Alfonso gripped hold of her arm tightly. Furiously, he shook her hard as he dragged her into the cabin.

'Shut up.'

'Please, I just wanted to go home.' Star pleaded to Alfonso who sneered at her before raising his hand and back-palming her. A large red mark was left on her cheek as she began to cry uncontrollably.

'I said shut the fuck up.'

Star's voice was staggered as she tried to catch her breath. 'I can't... I can't.'

Alfonso's hand slapped her again and she squealed, running into the corner as he let her go. She curled up tightly, too frightened to move.

'You can forget about going home. You ain't going to see Mummy and Daddy again, sweetheart, and you certainly ain't going to get out of this cabin till we get there. If you need to piss, piss in the corner.' With that, Alfonso slammed the door closed, locking it as he went. He stomped down the deck, checking to see they were anchored properly on the buoy.

He was in a foul mood. The little cow had given him a fright. All his efforts pissed away by some spoilt brat who thought she was clever. The sooner they delivered her, the better.

Alfonso turned to Julian angrily. 'I'm going to get some kip. We'll set off in the morning at first light.'

'Quiet.'

Star felt a heavy weight. Sleepily, she opened her eyes. A hand pressed on her mouth as Julian Millwood lay on top of her, staring coldly down.

'I want you to be very quiet. No screaming, do you understand?'

Star nodded, her eyes full of terror as she felt Julian pulling at her clothes.

'If I take my hand off, I don't want you to scream.'

Star nodded again, but the moment Julian released his hand she let out a cry. In less than a second her scream was muted by his hand slamming hard back down on her face. 'You stupid bitch, I told you to be quiet.' Angrily he pushed down his hand hard on her mouth, his face flushed with rage, the other hand pulling once more at her clothing.

'What the fuck are you doing?'

Julian jumped up, allowing Star to scramble to the side. He stared at his brother, who held the flick knife in his hand.

'I told you to leave her alone.'

'You ain't got any right to tell me what to do.'

'I have while half of her belongs to me.'

Julian, angry at the interruption and furious at being pushed around, stepped forward to Alfonso. 'Fuck you.'

Alfonso grabbed hold of Julian, overpowering him almost immediately with his strength. He held the blade against his throat. 'Don't fuck with me, Julian, because I won't think twice about slitting your throat.'

Unexpectedly, Julian pushed his weight to the side, causing Alfonso to lose his balance. Stumbling out of the cabin door and onto the deck, Alfonso brought his brother down with him.

Alfonso kicked out hard, slamming his elbow into Julian's face. His brother cried out in pain as blood spurted from his broken nose. About to bring the knife down, Alfonso froze. Standing just above him, holding a flare gun in her hands, was Star.

'Careful, sweetheart. Put that down; it's dangerous. Don't be silly, give it to me.' Alfonso spoke gently.

'Get up, both of you.' Star's voice trembled as she continued to point the flare gun at them.

Julian, still in agony from his nose, struggled up.

'Put yer hands up.'

Cautiously and slowly, Alfonso and Julian raised their hands in the air. Julian stepped forward to Star, blood trickling down his face. 'You're making a big mistake; you ain't got nowhere to go darlin'.' He stepped closer.

'Stay where you are!' Star waved the flare gun.

He laughed 'Or what?... Come here!' Julian leapt forward. Terrified, Star closed her eyes and pulled the trigger of the flare gun. She heard a scream. It was Julian. She opened her eyes just in time to see him dropping to his knees as he clutched his face, a yellow haze of smoke all around, the smell of burning flesh in the air.

She looked in horror at Alfonso who began to slowly walk towards her. She pulled the trigger again of the flare but nothing happened. She began to back away as he spoke, his voice sinister. 'Did you really think you could beat us?'

Star started to cry.

'Didn't I say no crying, Star? This time I'm going to teach you a proper lesson.'

From the corner of her eye, Star saw something on the floor catching the light of the cabin. Her heart raced as she looked at Alfonso. But as Alfonso took another step towards her, Star suddenly realised what she had to do. She had to be brave. Almost able to hear her dad's voice she bent down, grabbing hold of what was on the floor.

Alfonso's eyes widened, but he didn't move. 'Star, put it down. *That* isn't a flare gun.'

Star didn't take her eyes off Alfonso. She knew he was trying to trick her. But she wasn't going to believe him. He was a bad man who'd wanted to hurt her and now he was telling lies.

'Star, I'm *warning* you. Put it down. Give it to me.'

Alfonso held his hand out. It was shaking. He edged forward again, holding Star's gaze. He was only centimetres away from grabbing hold of her wrist when he made a sudden movement to grab her arm from the side. Petrified, Star jumped back, pulling the trigger. The trigger not of an SOS flare gun, like she thought she was holding, but the trigger of Alfonso's Smith & Wesson Magnum .397.

The bullet blasted through Alfonso's body. He held onto the gaping chest wound and for a split second locked eyes with Star, drained horror on his face as he realised his fate. He staggered to the side, blood pouring from his fatal wound as he fell onto the chain railing; then tipped over the side to plunge headlong into the dark waters below.

57

Star stood on deck, watching the sunrise. Still holding the gun in her hand. Still watching Julian who didn't move or make a sound, apart from the occasional groan of agony.

Her fear hadn't left her but with daylight erasing the night she didn't feel quite so scared. But she still didn't want to think of Alfonso or what had happened to him.

She hadn't been able to work the radio on board and her dad had only shown her how to work the sails, but this boat didn't have any. So she'd just have to wait. Wait until someone came to rescue her.

Through her spyglass, Star looked out to sea. She scanned the horizon. The sunlight dancing on the crystal waters. White clouds spinning in the blue sky. Birds hovering overhead. Then she paused. She rubbed the end of her spyglass just to make sure what she was seeing was real. Yes, there it was. There was a boat. But it wasn't *any* boat. It was her friend's boat. It was Teddy. Her friend had come to rescue her. She could see him waving madly. She waved back, her face ecstatic with excitement and relief. Almost immediately, Star began to cry again.

Teddy had come all this way on his own to find her. Her secret friend had battled with pirates and sea monsters to rescue her and all in a tiny boat.

Jumping up and down, Star continued to wave.

Teddy Davies saw the boat in front of him. He began to wave, desperately grateful he was going to be rescued, not bothering to fight back tears of relief. During the night as he'd floated in pitch-blackness, hearing strange sounds and noises, he'd actually thought he'd never be found. Lost at sea forever. Sinking without trace to the bottom of Davy Jones' locker.

He'd even started to reflect on his life. What he could've done differently. How he could've perhaps considered others a little bit more. And just before the dawn had broken, in desperation he'd resorted to recalling the Lord's Prayer, albeit only being able to remember the first three lines. But now all that didn't matter. He was going to be saved. Life could get back to normal.

With a huge smile between his tears, Teddy waved again. As his boat floated towards the yacht, he gawped. What the hell? He rubbed his eyes to make sure he hadn't begun to hallucinate. But it wasn't a hallucination, it was her. Right in front of him, standing on the deck was Star Barker-Williams, waving and grinning away. Teddy shook his head in amazement. Some things you just couldn't make up.

The greeting on the dock was a strange one as Teddy drove the boat into Puerto Banús. He'd radioed ahead explaining the situation. And there on the quayside, waiting to greet them, stood a line of people. Del, Milo, Claudia, Fat Man and an array of Del's and Milo's men – along with the

Spanish police waiting to take Julian into custody. A proper Kodak moment.

'Dad! Dad! Dad!' Star ran down the jetty, straight into Del's arms. He swooped her up, clinging onto her, unwilling to put her down as the tears rolled down his face.

'Let me look at you.'

'Don't cry, Daddy. I've been a brave girl, like what you said. I was a big girl, you should have seen me.'

Del's eyes scanned his daughter as her tiny hands wiped away his tears. Grime was etched on her face and her clothes were slightly torn. Her hair was mattered and she looked thinner than she had done before, but in her eyes he could still see a twinkling light. Star was back. Back in his arms where she belonged and he was never going to let her go.

'Where's Mum? Is she here?'

'She's in hospital, but she's fine and the baby's fine.'

Still in her father's arms Star squeezed her eyes shut and began to tremble. She was safe, but more importantly she was in her dad's arms. Loving and strong. Away from harm. After a moment she looked in Del's face, a small smile beginning to appear on her face. She spoke with quiet pride. 'Dad, Teddy saved me. He came all the way to save me. He wasn't even scared of the pirates or the monster that lives in the bottom of the sea. He was brave like me, Daddy.'

Del looked over his shoulder at Teddy. He'd received a garbled message from the Spanish police telling him Star had been found but they hadn't told him how or the circumstances surrounding it. So when he'd seen Teddy riding high on the boat coming into harbour he hadn't known what the hell was going on.

He walked up to Teddy, carrying Star in his arms, amazement in his face and total astonishment in his voice. 'Is this true?'

Teddy smiled nonchalantly, enjoying the glare of attention. He shrugged. 'What can I say, Del? It was nothing. All in the line of duty mate. All in the line of duty.'

FIVE MONTHS LATER

Star sat between her mum and dad, with Claudia sitting on the other side of them. She held her parents' hands squeezing them tightly. Full of excitement. Full of delight.

Sitting waiting on the front row, Star was hardly able to contain herself. She looked around, turning her head to see the hall full of people. She whispered to her dad. 'I've got butterflies in me stomach.' She grinned, her button nose crinkling up in happiness as she began to listen to the man on stage.

'And now, ladies and gentlemen, we come to a special award, given to a special person. Someone who has shown considerable courage against adversity. Confronting dangers both on dry land and on the high sea. Someone who kept going when there seemed to be no hope. Someone who scaled the heights of bravery most of us can only dream about. So without any further ado, it is with the greatest of pleasure I present this award to an exceptional individual. Ladies and gentlemen, I give you Detective Teddy Davies.'

Star stood up, whooping and clapping, her delighted face looking around at her parents. 'Stand up, Dad. Stand up.'

Del glanced at Bunny, who shrugged her shoulders. In a resigned manner Del stood up, followed by Bunny, then Claudia, until the whole room began to give Teddy a standing ovation.

Up on stage Teddy looked around the room. He caught Del's eye and winked at him, seeing the scowl on his face. He looked at Star; stupid kid but he was beginning to like her. He looked at Bunny and smirked, remembering, then he gazed outwards seeing the hundreds of people in the hall who'd come to see him. *Him.* Then he closed his eyes, revelling in the sound of the applause.

Finally, Teddy Davies felt he had the recognition he deserved

> *Kathleen Barker,*
> *A loving sister,*
> *A loving daughter.*
> *Sadly missed but never forgotten.*

Bunny stood next to Claudia, reading the gravestone. It was the first time she'd ever come here. The first time she'd seen her sister's grave and it was only now she was able to remember her how she wanted to. Full of life. Full of love and full of kindness. She had loved her sister with all her heart and Kathleen had loved her back with all hers.

Bunny suddenly bent forward.

'You all right?' Del put his hand on Bunny's large pregnant stomach. She smiled warmly. 'Yes, just the baby kicking.'

'I was thinking, if it's a girl why don't we call her Kate? What do you say, Bun?'

Bunny looked at the grave, a soft sadness in her eyes as she watched Star place a bunch of flowers on it. 'I say she'd have liked that very much.'

Star bounded up to Claudia. 'What was Auntie Kathleen like, Nanny?'

Claudia looked at Bunny, who nodded her head.

'Go on Mum, it's fine.'

Claudia looked at her daughter and then at her granddaughter. She smiled. 'Well Star, let me tell you. When your mummy and Auntie Kathleen were little, they were bleedin' toerags. Always getting into scrapes...'

Star and Claudia walked off towards the car, chattering away. Del gently pulled Bunny back.

'I'm not flying back to Marbella with you guys today. There's something I need to do first, but I'll see you tomorrow ... and Bronwin, you know how much I love you, don't you?' He kissed her on her forehead, before turning to walk away in the other direction.

The drab grey concrete tower blocks rose up into the air. Windows were boarded up. Misspelt graffiti sprayed over doors and walls. Abandoned supermarket trolleys lay amidst urine and discarded needles as Del stood knocking on the paint-peeling door.

Eventually the door was opened by a thin scruffy man, his eyes hollow and sunken, his skin pale and drawn. His hands trembled as his yellowed fingers held onto a cigarette. A little boy ran to the door and Del watched as the man's eyes lit up in warmth as he picked him up.

'Can I help you?' The man's tone was hostile and closed.

'Gary Cole?'

'Yeah?'

'You don't know me but I wanted to give you this.' Del handed the man a large brown envelope. 'I know it won't bring your daughter Julie back, but maybe you can buy her a proper gravestone.'

Gary Cole looked at Del. His eyes filled with tears. Embarrassed, he turned to his son, Zak, burying his head in his jam-smeared hair.

'I'm going to get off now, but I'm sorry about your daughter, mate. I really am.'

Del turned and walked away back to his car. What happened to Julie Cole had so nearly happened to Star. She had been one of the lucky ones. Knowing they'd found Alfonso washed up dead on the shore, with Julian living the remainder of his years banged up in a Spanish prison was a small comfort to Del, though he doubted it would be to Gary Cole. As for Edith's involvement in it all, she'd been lucky he hadn't called the police, but then her losing everything was punishment enough. Money was where it hurt her. And having none meant she'd be in a lot of pain.

'Mate! Mate! Stop!' It was Gary.

Del pulled up his car as Gary, carrying his son, waved frantically to him. It took Gary a moment to speak as he got his breath back, still holding onto the envelope Del had given him.

'Mate, I can't take this. There's a fortune in here.'

Del reached out of the driver's window to tickle Gary's son on the cheek before turning to look

Gary straight in the eyes.

'Keep it. It's yours. I wanted you to have it. Use it to get you and your son out of here... Good luck, Gary, and take care.'

Del put his car into drive, leaving Gary Cole standing in the middle of the car park, filled with a new sense of hope.

'Daddy, you're back!' Star shouted in delight as she sat on the wall by the pool looking though her spyglass at the Mediterranean Sea.

'What can you see, doll?' Del spoke as he threw down his bag, winking at Bunny who smiled in joy to see him.

'I'm looking at Milo's boat.'

'Pirates?'

Star giggled. 'Milo's not a pirate.'

Del ruffled her hair, a big grin appearing on his face.

'Some people might not agree with you there, babe.'

He sat down next to his daughter, moving her pet snails out of the way, feeling at peace. He nodded a greeting to Fat Man who was attentively pouring a glass of lemonade for Claudia, who looked as happy as he felt. This was all Del had ever really needed. Family and friends really were his everything.

Bunny sat on the lounger, feeling the baby kicking hard. She was happy they'd all decided to make the permanent move to Marbella. Everyone seemed more at ease. She smiled at Del, more in love with him than she'd ever been, but then she knew why. Finally, she'd faced up to her past.

Hidden secrets now broken. Hidden memories now exposed. She had forgiven herself. The past was no longer a shroud of anxiety; the future no longer a veil of mistrust. She, Bronwin – or as her sister Kathleen had called her, Bunny – for the first time since that day in the woods, she was happy.

Holding her stomach, Bunny looked across at Del, a twinkle of delight and joy in her eyes. 'Del?'

'Yes, doll?'

'Tell me something.'

'Like what?'

Bunny grinned. 'Anything.'

'Okay... Er, tomorrow I'm going into Puerto Banús.'

'I trust you.'

Del raised his eyebrows. 'The sun is going to shine tomorrow.'

Bunny grinned. 'I trust you.'

Del grinned back. 'All of us are going to have a barbeque tonight and Claudia's probably going to eat the lion's share.'

Bunny giggled. 'I trust you.'

Del took hold of Bunny's hand, staring into the deep pools of her blue eyes. 'But more importantly Bunny, you complete me – and all of us are going to be fine. Everything's going to be just fine.'

'Yes it is, babe, and it's because I trust you. Hear that? I can finally say it.' Bunny raised her voice, shouting the rest of the words loudly and happily. 'I trust you. Del Christian Williams, I trust you.'

Bunny's laughter mixed with Del's, soared into the air. Laughter and joy which stayed within the Williams' household for years to come.

The publishers hope that this book has given you enjoyable reading. Large Print Books are especially designed to be as easy to see and hold as possible. If you wish a complete list of our books please ask at your local library or write directly to:

Magna Large Print Books
Magna House, Long Preston,
Skipton, North Yorkshire.
BD23 4ND

This Large Print Book for the partially sighted, who cannot read normal print, is published under the auspices of

THE ULVERSCROFT FOUNDATION

THE ULVERSCROFT FOUNDATION

... we hope that you have enjoyed this Large Print Book. Please think for a moment about those people who have worse eyesight problems than you ... and are unable to even read or enjoy Large Print, without great difficulty.

You can help them by sending a donation, large or small to:

The Ulverscroft Foundation, 1, The Green, Bradgate Road, Anstey, Leicestershire, LE7 7FU, England.
or request a copy of our brochure for more details.

The Foundation will use all your help to assist those people who are handicapped by various sight problems and need special attention.

Thank you very much for your help.